Alexei Tolstoy

ORDEAL

A trilogy

Book Two
The Year 1918

Raduga

Publishers

Moscow

Translated from the Russian by *Ivy* and *Tatiana Litvinov*
Designed by *A. Yakovlev*

Алексей Толстой
ХОЖДЕНИЕ ПО МУКАМ

Трилогия
Кн. II. ВОСЕМНАДЦАТЫЙ ГОД
Роман
На английском языке

First printing 1953
Reprinted in 1965, 1967, 1976, 1981, 1982, 1984, 1991

Printed in the Union of Soviet Socialist Republics

$$\text{T} \frac{4702010201-037}{031(01)-91} 027-91$$

ISBN 5-05-003419-3
ISBN 5-05-003421-3

The Year 1918

THRICE WRUNG OUT IN WATER,
THRICE BATHED IN BLOOD,
THRICE BOILED IN CAUSTIC. WHO
SO CLEAN AS WE?

I

All was over. A chill wind was blowing rubbish along the streets of the subdued St. Petersburg—fragments of military orders, of theatre posters, of appeals to the "conscience and patriotism" of the Russian people—about the silent, deserted streets of Petersburg. Motley scraps of posters, with traces of paste on their backs, rustled ominously, fleeing before the wind, which drove the snow zigzagging over the pavement.

This was all that was left of the noisy and drunken hurly-burly which had so recently shaken the capital. The idle crowds had gone from the streets and squares. The Winter Palace* stood empty, its roof shattered by a shell from the cruiser Aurora**. The members of the Provisional Government, the influential bankers, the famous generals, had all vanished into thin air. The dashing carriages, the elegant women, the officers, the officials, the statesmen with their exalted ideas—all, all had gone from the streets, and the streets were shabby and grimy. The sound of hammers nailing boards over shop windows was heard ever more frequently in the night. Some windows still displayed pitiful relics—a bit of cheese here, a stale cake there. But this merely increased the yearnings for the vanished life. The timid pedestrian kept close to the wall, glancing furtively at the patrols—groups of resolute individuals striding along with red stars on their caps, their rifles slung over their shoulders, with the muzzles pointing downwards.

The north wind sent chill draughts through the darkened windows of houses, and forced its way into deserted porticoes, scattering the wraiths of past luxuries. Petersburg was a ghastly city in the end of 1917.

Ghastly, incomprehensible, unfathomable. All was over. The past was cancelled. A man in a torn hat carrying a pail and a

---

*Winter Palace—residence of the tsar and headquarters of the counter-revolutionary Provisional Government from February to October 1917.

**Aurora—a Baltic fleet cruiser; the storming of the Winter Palace began with artillery fire from the guns of the Aurora.

paint-brush, was running backwards and forwards across the wind-swept street. He kept pasting up ever new decrees on bills which made white patches on the ancient walls. Rank, distinctions, pensions, epaulettes, God, private property, the very right to live as one liked—all were gone. Cancelled! The bill poster shot ferocious glances from beneath the brim of his hat through plate-glass windows, behind which the inmates, in felt boots and fur coats, still paced the cold rooms, wringing their hands, and saying over and over again:

"What's it all about? What's going to happen? The ruin of Russia, the end of all.... Death."

When they went to the windows they saw a long furniture van drawn up in front of the house opposite, where His Excellency lived and where there had always been a policeman standing at attention, his eyes fixed on the grey façade; and they could see armed men carrying tables and chairs, carpets and pictures out of the wide-open doors of the house into this van. A flag of red bunting hung over the entrance, and there stood His Excellency, stamping about in a thin coat, his whiskers streaming, his grey head shaking. They were evicting him. Where was he to go in this cold? Wherever he liked.... And this was His Excellency—an essential cog in the mechanism of State!

And when night fell ... pitch-dark, not a lamp, not a light from a window. No coal, and yet they say the Smolny* is flooded with light, and they have light in the factory districts. The wind howls over the tortured, bullet-ridden city, whistling through holes in the roofs: "Woe! Woe!" And shots ring out in the darkness. Who is shooting, what for, and at whom? Isn't it over there, where a flickering glow is staining the snowy clouds? No, that's the wine cellars burning.... People are drowning in wine from broken barrels in basements.... To hell with them, let them burn alive!

Oh, Russian people, Russian people!

The Russian people, crammed into an endless stream of troop trains, were surging back in their millions from the front, to their homes, to the villages, the steppes, the swamps, the forests.... To the land, to their women.... They stood motionless in railway carriages with broken windows, so closely packed that a corpse could not be dragged through their ranks and thrown out. They travelled on the buffers, on the roofs. They froze stiff, fell beneath the wheels, got their heads broken against low-hanging bridges. Anything that had come to their hands was stuffed into chests and

---

Smolny—a building in Leningrad. In October 1917 the Smolny became the headquarters of the October Revolution.

bundles and carried away—you never know what'll come in handy: a machine gun, a rifle lock, odds and ends taken from a corpse, hand grenades, rifles, a gramophone, a bit of leather cut from the seat of a railway carriage. The only thing not taken was money—you couldn't even use it for rolling cigarettes.

The trains crawled slowly over the plains of Russia. They halted from sheer exhaustion at stations with broken windows and doors torn from their hinges. Every station was greeted with streams of obscenity. Men in long grey coats, clicking the locks of their rifles, leaped from the roofs of the carriages and rushed off to look for the stationmaster, to finish off this minion of the world bourgeoisie. "Come on, give us another engine! Are you sick of life, you son-of-a-bitch? Let the train pass!" Then, rushing to the engine, which was in the last stages of collapse, driver and stoker having escaped to the steppe, they would shout: "Coal! Wood! Break up the fences, chop up the doors and window-frames!"

Three years before, not many questions had been put as to whom and for what we were fighting. The heavens opened, and earth shook: mobilization, war! The people realized that the time for dreadful events had come. The old way of life was over. Take up your rifle! Come what may, there will be no going back to the old ways. The grievances of centuries came to a head.

By the end of three years people had discovered what war meant: a machine gun in front, a machine gun behind—and weltering in dung and lice, till one's turn came. Then a shudder passed over the people, their heads swam—Revolution! Recovering, they began to ask: "And what about us? Are we to be cheated again?" They listened to the agitators: "Aha! we were fools, were we? Then now we will be wise! We've fought enough—now let's go home and take our revenge. Now we know whose bellies our bayonets are intended for. There's no more tsar, and no more God. Nothing but us. Home—to divide the land!"

The troop trains from the front went like ploughs over the plains of Russia, leaving in their wake wrecked stations, shattered rolling stock, plundered towns. From villages and farmsteads came screeching metallic sounds—men were sawing the ends off their rifles. The Russian people were settling down on the land in good earnest. And once again, as in far-off days, the huts were lighted by burning flickering rushlights, while the women stretched their yarn on the hand looms of their great-grand-mothers. It seemed as if time were rattling back towards long-past ages. It was the winter of the year when the second revolution, the October Revolution, broke out.

Petersburg, famine-stricken, plundered by the villages, penetrated through and through by Arctic winds, surrounded by the enemy, shaken by plots, a city without coal or bread, its factory chimneys cold, a city like an exposed human brain, kept broadcasting from the Tsarskoye Selo radio station ideas as violent as bombshells.

"Comrades!" A lean fellow perched on a stone pedestal, his "Finnish cap" worn back to front, was shouting himself hoarse in the chill air. "Comrade deserters, you have turned your backs upon the imperialist reptiles ... we, the workers of Petersburg, tell you: you did right, Comrades! We're not going to be the hirelings of the bloody bourgeoisie. Down with the imperialist war!"

"Dow-ow-own...." The syllable rolled languidly over the groups of bearded soldiers. Their rifles on their shoulders, their bundles on their backs, they stood in heavy fatigue before the equestrian monument to Tsar Alexander III.

Snow lay on the black mass of the tsar's figure, and on that of the orator in his wide-open jacket, haranguing the crowd from beneath the muzzle of the stumpy bronze horse.

"We mustn't throw aside our rifles, though, Comrades! The Revolution is in danger. The enemy is rising against us from all the corners of the world. In his predatory hands are mountains of gold and terrible weapons of destruction. He trembles with joy to see us drowning in blood. But we will not flinch. Our weapon is our ardent faith in world social revolution. It is coming, it is near...."

The end of his sentence was borne away on the wind. A broad-shouldered man with his coat collar turned up stood near the monument. He seemed to be taking no notice of the monument, the speaker, or the soldiers with their bundles. But suddenly a chance phrase caught his ear, or rather, not so much the phrase itself, as the frenzied conviction with which it was yelled out from beneath the muzzle of the bronze horse:

"Get this into your heads—in six months the root of all evil—money—will be destroyed for good. There will be no more hunger, want, or humiliation.... Take what you need from the public treasury. And we'll make privies out of the gold ...."

Just then, however, a gust of wind drove the snow deep into the speaker's throat. Bending over in fretful vexation, he began coughing, and could not stop. His lungs seemed to be bursting. The soldiers stood where they were for a few minutes, and then, their high caps swaying, they dispersed, some to the stations, some right across the town, to the other side of the river. The orator crawled down from the plinth, his nails slipping on the frozen granite. The man with turned-up collar called out in a low voice:

"Hullo, Rublev!"

Vasili Rublev, still coughing, buttoned up his jacket. He did not put out his hand, but glowered at Ivan Ilyich.

"Well, what d'you want?"

"I'm just glad to see you...."

"Those blockheads," said Rublev, casting his eyes over the snow-blurred silhouette of the station, in front of which, beside their bundles, the vermin-ridden, bearded soldiers stood about in groups and clusters. "How can you get anything into their heads? They scuttle away from the front like cockroaches. Louts! A little terror is what is needed!"

His hand, chilled to the bone, grasped at the snowy air. And his fist pummelled an invisible something. A shudder passed over his frame, but his hand remained outstretched.

"Rublev, old man, you know me." (Telegin turned down his collar and bent towards Rublev's pallid countenance.) "Explain all this to me, for God's sake. We're running our heads into a noose. The Germans could be in Petrograd in a week's time if they liked. You know I never took any interest in politics—"

"What d'you mean you never took any interest?"

Rublev seemed to bristle all over, as he turned awkwardly towards Ivan Ilyich. "And what did you take an interest in? D'you know who the people are who take no interest now?" He looked furiously into Ivan Ilyich's eyes. "Neutrals are enemies of the people...."

"That's just what I wanted to ask you about. Can't you talk like a human being?"

Ivan Ilyich, too, bristled up. Rublev drew a deep breath through his nostrils.

"You're a queer chap, Comrade Telegin. Well, I've no time to talk to you—is *that* something you can understand?"

"Look here, Rublev, I'm in an awful state. Have you heard that Kornilov is raising the Don?"

"Yes, I have."

"Either I shall go to the Don, or stay with you...."

"How d'you mean—'*either*'?"

"I must find out for myself which side is right. You're for the revolution, I'm for Russia. And perhaps I'm for the revolution, too. I fought in the war, you know."

The fury in Rublev's dark eyes died down, and nothing was left in them but sleepless exhaustion.

"All right," he said. "Come to the Smolny tomorrow—ask for me. Russia!" He shook his head and laughed. "She's enough to drive one mad, this Russia of yours. She makes me see red! But after all we shall all die for her.... Go to the Baltic station. Three thousand deserters have been lying about the floor there for over a fortnight. Call meetings among them, make propaganda for the Soviets. Tell them: Petrograd needs bread, we need fighters...."

(His eyes began to burn again.)

"Tell them, if they just lie on the stove ledge, scratching their bellies, they're done for. They'll get the revolution in their backsides. Hammer that into their skulls. And tell them no one can save Russia and the revolution now but the Soviets.... Understand? There's nothing in the world now so important as our revolution...."

Telegin ascended the frozen staircase in the dark to the fifth floor. He groped for the door. He knocked three times, and then again. Someone approached from inside. After a moment's pause he heard his wife ask softly:

"Who's there?"

"It's me, Dasha."

A sigh came from the other side of the door. A chain rattled. There was evidently some trouble in turning the key in the lock. Dasha's voice could be heard whispering "Oh, my God!" At last she got it open, and went straight back along the corridor, and sat down.

Telegin locked the door, conscientiously seeing to all latches and bolts. He took off his galoshes. He felt in his pockets—"no matches damn it!" Still in his cap and coat, he stretched out his arms and followed the direction Dasha had taken.

"Again no light," he said, "it's a disgrace! Where are you, Dasha?"

After a slight pause she replied softly from the study:

"There *was* light, but it went out again."

He went into the study; it was the warmest room in the whole flat, but today even here it was cold. He looked round, but could make out nothing—he could not even hear Dasha's breathing. He was very hungry, and was longing for tea, but he felt sure Dasha had not got anything ready.

Turning down his coat collar, Ivan Ilyich sat down on the armchair near the sofa, his face towards the window. Out there, in the snowy darkness, wavered a dim light. From Kronstadt, or from somewhere nearer, perhaps, the searchlights were groping over the sky.

"I ought to light the stove," he said to himself. And he tried to think of a way of asking Dasha where the matches were, without irritating her.

But he could not bring himself to ask her. He wondered what exactly she was doing—crying or dozing? It was really too quiet. There was a tomblike silence throughout the many-storied house. The only sounds were an occasional faint shot. Six bulbs in the chandelier suddenly glowed, and a reddish light illuminated the room. Dasha was seen to be seated at the desk, a coat flung over whatever she had on, one foot, in its felt boot, thrust forward. Her head lay on the desk, one cheek resting on the blotting pad. Her face was thin and harassed, her eyes were open—she had not even closed her eyes!—she sat there awkwardly, uncomfortably, all hunched up....

"Dasha, you mustn't go on like that!" said Telegin thickly. He felt an intolerable pity for her. He went up to the desk. But the red filaments trembled and went out. The light had only lasted a few seconds.

He stood behind Dasha, and bent over her, holding his breath. It seemed as if nothing could be simpler than to stroke her hair without a word. But she might have been a corpse, for all the response his approach evoked in her.

"Dasha! Why do you torture yourself so?"

A month before Dasha had given birth to a baby boy, which had scarcely lived three days. The birth had been premature, the result of a terrible shock. Two men of superhuman height, in fluttering shrouds, had leaped upon Dasha in the dusk, on the Field of Mars. They must have been the notorious "hoppers", who, fastening springs to their feet, were, in those fantastic times, terrorizing the whole of Petrograd. They whistled and gnashed their teeth at Dasha, and when she fell down tore off her coat, and hopped away across Lebyazhi Bridge. Dasha had lain for some time on the ground. There were showers of driving rain, and the naked lime trees in the Summer Park rattled their branches frenziedly. Somewhere beyond the Fontanka River came long-drawn cries for help. The unborn child kicked out vigorously, as if asking to be admitted into the world.

He was so insistent that Dasha at last got up and crossed the Troitsky Bridge. The wind flattened her against the iron railing, and her damp dress clung to her legs. There were neither lights nor passers-by. Far below was the black, turbulent Neva. Dasha felt the first pains as she stepped off the bridge. Realizing that she would be unable to reach home, she thought only of getting to a tree for shelter from the wind. In Krasniye Zori Street she was stopped by a patrol. The soldier, rifle in hand, bent over her deathly pale countenance.

"They stripped her, the beasts! And she in the family way!"

He took Dasha home and saw her to the fifth floor, where he banged on the door with the butt end of his rifle. When Telegin opened the door and thrust out his head, the soldier shouted at him:

"Is that the way? Letting a lady go out alone at night! She almost had her baby out in the street! You devils, you bourgeois boobies!"

Labour set in the same night. A garrulous midwife appeared in the flat. The pains continued a day and a night. The child was born half-strangled, having swallowed water in the process of birth. They slapped him, rubbed him, blew into his mouth. He wrinkled up his face and cried. The midwife would not give up hope, though the child had begun to cough. He wailed, like a kitten, with shallow, pitiful cries, and would not take the breast. Then he stopped crying and only coughed. And on the morning of the third day Dasha put out her hand to the cradle, and drew it back hastily—the little body she touched was cold. She seized him with eager hands and unwrapped him. His fair, sparse hair was standing straight up from his peaked skull.

Dasha gave a frantic shriek. She flung away from the bed, making for the window—to break it, to throw herself out, to end her life....

"I failed him!" she exclaimed over and over again. "I can't bear it!" Telegin had difficulty in restraining her and laying her on the bed. The tiny corpse was taken away. Dasha said to her husband:

"Death came to him while I was asleep. Only think—his hair stood on end. He suffered alone. And I slept."

Nothing he said could dispel her vision of the child's solitary struggle with death.

"All right, Ivan, I won't go on any more," she would answer Telegin, so as not to have to listen to her husband's reasonable voice, not to have to see his healthy, rosy face, from which no distress could drive away the look of content.

Telegin's exuberant health enabled him to rush about the town in torn galoshes from morning to night, looking for odd jobs, food, firewood, and the like. Several times a day he would run home, all solicitude and kindness.

But these tender cares were what Dasha needed least of all just now. The greater the practical activities displayed by Ivan Ilyich, the more hopelessly estranged was Dasha. She sat all day alone in the cold room. An occasional nap was her greatest blessing. She

14

would doze, pass her hands over her eyes, and feel a little better. Then she would go to the kitchen, remembering that Ivan Ilyich had asked her to do something. But the simplest of tasks was beyond her abilities just now. The November rain drummed against the windows. The wind howled over Petersburg. And in this cold, in the cemetery on the seashore, lay the tiny dead body of her son, who had not even been able to complain....

Ivan Ilyich realized that she was mentally sick. It was enough for the electricity to go out for her to huddle up in a chair, her head covered with a shawl, silently absorbed in her mortal grief. But life had to be lived.... One must live.... He wrote to Katya, who was in Moscow, about Dasha, but the letters must have gone astray, for there was no answer. Perhaps Katya herself had had some mishap. Times were hard.

Standing behind Dasha, Ivan Ilyich moved his feet and trod on a box of matches. He understood it all immediately: when the light had gone out, Dasha, to combat the darkness and solitude, had lit matches every now and then. "Oh, the poor darling!" he thought. "Alone all day!"

Cautiously he picked up the box. There were still a few matches in it. He fetched from the kitchen the sticks made ready in the morning—the carefully sawed remnants of the old wardrobe. Squatting on his heels in the study, he began lighting the small brick stove from which a bent iron pipe stretched right across the room. The smoke from the burning splinters smelt nice. A little wind moaned through the crevices around the door of the stove. A trembling disc of light appeared on the ceiling.

These home-made stoves were afterwards nicknamed "Bourgeoise", or "Bumblebee", nicknames that spread far and wide. They served humanity honestly all through the period of military communism. The simpler ones were of iron, on four feet, with a single opening for cooking, or—in exceptional cases—with an oven, in which pancakes of coffee grounds, or even pies made with salt dried fish, could be baked. The more elaborate ones had tiles torn from the fireplace; but all of them heated and cooked, and chanted the immemorial song of fire to the accompaniment of the blizzard's howl.

People gathered round the burning embers as in times of old around the hearth, warming their frozen fingers, and waiting patiently for the lid of the kettle to start dancing. Conversations were carried on which, unfortunately, were never written down. Drawing their broken-down armchairs nearer, professors, their beards grown bushy, their feet in felt boots, blankets round their shoulders, or over their knees, wrote their remarkable books. Poets, grown almost transparent from hunger, composed verses about love and revolution; plotters, gathering in a circle, their heads almost touching, whispered fragments of news, each more terrible and fantastic than the one before. And housefuls of antique furniture flew up the iron chimneys in smoke during these years.

Ivan Ilyich had the utmost respect for his own stove, pasting up its cracks with clay, and hanging old tins under its chimney, to catch the soot which would otherwise have fallen on to the floor. When the kettle had boiled he extracted a screw of paper from his pocket, and put a generous sprinkle of sugar into a glass. From another pocket he drew a lemon, which had fallen into his hands by a miracle (a war invalid on Nevsky Prospekt had given it him in exchange for a pair of mitts), and placed in front of Dasha a glass of sweet tea with a slice of lemon.

"Look, Dasha—with lemon! I'll just light the blinker."

This was the name given to an appliance made from a tin can in which a wick was suspended in sunflower oil. When Ivan Ilyich brought it in, the room was dimly lighted.

Dasha was now sitting up properly in her chair and drinking tea. Telegin, delighted, seated himself near her.

"Guess who I met! Vasili Rublev! Remember there were Rublevs, father and son, in my workshop? We used to be great friends. The father had shrewd eyes, and his heart was always half in the village, half at the plant. A marvellous type! And Vasili was a Bolshevik even in those days. Clever chap, but as cross as a bear with a sore head. In February he was the first to lead our workers into the street. He climbed into garrets, looking for policemen. They say he killed half a dozen or so with his own hands. And since the October Revolution he has become a great man. Well, he and I had a talk ... are you listening, Dasha?"

"I'm listening," she said.

Setting down her empty glass and propping her chin on her slender fist, she sat gazing at the floating flame of the blinker. In her grey eyes could be seen indifference to everything in the world. Her face had lengthened, her delicate skin looked transparent, her nose, once independent to sauciness, looked peaked.

"Ivan," she said (and this must have been to show her gratitude for the tea and lemon), "when I was looking for matches I found a box of cigarettes behind some books. If you want them...."

"Cigarettes! Oh, Dasha, and they're my old favourites."

Ivan Ilyich displayed exaggerated delight, although he had himself hidden the cigarettes behind some books to provide against a rainy day. But he lit one now, casting sideways glances at Dasha's lifeless profile. "I must take her away somewhere, far away, to the south."

"Well, Vasili Rublev and I had a talk—he's helped me a lot, Dasha. I don't believe those Bolsheviks can just disappear. They have their roots in people like Rublev—if you know what I mean. It's true none of them were elected. And their power hangs by a thread, and that only in Petrograd, Moscow, and a few of the bigger district centres. But the secret of their strength lies in the *quality* of their power. And this power is closely bound up with men like Vasili Rublev. There aren't many of them for such a country as ours. But they have faith. He can be torn limb from limb by wild beasts, he can be burned alive, and he'll still go on singing the *Internationale* as fervently as ever...."

Dasha maintained an unbroken silence. Ivan Ilyich poked the fire. Squatting down at the door of the stove, he said:

"D'you know what I'm leading up to? We must join one side or another. One can't just sit and wait for things to come round, and it would be disgraceful to stand by the wayside and beg. I'm a perfectly healthy man. I'm no saboteur.... Candidly speaking I want something to do...."

Dasha sighed. A tear trickled slowly from between her tightly-closed lids. Ivan Ilyich breathed hard.

"Of course first of all we must decide what to do about you, Dasha. You must find the strength to live—shake off your troubles. The way you live now isn't life at all—it's just fading away."

He emphasized the words "fading away" with involuntary irritation. To this Dasha replied in a childish whimper:

"Is it my fault I didn't die then? And now I'm in your way. You bring me lemons.... I never asked you...."

"There's no talking to her," thought Ivan Ilyich.

He walked up and down the room, stopping every now and then at the window and drumming with his nails on the steamy glass. The snow was whirling in a maze, the tempest was howling, the fierce wind swept by with such rapidity that it seemed to be trying to overtake time itself, as if anxious to project itself into the future, there to proclaim extraordinary events.

"Should I send her abroad?" thought Ivan Ilyich. "To her father in Samara? How difficult it all is! Anyhow we can't go on like this."

Dasha's sister Katya had taken Roshchin, now her husband, to her father in Samara, where they could live in peace till the spring, without watching every crumb they ate. By spring, of course, the Bolsheviks would have come to an end. Dr. Dmitri

Stepanovich Bulavin had even named a date—between the time when the frost melted and the roads became impassable, the Germans would launch an offensive along the whole front, where the remnants of the Russian armies were now holding meetings, and the soldiers' committees were vainly endeavouring to find new forms of revolutionary discipline amidst chaos, treachery, and wholesale desertion.

The last few years had aged Dmitri Stepanovich, who had had a hard time, and had become still more fond of talking politics. He was delighted at the arrival of his daughter, and started instantly upon Roshchin's political reeducation. They would sit for hours in the dining room, beside the samovar, a capacious battered vessel, which had yielded a veritable lake of boiling water in its time; it seemed to improve with age—you only had to throw a handful of charcoal into it for it to start singing the endless song of a samovar in a country town. Dmitri Stepanovich, in his fusty clothes, himself grown flabby and dingy, with tangled grey curls, smoked foul-smelling cigarettes, coughed himself red in the face, and talked incessantly.

"Our poor old country's gone to the dogs.... We've lost the war.... No offence meant, Colonel! Peace should have been concluded in 1915.... And we should have submitted ourselves to German rule and training. Then they would have taught us something, then something might have been made of us. But now everything's over.... Medical science is powerless in such a case, as they say.... What you say is nonsense! What are we to arm ourselves with—three-pronged pitchforks? This very summer the whole southern and central parts of Russia will be occupied by the Germans—Siberia by the Japanese; and our muzhiks, with their famous pitchforks, will be chased to the tundra of the Arctic Circle, and then a period of order, culture, and respect for humanity will set in. And our country will become Russland—and I, for one, shall be extremely pleased."

Dmitri Stepanovich was an old liberal and now mocked in bitter irony at what he had once held sacred. His very house bore the impress of his self-contempt. The rooms, with their dusty windows, were never swept and cleaned, the portrait of Mendeleyev* in his study was thickly veiled with spiders' webs, the plants withered in their tubs, while books, carpets, and pictures were still in boxes beneath sofas, as they had been when Dasha had visited him in the summer of 1914.

Dmitri Ivanovich Mendeleyev (1834-1907)—great Russian chemist, famous also in other branches of science. Discoverer of the periodic law and inventor of the Periodic System.

18

When power was taken over by the Soviets of Soldiers' and Workers' Deputies in Samara, and most of the doctors refused to work for the deputies of the "soldiery and the rabble", Dmitri Stepanovich had been offered the post of director of all municipal hospitals. Since, according to his calculations, the Germans would be in Samara by spring anyhow, he accepted the appointment. Medicaments were in a bad way, and Dmitri Stepanovich prescribed nothing but enemas. "All troubles come from the bowels," he told his assistants, darting ironical, supercilious glances at them through his cracked pince-nez. "During the war the population neglected its bowels. If you dig about among the primal causes of our esteemed anarchy, you're sure to come up against constipation of the bowels. Yes, gentlemen, the strict and wholesale application of the enema...."

These talks at the tea table made a painful impression on Roshchin. He had not completely recovered from an injury which he had received on the first of November in Moscow, during street fighting. He had been in command of a company of cadets defending the approaches to Nikitsky Gate. Sablin, fighting on the Bolshevik side, had attacked from Strastnaya Square. Roshchin had known him from his Moscow days—a cherubic schoolboy with blue eyes, and a tendency to blush. It seemed incredible that this lad from an old Moscow family could be the ferocious Bolshevik or Left Socialist-Revolutionary (whatever they called themselves!), shouldering his rifle and dodging behind the lime trees of Tverskoi Boulevard—the Tverskoi Boulevard hallowed by the poems of Pushkin, where Sablin himself, a grammar book under his arm, had once walked so sedately. "The betrayal of Russia, of the army, to clear the way for the Germans and release the wild beast—that's what you're fighting for, Mr. Sablin! The lower ranks, mere grovelling swine, may be forgiven, but you...." Roshchin himself was working a machine gun (in the trenches dug at the corner of Malaya Nikitskaya, in front of Chichkin's dairy), and when the slim figure in the long coat dodged out from behind the trees again, he peppered it with bullets. Sablin dropped his rifle and sank to the ground, clutching at his thigh. Almost at the same moment a fragment of shell carried off Roshchin's cap. He was out of action.

On the seventh night of street fighting, Moscow was enveloped in a thick yellow fog. The gurgling of shells had quieted down. Isolated groups of cadets, students and officials, still kept up a desultory firing, but the Committee for Public Safety, with a Zemstvo doctor named Rudnev at its head, had ceased to exist. Moscow was occupied by the troops of the Revolutionary Committee.

2*

The very next day young men in civilian clothes, carrying bundles, were to be met with in the streets, making for the Kursk and Bryansk railway stations. There was an ominous expression in their eyes, and though they wore puttees or cavalry boots, no one stopped them.

But for his injury Roshchin would have gone, too. He had had a slight paralytic stroke, followed by temporary blindness and heart trouble. He kept waiting for the moment when the troops from General Headquarters should suddenly appear, and start firing on the Kremlin from Vorobyovy Hills. But the revolution was only just beginning to strike root among the masses. Katya persuaded her husband to leave, to forget for a while both Bolsheviks and Germans. Then they would see....

Vadim Petrovich obeyed her. Once he had settled down in Samara, he never left the doctor's flat. He ate and slept. But how was he to forget? Every morning, opening the *Samara Soviet News*, which was printed on wrapping paper, he set his jaws. Every line seared him like a lash....

"...the All-Russia Congress of Soviets of Peasants' Deputies appeals to the peasants, workers and soldiers of Germany and Austro-Hungary to offer ruthless resistance to the imperialist demands of their governments.... We appeal to the soldiers, peasants and workers of France, England and Italy, to force their blood-thirsty governments to conclude an immediate, democratic, just peace with all nations.... Down with the imperialist war! Long live the fraternal ties between workers of all countries!"

"Forget! Oh, Katya! I should have to forget myself first! Forget the immemorial past! Our former greatness!... Less than a century ago, Russia was imposing her will upon Europe.... And are we to meekly lay all this at the feet of Germany now? Dictatorship of the proletariat! Oh, what words! Stupidity! Oh, Russian stupidity! And the muzhik? Oh, the muzhik! He will pay dear for all this...."

"No, Dmitri Stepanovich," Roshchin would reply to the doctor's endless arguments at the tea table, "there are still forces left in Russia.... We're not dead yet.... We're not mere dung for your Germans.... There's fight in us yet! We'll defend Russia—defend her to the death.... Only give us time!"

Katya, who was the third member of the party around the samovar, deduced only one thing from all these arguments—Roshchin, her beloved, was unhappy. He suffered as if under slow torture. His round cropped head had become touched with silver. His haggard face, with the dark sunken eyes, looked almost charred. When he said, clenching his heavy fists on the tattered oilcloth: "We will avenge ourselves! We will punish!", all Katya

20

understood was that he had come back home angry, powerless, wretched, and was threatening somebody: "Just wait—we'll be even with you!" But upon whom could Roshchin revenge himself—this gently bred, delicate, mortally weary man? Surely not upon those ragged Russian soldiers, begging for a crust and a cigarette in the cold streets? Katya would sit down gently beside her husband and stroke his hand. She was overcome with tenderness and pity for him. She could never understand evil—if she encountered it in another she was always ready to blame herself.

She understood nothing of what was going on. For her the revolution was like a stormy night which had descended upon Russia. There were a few words of which she was afraid: Sov. Dep. (Soviet of Deputies), for instance, seemed to her a ferocious word, Rev. Com. (Revolutionary Committee) a terrifying one, like the roar of a bull, thrusting its shaggy head through a wattle fence into the garden where the little Katya was standing. (There had been an incident like this in her childhood.) When she unfolded the single brown sheet of newspaper and read: "French imperialism, with its predatory plans and rapacious allies..." she conjured up Paris, with its still, bluish summer mists, its vanilla-flavoured melancholy, the gurgling rills in its gutters; she remembered the stranger who had followed her about and had spoken to her on the park bench the day before he died: "You mustn't be afraid of me, I have angina pectoris, I'm an old man. A great misfortune has come upon me—I have fallen in love with you. Oh, what a sweet face you have!"

"Surely *they're* not imperialists!" thought Katya.

Winter was drawing to an end. The town was full of rumours, each more fantastic than the last. It was said that the English and French were making a secret peace with Germany, in order to fall upon Russia with their combined forces. Legendary victories were ascribed to Kornilov, who was said to be breaking up, with a handful of officers, the thousand-strong battalions of the Red Guards, capturing Cossack villages, which they immediately relinquished as of no use to them, and preparing for a general summer offensive on Moscow.

"Oh, Katya!" cried Roshchin, "and I sit here in comfort while fighting is going on. It won't do!"

On the 4th of February a crowd bearing flags and slogans swept by the windows of the doctor's flat. Thick snow was falling, and a blizzard was beginning, and the brass trumpets blared out the *Internationale*. The doctor tumbled noisily into the dining room, his cap and coat sprinkled with snow.

21

"Peace with the Germans, friends!"

Glancing silently at the broad, glistening countenance of the doctor, with its expression of pawky defiance, and at his smugly triumphant smile, Roshchin turned to the window. Out there, enveloped in the blizzard, an immense crowd was tramping by—arm in arm, in groups, shouting and laughing. Greatcoats, wadded jackets, women, little boys, passed in endless procession, the real, the dingy Russia.... Where did they all come from?

The back of Roshchin's silvery head, tense and indignant, seemed to sink into his shoulders. Katya put her cheek against his shoulder. The life passing outside the window was quite incomprehensible to her.

"Look, Vadim!" she said, "how happy their faces are! Is it really the end of the war? It's hard to believe in anything so marvellous."

Roshchin moved away from her, his hands clasped tight behind his back. His mouth was set in a cruel line....

"Just you wait!"

Five men, in crumpled jackets and shirts of army cloth, were sitting at a table in a small, vaulted chamber. Their faces were dark from want of sleep. Telephones and glass tumblers stood about, among the papers, cigarette butts, and bits of bread with which the scorched baize on the table was littered. Occasionally the door into the long corridor opened letting in a buzz of talk, and a broad-shouldered military man wearing a cartridge belt would bring in a heap of papers for signature.

The chairman, the fifth man at the table, a stocky individual in a short grey jacket, sat in an armchair too high for him, and seemed to be dozing. His left hand rested on his forehead, covering the eyes and nose; all that could be seen of his face was a straight mouth with bristly moustache, and an unshaven cheek with twitching muscles. Only those who knew him well could discern between the interstices of the fingers so wearily covering his face, the keen, shrewd glances he kept casting at the speaker, and at the faces of the other three.

The telephones rang incessantly. The same broad-shouldered military man with the cartridge belt would lift the receiver, and jerk out, under his breath: "Sovnarcom* .... Meeting.... Impossible...." From time to time somebody in the corridor bumped against the door, and the brass knob would be turned. Outside,

---

*Council of People's Commissars.—Tr.

the wind from the sea raged, beating rain and particles of frozen snow against the windowpanes.

The speaker finished what he was saying. The men around the table sat with drooping heads or supported them on their hands. The chairman moved his hand higher up his bald skull, and scribbled a note, underlining one word so violently that the pen went through the paper. He threw the note to the man sitting next but one, a gaunt individual with a black moustache and bristling hair.

The latter read it, smiled into his moustache, and wrote a reply on the note....

The chairman, looking out of the window at the raging blizzard, quietly tore up the note into little bits.

"The speaker is right—we have no army, and no supplies," he said in a rather muffled voice. "We are moving in a vacuum. The Germans are advancing, and will continue to advance. The speaker is right."

He was interrupted by several people speaking at once:

"But this is the end! What's to be done? Capitulate? Go underground?"

"What's to be done?" he narrowed his eyes. "Fight! Fight ruthlessly! Defeat the Germans! If we can't beat them now—we will retreat to Moscow. And if the Germans take Moscow, we'll retreat to the Urals. We'll create a Ural-Kuznetsk Republic. There's coal and iron there, and a militant proletariat. We'll evacuate the Petrograd workers there. That'll go fine. And if need be, we'll retreat all the way to Kamchatka. One thing must never be lost sight of—we must preserve the flower of the working class, we mustn't let it be destroyed. And we'll occupy Petrograd and Moscow again.... The situation will change again and again in the west.... It's not the Bolshevik way to hang one's head and tear one's hair...."

He sprang out of the high chair with surprising vivacity, ran—his hands in his pockets—to the folding oak doors, and opened one leaf. The gaunt faces of Petrograd workers, their eyes glowing in the dim light of the corridor, turned towards him out of the steaming atmosphere. He raised a big ink-stained hand:

"Comrades, the socialist native land is in danger...!"

II

Early in the winter two streams of humanity were continually meeting at the South-Russian railway junctions. From the north came amateur politicians, officers in mufti, businessmen, policemen, proprietors escaping from burning estates, adventurers, actors, writers, government officials, adolescents who felt that the times of Fenimore Cooper were returning—in short the population, only lately so noisy and varied, of both capitals, fleeing from the chaos prophesied in the Apocalypse, to the rich grain districts of the Don, the Kuban, the Terek. From the south they were met by the immense Transcaucasian Army, pushing north with arms, machine guns, ammunitions, and truckloads of salt, sugar, textiles. When these streams met, there was a dense crowd, in which White Guard spies got to work. The Cossacks came from their villages to the trains to buy arms, rich peasants exchanging grain and lard for textiles. Everywhere were bandits and pickpockets. Those who got caught were "liquidated" on the spot, right on the rails.

The Red Guard covering detachments were quite ineffective, and were swept away like cobwebs. Here was the steppe and freedom. Cossacks had been striding about here from time immemorial. All was flimsy, all was in a state of flux, indefinite.... Today, outsiders and landless peasants prevailed and elected a Soviet, the next day the Cossacks from the villages drove back the Communists with cold steel and sent a messenger with a dispatch hidden in his cap to Ataman Kaledin in Novocherkassk. Nobody gave a fig for the Petrograd authorities here.

But towards the end of November Petrograd was beginning to make its power felt. The first revolutionary detachments were created—sailors, workers, homeless soldiers from the front—travelling from place to place in dilapidated troop trains. They were undisciplined and riotous, and though they fought savagely, they retreated at the slightest failure, and threatened, at the stupendous meetings held after a battle, to tear their commanders limb from limb.

The plan drawn up provided for the encirclement of Don and Kuban districts in three main directions: Sablin was to advance from the north-west, cutting the Don off from the Ukraine, Sievers' troops were to approach Rostov and Novocherkassk in a semicircle, and detachments of Black Sea sailors were to press on from Novorossiisk. In the interior, a rising was being prepared in the industrial and mining districts.

In January the Red detachments approached Taganrog, Rostov, and Novocherkassk. The breach between Cossacks and outsiders had not yet assumed threatening dimensions in the Don villages. The Don was still passive. The sparse troops of Ataman Kaledin abandoned the front without putting up a fight, under pressure from the Red troops.

The Red forces were a desperate menace to the foe. The workers in Taganrog rose and drove Kutepov's volunteer regiment out of the town. Sergeant Podtelkov's Red detachment completely routed the last ataman's covering force at Novocherkassk.

Then Ataman Kaledin made a last desperate appeal to the Don Cossacks to send Cossack volunteers to the only stable military formation—the Volunteer Army, formed in Rostov by generals Kornilov, Alexeyev, and Denikin. But no one responded to the Ataman's appeal.

On the twenty-ninth of January Kaledin summoned the ataman government in the palace of Novocherkassk. The fourteen Don Cossack colonels, famous generals and representatives of the "Moscow Centre for the Struggle Against Anarchy and Bolshevism", sat at the half-moon table in the white hall. The Ataman, a tall morose individual with a drooping moustache, said with sombre tranquillity:

"I have to inform you, gentlemen, that our position is hopeless. The forces of the Bolsheviks are increasing from day to day. Kornilov is withdrawing all his troops from our front. His decision is irrevocable. Only a hundred and forty-seven men responded to my appeal for the defence of the Don district. The population of the Don and the Kuban not only refuse us their support—they are hostile. Why is this? How are we to account for this shameful state of affairs? Corruption has been our ruin. There is no more sense of duty, no more honour. I propose, gentlemen, that you resign and hand over your authority to others." He took his seat, and added, not looking at anyone: "Be brief, gentlemen, time presses...."

Mitrofan Bogayevsky, the Ataman's assistant, cried out furiously:

"In other words you propose handing over the power to the Bolsheviks!"

To this the Ataman replied that the Cossack government could do as it saw fit, and left the meeting on the spot, going out with heavy footsteps through a side door to his own quarters. There he gazed through the window at the bare swaying tops of trees in the park, and dreary snow clouds, and called to his wife. She did not reply. Then he went into the bedroom, where a fire was glowing in the open grate. He removed his jacket and cross, and, for the last time, as if he could not yet quite believe it, stared hard at the war map hanging over the bed. The Don and Kuban steppes were surrounded by thick clusters of tiny red flags. The only place which bore the tricolour was the black point marking Rostov. The Ataman drew the warm, flat Browning gun from the hip pocket of his blue trousers with the officers' stripes and shot himself in the heart.

On the ninth of February General Kornilov left his small Volunteer Army, composed entirely of officers and cadets, accompanied by cartloads of generals and some of the most important refugees, out of Rostov into the steppes, beyond the Don.

The General, a short, angry-looking man with Mongol features, marched at the head of the troops, a soldier's knapsack on his back. On one of the carts in the line the unfortunate General Denikin lay beneath a stripy rug, struck down by an attack of bronchitis.

The brown steppe, denuded of snow, floated past the windows of the railway carriage. A chill wind, smelling of the thawing earth, blew in through the broken glass. Katya was looking out of the window. Her head and shoulders were enveloped in a downy Orenburg shawl, knotted at the small of her back. Roshchin, in a soldier's greatcoat and tattered peaked cap, lay dozing on the seat. The train was going very slowly. Tall trees came in sight, their enmeshed branches thickly clustered with nests. Clouds of rooks were circling above them, or swaying on the branches. Katya moved closer to the window. The rooks cawed in vociferous anxiety, as in spring as they had cawed when Katya was a little girl—about the torrents released in spring, the mists, the first storms....

Katya and Roshchin were travelling south. They were going they knew not where—to Rostov, to Novocherkassk, to the Don villages. To some place where the knot of civil war was being tied. Roshchin slept, his head drooping, his unshaven face thin, the harsh lines showing round his fastidiously compressed lips. Katya felt a sudden panic. It was not *his* face, this unfamiliar countenance with the peaked nose....The wind bore the sound of the cawing of the rooks through the window. The train went slowly on, clattering over the points. Over a muddy path slanting across the steppe, there stretched a train of carts—shaggy ponies, farm carts plastered with mud, and in them bearded men, of unfamiliar, terrible aspect. Roshchin gave utterance in his sleep to something between a snore and a moan, a hoarse, painful sound. Katya touched his face with trembling fingers.

"Vadim, Vadim!"

The alarming sounds ceased abruptly. He opened eyes perfectly void of expression.

"Hell! I do have such beastly dreams!..."

The train came to a stop. Now the sound of voices mingled with the cawing of rooks. Women in men's boots, with sacks on their shoulders, came running up, pushing their way, exposing their white thighs as they climbed on to the goods truck. A tousled head in a greasy peaked cap, with a shaggy beard growing right up to the eyes, thrust itself into the window of the carriage where Katya was sitting.

"You don't happen to have a machine gun for sale?"

There was a sound of loud coughing from the upper berth, as someone there turned heavily, and a jovial voice replied:

"The machine guns are all sold, but we have some cannon."

"We have no use for them," said the peasant, his beard sticking out like a broom when he opened his big mouth. He thrust his head and shoulders into the carriage, and cast a shrewd glance around. "Anything to be had here?" A tall soldier jumped down from the top berth—he had a broad face, insolent blue eyes, and a shapely, shaven skull. He tightened the belt of his coat with an energetic gesture.

"You shouldn't be fighting, Dad, your time has come to fart on the stove ledge...."

"That's where I ought to be," agreed the peasant. "But there's no sleeping on the stove ledge now, soldier. Nobody's going to let you, and one has to get food some other way."

"By robbing?"

"Tut-tut!"

"What d'you want a machine gun for?"

"Well now..." the peasant rubbed his nose and passed a gnarled hand over his whiskers to hide the gleam and the sly laughter in his eyes. "My son has come back from the war. 'You go to the station,' he told me, 'and find out the price of a machine gun. I'd go up to four poods of wheat....' Well?"

"Kulaks!" laughed the soldier. "Fat devils! How many horses have you got, Dad?"

"God gave me eight. Hasn't anyone got anything to sell—arms or something?" Once more he glanced at the passengers, and suddenly his smile vanished, and his eyes went dull, and, turning away as if the people in the railway carriage were so much dung, he stumped back through the mud of the platform, flourishing his whip.

"Get that?" said the soldier, looking frankly at Katya. "Eight horses! And probably has twelve sons. He just gets them into the saddle, and off they go over the steppe—plunderers. And he lies on the stove ledge, resting his backside on the grain, keeping guard on the booty."

The soldier transferred his glance to Roshchin, and suddenly his brows lifted, and his face lit up.

"Vadim Petrovich—is it you?"

27

Roshchin glanced swiftly at Katya but there was no help for it. He had to stretch out his hand in greeting. The soldier pressed it warmly, and sat down beside him. Katya could see that Roshchin was put out.

"So we meet again," he said sourly. "Glad to see you looking so well, Alexei Ivanovich. You see how I've had to rig myself out!"

Then Katya understood that this soldier was Alexei Krasilnikov, Roshchin's former orderly. Vadim Petrovich had often spoken of him, and considered him a splendid specimen of a talented and intelligent Russian peasant. She wondered why he was so cold to him. Krasilnikov, however, seemed to understand. Smiling, he lit a cigarette, asking in a low, matter-of-fact voice: "That your wife?"

"Yes, I'm married. Let me introduce you. Katya, this is my guardian angel—you remember me telling you about him. Well, we fought the good fight together, Alexei Ivanovich, and now allow me to congratulate you on the filthy peace. The Russian eagles...." (He laughed bitterly.) "And now my wife and I are making for the South ... nearer to the sun...." (The words sounded false in his own ears, and Roshchin frowned. Krasilnikov gave not the slightest sign of emotion.) "Nothing else left now.... Our grateful country has rewarded us with a bayonet in our bellies...." (He shuddered, as if bitten all over by lice.) "Outlawed, enemies of the people.... That's what we are...."

"You're in a difficult situation!" Krasilnikov wagged his head, looking out of the window through narrowed lids. On the other side of a broken fence a crowd was gathering on the plot of ground belonging to the station. "Just as if you were a foreigner. *I* understand you, Vadim Petrovich, but not everybody would. You don't know our people!"

"What d'you mean by that?"

"Simply that you never did know them. And you've been deceived all along."

"By whom?"

"By us, us soldiers and muzhiks.... The moment you turned your back, we laughed. Vadim Petrovich! Selfless heroism, love for the tsar, for the native land—the gentry invented all that, and we were made to repeat it in the army.... I'm just a muzhik. I'm going to fetch my younger brother in Rostov. He's lying there wounded, with an officer's bullet in his chest. I'm going to take him back to the village. Perhaps we shall till the soil, or perhaps we'll fight.... We'll see when we get there. But if we do fight, it'll be of our own free will, without any drums, and we'll fight like hell! Better not go south, Vadim Petrovich. I don't think it'll agree with you."

Roshchin gazed at him with shining eyes, passing his tongue over his parched lips. Krasilnikov was looking more and more attentively at what was going on at the other side of the fence. The buzz of angry voices was getting louder and louder. A few people climbed trees, to get a better view.

"You won't be able to manage the people, I tell you! You're no better than foreigners, you bourgeois. That's a bad word nowadays, like saying—horse thief. An old soldier like Kornilov—he pinned the St. George's cross on my tunic with his own hands—tried to get the Cossacks to fight for the Constituent Assembly, and what has come of it—nothing! He couldn't find the right words, though you'd think he knew the people.... Now they say he's roaming about the Kuban steppe, like a dog among a pack of wolves.... The muzhiks say: 'The bourgeois are furious at not having their way in Moscow....' They're keeping their rifles oiled and clean in case of anything happening. Make no mistake about it! No, no, Vadim Petrovich, you go back to the capital, you and your wife.... It'll be safer for you there than here, among the muzhiks.... Just look at them...." (Suddenly he raised his voice, frowning.) "They'll kill him..."

Behind the railings things seemed to be coming to a head. Two stocky soldiers with ferocious expressions on their faces, were firmly holding a frail man dressed in a torn jacket made from a flannel blanket. His unshaven face was deathly pale, the nose swollen, and blood was trickling down from the corner of his quivering lips. He was watching the movements of an infuriated young woman, from eyes in which there was a pale gleam. She kept tearing her thick shawl from her head, squatting down and spreading out her skirts, and throwing herself upon the man with the pale face, seizing him by his bristling hair, and screaming almost exultantly:

"He stole it, he got it from under my petticoats, the beast! Give me back my money!"

Then she clutched at his cheeks, holding on like grim death. The pale man jerked himself free, but the soldiers held him down. The woman gave a squeal. And then, pushing people out of his way, the peasant with the bearlike head made his appearance upon the scene, shoved the woman aside with his shoulder, struck the pale man neatly in the mouth, and gave a loud grunt. The latter sank to the ground. A man with long coat sleeves, perched on the nearest tree, bent down, shouting: "Murder!" The crowd immediately began to press forward. People bent over the body and straightened themselves again, shaking their fists.

The window of the railway carriage floated past the crowd. At last! A suppressed cry seemed to stick in Katya's throat. Roshchin frowned his disgust. Krasilnikov shook his head.

"Tchk! Tchk! And they killed him all for nothing, probably!" he said. "Those women would drive anybody crazy. They're worse than the men. Nobody knows what's come over them these last four years. We come back from the war, and what do we find—our women have quite changed. You dare not so much as tickle them with the reins—you have to look out for yourself. Oh how uppish the women have become!"

At first sight it was difficult to understand why the "organizers of the salvation of Russia"—Commanders in Chief Alexeyev and Lavr Kornilov—should have led a handful of officers and cadets (five thousand in all), with the most wretched artillery, and practically no shells or cartridges, to the south, to Ekaterinodar, into the very thick of the Bolshevik forces, which formed a semicircle around the capital of the Kuban Cossacks.

No strict strategical plan could be discerned in this. The Volunteer Army had been violently ejected from Rostov, which they had been unable to hold. It had been swept into the Kuban steppe by the wave of revolution. But a political plan there was, and two months later this plan was justified. The rich Cossacks were inevitably bound to rise against the outsiders—by which was meant the new population, who rented Cossack lands, but enjoyed no rights or privileges whatever.* There were one million six hundred thousand "outsiders", as against one million four hundred thousand Cossacks.

The "outsiders" were inevitably bound to strive for land and power. The Cossacks, just as inevitably—to rise in arms in defence of their privileges. The "outsiders" were led by the Bolsheviks. At first the Cossacks would recognize no authority over themselves. They would live as proprietors in their own villages— what could be better? But in February, Golubov, a Cossack adventurer with twenty-seven Cossacks at his back, broke in upon a conference at the field headquarters of Ataman Nazarov in Novocherkassk, and, brandishing his rifle, shouted, amidst the click of gunlocks: "Stand up, you blackguards! Soviet Ataman Golubov has come to take power!" The next day Ataman Nazarov and his staff were taken out and shot in a copse on the outskirts of the

---

* *Cossack privileges.* The most important of the privileges introduced by the tsarist government in 1835, was that of allotting land for life to landless Cossacks, according to their rank.

town, and Golubov, to secure for himself the ataman's mace, after having about two thousand Cossack officers shot, galloped into the steppe to get Mitrofan Bogayevsky, whom he then dragged about to meetings, to speechify on behalf of a free Don and his own leadership. But when Golubov himself was killed soon after, at a meeting held in the village of Zaplavskaya, in February, the Cossacks found themselves leaderless. And from the north they were menaced by Great Russia—dishevelled, impatient, famished.

To direct the Cossack movement from Ekaterinodar, to mobilize a regular Cossack army, to cut off from Bolshevik Russia the Caucasus, and the Grozni and Baku oil fields, to emphasize their loyalty to the Allies, such were the initial plans of the command of the Volunteer Army, when embarking upon what was later known as the "Frost Campaign".

Seaman Semyon Krasilnikov (the brother of Alexei) lay with others like him, in a ploughed field on the edge of a ravine not far from the railway line. Beside them a soldier, diligent as a mole, was digging with a spade. When he had got himself entrenched he shoved his rifle in front of him, and turned to Semyon.

"Dig deeper, brother."

Semyon had difficulty in digging away the sticky clods from beneath him. Bullets were whistling overhead. The spade struck a brick. Swearing, Semyon rose to his knees, and instantly received a stinging blow in the chest. Gasping and choking, he fell face downwards into the hollow he had dug.

It was one of the innumerable brief battles to stop the advance of the Volunteer Army. The Red forces, as almost always, were numerically stronger. And, while perfectly capable of fighting, it was no great catastrophe for them to retreat. During the early period of the Civil War, victory was not of the first importance to them. Should a position be inconvenient, or the cadets be for the moment too great a menace, it didn't matter much. They could wait till next time—and they would let Kornilov pass.

For the Volunteer Army, however, each battle was a matter of life and death. It was compelled to win a battle and move its baggage carts and its wounded in a single day's march. There was no possibility of retreat. And the Kornilov troops conquered by the force of sheer despair. This time, too, the same thing happened.

On a last year's haystack, about a quarter of a mile from the lines under machine-gun fire, stood Kornilov, his legs straddled. Raising his elbows, he looked through field glasses. A canvas knapsack quivered on his back. His sheepskin coat, black with grey trimmings, was unbuttoned. He was hot. His chin, which was covered with grey stubble, stuck out obstinately beneath the field glasses.

Below, hugging the side of the haystack, stood Lieutenant Dolinsky, the Commander's aide, a large-eyed, black-browed youth wearing an officer's greatcoat and a jauntily dented peaked cap. Swallowing the excitement rising in his throat, he looked up at the Commander's grey chin, as if the only hope of survival was in this stubble—so human, so familiar!

"Excellency, come down, I implore you—you'll be shot," said Dolinsky over and over again. He saw Kornilov's purple lips part, baring his teeth convulsively. This meant things were bad. Dolinsky no longer looked over there, where the tiny black figures of the Bolshevik lines kept moving and running over the brown-green steppe. Bursts of shrapnel poured over them with protracted hisses. But he knew very well how few—God, how few!—shells there were. Beyond the bridge, which had been blown up, sounded the grave "boom!" of the Bolshevik heavy gun... A machine gun chimed in with its hurried raprap. And bullets buzzed like bees all round the Commander's head.

"You'll be shot, Excellency...."

Kornilov let the field glasses fall to his side. He puckered up his tanned Mongolian face, with the black birdlike eyes. Stamping over the hay, he turned and leaned towards a group of dismounted Turkmen who were standing behind the haystack. These were his bodyguard. They were lean, bowlegged men in huge round sheepskin caps and striped, salmon-coloured Circassian tunics. They stood motionless as statues, holding the bridles of their lean horses.

Kornilov barked out an order in his harsh voice, and pointed to the ravine. The Turkmen scrambled into their saddles like cats, one of them uttered a characteristic guttural cry, and they all waved their crooked swords, and set off, first at a trot, then at a gallop, for the steppe, in the direction of the ravine, where there was a strip of black ploughland, and, beyond it, the railway line.

Semyon Krasilnikov lay on his side now—he felt easier that way. Only an hour ago strong and full of fury, now he lay groaning feebly, spitting up blood with an effort. To his right and left his comrades were firing spasmodically. Like him, they were all looking at the brown slope on the other side of the ravine. About fifty horsemen were pouring in lava formation down its side. This was the charge of the cavalry reserve.

A man ran up from behind, and fell on his knees beside Krasilnikov, shouting himself hoarse and brandishing a Mauser. He wore a black leather jacket. The horsemen made a clattering descent of the ravine. The man in the leather jacket was shouting, in quite unmilitary but extremely insistent tones:

"Don't you dare retreat—stand your ground!"

Huge caps now began to show on the near side of the ravine, and a drawn-out cry, like the howling of the wind, was heard. It was the Turkmen dashing up. In their striped quilted jackets, almost prone on their horses' necks, they galloped over the glutinous ploughland, in the furrows of which there were still patches of grimy snow. Clods of mud were hurled into the air by the horses' hoofs. Blood-curdling cries issued from the throats of the little men in the tall caps, their bared teeth set in fierce grins on their tanned, moustached faces. Now the watery gleam of their crooked swords could be seen. How were the Reds to repel a cavalry attack? The grey-coated figures rose from the ploughland. They fired, retreating. The Commissar in the leather jacket was in a frenzy—he leaped forward and struck one of them in the back:

"Forward—charge with the bayonets!"

It seemed to Krasilnikov that one of the stripy-robed figures had rolled off his horse on purpose, while the good steed, turning a terrified eye over its shoulder, galloped away. A metallic clashing sound, clouds of smoke, and the yellow lightning of shrapnel burst over the line. And Vaska, the wag in the outsized greatcoat, suddenly threw down his rifle in a panic, staring pale and open-mouthed, as death came thundering up. The horsemen drew nearer, getting larger and larger. One of them was tearing ahead, his horse almost hugging the ground, holding its head down like a dog. Its rider straightened up, and stood in the stirrups, the skirts of his robe flying apart.

"The swine!" Krasilnikov reached for his rifle. "Our Commissar's in for it!" The horseman charged at the leather jacket. "Shoot him, shoot him—can't you?"

Krasilnikov only had time to see the crooked sword come sweeping down on the leather jacket.... And the next minute the whole stream of cavalry fell upon the line. There was a hot whiff of horses' sweat.

The Turkmen overran the line and turned to the flanks. At the same time men in light-grey and black greatcoats, their officers' shoulder straps gleaming, came running out of the ravine, and stumbled across the field.

"Hurrah-ah-ah!"

The fighting moved nearer to the railway line. For a long time Krasilnikov could only hear the groans of the wounded Commissar. The shots grew more and more infrequent. The guns fell si-

3–559

lent. Krasilnikov closed his eyes—there was a buzzing in his head, and he had a pain in his chest. He felt a wave of self-pity, he did not want to die. His body seemed to be getting heavier, to be sinking into the ground. He thought pityingly of his wife, Matryona. She would be lost without him. How she had longed for him, forever writing to him in Taganrog—come, oh, come! If his Matryona were with him now she would bind up his wound, and bring him a drink. How nice a glass of cold water would be ... and then a bowl of curds....

When Krasilnikov heard voices swearing—officers' voices, not his comrades'—he opened his eyes cautiously. There were four of them walking together—one in a grey Circassian tunic, two in officers' greatcoats, and the fourth in a students' overcoat with NCO shoulder straps sewn on to it. They held their rifles under their armpits, as hunters do.

"Look, a sailor—finish him off, the bastard," said one.

"Leave him alone—he's dead. That one over there's still alive."

They stood still, looking at the prostrate figure of Vaska, the wag. The one in the Circassian tunic suddenly barked out: "Get up!" and gave Vaska a kick.

Krasilnikov saw Vaska get up, one half of his face streaming with blood.

"Ten-shun!" shouted the one in the Circassian tunic and hit Vaska in the mouth. And instantly all four held their rifles atilt.

"Spare me, kind Uncle!" cried Vaska in a weeping voice.

The one in the Circassian tunic leaped away from him, and, drawing the air through his nostrils with a loud sound, thrust his bayonet into Vaska's stomach. Then he turned and walked away. The others bent over Vaska and dragged off his boots.

When the Volunteers, after shooting their prisoners and setting fire to the village council to teach the people to know better next time, proceeded on their way southward, Semyon Krasilnikov was picked up from the ploughland by Cossacks. The cadet lines had hardly disappeared beneath the low horizon, leaving behind them the steppe, just beginning to show pale green sprouts, when the Cossacks with their wives, children and cattle, returned to their village.

Semyon did not want to die among strangers. He had some money on him, and found a man to take him in a cart to Rostov. From there he wrote to his brother that he was severely wounded and was afraid of dying among strangers, adding that he would like to see Matryona. The letter was taken by a man from Semyon's village.

Up to 1918 Semyon had served in the Black Sea Fleet, as a

sailor on the destroyer *Kerch*. The fleet was under the command of Admiral Kolchak. For all his intellect, education, and what seemed to him his selfless love for Russia, Kolchak understood nothing of what was going on, or of what was bound to take place. He knew the strength and armaments of all the world's navies, could recognize the silhouette of any warship in a sea fog, was an expert on mines, and one of the initiators of the campaign for raising the efficiency of the Russian navy after the catastrophe of Tsushima.* But if anyone had spoken to him before 1917 about politics, he would have replied that he was not interested in politics, that he did not understand them, and considered them the business of students, dingy blue stockings, and Jews.

For him, Russia was a smoking column of battleships (existing and to be), with the St. Andrew's flag proudly fluttering from the flagship, making Germany quake in her shoes. He loved the severe Empire style entrance to the building of the Ministry for War, with its familiar hall porter, who would help him off with his coat with paternal care and say: "Nasty weather, Alexander Vasilyevich!"; he loved his well-bred elegant colleagues, and the reserved, friendly spirit of the Officers' Club. The tsar was the fountainhead of this system, of these traditions.

And there was another Russia, which Kolchak loved no less: the Russia which lined up on the quarter-deck—sailors in ribboned caps, broad-faced, tanned, strong-limbed; the Russia which could be felt in the splendid voices singing the evening prayer, when the flag was lowered at sunset; the Russia which knew how to lay down her life without a murmur when she was told to do so. It was a country to be proud of.

In 1917 Kolchak took the oath of fealty to the Provisional Government without a moment's hesitation, and went on commanding the Black Sea Fleet. With embittered submission bowing to the inevitable, he endured the fall of the head of the Empire, and, clenching his teeth, recognized the Seamen's Committees and the revolutionary order, all for the sake of keeping the navy and Russia in a state of war with Germany. He would have gone on fighting so long as he had a single torpedo boat left. He went to seamen's meetings in Sevastopol, and, replying to the incendiary speeches of local and visiting orators—workers, all of them—said that he personally had no need of the Dardanelles and the Bos-

*****

Tsushima—island in the Korean Straits. During the Russo-Japanese war of 1904-05, the Russian squadron, owing to the inept strategy of the tsarist High Command, suffered grave defeat at the Battle of Tsushima. The losses of the Japanese fleet were also severe.

phorus, since he had neither lands nor factories, and nothing to export, but that he demanded war, war, war, "and not as a hireling of the bourgeoisie" (here a fastidious grimace distorted his clean-shaven face, with the strong chin, weak mouth and sunken eyes), "but as a Russian patriot".

The seamen laughed. It was appalling! Only the day before zealously ready to go through fire and water for their country and for the flag of St. Andrew, they were now shouting at their Admiral: "Down with the hirelings of imperialism!" He had uttered the words "Russian patriot" with force, with a frank gesture, ready at that moment to lay down his life, and the seamen—the devil must have got into them—had listened to the Admiral as if he were an enemy trying to entrap them with his wiles.

At meetings Semyon Krasilnikov learned that it was not "patriots", but industrialists and big landed proprietors who wished to prolong the war, which was yielding them great profits, and that the people did not need the war. He learned that the Germans were peasants and workers like the Russians, only fighting because they had been deceived by their own bloodthirsty bourgeoisie and Mensheviks. At meetings the sailors worked themselves up into a frenzy of hate: "They have been deceiving the Russian people for a thousand years! They have been drinking our blood for a thousand years! The landowners, the bourgeoisie—oh, the vipers!" Eyes were opened: *that's* why we have always lived worse than cattle ... *that's* where the enemy lurks! And though Semyon was terribly homesick for his abandoned farm and his young wife, he clenched his fists as he listened to the speakers, grew drunk like all the rest on the wine of revolution, and in this intoxication forgot his homesickness, and his longing for the beautiful Matryona....

One day a famous agitator, Vasili Rublev, came from Petrograd. He put the question: "Are you going to play the fool for ever, brothers, and be content with showing your teeth at meetings? Kerensky has long ago sold you to the capitalists. They'll give you a little more time for holding forth, and then the counterrevolutionaries will begin chopping off everybody's heads. Get rid of Kolchak before it's too late, take the navy in your workers' and peasants' hands...."

The next day a radio message was sent out from a battleship: "disarm all officers." A few officers shot themselves, the rest surrendered their arms. On flagship *St. George the Conqueror*, Kolchak had the entire crew called to the upper deck. The sailors, laughing, came up on the quarter-deck. Admiral Kolchak stood on the bridge dressed in full uniform.

"Sailors!" he cried in a shrill, cracked voice. "An irreparable misfortune has occurred. The enemies of the people, secret German agents, have disarmed the officers. And who is such a fool as to speak seriously of an officers' counterrevolutionary plot? Generally speaking I am bound to say that there is no such thing as counterrevolution—it doesn't exist."

Here the Admiral began pacing the bridge, his sword clattering, the better to give rein to his feelings.

"I regard all that has occurred as first and foremost a personal insult to myself, as your senior officer, and naturally I neither can nor will go on commanding the navy and shall immediately send a cable to the Government. 'Giving up the navy and leaving.' I've had enough!"

Semyon saw the Admiral seize the gold hilt of his sword in both hands, try to unfasten it from his belt, and, finding it entangled, tug at it violently. His very lips were blue.

"Every honest officer would do the same in my place!"

He raised his sword and cast it into the sea. But this heroic gesture made not the slightest impression on the sailors.

From that moment the navy was in a turmoil, and storms were in the offing. The sailors, closely united by life at sea, healthy, audacious and agile, having seen oceans and foreign lands, were less backward than the soldiers, and more alive to the impassable gulf between the wardroom and crew's quarters, and all this made of them a highly inflammable element. And the revolution was quick to make use of them. The sailors threw themselves into the heat of the struggle with all their unspent passion, themselves spurring to action a foe which had up to then been vacillating, procrastinating, still mustering its forces.

Semyon had no time for thoughts of home and wife now. By October, speechifying was over and the rifles began to speak. The enemy was to be met at every hand. Death lurked in every terrified, furtive glance of hate. From the Baltic to the Pacific, from the White Sea to the Black Sea, Russia was tossed in turbid confusion. Semyon slung his rifle over his shoulder and set off to combat the "hydra of counterrevolution".

Carrying a bundle and a kettle, Roshchin and Katya threaded their way through the crowds at the station and were borne along by the tide of humanity between the threatening bayonets of the outposts. Once outside, they sauntered aimlessly up Rostov's principal street. Only six weeks before, the flower of Petersburg society had been strolling from shop to shop here. The pavements had been gay with guardsmen's caps and the jingling of spurs, snatches of French could be heard, and elegantly attired ladies snuggled into expensive furs to shield their noses from the chill damp. With incredible frivolity they thought only of wintering here, and returning in time for the white nights to their Petersburg flats and mansions, with the respectful hall porters, pillared drawing rooms, carpets, and blazing fires. Oh, Petersburg! In the end everything was bound to turn out all right! Certainly the elegantly attired ladies were in no way to blame!

And suddenly, as if some great stage manager had clapped his hands, everything disappeared, as on a revolving stage. The scenery was entirely changed. The streets of Rostov were deserted. The shops were boarded up, their plate-glass windows punctured with bullet holes. The ladies hid away their furs and bound up their heads in kerchiefs. Some of the officers left with Kornilov, but the greater part became, with dramatic rapidity, harmless townsmen, actors, cabaret singers, dancing teachers, and the like. And the February wind drove the rubbish in clouds over the pavements.

"We came too late," said Roshchin.

He walked with drooping head. He felt as if the body of Russia had been broken into a thousand bits. The dome which had protected the Empire had been smashed to smithereens. The people had become a herd. History and the great past had vanished like a transparency in front of a stage setting. The naked, scorched desert, now dotted all over with graves, was exposed. The end of Russia.... He felt as if something within him had been shattered, and that its sharp fragments were piercing that which he had always considered indestructible, the very axis around which his life revolved. He kept a pace behind Katya, stumbling as he walked. "Rostov has fallen, Kornilov's army, the last wandering remnant of Russia, is on the eve of annihilation, and when this happens there will be nothing left but to put a bullet in one's brains."

They were walking at random. Roshchin remembered the addresses of some of his former regimental comrades. But they, too, might have run away or been shot. Then there remained only death in the road. He glanced at Katya. She was stepping out serenely and modestly in her short cloth jacket and Orenburg shawl. Her sweet face, with the great grey eyes, kept turning with naive wonder from the torn notices to the broken shop windows. The ghost of a smile hovered over the corners of her lips. "Can it be she doesn't realize how terrible it all is? I can't understand this spirit of universal forgiveness."

A group of unarmed soldiers stood at a corner. One of them, a pock-marked fellow with a black eye, held under his armpit a loaf of greyish bread, from which he was slowly tearing off a bit at a time, and as slowly munching it.

"You can't make out what the power is here—Soviet or something else," another was saying to him. This one had a wooden chest to which was tied a pair of worn felt boots. The one eating the bread replied:

"The power belongs to Comrade Broinitsky. Let's go and find him, he'll give us a train, and we'll go away. If we don't we'll have to rot here till kingdom come."

"Who is he? What's his rank?"

"Military Commissar, or something...."

Roshchin approached the soldiers and asked them the way to the address he was seeking. One of them answered in unfriendly tones:

"We're strangers ourselves."

Another said:

"You've come to the Don at a bad time, officer."

Katya tugged at her husband's sleeve and they crossed to the opposite pavement. There, on a broken bench beneath a leafless tree sat an old man in a threadbare coat and straw hat, resting his unshaven chin on the handle of his stick. He was shaking convulsively, and tears were running down his hollow cheeks from his closed eyes.

A tremor passed over Katya's face. Roshchin pulled her by the sleeve.

"Come on, you can't pity everyone...."

They roamed the dirty, dilapidated town for hours before they found the number of the house they wanted. Turning into the gate they came upon a short man with fat legs and a skull as bare as an egg, in a soldier's wadded sleeveless vest, covered with grease spots. He was carrying a vat, his face averted from the stench arising from it. It was Lieutenant Colonel Tetkin, a brother officer of Roshchin's. Placing the vat on the ground he embraced Vadim Petrovich, and bringing his heels together, pressed Katya's hand.

"I see everything, don't say a word—I'll get you settled. But you'll have to share a room. Still, there's a three-leaved mirror, and an aspidistra. My wife comes from these parts, you see.... At first we lived there" (he pointed to a two-storey brick house), "and then we moved over here, in quite a proletarian way." (He pointed to a rickety wooden annex.) "And I, as you observe, make boot polish. I registered at the labour exchange as unemployed.

So long as the neighbours don't inform on us we'll see it through somehow. We're Russians, we're used to this sort of thing."

He laughed, opening his big mouth and displaying a splendid set of teeth. Then he said thoughtfully: "See what we've come to!" and rubbed his skull with his hand, smearing it with boot polish.

His wife, as short and stocky as himself, welcomed the guests in a melodious voice, but they could see in her hazel eyes that she was not enraptured. Katya and Roshchin were shown into a low room with torn wallpaper. In the corner there really was a shabby three-leaved mirror, its glass turned to the wall, an aspidistra, and an iron bedstead.

"We turned the glass to the wall for safety's sake, it's a valuable thing, you know," said Tetkin. "If they came to raid the place they'd smash the glass to smithereens. They can't bear to see their own faces." He laughed again, rubbing his skull. "And in a way I understand them, you know. A mirror in the midst of all this breakage—of course one would smash it."

His wife laid the table neatly, but the forks were rusty, the plates broken—they must have hidden away their best things. Vadim and Katya enjoyed the savour of dried fish, white bread, and eggs fried in lard. Tetkin fussed round them, filling their plates with food. His wife, her plump arms folded under her chest, complained of everything.

"Such disgraceful goings-on, such oppression, it's simply excruciating! I haven't been out of the house for over a month.... If only they'd drive away those Bolsheviks! What are they saying about it in the capital? Will they soon crush them?"

"You be careful," said Tetkin anxiously. "You won't be patted on the head for such words, Sofia Ivanovna, these days!"

"I'm not going to hold my tongue—let them shoot me!" Sofia Ivanovna's eyes grew round, and she hugged herself still tighter. "The tsar will come back, he will!" She turned on her husband, her bosom heaving. "You're the only one who can't see that!"

Tetkin frowned apologetically. When his wife flounced angrily out of the room, he whispered:

"Take no notice, she's a good-hearted woman and a splendid housewife, but all these things have made her almost crazy..." (he glanced at Katya's face, flushed from drinking tea, and at Roshchin, who was rolling a cigarette). "Ah, Vadim Petrovich, it's all so complicated! You can't reject everything pell-mell. I come in contact with people, I see a lot.... I'm often at Bataisk, on the other side of the Don—it's mostly poor people, workers, who live there. They're not scoundrels, Vadim Petrovich. No, no, they're oppressed, insulted human beings. How they've been waiting for the

40

Soviet power! For God's sake, don't think I'm a Bolshevik or anything of that sort..." (he pressed his stumpy, hairy hands imploringly to his chest, as if in deep apology). "Rostov has been handed to the Bolsheviks by supercilious and incapable rulers. You should have seen what went on here under Ataman Kaledin. The guards, dissipated and arrogant, strolled up and down Sadovaya Street! 'We'll drive those swine down to the cellars!' That's the way they talked. And those swine are the entire Russian people. They resisted, they didn't want to go down to the cellars. I was at Novocherkassk in December. Remember the guardhouse on the principal avenue there? They say it was built by Ataman Platov* in the time of Alexander the Blessed—a small building in the 'Empire' style. I can shut my eyes, Vadim Petrovich, and see before me the steps of this portico, running with blood.... As I passed it I heard a terrible shriek—the shriek of a man under torture. In the daytime, in the middle of the capital of the Don.... I went nearer. There was a crowd—Cossacks standing by their horses, in front of the guardhouse. They were all looking on in silence— floggings were going on at the pillars, to intimidate the population. They were taking two at a time from the convoys, workers arrested for sympathizing—only for sympathizing, mind you—with the Bolsheviks. Their wrists were immediately twisted and bound to the pillars, and four sturdy Cossacks were lashing them on the backs and buttocks. The whip whistled, and, first fragments of shirts and trousers, and then pieces of flesh, flew up into the air, and blood streamed down the steps, like at a slaughter house.... I'm not easily shocked, but this time I was.... Their cries were terrible. People don't shriek like that from physical pain alone...."
Roshchin listened to him with lowered eyelids. His fingers trembled as they held the cigarette. Tetkin scratched at a mustard stain on the tablecloth.

"And there you are—the Ataman is no longer alive, the flower of the Cossack nobility lie buried in the gully outside the town, the blood on the steps cries for vengeance. The power of the poor.... I myself don't care whether I make boot polish or do something else.... I escaped with my life from the world war, and the only thing I value is the breath of life. Excuse the phrase. I read a lot of books in the trenches, and my phrases have become literary.... So you see...." (He glanced towards the door and lowered his voice.) "I reconcile myself to any regime so long as I see people are happy ... I'm not a Bolshevik, understand that, Vadim Petrovich...." (Again his hands spread imploringly over his chest.) "I

*Ataman Platov—famous Cossack general, hero of the 1812 Patriotic War.

myself don't need much—a bit of bread, a pinch of tobacco, and genuine spiritual contacts..." (He smiled apologetically.) "But that's just the point—the workers grumble, not to mention the man in the street.... Have you heard of Comrade Broinitsky, the Military Commissar? My advice is—if you see his car—hide! He came to the top immediately after the taking of Rostov. At the slightest word he shouts: 'Comrade Lenin knows my worth, I'll send a personal telegram to Comrade Lenin....' He's surrounded himself with the criminal element, who are continually carrying out requisitions and taking people out to be shot. They strip anyone they meet at night. He behaves like a bandit... Disgraceful! And where does the requisitioned property go? And the Revolutionary Committee can't do a thing with him, you know! They're afraid.... I don't believe he's a man of principle. He does more harm than good to the proletarian cause...." (But here Tetkin, seeing he had gone rather far, turned aside, gave a sniff, and again, this time without a word, laid his hand on his chest.)

"I don't understand you, Colonel," said Roshchin coldly. "The Broinitskys and their lot are 96 carat Soviet power. We don't try to justify them, we fight them at the peril of our lives.... "

"In whose name?" asked Tetkin quickly.

"In the name of Great Russia, Colonel!"

"And what's that? Great Russia according to whose conception? I should like you to be a little more precise. That of Petrograd society? That's one meaning. Or that of the infantry regiment in which you and I served, dying heroically on the barbed-wire entanglements? Or that of the Moscow Commercial Conference? Remember how Ryabushinsky sobbed over Great Russia in the Bolshoi Theatre? That's a third meaning. Or that of a worker who realizes the greatness of Russia on holidays, as he sees it from the dirty tavern? Or that of the hundred million peasants who...."

"What the devil...." (Katya gave Roshchin's hand a quick squeeze under the table.) "Excuse me, Colonel! Till now I knew that Russia was called one sixth of the earth's surface, inhabited by a people with a great history.... Perhaps that's not the Bolshevik view.... I ask your pardon...." (He gave a bitter laugh, suppressing with difficulty his swelling irritation.)

"That's precisely my view. I'm filled with pride. Personally I'm quite satisfied when I read the history of the Russian State. But the hundred million peasants haven't read those books. And they're not filled with pride. They wish to have their own history, to be developed, not in the past, but in the future.... The history of prosperity ... and there's nothing to be done about it. And they have leaders—the proletariat. These go still further—they are venturing to create what you might call world history.... There's nothing to be done about that, either.... You accuse me of Bolshevism, Vadim Petrovich. I accuse myself of mere passive contemplation—a grave fault. But my excuse is the prostration setting in after life in the trenches. In time I hope to become more active and then, perhaps, I shall not refute your accusation...."

Tetkin bristled up, and drops of sweat stood out on his flushed skull. Roshchin hastily put on his coat, fastening the hooks in the wrong eyes. Katya, her face creased with anxiety, looked from her husband to Tetkin. After a painful pause Roshchin said:

"I regret to have lost a comrade. Allow me to tender my humble thanks for your hospitality...."

He went out of the room without extending his hand. Then it was that Katya, always so silent and lamblike, almost shouted, clenching her fists:

"Vadim, wait a moment, please...." (He turned, raising his eyebrows.) "Vadim, you're in the wrong, this time...." (She flushed violently.) "Nobody can live with your feelings, with your views...."

"Oh, indeed!" said Roshchin menacingly. "My congratulations."

"Vadim, you have never asked me what I thought and I demanded nothing, never interfered in your affairs. I believed in you. But do understand, Vadim, dear one, what you think is not right. I've been longing to tell you for ages. Something quite different must be done. Not that for which you came here.... First you've got to understand. And only then, if you are quite sure..." (dropping her hands in excitement, she cracked the joints under the table). "If you are sure your conscience will allow you—then go out and kill..."

"Katya!" cried Roshchin harshly, wincing as from a blow. "Kindly hold your tongue!"

"I won't! I'm saying this because I love you dearly. You mustn't be a murderer, you mustn't, you mustn't...."

Tetkin, not venturing to rush up to either of them, kept whispering:

"My friends, my friends, let's talk it all over. We'll agree in the end."

But it was too late to come to an agreement. The furious hate which had been accumulating in Roshchin for the last few months, suddenly burst out violently. He stood in the doorway, his neck craned, his teeth bared, and looked at Katya.

43

"I hate you!" he hissed. "Go to the devil! You and your love! Find yourself a Yid ... a Bolshevik! Go to the devil!"

From his throat came the same painful sound Katya had heard in the railway carriage. He seemed to be on the verge of breakdown, and the air was heavy with catastrophe.... (Tetkin actually moved up to get in front of Katya), but Roshchin, his eyes slowly narrowing, went away.

Semyon Krasilnikov, sitting up in his hospital cot, listened sombrely to his brother Alexei. The presents sent by Matryona— lard, poultry, pies—lay at the foot of the bed Semyon did not so much as look at them. He was lean, his face sickly, unshaven, his hair unkempt from lying so long, his legs in the yellow calico underdrawers, thin. He was rolling a red egg from one hand to the other. His brother Alexei, tanned, his beard tinged with gold, sat on a stool, his legs in their good boots wide apart; he was speaking kindly and pleasantly, but at every word Semyon's heart became more and more estranged from him.

"The peasants have their own line, brother, and the workers have theirs," Alexei was saying. "The workers went down into the 'Deep Mine', and it was flooded, the machinery out of order, the engineers all run away. And we've got to eat, haven't we? So all the workers went into the Red Guard. It means it's to their interest to drive the revolution deeper, doesn't it? But our peasant revolution is—ten inches deep of good soil. And we must deepen it by ploughing, sowing, reaping. Am I right? If we all go and fight, who's going to do the work? The women? It's a lot if they can manage the cattle all by themselves! And the earth requires care and cherishing. That's how it is, brother. We'll go home and you'll recover quicker on our own food. We have land of our own now. And there's no one to work. To harrow, to sow, to harvest— how can Matryoná and I manage alone? We have eighteen boars now, and I have my eye on a second cow. And hands are needed for all this".

Alexei drew from his pocket a pouch filled with homegrown tobacco. Semyon declined to smoke with a shake of the head. "My chest still aches." Alexei, still trying to persuade his brother to go back to the country, began turning over the presents, and touched a flaky pie with his finger.

"Eat this—Matryona used a whole pound of butter in it."

"Look here, Alexei Ivanovich," said Semyon. "I don't know how to answer you. I'd go home with pleasure till my wound healed. But I'm not going to stay and work the land, so don't think it."

44

"H'm. And may I ask why?"

"I couldn't, Alyosha." (Here a convulsion distorted his mouth, but he overcame it with an effort.) "You've just got to believe I couldn't. I can't forget my wound. I can't forget how they tortured my comrades." (He turned towards the window, still trembling, fury in his eyes.) "You must try and put yourself in my place. I can think of nothing but those vipers...." He whispered a few words, and then, the red egg clutched in his hand, spoke aloud: "I'll never rest as long as those vipers are drinking our blood. I'll never rest!"

Alexei Ivanovich shook his head. He spat on the end of his cigarette and extinguished it between his fingers; looking round for somewhere to put it, he threw it under the bed.

"Well, Semyon, it's your business, and your cause is a just one. Come home and get well. I won't try and keep you by force. "

Alexei Krasilnikov had hardly left the hospital before he met his fellow countryman, Ignat, a war veteran. They stopped to shake hands and exchange greetings. Ignat said he was working as a chauffeur for the Executive Committee.

"Come with me to the 'Soleil'," suggested Ignat. "You can come back with me for the night. There's a fight going on there today. Have you heard of Commissar Broinitsky? I wonder what he'll find to say for himself today. His chaps are such hoodlums, the whole town is groaning. They cut up two children, schoolboys, in full light, yesterday, over there, at the corner—for no reason at all—just fell on them with their swords. I was standing by that post—it fairly made me vomit."

They talked all the way to the "Soleil" cinema and, pushing their way through the crowd inside, took up their stand beside the orchestra. A pale, round-shouldered man with a shock of black hair was pacing up and down the small stage with short steps like a caged animal, in front of the table placed for the presidium, which consisted of a round-faced woman in a soldier's coat, a gloomy soldier with a dirty bandage round his head, a withered-looking old worker in spectacles, and two young men in soldiers' tunics. The pale man was speaking, monotonously sawing the air with a feeble fist, a bundle of newspaper cuttings clutched in his other hand.

"A teacher—from our Soviet," whispered Ignat to Krasilnikov.

"We cannot be silent ... we must not be silent.... Has our town got that Soviet power for which you fought, Comrades? We have nothing but violence. A despotism worse than the tsar's.... Breaking into the houses of peaceful citizens.... It's dangerous to go out

45

after dusk, you might be stripped, robbed. Children are killed in the streets. I have spoken about this at the Executive Committee, I've spoken about it at the Revolutionary Committee. They are powerless.... The Military Commissar covers all these crimes with his unlimited power. Comrades...." (He smote himself convulsively on the chest with the bundle of cuttings.) "Why do they kill children? Better shoot *us*.... Why do you kill children?''

His last words were lost in an excited hum throughout the hall. His hearers exchanged glances of fear and agitation. The speaker seated himself at the table, hiding his lined face behind the sheets of a newspaper. The chairman, the soldier with the bandaged head, glanced towards the wings.

"Comrade Trifonov, Commander of the Red Guard, will speak."

The audience applauded, clapping with their hands high above their heads. Some women's voices from the middle of the hall cried: "Comrade Trifonov!" A bass voice barked out: "Three cheers for Trifonov!" And just then Alexei Krasilnikov noticed a tall, slender man in a smart leather jacket with officer's straps crossed over the front of it, who had been standing right up against the orchestra with his back to the audience, and who now, suddenly drawing himself up, turned to face the clamourers. As his prominent steel-grey eyes travelled mockingly, coolly over the faces before him, hands were dropped, heads were drawn into shoulders, and there was no more clapping. Somebody went rapidly, with a crouching gait, towards the exit.

The man with the steely eyes laughed scornfully and settled his holster with a quick movement. He had a long, clean-shaven, actor's face. Once more turning towards the platform, he placed his elbows on the orchestra barrier. Ignat nudged Krasilnikov.

"That's Broinitsky. He only has to look at you to make your heart sink!"

From the wings, his heavy boots making a loud noise, came Commander of the Red Guard Trifonov. There was a red armlet on the sleeve of his flannel jacket, and something red round the band of the cap he held in his hand. Sturdy and serene, he approached the very edge of the platform with unhurried steps. The greyish skin on his shaven skull twitched. His eyes were hidden in the shadow cast by his overhanging brows. He raised his hand (complete silence ensued) and pointed with his half-clenched fist at Broinitsky standing below.

"See, Comrades, Comrade Broinitsky, the Military Commissar, is here. Good! Let him answer that last question. And if he doesn't want to, we'll make him...."

46

"Oho!" came from Broinitsky in menacing tones from below.

"Yes—make him! We are the power of the workers and peasants, and he is bound to obey. It's hard to get to the bottom of everything at once in these times, Comrades.... They're confusing times.... And, as is well known, muck always rises to the surface. This leads us to the conclusion that all sorts of blackguards attach themselves to the revolution .... "

"Name who you mean!" shouted Broinitsky with a strong Polish accent. "Give the name!"

"We'll come to names, don't be in a hurry.... By the self-sacrificing efforts of the workers and peasants we have cleared Rostov of White Guard bands.... The Soviet power stands firm on the Don. Why are protests coming in from all sides? The workers are restless, the Red Guard are dissatisfied.... The troops in the trains are raising hell—they want to know what they are rotting in the sidings for. We have just heard the voice of a representative of the intellectuals" (pointing to the previous speaker). "What's the matter? Everybody seems to be dissatisfied with the Soviet power. 'Why do you plunder?' they ask. 'Why do you get drunk, why do you murder children?' The previous speaker even asked to be shot...." (Laughter from some, a slight outburst of applause.) "Comrades! The Soviet power does not plunder and murder children. But there are swine who hang on to the Soviet power, who do plunder and do murder. And by this they are undermining faith in the Soviet power, and putting a keen weapon into the hands of our foes...." (A pause, not even the breathing of so many hundreds of people is audible.) "And now I want to put a question to Comrade Broinitsky: Are you aware of the murder of two boys yesterday?"

An icy voice from below:

"I am."

"Good! And are you aware of the nightly looting, of the drunken orgies in the Palace Hotel? Are you aware whose hands requisitioned property falls into? You do not speak, Comrade Broinitsky? You have no answer to make. The requisitioned goods are squandered on drink by a gang of bandits...." (A buzz in the hall. Trifonov raised his hand.) "And here is something else we have discovered. Nobody gave you power in Rostov, your mandate is forged, your references to Moscow, not to speak of Comrade Lenin, are insolent lies...."

Broinitsky now stood erect. Tremors passed over his handsome face, now deathly pale.... Suddenly he leaped aside to where a flaxen-haired young soldier stood open-mouthed; tugging at his coat, and pointing to Trifonov, Broinitsky shouted ferociously:

47

"Shoot that scoundrel!"

The youth's face was distorted by a ferocious scowl as he tore his rifle from his shoulder. Trifonov stood motionless, his legs wide apart, and merely bent his head with a bull-like movement. A worker ran out from the wings and stood beside him, hastily clicking the lock of his rifle. He was followed instantly by another, and another, till the whole platform was black with jackets and greatcoats, and alive with the jingling of clashing bayonets. The chairman then jumped up on to the chair and, pushing back the bandage which was falling over his eyes, cried in a rheumy voice:

"Comrades, we don't want any panic—nothing unforeseen has occurred. Shut the door there at the back, please. Comrade Trifonov is quite safe. Comrade Broinitsky is requested to speak."

But Broinitsky had disappeared, and only the flaxen-haired soldier remained standing next to the orchestra, his lips parted in astonishment.

III

At the village of Korenovskaya the Volunteer Army met with extremely serious resistance. The village was, however, taken, though great losses were sustained, and here the news feared above all else by the Whites could no longer be kept from the army—a few days before, Ekaterinodar, the capital of the Kuban, the object of the whole campaign, the only hope for rest and a base for further struggle, had surrendered to the Bolsheviks without a shot being fired. Pokrovsky's Kuban Volunteers, the Kuban Ataman, and the Rada itself, had escaped—where, nobody knew. Thus the army was suddenly trapped, when only a three days' march from the goal of the campaign.

And the hopes of a friendly welcome in Kuban were also thwarted. The Cossacks apparently had decided to puzzle out the meaning of events without the help of the cadets, and the homesteads lying in the army's path were abandoned, there were ambushes in every village, and a machine gun behind the crest of every hill. What was there for the Volunteer Army to hope for now? Surely not for the Kuban Cossacks—Ukrainian settlers, Circassians, bred in traditional enmity to the Russians, or the remnants of the Caucasian army, held up in the rich Kuban, to join the dazzling officers and beardless cadets, in a cry of "Three cheers for Kornilov, for our country, for our faith!" And this formula, as faded and inedible as tsarist pennies, was all the Volunteer Army had to offer both the rich Cossack villages, already on the alert ("Hasn't the time come for us to declare our own Cossack independent republic?"), and the emigrant population, rallying to the red banners, to fight for equality of rights to the Don and Kuban lands and fisheries, for village Soviets....

True, the army had in its train the famous agitator, the sailor Fedor Batkin, a bowlegged, swarthy fellow in a reefer jacket and seaman's cap adorned with the ribbon of St. George. The officers had again and again tried to have him shot as a Yid and a Red son-of-a-bitch. But Kornilov himself had protected him, considering that the famous sailor Batkin fully compensated for all the ideologically weak places in the army. Whenever the Commander in Chief had to address the people (in the villages), he made Batkin begin, and the latter artfully explained to the villagers that it was Kornilov who was for the revolution, while the Bolsheviks, on the contrary, were counterrevolutionaries and hirelings of the Germans.

The Volunteer Army could not surrender, there was no such thing as taking prisoners at that time. And if they dispersed they would be killed one by one. There was a plan for crossing the Astrakhan steppe to the Volga, and getting into Siberia. But Kornilov insisted: continue the campaign against Ekaterinodar and take the town by storm. At Korenovskaya the army veered southwards, crossing the river Kuban, swollen and turbulent at this season, after heavy fighting at the village of Ust-Labinskaya. It forged ahead without halting by the way, carrying in its train great numbers of wounded. But it was still dangerous, and still capable of striking back with such painful effect that the ring of the Red troops broke to let it through at every encounter.

The Volunteer Army moved in the direction of Maikop, to throw dust in the enemy's eyes, but at the village of Filippovskaya it crossed the river Belaya, and turned sharply westwards, towards the rear of Ekaterinodar. On the other side of the Belaya it was outflanked in the narrow pass by strong Red forces. The situation appeared hopeless. Rifles were distributed among the slightly wounded.... The fight continued all day. The Reds fired their cannon from the heights above, peppering crossings and baggage trains from machine guns, and preventing the enemy from ascending. When dusk fell, however, and the dishevelled Volunteer units made a last desperate effort at a counterattack, the Reds retreated from the heights and let the Kornilov troops pass westwards. History was repeating itself: military experience, and the consciousness that the issue of the battle was a matter of life or death, gained the day.

All round, villages flamed through the night. The weather had broken up, and a north wind was blowing. The sky was blanketed with thick, impenetrable clouds. Rain set in, pouring in torrents all night. On the fifteenth of March, the Volunteer Army, moving on Novo-Dmitrovskaya, was confronted by a boundless expanse of water and liquid ooze. Infrequent hills threaded by narrow paths were lost in the mist enveloping the ground. Men went knee-deep in water, carts and guns sunk to the hub. A wet snow was falling, gradually working up into a terrific blizzard.

Roshchin crawled out of the goods truck. Adjusting his rifle and knapsack, he looked about him. A group of soldiers from the Varnav Regiment were shouting and clattering on the tracks. Some were in greatcoats, some in sheepskins, some in civilian overcoats, belted with string. Many were carrying machine-gun bolts, hand grenades, revolvers. Some wore on their heads ordinary peaked caps, some, high conical fur caps, and some, bowler hats confiscated from speculators. The sticky mud was churned by broken boots, felt boots, feet wrapped in rags. Bayonets met and clashed, and confused cries mingled in the air: "Off to the meeting with you, lads! We'll work this out for ourselves! Time we stopped being driven to the slaughter!"

The excitement arose owing to rumours, as always in such cases, exaggerated, of the defeat of the Red units at Filippovskaya. There were shouts of: "Kornilov has fifty thousand cadets, and our regiments are being sent one at a time against him to their death.... Treachery, lads! Get the Commander."

The soldiers were running up to the station yard, which came to an end, just beyond the village, in the mist-veiled steppe. The doors of the goods trucks clattered continually, as half-crazed men with rifles on their backs jumped to the ground, and ran eagerly towards a place where the wind was whistling through the bare branches of the Lombardy poplars, and rooks were cawing and circling overhead. The speakers scrambled on to the roof of a turf-covered icehouse, shaking their fists and shouting: "Comrades, why do the Kornilov bands beat us? Why are the cadets being allowed to pass through to Ekaterinodar? What sort of plan is this? Let the Commander tell us!"

The thousand-strong crowd echoed: "The Commander!" so thunderously that the rooks flew right up to the clouds. Roshchin, standing on the station steps, could see the crumpled cap of the Commander floating towards the turf-covered icehouse through the mass of moving heads. His gaunt, pallid clean-shaven face, and fixed gaze were tense with determination. Roshchin recognized his old acquaintance, Sergei Sergeyevich Sapozhkov.

There had been a time, before the war, when Sapozhkov had spoken on behalf of the "People of the Future" group, making mincemeat of the old moral system. He had appeared in bourgeois society with seductive drawings on his cheeks, wearing a frock coat of bright green fustian. During the war he had volunteered for the cavalry, become famous as a reckless scout and duellist, and been made a second lieutenant. And quite unexpectedly, in the beginning of 1917, he had been arrested, sent to Petrograd, and sentenced, to be shot for membership of a secret organization. Set free by the February Revolution, he had for a short time identified himself with the anarchist group in the Soviet of Soldiers' Deputies. Then he disappeared, reappearing in the end of October to take part in the seizing of the Winter Palace. He was one of the first regular officers to join the Red Guard.

And now, slipping and losing his hold, he clambered on to the turf roof. Once there, he thrust his thumbs into his belt, his chin resting on the folds in his neck, and let his gaze rove over the thousands of heads craning towards him.

"D'you want to know, you yelling devils, why the gold-epauletted bastards beat you? It's because of all this noise and to-do." He spoke mockingly and not very loud, but his voice could be heard by all. "Not only do you disobey the orders of the Supreme Command, not only do you start yelling on the slightest provocation, but some of you are panic-mongers, as well. Who told you we were beaten at Filippovskaya? Who told you Kornilov is moving on Ekaterinodar owing to treachery? Was it you? " (He threw out a hand, holding a revolver, with a rapid movement, pointing to one of those standing in front.) "Come on up, then, let's have a talk! Aha-ah, so it wasn't you!" (He reluctantly returned his revolver to his pocket.) "D'you take me for a milksop, d'you think I don't know what you're yapping about? D'you want me to tell you? Fedor Ivolgin, that's one, Pavlenkov, that's two, Terenti Dulya, that's three, and they all had direct information that there are vats full of booze at the village of Afipskaya...." (Laughter. Even Roshchin smiled wryly: "He got out of it ingeniously, the rascal!") "Well, of course, these chaps are all eager for the fight. It's as plain as day our Commander in Chief's a traitor—supposing those vats of booze were to fall into the hands of Kornilov's officers.... Wouldn't that be a disaster for the republic?" (A burst of laughter, sending the rooks skyhigh once more.) "I consider the incident closed, Comrades. I will read the latest field bulletin."

Sapozhkov drew out some leaflets and began reading in a loud voice. Roshchin turned and went through the station to the platform, where, sitting down on a broken bench, he began rolling home-grown tobacco in a scrap of paper. A week before (presenting forged papers), he had joined a Red Guard unit going to the front. He and Katya had come to some sort of an arrangement. After the painful conversation over the teacups with Tetkin, Roshchin had wandered about the town for the rest of the day, returning at night to Katya, and, averting his eyes from her face for fear of showing signs of weakness, said severely:

"You will live here for a month or two—I don't know exactly.... I hope you and Tetkin will find yourselves entirely in agreement. At the first opportunity I will pay him for your keep. But kindly inform him immediately that he will be paid, I want no charity. Well—I mean to disappear for a time."

Katya asked, scarcely opening her lips:

"Are you going to the front?"

"Excuse me, but that concerns no one but myself."

Things were going badly with Katya, very badly. Only last summer, one July day on the embankment, when the outlines of the bridges and the colonnades on Vasilyevsky Island were reflected in the mirrorlike Neva—on that far-off, sunny day, Roshchin had said to her, sitting on the stone bench by the water: "Wars will pass, revolutions will disappear, and only your warm, loving heart will remain." And now they had parted enemies, in the dirty yard.... Katya deserved a better ending to her romance.... "But when the whole of Russia is coming to an end, what the devil does it matter!"

Roshchin's plan was quite simple: to go with a Red Guard unit to the battle area against the Volunteer Army, and go over to the other side at the first opportunity. In the army he was personally known to General Markov and Colonel Nezhentsev. He could give them valuable information as to the disposition and condition of the Red troops. But most important of all, he would feel himself among his own people, could cast off the accursed mask, breathe freely once more, and spit out, together with a clip of bullets, his violent contempt into the face of those "wretched dupes, those unruly savages...."

"The Commander was right about those spirits. We make a lot of noise. We're making a hell of a row, and we'll have no end of trouble, trying to find out what's it all about!" said an insignificant-looking individual in a sheepskin jacket with tufts of wool sticking out here and there. He seated himself on the bench next to Roshchin, and asked him for a pinch of tobacco.

"I'm an oldster—I smoke a pipe." (He turned towards Roshchin a shrewd, weather-beaten face, with a bleached-looking beard and screwed-up eyes.) "I used to work in the barns for Nizhni merchants, and learned to smoke a pipe there. I've been fighting since 1914 and can't give it up—I'm a fighter, brother, that's what I am."

"It's time for you to rest," said Roshchin with inward distaste.

"Rest? Where is that to be found? You come from the wealthy, my lad, I can see that. Oh, no, I'm not going to give up fighting! I've had my fill of grief from the bourgeois. I've been in service since I was sixteen, all the time a watchman. I was promoted to coachman when I was working for the Vasenkovs—they were merchants, perhaps you've heard of them—but I ruined their pair of bays, good horses they were, by watering them wrong. I ruined them, I admit it. Of course I was sacked. My son was killed, my wife died long ago. You tell me, now, who am I to fight for—the Soviets or the bourgeois? I'm well fed, and last week I took a pair of boots from a corpse. Good stuff—look at them! They don't let the damp through. All I have to do now is shoot a bit and shout 'hurrah'. Then I can go and sit by the soup cauldron. And here one is working for one's own side, my lad! The poor, the portionless, the barebacked, those whose constant companions are grief and misfortune—that's our army. And the Constituent Assembly—I saw who they elected to it in Nizhni—just the gentry and the wiseacres".

"You *have* learned to wag your tongue," said Roshchin, glancing furtively at his interlocutor. His name was Kvashin. They had jolted together a whole week in the same railway carriage, sleeping side by side on the top berth. The carriage knew Kvashin by the name of Grandad. He was always settling down somewhere with a newspaper, adjusting gold pincenez on his withered nose, and reading under his breath.

"I got this pince-nez," he was fond of relating, "in Samara, on an order. The millionaire Bashkirov ordered this pince-nez for himself, and I'm using it."

"I've learned to wag my tongue, it's true," he replied to Roshchin. "I never miss a single meeting. At every station I read the decrees and edicts. Our proletarian strength is in *talk*. What would we be worth if we couldn't speak, if we weren't class-conscious? Mere small fry!"

He took out a newspaper, unfolded it carefully, put on the pince-nez with slow dignity, and began reading the leading article, pronouncing the words as if they came from a foreign language.

"...Remember that you are fighting for the happiness of all

toilers and oppressed, you are fighting for the right to build up a better, juster life...."

Roshchin turned away without noticing that Kvashin, while uttering these words, was gazing intently at him over his pince-nez.

"Anyone can see, my lad, that you come from the rich," said Kvashin in quite different tones. "You don't like my reading. You're not a spy, are you?"

From Afipskaya the column of the Varnav Regiment moved on foot towards the village of Novodmitrovskaya. In the dark of the night the wind whistled among the bayonets, tore at clothing, blew icy pellets of snow into men's faces. The feet sank through the upper crust of snow, into the sticky mud. The howling of the wind was interspersed with cries: "Stop! Easy there! Don't shove so, you devils!"

The cold penetrated the thin coats, chilled men's bones. Roshchin thought: "The only thing is not to fall. That would be the end, I should be trampled...." Worst of all were the sudden halts and cries from in front. It was obvious they had lost their way, and were wandering along the edge of a ravine, on the bank of a river. "I can't go on any longer, brothers," came in a broken voice from somewhere near. "Could that have been Kvashin? He was beside me all the time. He guesses what I am, he doesn't believe a word I say." (Roshchin had shaken him off with difficulty the evening before.) "Now they've stopped again in front." Roshchin's nose was pressed against the frost-stiffened coat of the man before him. His numbed hands thrust into his sleeves, his head bowed, he stood and thought: "I've been fighting fatigue, tramping thousands of miles, all in order to kill. That's very important and significant. I cast Katya off in anger—that's of lesser importance. Today or the next day I shall go over to the other side and start killing these people, these Russians, in a blizzard just like this. Queer! Katya always said I was a kind and magnanimous person. Queer, very queer!"

He took note of his thoughts with curiosity. Suddenly their thread was broken. "Aah!" he thought. "A bad job! I'm freezing. The last, the most important thoughts are passing through my mind. It means I'll soon be lying in the snow. "

But the frozen back in front of him swayed and moved forward. And Roshchin swayed and moved forward behind it. Now he was knee-deep in mud. He could hardly drag his boot, which seemed a ton-weight, out of the clay. The wind bore a fragmentary cry to his ears: "A river, lads!" Curses rolled out. And the wind went on whistling through the bayonets, blowing strange thoughts into men's minds. Vague bent figures lurched past Roshchin. He gathered up his remaining strength, dragged out his foot with a groan, and staggered on.

A turbulent stream made a dark line across the snow, further all was veiled by the blizzard. Feet slipped on the slope of the bank. The dark water rushed impetuously on. There were shouts: "The bridge is flooded.... Shall we go back?" "Who said—back? Was it you? Did you say—back?" "Let go! Let go, Comrade!" "Give him one with the butt!" "Oh-oh-oh!".

On the edge of the bank beneath, a cone of light from an electric torch shone out. It lighted up the humped bridge, washed by the grey, rushing waters, and a broken-off fragment of railing. The torch waved high, zigzagging from side to side, and went out. A voice cried, hoarse, blood-curdling:

"Squad.... Cross the river.... Rifle and cartridges on your heads. Don't push—two at a time.... On!"

Raising his rifle, Roshchin waded up to his waist in the water, which was after all not so cold as the wind. The waves beat powerfully against his right side, almost knocking him down, as if they would carry him into that grey-white darkness, into the deep waters. His feet slipped on the bridge, he could scarcely feel the broken planks beneath him.

The Varnav Regiment was sent to Novodmitrovskaya to reinforce the local forces. The whole population was digging trenches, fortifying the village council and other buildings, stationing machine guns. The heavy artillery was further south, in the village of Grigoryevskaya. In the same neighbourhood was the Second North Caucasian Regiment under the command of Dmitri Shelest—it had been pursuing the Volunteer Army all the way from Rostov. To the west, at Afipskaya, was a garrison, with artillery and armoured trains. Red forces were widely dispersed—which should never have been allowed, with the ground and the roads made impassable by melting snow.

Towards nightfall a Cossack, covered with wet snow and mud, galloped up to the village council. He drew rein at the porch. Steam was rolling upwards from the distended sides of his horse.

"Where's the Comrade Commander?"

Several men rushed out into the porch, hastily fastening their coats. Sapozhkov made his appearance, clad in a sheepskin cavalry jacket.

"I'm the commander," he said, pushing them aside.

The Cossack, stopping to take breath, said, leaning on the pommel:

"The entire outpost has been killed. I'm the only one who got across."

"What else?"

"This: you can expect Kornilov here tonight, with all his forces...."

Those on the porch exchanged glances. Amongst them were Communists, the organizers of the village defences. Sapozhkov sniffed, the skin under his chin gathering into folds.

"I'm ready—what about you, Comrades?"

The Cossack, alighting from his horse, began telling them how the Circassians from General Erdeli's brigade had cut down the outpost. Soldiers, Cossack women and little boys crowded round the porch. All listened in silence.

Roshchin, his head swathed in the folds of his hood, came up too. He had managed to get a sleep and dry his clothes in a hot and stinking hut, in which about fifty Red soldiers lay huddled on the floor among leggings and wet clothes. The woman of the house had baked bread at dawn, cutting it up with her own hands, and distributing slices all round.

"Fight well, soldiers! Don't let the officers get into our village!"

The Red soldiers had answered the young housewife:

"Don't you be afraid! The only thing you have to fear is..." Here they used a word which made her brandish the loaf at them:

"You bulls, you! On the eve of death, too! Always the same..."

Every bone in Roshchin's body was aching after the night's march. But his determination was firm. He had been digging the frozen ground in the vegetable plots ever since morning. Then he had carried ammunition boxes from the carts into the village council. Everyone got a cup of spirits with dinner, and the fiery liquid had driven away his aches and soothed the pain in his joints; he decided not to postpone matters, but to finish off what he had to do that very day.

And now he was hanging about the porch, seeking an opportunity to get himself detailed to one of the outposts. Everything had been thought out, to the captain's shoulder straps sewn into the front of his tunic. It all turned out as he had expected. The stocky sailor standing beside Sapozhkov came down from the porch and began appealing for volunteers for the dangerous job.

"Brothers!" he cried in a thunderous voice. "Is there anyone here ready to risk his life?"

An hour later Roshchin left the village with one of the parties of fifty soldiers, and set out for the mist-enveloped plain rolling drearily ahead. The languid dusk was falling. The snow had stopped and the wind lashed their faces with gusts of heavy rain.

They marched over a pathless sheet of water as if they were passing through a lake, towards some mounds where trenches had to be dug.

A flash as of lightning, followed by a boom and a wail, rent the damp morning mist. And the next moment shots rang out in confusion over the mounds and the bank of the river. Again a flash of lightning, a shell burst, and the crack-crack of a machine gun from somewhere in front.

This was Kornilov approaching. His leading units were already at the other side of the river. Roshchin thought he could distinguish a few stooping figures, running right up to the bushes next to the water. His heart beat. He leaned out of the shallow trench dug in the bank of the stream.

The turbid yellow-green water whirled by level with the banks. In the middle of the stream, to the left, could be seen a half-flooded bridge. A score or so of those vague figures clambered on to it from the water, and ran crouching along it. The firing from the mounds grew more and more confused and frequent over the river and the bridge. Quite near, on the other side, a long tongue of fire came from a gun. Shrapnel burst over the trench in which Roshchin was crouching. Figures, some grey, some black, rose from the crest and made for the crossing—running, sliding down on their buttocks, rolling and falling. Roshchin could already make out the narrow strips of their shoulder straps.

There was another shell-burst, and a jagged roar over the trench. "Brothers, brothers—oh-h!" a voice sang out. Amidst the crackling of shots a wail could be heard: "They're trying to surround us! Back, lads!"

"Here it comes, the longed-for moment," thought Roshchin. He flung himself prone, and lay motionless. Thoughts ran wildly through his brain: "...no handkerchief ... a bit of shirt on my bayonet ... and be sure to shout in French...." Then someone fell heavily on to his back, seized him round the neck, grunting and digging his fingers into his throat. Roshchin started—at his shoulder he saw a face covered with blood, a bulging eye, a toothless, open mouth. Kvashin again. He was shouting over and over again, as if in a frenzy:

"Crossing yourself! You've seen your own people!"

Roshchin, shaking him off his back, stood up straight swaying. Kvashin's fingers sank into his shoulders like a tick. Struggling to free himself, Roshchin threw himself against the parapet of the trench, digging his teeth furiously into the stinking sheepskin jacket. He could feel his elbows and knees beginning to slip on the liquid mud—the edge of a ravine was only a step or two away.

"Let go!" roared Roshchin in desperation. The ground gave way beneath him and the two of them rolled down the side of the ravine into the river.

All around hummed from the gunfire, the earth trembling from explosions. The main forces of the army were crossing the river. The artillery from the village of Grigoryevskaya was firing on the ford. The snowy field was strewn with hand grenades, and columns of water rose whenever one fell into the river.

The White infantry were fording the river two men on each horse. The horses reared as they plunged into the rapid river, and had to be urged forward with bayonets. A horse-drawn gun clattered down the steep slippery bank. Swaying from side to side it disappeared beneath the water. Lashed by cavalry whips, the lean horses managed somehow or other to hoist it on to the hump of the half-flooded bridge. Shells fell on every side, the water hissed. The horses reared violently, their hind legs entangled in the traces.

Machine-gun carriers rattled downwards, past the bridge, to the river, where they floated and whirled round helplessly. One overturned, and was swept past together with horses and men, the latter hanging frantically to the wheels. Into this swirling mass a grenade slid down from the sky, sending fragments of wood and chunks of flesh flying high into the air in a waterspout.

A short man with a clipped beard, wearing a brown flannel jacket and a tall white fur hat pulled well over his eyes, was waltzing about on the bank, seated on a small, shaggy horse. Brandishing his whip menacingly, he was shouting in a high, affected voice. This was General Markov, in charge of the fording of the river. Fantastic tales were told of his courage.

Markov was one of those who had fought in the World War and been poisoned through and through by its sinister breath. On horseback, his field glasses at his eyes, or commanding the terrible game of war, at the head of his men, sword in hand, he doubtless experienced incomparable ecstasies. He could have brought himself to fight any foe for any cause. A few ready-made formulae about God, the tsar, and the native land had found a place in his brain. These were absolute truths for him, he required nothing more. Like a chess player for whom nothing but the chess board exists, the whole world for him was narrowed down to a given area over which figures could be moved.

He was ambitious—harsh and overbearing to subordinates. He was feared in the army, and many cherished rancour against this man who regarded human beings as mere pawns. But he was brave, and knew well those critical moments of battle when the outcome of the day depends on the commander being able to gamble with his life, heading his troops, whip in hand, beneath a shower of bullets.

The fording took several hours. The river and its banks were again enveloped in a snow storm. The wind increased, turning northwards. The frost was gaining in intensity. Roshchin, lying with a dislocated shoulder beneath the steep bank of the river, had long given up hope of being noticed. Despite the pain, he managed to drag the straps from out of the breast of his tunic, to fix them roughly on to the shoulders of it with pins, and to tear the five-pointed star from his cap. The river had long carried away the corpse of Kvashin. There were wounded lying about everywhere—nobody had time for them now.

Once across, the army fought its way to Novodmitrovskaya without halting. The clothing froze on men's bodies, and was covered with a layer of ice. The frozen earth rang beneath hoofs and wheels, boots were broken and feet flayed by the mounds and ruts in the road.

Some of the wounded got up and crawled on to the steep bank, hanging on for dear life, and sometimes slipping back. Roshchin felt his feet being frozen to the ground. Setting his teeth (he had pain in his shoulder, and in the small of his back, and his kneecap was broken), he, too, got up and staggered in the wake of the wounded. Nobody paid any attention to him. It cost him enormous trouble to get to the top of the bank. Up there the blizzard howled, and bullets whistled. A round-shouldered man just in front of him, in a frozen officer's greatcoat and peaked hood, suddenly stumbled aside and fell. Roshchin merely bent lower, to get out of the teeth of the wind.

A horse's carcass lay covered with snow, one rigid hind leg protruding. Two miserable hacks stood beside an abandoned gun, with drooping heads. Their sides were frozen to each other, their backs saddled with snow. And the rapping of machine guns ahead was growing more insistent and ominous. The Volunteer Army was fighting desperately in the hope of reaching warm huts by nightfall, and escaping death in the blizzards raging over the field.

The artillery from Grigoryevskaya were now firing upon the attackers. But the rest of the Red forces, including the reserves from Afipskaya, were not thrown into the battle. The Second Caucasian Regiment had received the order to attack only after the Varnav Regiment was surrounded in Novodmitrovskaya, where it had fared badly in hand-to-hand street fighting. The Second Caucasians marched six miles over unbroken swamp and flooded ground, losing a whole company by drowning and frostbite, and struck at the enemy's rear, thus enabling the remainder of the Varnav Regiment to break out of encirclement.

The same state of confusion and disorder prevailed among the Whites, too. Pokrovsky's Kuban detachment, which was to have attacked the village from the south, refused pointblank to march through the swamps. And Pokrovsky himself, who had received his general's epaulettes not from the tsar, but from the Kuban government, was violently offended with General Alexeyev, who had said to him with aristocratic scorn, at a military conference: "That'll do, Colonel—sorry, I don't know what to call you now...." It was because of this "Colonel", that Pokrovsky had not led his detachment through the swamps. The cavalry of General Erdeli, sent to surround the village from the north, were unable to wade through the flooded ravine, and returned towards nightfall to the ford.

The first White forces to arrive at Novodmitrovskaya was the regiment of officers. Half frozen, and in a state of frenzy, the veteran officers, scenting the welcome odour of newly-baked bread, and seeing the warm glow from the windows, trampled through the squelching mass of snow and mud, and waded through sheets of water thinly crusted over with ice, without waiting for reinforcements. They were espied at the very approach to the village, and machine-gun fire was opened on them. The officers made a furious bayonet charge. Each one of them knew what to do and how to do it at any given moment. Markov's tall white hat was seen everywhere. It was a battle between regular officers and a poorly-led, undisciplined mob of soldiers.

The officers broke into the village, and entered upon hand-to-hand combat with the Varnav men and the guerilla fighters. In the darkness and scuffle the machine gunners were bayonetted or blown up by grenades at their posts. The Whites were continually receiving reinforcements. The Reds were surrounded and began retreating to the town square where the Revolutionary Committee was quartered in the village council.

Shots came from every scrap of cover, fighting went on at every street corner. A gun carriage, raising fountains of mud, came galloping up. Swinging round the square, the gun pointed its muzzle straight at the village council, sending a shell right into it. People began jumping out of windows, yellow smoke billowed out—crates of cartridge cases inside the building had been touched off by the artillery fire.

The Second Caucasian Regiment was at that very moment firing on the attackers from the east. The Varnav men heard the battle going on in the enemy's rear and took heart of grace again. Sapozhkov, whose voice was almost gone from shouting and swearing, tore the banner from the standard-bearer's hands, rolled up as it was in oilcloth, and, shaking it free and waving it, ran across the square to the high, swaying poplars, where the Whites were most thickly concentrated. The Varnav men dashed out from all directions with rifles atilt, broke through, and got out of the village on the western side.

Roshchin spent the night burrowed into the hay on an abandoned cart, from which he had first had to drag two frozen corpses. All night, guns boomed and shrapnel burst over Novodmitrovskaya, and then, after having spent the night in Kaluzhskaya, the baggage carts and trains of wounded of the Volunteer Army proceeded at daybreak. Roshchin crept out of the cart and got behind them. His excitement was so great that he did not notice his pain any more.

The wind, still strong, was now blowing from the east, dispersing the snow and rain clouds. By eight in the morning the sky showed clean between the high-piled clouds. The sunlight fell in warm, swordlike rays. The snow began to melt. The steppe showed darker and darker, crossed here and there by emerald strips of sprouting crops, and golden strips of stubble. Everywhere gleamed water, and the ruts in the roads had become streams. Corpses drying in the mounds stared at the azure sky with unseeing eyes.

"Look—it's Roshchin! By God, it is! Roshchin, how did you get here?" cried someone from a passing cart. Roshchin turned. Three men, their heads bandaged, their arms in slings, sat in a filthy rickety cart, driven by a gloomy Cossack with a rotting sheepskin thrown over his shoulders. One of the three, a lean, lanky individual whose neck seemed to be craning out of his collar, greeted Roshchin with rapid nods, his cracked lips parted in a smile. Roshchin had difficulty in recognizing in him his regimental friend Vaska Teplov, once a rosy-cheeked reveller, a woman chaser, and a tippler. He approached the cart in silence, and embraced him.

"Who ought I to go to, Teplov, tell me that! Who's your chief of staff? You see my shoulder straps are only pinned on. I only crossed the lines yesterday...."

"Get in! Stop! Pull up, you swine!" shouted Teplov to the driver. The Cossack grumbled but obeyed. Roshchin swung himself on to a corner of the cart and sat with his legs hanging over the wheel. It was bliss to be riding beneath the warm sunshine.

He related his adventures from the moment of leaving Moscow with the impartiality of a report. Coughing slightly, Teplov said

"I'll take you to General Romanovsky myself.... We'll go to the village and get a feed and I'll fix you up in no time.... Did you really think you could go straight to him, you poor sap? 'Please I've come from the Red gang...' You don't know our lot. They'd have bayonetted you on the way to headquarters. Look! Look! (He pointed to a long corpse in an officer's greatcoat lying by the roadside.) "That's Mishka, Baron Korff ... remember him? Ah what a chap he was! Got any cigarettes? God, what a glorious morning! The day after tomorrow, old man, we'll be entering Ekaterinodar, we'll sleep in beds and then make straight for the park. Music, girls, beer!"

He gave a loud, hysterical laugh. His sickly face, the skin drawn tightly over the bones, broke into wrinkles, and feverish spots burned on his cheekbones.

"And it'll be music, girls, beer, all over Russia. We'll rest a month in Ekaterinodar, and clean ourselves up, and then for reprisals! Ha! We're not such fools any longer, old boy.... We've purchased with our blood the right to do what we think fit with the Russian Empire. We'll show them what order means.... The bastards! Look at that one over there!" He pointed to the edge of a ditch where, his limbs extended unnaturally, lay the body of a man in a sheepskin jacket. "He was probably one of their Dantons...."

The cart was overtaken by a clumsy wicker phaeton. In it were two persons, covered with mud, with the collars of their coats thrown back, and wet fur caps on their heads: one was a huge stout man with a dark flabby face, the other, who had an unkempt grizzled beard and bags under his eyes, held a long cigarette holder between his sagging lips.

"The saviours of their country," said Teplov, nodding toward them. "We put up with them for want of any better. They might be of use."

"The fat one's Guchkov, isn't he?"

"Yes, he is, and he'll be shot all in good time, don't worry! The one with the cigarette holder is Boris Suvorin, his record's none too good, either. He's for a monarchy, you know, but not exactly a monarchy. He's a wriggler, but a clever journalist. We won't shoot *him*."

The cart turned into the village. The huts and houses behind the garden plots seemed deserted. The remains of fires were still smoking. A few corpses lay on the ground, half trodden into the mud. Isolated shots rang out, signalizing the finishing-off of the "outsiders" dragged from cellars and haylofts. A train of carts stood in confusion on the square. The cries of the wounded arose from the carts. Nurses in dirty men's greatcoats, exhausted and at their wit's end, threaded their way among them. Inhuman shrieks and the sound of lashing came from a yard in the neighbourhood. Horsemen were galloping about. A group of cadets were standing by a fence, drinking milk from a tin pail.

The sun shone ever more brightly and warmly from the blue, wind-swept depths of the sky. Dangling from a bar fixed between a tree and a telegraph pole, were seven long corpses, their necks dislocated, the toes of their bare feet pointing downwards. These were Communists from the Revolutionary Committee and the Tribunal.

It was the last day of the Kornilov campaign. Mounted scouts, shading their eyes from the rays of the sun, could make out, through the mists of morning, the golden domes of Ekaterinodar beyond the turbid Kuban River.

The task before the leading cavalry unit was to get away from the Reds the only ferry on the Kuban, at the village of Elizavetinskaya. This was a new manoeuvre of Kornilov's. He could have been expected to attack from the south, at Novodmitrovskaya, or from the southwest, on the Novorossiisk-Ekaterinodar railway. But that he would choose the extremely dangerous detour on the west side of the town, and attempt to cross, with his whole army, the turbulent waters of the Kuban at a place where there were no bridges, and only a single ferry, so that there was no possibility of retreat, was a strategic step which the Red headquarters of Commander in Chief Avtonomov could not possibly have foreseen. And it was precisely this, the most feebly defended route, allowing two or three days' respite from fighting, and leading the army straight to the orchards and vegetable plots of Ekaterinodar, which was chosen by the wily Kornilov.

Deficits in the supply of munitions were made good during the occupation of the railway station at Afipskaya, where the Volunteers blew up the line to secure themselves against being fired upon from armoured trains. Despite this, machine guns from one of the Red trains overtook the flank of the attackers as they were wading through the sheets of water left by the melting snow. When a line of bullets, raising great waterspouts, fell among them, they plunged into the water like ducks, head first. Then they stuck out their heads again, and ran on. The Afipskaya garrison put up a desperate resistance. But the Reds were doomed—they were only on the defence, and the enemy was attacking.

The Volunteer units surrounded and detoured Afipskaya in slow, serpentine lines. The bright sunlight streamed over the watery blue plain, from which trees, hayricks, and the roofs of homesteads protruded, while the shadows of spring clouds chased one another across the floodwaters. In his short sheepskin jacket with the soft general's shoulder straps, armed with field glasses and a map, Kornilov moved on horseback through this mirage-like atmosphere. Every now and then he gave orders to aides, who galloped off in a whirlpool of splashes. At one time he was under fire, and General Romanovsky, at his side, was slightly wounded.

When the station was outflanked from the west, and the general attack had begun, Kornilov whipped up his horse and trotted straight into Afipskaya. He had never for a moment doubted that victory would be his. There, on the railway lines, amidst abandoned trains, station buildings, warehouses and barracks, the Volunteer units slaughtered the trapped Reds.

This was the last and the bloodiest of the Volunteer Army's victories.

Colonel Nezhentsev, red-cheeked, youthful-looking, elated, bounded up to Kornilov, hopping over corpses. The glass in his pince-nez twinkling, he reported:

"The station of Afipskaya is occupied, Your Excellency!"

Kornilov interrupted him with an impatient:

"Has ammunition been seized?"

"Yes, Your Excellency! Seven hundred shells and four truck-loads of small arms and ammunition."

"God be thanked!" Kornilov crossed himself with sweeping gestures, the nail of his little finger scratching the stiffened surface of his coat. "God be thanked...."

Nezhentsev then indicated with a movement of his eyes the group of shock fighters crowding at the station—a special regiment of daredevils, with tricolour rectangular stripes sewn on their sleeves. They stood leaning on their rifles, like men resting after a difficult ascent. Their faces were set in lines of fury, the eyes roving, and their hands, and the very faces of many, were covered with blood.

"Twice they saved the situation, and were the first to rush in, Your Excellency!"

"Aha!" Kornilov smote his horse and galloped at full speed to the shock troops, though the distance was not great. A flutter passed over the group of men, and they fell into rank precipitately. Kornilov reined in his horse with dramatic violence, like a horse-man on a monument, and shouted in jerky accents throwing back his head:

"Thanks, my eagles! I thank you for the brilliant work you have done, and again for seizing the munitions.... I bow low before you...."

Having received a fresh supply of munitions, the Volunteer Army began crossing the Kuban on a ferry of planks seized by a leading cavalry unit. At that time it numbered nine thousand men, and four thousand horses. The crossing took three days. Troops, carts, ordnance depots and munitions stretched on either side of the ferry in a vast camp. The spring breeze fluttered the rags of laundry hung on shafts to dry. Smoke arose from camp-fires. Hobbled horses pastured in the meadows. Elated officers leaped on to carts, endeavouring through their field glasses to make out in the blue distance, the orchards and domes of the promised city.

"Upon my word, we're like the crusaders entering Jerusalem!"

"Ah, but there were Jewesses there, gentlemen, and here there are proletarianesses."

"We'll announce the socialization of women.... Ha-ha-ha...."

"Baths, parks, beer shops...."

No attempt was made from the Ekaterinodar side to prevent the crossing, though every now and then scouts would take a pot shot. The Reds had decided to defend the town. The whole population—men, women, and children—hastened to dig trenches, make wire entanglements, post guns. Troops of Black Sea sailors arrived from Novorossiisk with guns and munitions. The commissars spoke to the troops of the class nature of Kornilov's Volunteers, backed up as they were by a "ruthless world bourgeoisie, against which, Comrades, we are waging a relentless war", and swore to die rather than surrender Ekaterinodar.

On the fourth day of their march the Volunteer Army moved to the storm of the capital of the Kuban.

The furious attacks of the Volunteers encountered hurricane fire from the batteries at the Black Sea railway station and the Kuban landing stages. But thanks to the unevenness of the ground, and the protection afforded by orchards, ditches, hedges, and the beds of streams, the attackers reached the town with only slight losses.

Here the battle began. Near a white house known as "The Farm", at the outskirts of a still leafless poplar grove on the high bank of the Kuban, the Reds put up a stubborn resistance, and, beaten off, again rushed upon the enemy's machine guns in great numbers and seized the farm, only to be beaten off an hour later by the Kuban Cossack scouts of Colonel Ulagai.

Kornilov and his staff immediately set up their headquarters in

65

the one-storey building. From there the straight streets of Eka-terinodar, the high white houses, the fences, the cemetery, the Black Sea station, and, in front of all, the long rows of trenches, could be seen at a glance. It was a bright, windy spring day. Everywhere floated the smoke following upon shots, and the blue haze thundered throbbingly with the incessant roar of the guns. Neither Reds nor Whites spared their lives on that day.

A corner room, set apart in the white house for Kornilov, was equipped with field telephones, a table and a chair. He went into it immediately, sat down at the table, unfolded the map, and became absorbed in contemplation of the next moves of the game. Two of his aides, Second Lieutenant Dolinsky and Khan Khad-zhiev, were with him, one taking up his station at the door, the other at the telephones.

Never had the wrinkled Mongolian countenance of the Com-mander in Chief been so gloomy. His greying hair stood up stiffly, and his small, parchment-skinned hand, with the gold signet ring on the fourth finger, lay motionless on the map. He alone had insisted on this storming of the town, against the advice of Alex-eyev, Denikin and the other generals, and now, at the end of the first day, his self-assurance was shaken. But he would not have admitted this even to himself.

Two mistakes had been made: the first had been to leave a third of the troops, under General Markov, at the crossing to guard the trains—owing to this, the initial blow struck at Ekaterinodar had been insufficiently concentrated and failed to yield the expected results, the Reds having withstood it, and clinging to their posi-tions, in which they were apparently firmly entrenched. The sec-ond mistake had been to apply the same punitive-expedition tac-tics in Ekaterinodar as had been used in the villages taken on the way; the town was surrounded (on the right flank, by an infantry division and scouts along the river towards the tanneries, on the left by deep cavalry penetration under General Erdeli), so as to close all exits and entrances, and take reprisals against the defen-ders of the town and the population—shooting, hanging and beat-ing them, as "ban-dits" and "mutinous swine". Such tactics brought the defenders to the conclusion that it would be better to fall in battle than die on the gallows. (The word spread like wild-fire through the town—"Kornilov is going to kill everyone".) Women, girls, children, the young and the old, rushed beneath showers of bullets to the trenches with jugs of milk, cream-cheese fritters, and pies. "Eat, sailors, eat, soldiers, eat, dear comrades, defend us...." And they continued to carry food and ammunition boxes to the defenders, even when horsemen were galloping about everywhere, especially towards evening, shouting: "Clear the streets! To your houses! Extinguish all lights!"

Thus the first day ended with a balance in favour of the Reds. On that day the Whites lost three of their best commanders, about a thousand officers and rank and file, and exhausted, without appreciable advantage, more than a third of their ammunition.

And from Novorossiisk, moving through a curtain of fire, dilapidated trains full of sailors, shells and guns, arrived one after another. The men leaped straight out of the trucks into the trenches, the too great compactness of their onrush and lack of leadership resulting in enormous losses.

Kornilov sat poring over his map in the corner room. He already realized that there was no other way out—either the town must be taken, or they must all die. His thoughts touched upon the idea of suicide. The army, of which he had been the sole commander, was melting like tin soldiers thrown into a stove. But this dull, fearless man was as obstinate as a bull.

About a score of wounded officers sat in the burning sun on the church steps in the village of Elizavetinskaya. The sound of cannon fire, now louder, now softer, came from the east. But here, pigeons were rising into the cloudless sky above the shell-shattered belfry. The square in front of the church was empty. The huts with their broken windows were abandoned. A half-buried corpse, covered with flies, lay beside the wattle fence, where the buds were bursting on the lilac bushes.

A subdued conversation was going on on the church steps.

"I had a sweetheart, a lovely girl, a darling. I can just see her, in her pink, frilly dress. Where she is now, I don't know."

"Love.... It seems incredible.... And how one longs for the old life.... Clean women, oneself well dressed, sitting quietly in a restaurant. Ah, how good it was, gentlemen...."

"The little Bolshevik is stinking. It is time he was buried."

"The flies will eat him up."

"Sh! Listen, gentlemen! Hurricane fire again."

"It's the end, believe me! Our chaps are in the town already!"

Silence. All turned, looking towards the east, where a grayish yellow cloud of smoke and dust hung over Ekaterinodar. A red-haired officer, thin as a skeleton, hobbled up and sat down beside them.

"Valka's just died...." he said. "He kept crying: 'Mamma, Mamma, can you hear me?' "

A harsh voice came from the top of the steps:

"Love! Girls in frilly dresses.... R-r-rubbish! Campfire talk!

5*

My wife was prettier than your sweetheart with her frills ... and I sent her to..." (he snorted angrily). "And it's all a pack of lies, you never had any sweetheart. A revolver in your jacket, a sword at your side—that's your entire family and belongings."

Roshchin, on sentry duty in front of the church, halted in his pacing to and fro to gaze steadily at the speaker, a blond fellow with a boyish face and snub nose, harsh lines on either side of his mouth, heavy, old-looking, clouded blue eyes, the eyes of a sleepless murderer. Roshchin leaned on his rifle—his leg still ached—and importunate thoughts besieged him. The memory of the forsaken Katya returned with a rush of pity. He pressed his forehead against the cold steel of the bayonet. "Enough! This is weakness,—it's not what's wanted...." Giving himself a shake he strode on again over the fresh green grass. "These are no times for pity or for love...."

A stocky, frowning individual stood beside a shell-shattered brick wall, looking through field glasses. His smart leather jacket, leather breeches, and soft Cossack riding boots, were bespattered with dried mud. Every now and then a bullet struck the brick wall beside him with a click. Below him, about a hundred paces away, were a battery and piles of green munition cases. Some horses which had just been led up to the wall stood with their heads hanging down, dropping steaming excrements. The gun crew, perched laughing and smoking on a gun carriage, glanced every now and then towards the commander with the field glasses. Almost all the men were sailors, with the exception of three ragged and bearded artillerymen who had got among them.

The horizon, the lines of trenches, folds in the earth, orchards, were veiled in smoke and dust. Whatever it was that the commander saw, kept appearing and reappearing in his field of vision. A copper-coloured sailor, clad in a vest and trousers, came out of the house in front of which the commander was standing, slunk catlike along the wall, and squatted down at the feet of the stocky man, embracing his knees with strong, tattooed arms.

"See those two trees right on the bank?" he asked, screwing up his amber, hawklike eyes.

"Well?"

"There's a little house just behind them, you can see its white walls."

"Well? "

"It's a farm."

"I know."

"And to the right, there's a grove. And over there—a road."

68

"I see it."

"At four o'clock some men on horseback galloped up, and people began stirring. In the evening two carriages arrived. That's where the devil sits, and nowhere else."

"Now go down!" said the stocky man imperiously, and called the commander of the battery to him. A bearded man in a sheepskin coat clambered up to the top of the mound. The stocky man handed his field glasses to him, and he looked long through them.

"The Slusarev homestead—the farm," he said in rheumy accents. "Four and a half miles away. We could direct fire on Slusarev."

He returned the glasses, clambered clumsily back down the slope, and, drawing a deep breath, shouted:

"Battery make ready! Range.... First salvo.... Fire!"

The brazen throats of the guns thundered the tubes jerked, releasing a flame of fire, and the heavy shells went their way, muttering a death refrain, towards the high bank of the Kuban, to the two bare poplars, where Kornilov sat gloomily before a map in the little white hut.

General Markov and his officers' regiment were summoned from the baggage train on the second day of the assault. Roshchin was a rank-and-file soldier in this column. The six miles or so to Ekaterinodar, which was still more thickly enveloped in the dust and smoke of the cannonade than it had been the day before, were covered in an hour's time. Markov strode in front, his wadded jacket unbuttoned, his tall fur hat pushed far back on his head. Addressing the staff colonel, who could hardly keep up with him, he swore and cursed at the High Command:

"They broke up the brigade, left me to hang about with the transport...." (Here he emitted a stream of obscenities.) "If they'd let me go with the brigade, I'd have been long ago in Ekaterinodar." (More obscenities.)

Leaping across a ditch, he raised his whip and, turning to the column which stretched far over the green field, uttered a command, the veins on his neck swelling as he shouted.

Panting officers, with grave, sweating faces, set off at a run, and the column turned as if on an axis, stretching across the field in four quivering ribbons, in full view of the city. Roshchin found himself quite close to Markov. They stood for a few minutes. Locks were tested on rifles. Cartridge pouches were inspected. Markov uttered another command, dragging out the vowels. An advance guard was formed, and started at a run far ahead. The lines moved in their wake.

Wretched carts met them from the left, jogging wounded men over the slippery road. Some of the wounded were walking, their heads bent. Many were seated on the sides of ditches, or on overturned carts. There seemed to be no end to carts and wounded, as if the whole army was made up of them.

A tall obese man on a black horse, with a moustache, a red band round his cap, and the shoulder straps of the military stables on his smartly cut tunic, overtook the regiment. He shouted something gaily to General Markov, who turned his head aside without replying. It was Rodzyanko, who had got permission to leave the transport, to have a look at the storming of Ekaterinodar.

The regiment again halted. The command came from afar—many lit up and began smoking. All looked in silence towards the place where, amidst ditches and mounds, the advance guard was hidden. General Markov, brandishing his whip, set off in the direction of the tall poplars. There, from the depths of the almost imperceptible green haze of the trees, shaggy columns of smoke rose at short intervals, and branches and clods of earth flew high into the air.

They had a long wait. It was past four now. A horseman emerged from the grove at a gallop, bending low over his horse's neck. Roshchin saw the foaming horse waltz about at the edge of a ditch, as if afraid to cross it, and then, with a wave of the tail, jump over it, the rider losing his cap. Galloping up to the regiment, he cried:

"Attack ... the artillery barracks ... the General is in front, over there...."

He flung his hand in the direction of a mound where a few figures came and went, one of them wearing a high fur cap. The command rang out:

"Lines ... forward!"

Roshchin's throat contracted, and his eyes burned; he knew a second of fear and ecstasy, in which his flesh seemed to melt, and he felt a desire to run, to shout, to shoot, to pierce, a desire for his heart to fill with blood, to sacrifice his heart....

The first line moved ahead, with Roshchin on the left flank. And there was the mound upon which stood Markov, legs astraddle, facing the advancing regiment.

"On, on, friends!" he kept crying, and his eyes, usually narrowed, now seemed expanded ... terrible....

Then Roshchin saw the dry stems of grass sticking out of the earth. Everywhere motionless bodies in soldiers' tunics, sailors' jackets; officers' greatcoats, lay among the stalks, like sacks, some prone, some on their sides. In front of him were a low wattle fence and leafless brambles. A long-faced individual in a soldier's wadded vest was sitting with his back to the fence, opening and shutting his mouth.

Roshchin jumped over the fence and saw a broad road, along which columns of dust were advancing rapidly. It was the Bolsheviks firing on the attackers from machine guns. He stopped short, backed, drew a breath, and looked behind him. Those who had jumped over the fence were lying down. Roshchin did the same, pressing his cheek against the prickly earth. He forced himself with an effort to raise his head. The whole line was lying on the ground. About fifty paces away, in the field, rose the mound of a ditch. Roshchin leaped to his feet and, crouching low, ran these fifty paces. His heart was beating furiously. He fell into the sticky mud of the ditch. The whole line came after him, one by one. One or two fell down on the way. All breathed heavily as they lay in the ditch. The bullets flew over their heads.

But suddenly there was a change ahead of them—from somewhere or other shells began whistling past towards the barracks. The machine-gun fire grew weaker.

With an effort the men in the ditch got up and moved ahead. Roshchin could see his own shadow, reddish-black, slip over the uneven field. It kept changing, now getting shorter, now shooting far away. "Queer!" he thought. "I'm still alive—I even have a shadow."

The firing from the other side grew stronger again, but the thinning ranks now lay a hundred paces from the barracks in a deep gully. Markov was striding up and down the grey, clayey bottom his eyes ghastly.

"Gentlemen!" he was crying. "A breathing space ... smoke, damn you! And a final effort.... It's nothing, a mere hundred paces...."

A short, bald officer next to Roshchin, looking up at the top of the gully, which was smoking from exploding bullets, repeated the same curses again and again under his breath. Some of the men were lying down covering their faces with their hands. One, squatting on his heels and clutching his forehead, was spitting blood. Many were striding up and down the bottom of the gully like caged hyenas. The command: "Forward!" rang out. No one seemed to hear it. Roshchin pulled in his belt with spasmodic movements, seized the branches of a bush, and crawled upwards. He slipped, but went on again, setting his teeth. When he got to the top he saw Markov squatting on the crest of the gully, and shouting:

"Advance to the attack! On!"

A few paces ahead Roshchin could see the twinkling soles of Markov's boots, and the holes in them. A few men overtook him.

71

The brick wall of the barracks was suffused with the rays of the setting sun. The fragments of glass left in the windows were crimson. Figures were running out of the barracks over the field to some distant cottages, with little gardens in front.

A group of civilians and soldiers were standing around the broken gymnastic apparatus on the sandy yard of the artillery barracks. Their faces were pale, strained, absorbed, their eyes lowered, their hands hung lifeless at their sides. In front of them was a smaller group—leaning on their rifles. These were officers. They were gazing with brooding hatred at the prisoners. Both groups remained silent and expectant. Suddenly Captain von Mecke (Roshchin recognized him as the man with those murderer's eyes dulled by lack of sleep) came rapidly towards them with a skipping gait.

"All of them," he shouted gaily. "The order's for all.... Ten of you come here, gentlemen...."

Before the ten officers, rattling the locks of their guns, had time to step forward, there was a movement among the prisoners. One, tall and broad-chested, pulled his cloth tunic off, over his head. Another, a civilian, consumptive-looking, toothless, with a straight black moustache, cried in a breaking voice:

"Drink the blood of the workers, parasites!"

Two embraced closely. A hoarse voice intoned unmelodiously:

"Arise, ye prisoners...."

The ten officers settled their rifles against their shoulders. Roshchin suddenly felt that someone was looking fixedly at him. He looked up. (He was sitting on a box, taking off his boots.) A pair of eyes (he did not notice the face) was gazing at him with a dying reproach, with lofty significance. "Grey eyes—oh, God! Eyes that were so near, so dear!"

"Fire!"

The shots rang out hastily, one after another. Groans and cries were heard, Roshchin bent low, bandaging his leg, which had been grazed by a bullet during the fighting, with a dirty strip of rag.

Like the first, the second day did not bring victory to the Volunteers. True, on the right flank the artillery barracks had been occupied, but they did not advance a step in the centre, and on that sector the Kornilov Regiment lost in battle its commander— Colonel Nezhentsev, the General's favourite. On the left flank Erdeli's cavalry was retreating. The Reds were displaying unprecedented resistance, though there were wounded in almost every house in Ekaterinodar. Women and children in great numbers were killed near the trenches and in the streets. If, instead of

72

Avtonomov, there had been an able commander to organize a general attack by the Red troops, the battered Volunteer Army, its units in hopeless disorder, must inevitably have been overrun and destroyed.

On the third day the Volunteer regiments, their ranks more or less inadequately replenished, were once more sent to the attack and once more hurled back to their point of departure. Many of them, throwing down their rifles, sought refuge in their rear, among the baggage trains. The generals lost heart. Alexeyev came to inspect the positions, shook his grey head, and departed. But nobody had the courage to go and tell the Commander in Chief that the game was already up, and that, even if by some miracle they should break through to Ekaterinodar, they could now never hold the city.

Kornilov, after he had pressed his lips to the cold brow of his favourite, Nezhentsev, whose body was brought on a cart up to his window in the farm, never opened his mouth, and spoke to no one. When, however, some shrapnel burst close to the house and a bullet from it, flying through the window, lodged itself in the ceiling, he pointed to it gloomily with his leathery finger, and for some reason or other said to the aide-de-camp Khadzhiev: "Keep that, Khan!"

On the night of the fourth day the Commander in Chief's order was transmitted over all field telephones: "Continue the assault."

By now, however, it was clear to all that the tempo of the advance had been greatly decreased. General Kutepov, who had taken the post of the fallen Nezhentsev, was unable to induce the Kornilov Regiment (the best in the army) to leave the vegetable plots in which they were lying. The troops fought languidly. Erdeli's cavalry continued to retreat. Markov, who had strained his voice by shouting and swearing, kept falling asleep on the way, his officers could not move a step beyond the barracks.

In the middle of the day a military council was called in Kornilov's room, attended by generals Alexeyev, Romanovsky, Markov, Bogayevsky, Filimonov and Denikin. Kornilov, his small silvery head shrinking into his shoulders, listened to Romanovsky's report:

"No shells, no cartridges. The Cossack volunteers going back to their villages. All regiments in disorder. Morale low. Many unwounded leaving the battlefield for the rear..." and so on, and so on.

The generals listened with lowered eyes. Markov, his head reposing against somebody's shoulder, slept. In the dusk (the window was curtained), Kornilov's high cheekboned face was like that of a shrivelled mummy. He spoke in a muffled voice:

"And so, gentlemen, the situation is indeed serious. I see no way out but the seizure of Ekaterinodar. I have decided to storm the town tomorrow at dawn, with combined forces along the whole front. The Kazanovich Regiment is in reserve. I will lead it to the attack myself."

The snort with which he ended his words was entirely unexpected. The generals remained in their seats, their heads bent. General Denikin, stout, wheezy, grey-bearded, in appearance resembling a hard-working clerk, exclaimed involuntarily: "Oh, God, oh, God!", and, giving way to a fit of coughing, made for the door. Kornilov's black eyes shot a glance after him. He listened to everyone's objections, then rose and declared the council over. The decisive assault was fixed for the first of April.

Half an hour later Denikin came back to the room, the usual whistling sounds escaping from his lungs. He sat down and said, in tones of tender consideration:

"Your Excellency, may I put a question to you, as man to man?"

"Go on, Anton Ivanovich."

"Lavr Georgievich, why are you so inexorable?"

Kornilov replied immediately as if he had long been expecting such a question, and had his answer ready:

"There's no other way out. If we don't take Ekaterinodar, I shall put a bullet through my brains." With a finger on which the nail was bitten to the quick he pointed to his right temple.

"You wouldn't do that!" Denikin raised his plump, white hands and pressed them against his chest. "Before God, before your native land.... Who would lead the army, Lavr Georgievich?"

"You, Your Excellency."

With an impatient gesture Kornilov gave his interlocutor to understand that he would say no more.

The morning of the 31st of March dawned warm and cloudless. A fine mist rose from the earth, which was just beginning to be covered with green sprouts. The turbid yellow waters of the Cuban flowed lazily between its steep banks, their calm only broken now and then by the leaping of a fish. All was still. The only sounds were an occasional rifle shot, or the rumbling of a distant gun, followed by the whistling of a shell. Everyone was resting, in order, on the morrow, to embark upon a new and bloody battle.

Lieutenant Dolinsky was smoking in the porch in front of the house. He was thinking to himself: "I ought to wash my shirt, my underclothes ... my socks, too. It would be nice to have a bath...." There was actually a bird gaily twittering in the grove. Dolinsky raised his head. Phee-ee-eet!—a shell landed right in the middle of the green grove, exploding with metallic clatterings. The bird had stopped singing. Dolinsky flung the end of the cigarette at a silly hen which had somehow or other escaped the pot, sighed, turned into the house, and sat down near the door, but the next minute he jumped up and went into the darkened room. Kornilov was standing at the table, hitching up his trousers.

"Tea not ready yet?" he asked softly.

"It'll be ready in a minute, Your Excellency, I've ordered it."

Kornilov sat down, put his elbows on the table, and, raising his parchment-skinned hand to his forehead, mopped at his wrinkles.

"There was something I wanted to say to you, Lieutenant. But it's no good, I can't remember.... It's awful...."

Dolinsky, wondering what he wanted to say, bent over the table. It was all so unlike the Commander in Chief—the quiet voice, the distrait manner—that he was quite alarmed.

Kornilov repeated his last words:

"Awful! Awful! It'll come back to me, don't go away. I've been looking out of the window. A lovely morning... Oh, yes, now I remember...."

He stopped speaking and raised his head as if listening. Now Dolinsky, too, could make out the ever-nearing, blood-curdling howl of a shell, which seemed to be coming right through the curtained window. Dolinsky retreated a step. There was a terrific explosion overhead. The air shook. The lamp flame shot up. The body of the Commander in Chief, all the limbs extended, flew up into the air....

Dolinsky was flung out of the window. He found himself on the grass, white with lime, his lips trembling. People came running up to him....

A doctor, squatting on his heels, was busying himself over the body of Kornilov, which lay on a stretcher, half-covered with a sheepskin cloak. A short distance away stood a group of staff officers, and, close to the stretcher, Denikin, a peaked cap stuck awkwardly on his head.

A minute before Kornilov had been breathing. There were no visible marks of injury on his body, except for a slight scratch on one temple. The doctor was an insignificant individual, but at this moment he realized that the eyes of all were fixed upon him, and though he knew everything was over already he went on examining the body with an important air. Then he rose to his feet unhurriedly, adjusted his glasses and shook his head, as if to say: "Unfortunately medicine is powerless in this case...."

Denikin went up to him, and asked in a strangled voice:

"Can't you give us a word of comfort?"

"Hopeless!" the doctor threw out his hands. "It's the end."

Denikin drew out his handkerchief with convulsive movements, pressed it to his eyes, his shoulders heaving. His stout frame seemed to sag. The group of officers went up to him, looking not at the corpse, but at him. Dropping on to his knees, he made the sign of the cross over the yellow, waxen-coloured features of Kornilov, and kissed him on the forehead. Two officers helped him to get up. A third muttered nervously: "Who will take over the command gentlemen?"

"I will, of course. I will take it over," cried Denikin in a shrill, breaking voice. "Lavr Georgievich left orders about it, we spoke about it only yesterday."

That same night the whole Volunteer Army silently abandoned its positions, and moved north with its infantry, cavalry, baggage, carts, hospital units, and carts full of political supporters, towards the Gnachbau farmsteads, carrying with them two corpses—those of Kornilov and Nezhentsev.

Kornilov's campaign had failed. Its principal leaders and half of those who had participated in it, had perished. It looked as if future historians would be able to dismiss the whole affair in a few words.

In fact, however, Kornilov's "Frost Campaign" was of immense importance. The Whites found in it their first individual expression, their traditions, their military terms—culminating in the newly-created White Order, a sword, and a crown of thorns, on a St. George ribbon.

Subsequently, during recruiting and mobilization, in unpleasant arguments with foreign powers, and misunderstandings with local populations, they advanced as their first and highest justification, the martyr's crown. No objections could be raised against this: what if—to give an example—such and such a general *did* have the entire population of the district ramrodded (as the process was called). Those who did it were martyrs themselves and martyrs should not be judged by ordinary standards.

Kornilov's campaign had been the opening scene of the tragedy, the moment when, following on the prologue, the curtain rises, and the scenes, each more hair-raising and catastrophic than the one before, pass before the spectators in agonizing profusion.

IV

Alexei Krasilnikov jumped off the footboard of the truck, lifted his brother in his arms as if he were a child, and set him on the platform. Matryona was standing at the door of the station, beside the bell. Semyon did not recognize her at first; she wore a townmade coat, and her shining black hair was covered with a clean white kerchief, bound round her head in the new Soviet fashion. Her face, young, round, beautiful, wore a frightened expression, and her lips were pressed tightly together.

When Semyon, supported by his brother, approached her, his feet scarcely moving, Matryona's hazel eyes blinked, and a tremor passed over her face....

"My God!" she said softly. "How bad he looks!"

Semyon, with a gasp of pain, placed his hand on his wife's shoulder and touched her cool clean cheek with his lips. Alexei took the whip out of her hand. They all stood in silence. At last Alexei said:

"Here's your husband back again! They tried to kill him, but they couldn't quite. Never mind—we'll be reaping together soon. Come on, then, dear relatives."

Matryona put her strong, loving arm round Semyon's waist and led him to the cart, in which were embroidered cushions laid on a homespun rug. Seating him, she took her place beside him, stretching her feet, in the new, townmade boots, in front of her. Alexei, fixing the breechband, said gaily:

"A soldier from a cavalry troop train got left behind in February. I filled him with *samogon* two whole days. Then I gave him five hundred rubles in Kerensky notes, and look what a horse I got!" He clapped the sturdy chestnut gelding on the rump. Then, jumping on to the driver's seat, he settled his sheepskin cap firmly on his head, and gave a tug at the reins. They drove over a field path through the faintly sprouting fields, over which a lark was singing thrillingly in the sunlight, its wings quivering. A smile crept over Semyon's unshaven pallid face. Matryona, pressing him closer to her, questioned him with her eyes, and he answered:

"You people are doing yourself proud, aren't you?"

Semyon enjoyed going into the spacious, newly whitewashed house. There were green shutters on the small windows, and a new, shingled porch, and on passing through the familiar low door, Semyon was struck by the coziness and prosperity of it all— the warm whitewashed stove, the sturdy table with the embroidered cloth, the uncountrified pots and pans on the shelf, some nickelled, some chinaware, Matryona's bedroom with the iron bedstead and the lace quilt, the mattress topped by a pile of fluffed-out pillows, and, to the right, Alexei's room (formerly the room of their late father), with the bridle and saddle, shining new harness, a sword, a rifle, and framed photographs on the walls. And in all three rooms, the lovingly placed flowers in pots, the aspidistra and the cactus.... He had been away from home for eighteen months, and now there were aspidistras, and a bed fit for a princess, and Matryona in a townmade coat!

"You live like the gentry," he said, sitting down on a bench and unwinding his scarf with an effort. Matryona put away her fine coat in the chest, tied on an apron, turned the tablecloth on to its other side, and rapidly laid the table. She shoved the great oven prongs into the stove, and, bowing beneath the weight, her arms, bare to the elbow, suffused with colour, drew out the iron pot of borshch. There were already lard, smoked goose, and dried fish on the table. Matryona turned her gleaming eyes towards Alexei, he winked, and she brought in an earthenware jug full of *samogon*.

Then the brothers drew up to the table. Alexei handed the first glass to his brother. Matryona bowed low. And when Semyon drank the burning raw spirits, which almost took his breath away, they both—Alexei and Matryona—wiped their eyes. This meant they really were glad Semyon was alive and sitting at the table with them.

"We don't live like princes, brother," said Alexei when they had finished their borshch. "But we're comfortable."

Matryona cleared away the used plates and sat close to her husband.

"Remember the field near the copse, on the prince's estate?" continued Alexei. "The land with the rich soil? I made a great to-do in the village, stood the peasants six pails of *samogon* and they allotted the land to me. Now Matryona and I have ploughed it. And we got a fairly good crop from the strip along the riverbank last summer. All these things—bed, mirror, coffeepots, spoons and forks, and the rest of the odds and ends—we got all of them this winter. Matryona's a rare housewife. She never misses a market day. I still stick to the old ways, and sell for money. But she doesn't! She'll slaughter a cow, or kill a couple of hens in a jiffy, and on to the cart with them, with a sack of flour, and some potatoes, and off she goes to town.... And she doesn't go to the market place, but straight to the houses of the former gentry, her eyes rolling: 'For the bedstead,' she tells them. 'Two pods of flour and six pounds of lard.... And for the bedspread a sack of potatoes....' You'd die of laughing to see us coming home from the market— proper gypsies—our cart loaded up with a lot of fancy trash."

Matryona, pressing her husband's hand, said:

"Remember my cousin Avdotya? She's a year older than me— we want her to marry Alexei."

Alexei laughed, fumbling in his pocket.

"The wenches have settled it without me. But you know, brother, I'm tired of widowhood. Drinking and whoring, and then the filth seems to stick to you...."

He drew out a pouch and a charred pipe, with copper trinkets hanging from it, and began filling it with home-grown tobacco, and puffing smoke all over the hut. Semyon's head was going round from the talk and the *samogon*. He sat in his place, listening and marvelling.

Towards dusk Matryona took him to the bathhouse, soaped him well, enveloped him in clouds of steam, whipped him all over with a bundle of twigs, wrapped him in a sheepskin coat, and once again they all sat down to table, and had supper, finishing up the earthenware jug to the last drop. Still weak, Semyon went to bed with his wife, and slept with her warm arm round his neck. And when he opened his eyes the next morning the hut was neat and warm. Matryona, the whites of her eyes, and her teeth gleaming in a smile, was kneading dough. Alexei would soon be back from the fields for his breakfast. The spring sunshine was pouring through the brightly-polished windowpanes, and the leaves of the aspidistra gleamed. Sitting up in bed Semyon stretched himself: he felt that the day and night passed in Matryona's company had almost restored his health. He dressed and washed, and asked where his brother kept his razor. He shaved at the window in Alexei's room, in front of a fragment of glass. Then he went out and stood at the gate, greeting a man seated in a neighbour's garden, an old man who could remember four tsars. The old man took off his cap with a dignified bow; his numb legs in the felt boots were stretched out in front of him and his veined hands were folded symmetrically on the handle of his stick.

The familiar street was empty at that hour. Between the huts could be seen strips of green, extending far into the distance. On mounds, silhouetted here and there against the horizon, stood unharnessed carts. Semyon glanced to his left—two windmills were lazily swinging their sails over the chalky sides of a gully. Lower down, on the slope, amidst orchards and straw thatches, the belfry tower gleamed white. Beyond the copse, still so leafless as to be almost transparent, the windows of what had formerly been a nobleman's mansion blazed in the sunshine. Rooks were cawing around their nests. The copse and the handsome façade of the house were reflected in the flooded pond. Cows lay at the waterside, and children played about. Semyon stood looking from under his brows, his hands thrust into the capacious pockets of his brother's jacket. As he looked, sadness took possession of his heart, and gradually, through the transparent waves of heat streaming over the village, the bluish orchards, and the ploughed lands, another world, far from this tranquillity, began to form itself before his eyes. Alexei drove up in a cart, hailing him gaily from afar. He looked steadily at Semyon as he opened the gate. After unharnessing the gelding, he went to the yard to wash his hands beneath the hanging washstand.

"Never mind, brother, it'll pass," he said kindly. "When I came back from the German front I didn't want to look at anything either. Blood in my eyes, grief in my heart.... Damn the war.... Come and have breakfast."

Semyon said nothing. But Matryona, too, could see that her husband was out of spirits. After breakfast Alexei went back to the fields, and Matryona, barefoot, her skirts hitched up, carted away the dung. Semyon lay down on his brother's bed. He tossed and turned, but could not sleep. His heart was assailed by melancholy. Setting his teeth he told himself: "They wouldn't understand—it's no use trying to talk to them." But in the evening, when they all three went out to sit on some logs lying at the gate, Semyon could not resist saying:

"You might at least keep your rifle cleaned, Alexei."

"To hell with it.... We're not going to fight now, brother, for another hundred years."

"You're rejoicing too soon. It's too early to be growing aspidistras."

"And don't you be angry too soon, Semyon," Alexei pulled at his pipe and spat between his feet. "Let's talk like peasants, we're not at a meeting. I know all the things they say at meetings—I've shouted myself hoarse at them. You've got to know how to hear what you need, and take no notice of what you don't need. The land to the toilers, now! That's perfectly right. And now—Poor Peasants' Committees. In our village we've taken these committee persons in hand. But the Poor Peasants' Committee at Sosnovka does just what it likes, and the requisitions and outrages are something awful. Count Bobrinsky's estate all went to the sovkhoz, the peasants didn't get a foot of land. And who was in the committee? Two single men, with no horses, and the rest God knows who—strangers, convicts or something. D'you understand me?"

"Oh, that's not what I was talking about!" said Semyon, turning away.

"That's just it, but it is what I'm talking about! In 1917 I ran about the front shouting against the bourgeoisie, too. God bless the one who sent a bullet into my foot, I was straightaway evacuated home. The way I look at it—however much you eat, you want to eat again the next day. A man's got to work."

Semyon tapped with his nails against the log.

"The earth is burning beneath you, and you lie down and sleep."

"Perhaps in the navy," said Alexei firmly, "or in the towns, the revolution is not over yet. But it was over here the moment the land was divided up. This is how it will be from now on: first we'll get in the crops, and then we'll start on the committees. By St. Peter's day there won't be a single Poor Peasants' Committee left. We'll bury them alive. We're not afraid of the Communists. We're not afraid of the devil himself, remember that...."

"Stop it, Alexei Ivanovich, look, he's all of a tremble," said Matryona softly. "What can you expect of a sick man?"

"I'm not sick! I'm a stranger here, that's what it is!" shouted Semyon, rising and walking over to the wattle fence.

The conversation went no further.

Two bats flittered across a strip of the dying sunset glow like two disembodied spirits. Here and there lights burned in windows—supper was over. Songs—the voices of girls—came from a long way off. The singing broke off abruptly, and the tippety-tip of horse's hoofs was heard on the broad twilit street. The rider halted, called out something, and gave rein to his horse. Alexei took his pipe out of his mouth the better to hear, and rose from his seat on the logs.

"What can have happened?" asked Matryona in tremulous accents. At last the rider came in sight and galloped up to them—a hatless, barefoot lad.

"The Germans are coming!" he yelled. "Four people have been killed in Sosnovka."

After the conclusion of peace, about the middle of March, New Style, the German troops started an offensive against the Ukraine and the Donbas from Riga to the Black Sea.

Under the terms of the Peace Treaty the Germans were entitled to 75 million poods of grain from the Central Rada, 11 million poods of live cattle, 2 million geese and hens, two-and-a-half million poods of sugar, 20 million litres of spirits, two-and-a-half thousand truckloads of eggs, four thousand poods of lard, in addition to butter, hides, wool, timber and the like....

The Germans attacked the Ukraine according to all the rules of war, in khaki-clad and steel-helmeted columns. The weak covering detachments of the Reds were mowed down by the German heavy artillery.

Troops passed, followed by motorized transport, vast artillery parks, the guns camouflaged in brightly coloured zigzag lines; tanks and armoured cars clattered by, pontoons, whole bridges for crossing rivers were borne past. Aeroplanes buzzed incessantly overhead. It was the march of technique against an almost un-

81

armed people. The Red detachments, composed of war veterans and peasants, miners and industrial workers, badly organized and numerically inferior to those of the Germans, retreated, fighting, to the north and east.

The Central Rada, which had sold the Ukraine to the Germans, was substituted at Kiev by General Skoropadsky, late of the tsar's suite. Clad in the traditional Ukrainian blue coat so dear to the Ukrainian nationalists, he held the hetman's mace and struck heroic poses: "Long live the Ukraine! From now on and ever after—peace, order and prosperity! Workers—to the lathes, peasants—to the plough! Red devils—begone!"

A week after the herald of disaster had galloped along the main street of the village of Vladimirskoye, a mounted patrol appeared early one morning beside the windmills on the chalky slopes. It was composed of twenty riders on tall black steeds—tall, un-Russian looking fellows, in short, greenish jackets and braided Uhlan caps. They looked down at the village, and dismounted.

There were still people in the village—many had not gone out into the fields that day. At sight of the horsemen little boys ran from gate to gate, the women shouted to one another over the wattle fences, and soon a crowd had gathered on the open space in front of the church. By looking up they could clearly see the Uhlans posting two machine guns beside the mills.

And almost immediately after, from the other side, iron-rimmed wheels clattered over the village street, a whip cracked, and a pair of foam-covered horses harnessed to a military cart, came at full trot into the square. A clumsy-looking soldier with light eyes and a protruding jaw, wearing a fatigue cap and a tight uniform, was in the rider's seat. Behind him, arms akimbo, sat a German officer, a strange, fierce-looking gentleman, with a glass in one eye, and a cap that looked as if it had just come out of the shop. Huddled against his left side was an old acquaintance—the prince's bailiff, who had run away from the estate the previous autumn in his underclothes.

There he sat, Grigori Karlovich Miel, glowering at them in his good coat and warm cap—round-faced, freshly shaved, wearing gold-rimmed spectacles. The peasants felt their skins tingle when they saw Grigori Karlovich.

"Caps off!" shouted the strange officer suddenly in Russian. Some—those nearest to the carriage—sulkily pulled off their caps. Silence reigned in the square. The officer, still sitting with his arms akimbo, his monocle gleaming, began to speak, dropping out each syllable separately, and pronouncing the words with difficulty, but correctly:

"Agricultural workers of the village of Vladimirskoye, you see up there on the top of the hill, two German machine guns. They are in splendid working order.... You are, of course, rational agricultural workers. I should be sorry to do you any harm. It is my duty to inform you that the German troops of the Emperor Wilhelm have come to you to re-establish among you the life of honest people. We Germans don't like the property of others being stolen, we punish such actions ruthlessly. The Bolsheviks taught you differently, didn't they? That's why we have driven the Bolsheviks away, they will never come back to you any more. I advise you to think well over your bad deeds, and to make up your mind to return to the owner of this estate without delay all that you have stolen from him."

These words evoked diverse grunts from the crowd. Grigori Karlovich sat there all the time, the peak of his cap pulled over his eyes, looking steadily at the peasants. Once a triumphant smile appeared for a second on his plump face—apparently he had recognized somebody. The officer stopped talking. The peasants held their peace.

"I have fulfilled my duty. You speak to them now, Mr. Miel," said the officer, turning to the bailiff.

Grigori Karlovich politely declined this proposal.

"I have nothing to say to them, Lieutenant. They understand everything perfectly."

"Good!" replied the officer, who didn't care either way. "Drive on, Augustin."

The driver cracked his whip, and the military cart rolled through the crowd, which made way on all sides, towards the prince's mansion, where, only three days before, the Volost Executive Committee had been housed. The peasants looked after the departing cart:

"The German's perked up again," came from the crowd.

"Grigori Karlovich wouldn't talk, mates."

"Give him time—he'll talk!"

"Oh, God, what a calamity—what have we done?"

"The police officer will be upon us soon."

"He's come to Sosnovka already. He called a meeting and started swearing at the muzhiks—you so-and-so, you robbers and bandits, have you forgotten 1905? He rated them for three solid hours, swearing all the time. He showed them what politics meant."

"What's going to happen now?"

"Floggings—that's what."

"And what about the land? Whose will it be now?"

"Half-and-half. They'll let us bring the harvest in, and take half of it for the prince."

"What the hell—I'm going away."

"Where to, fool?"

The peasants talked a little more, and then dispersed. And by night, sofas, beds, curtains, gilt-framed mirrors and pictures were carried back to the landowner's mansion.

The Krasilnikovs had supper in the dark. Alexei kept laying down his spoon, looking out of the window, and sighing. Matryona went about, quiet as a mouse, between the stove and the table. Semyon sat with bowed shoulders, his dark curly hair falling over his forehead. Every time she cleaned up the fragments, or put a dish with something else on the table, Matryona would brush against him with her arm, or with her breast. But he maintained a stubborn silence, not even lifting his head.

Suddenly Alexei staggered to the window, tapped on the glass with his fingernails, and looked out. In the stillness of evening a long, wild shriek could now be clearly heard. Matryona dropped on to a bench, squeezing her hands between her knees.

"They're flogging Vaska Dementyev," said Alexei quietly. "They came for him and took him to the prince's house."

"That'll be the third," whispered Matryona.

They listened in silence. A shriek hung in the air over the nightbound village, striking the same note of horror and despair.

Semyon rose abruptly, tugging at his trouserbelt with an abrupt movement, and went into his brother's room. Matryona, equally silent, rushed after him. He had taken the rifle down from the wall. Matryona put her arms round his neck, hung on him, throwing back her head and setting her white teeth, and there she froze. Semyon tried to push her away, but could not. The rifle fell on the earthen floor. Semyon threw himself on the bed, burying his head in a pillow. Matryona sat down beside him, stroking his rough locks with rapid movements.

Not trusting to the strength of the guards and the Gaidamaks, as the new hetman troops were called, Grigori Karlovich, the bailiff, asked for a garrison to be sent to Vladimirskoye. The Germans were always ready to help in such cases, and two platoons with machine guns entered Vladimirskoye.

The soldiers were billeted in the village. People said it was Grigori Karlovich who named the homesteads to be used. However that may have been, every peasant who had participated in the previous year's looting of the prince's mansion, and every non-party member of the former Volost Executive Committee (ten of the younger ones had left the village before the appearance in it of the Germans) was made to quarter and support a soldier and a horse.

And so a gallant German soldier, in field equipment, rifle on shoulder and helmet on head, knocked at the gate of the Krasilnikov home. Uttering incomprehensible words, he showed Alexei his order, and clapped him on the shoulder:

"Gut, Freund...."

He was assigned Alexei's room, after the harness and arms had been removed. He settled down at once, spreading a good blanket on the bed, hanging a photograph of Wilhelm on the wall, and ordering the floor to be swept clean.

While Matryona was sweeping he collected his dirty linen and asked for it to be washed. *"Schmutzig—pfui!"* he said. *"Bitte waschen."* Then, well pleased, he threw himself down on the bed in his boots, and lit a cigar.

The soldier was a fat man with a sleek upturned moustache. His clothes were of good quality and comfortable. And he was as greedy as a hog. He devoured everything Matryona brought to him. Best of all he liked the salt bacon. Matryona could hardly bear to feed a German on her bacon, but Alexei said: "Never mind that! Let him guzzle and sleep, so long as he doesn't go poking his nose into things."

In his leisure time the soldier hummed military marches, or wrote home on picture postcards of Kiev. He behaved quite decently, but tramped about in his boots as if the place belonged to him.

The Krasilnikovs lived as if there were a corpse in the house. They sat down to meals and rose from table in silence, and Alexei was always glum, wrinkles had appeared on his forehead. Matryona went about with a drawn face, sighing and furtively wiping away tears with her apron. She was in continual terror that Semyon would lose control of himself in an outburst of rage. But Semyon had fallen silent these days, and seemed to have retreated within himself.

Every day now the house of the Volost Administration and the gates of farmsteads were freshly plastered with the Hetman's orders for the return of livestock and lands to the owners, for requisitions and seizures, and the compulsory sale of bread, notices of ruthless penalties for attempts to organize riots, aid to Communists, and so on....

The peasants read the notices and held their tongues. Then ominous rumours began to be spread that in some village purchasers with an escort of German cavalry had even taken away un-milled grain, paying for it with un-Russian paper money which even the women would not take, that in another village they had driven away half of the livestock, and in yet another had not left behind them enough food to keep a sparrow alive.

The peasants began gathering in small groups at night in secret places, exchanging rumours and grunting. What was to be done? Was there no way out? The force which had descended upon them was so overpowering that there seemed nothing for it but surrender without a murmur.

Semyon began attending these gatherings in backyards, on the bank of a stream, beneath a willow. He would sit on the ground, his coat thrown over his shoulders, smoking and listening. He sometimes longed to leap to his feet, throw off his coat, square his shoulders, and cry out: "Comrades!" But what would be the good? They'd only be frightened, and run away with their trousers flapping.

Once he came across a man, standing and grinning at him. Semyon would have gone on, but the man cried softly: "Brother!"

Semyon gave a start. Could it be a friend?

"What d'you want?" he said, casting an oblique glance at him.

"Aren't you Alexei's brother?"

"Well, and if I am?"

"You don't know your own people.... Remember the crew on the *Kerch*?"

"Kozhin? Is it you?"

Semyon thrust his hand vigorously into the other man's.

They stood looking at one another. Kozhin, with a quick look aside, said:

"Are they sawing their guns?"

"No. Things are quiet so far."

"Are there any lively lads here?"

"Who knows? I haven't seen any yet. We must wait and see."

"What are you fellows doing?" said Kozhin, his eyes continually on the move, peering about among the twilight-muffled outlines of objects. "What are you thinking about? You allow yourselves to be plucked like geese. Are you aware that everything in Uspenskoye, where I come from, has been burned down by artillery fire? The women and children have all run away somewhere, the men are in the woods... The people are running away from Fedorovka, from Gulyai-Polye, and they all come to us...."

"What d'you mean—'us'?"

"Know the Dibrivski woods? That's where we meet.... Well, all right.... Just whisper in the ears of some of your lot: Vladimirskoye must supply forty sawed-off rifles, ten rifles with cartridges, as many hand grenades as you can muster.... And all that must be hidden among the haycocks, in the fields. Understand? They've got it all hidden in the hay at Sosnovka, the lads are only waiting for me.... At Gundayevka thirty peasants are waiting with horses. We must get away."

"But where to? Who to?"

"To the Ataman.... Shchuss, he's called. We're forming detachments all over the Ekaterinoslav region. Last week we defeated the Gaidamaks and set fire to the estate.... That was good sport, brother! We threw the spirits and the sugar to the peasants, free.... Remember, I shall be back in a week. "

He winked at Semyon, leaped over the wattle fence and ran with a crouching movement towards the reeds, where the frogs were croaking vociferously.

Rumours of the atamans and of raids had already reached Vladimirskoye, but no one had believed them. But here was a living witness. Semyon confided in his brother the same evening. Alexei heard him with a grave face.

"What's that ataman's name?"

"Shchuss, he says."

"Never heard of him. They say Nestor Ivanovich Makhno has a gang of twenty-five daredevils who raid the estates. But I never heard of Shchuss. He may be all right—the muzhik's capable of anything nowadays. Anyway—whether it's Shchuss or another man, the cause is good.... But Semyon, don't tell the muzhiks yet. When the time comes I'll tell them myself."

Semyon shrugged his shoulders, smiling.

"You'll wait till they've picked your bones clean."

Apparently Semyon was not the only one who had met Kozhin. Whispers of sawed-off guns, hand grenades, ataman bands stole about in the village. A keen ear could have made out the rasp of the file at night, in the farm yards. But so far all remained quiet. The Germans even established order, issuing the command—the village street to be cleaned on Saturday nights. Nobody murmured, and the street was swept.

Then came misfortune. Early one morning, before the cattle were driven to the watering place, gendarmes and soldiers with badges on their chests went along the clean street, knocking on windowpanes.

"Come out!"

Peasants began running out of their gates, barefoot, buttoning their clothes, and were handed an official notice: so much grain, wool, lard and eggs from the farmsteads named, to be handed over to the German authorities for a given sum in Reichsmarks. A train of army carts was already standing in the square, in front of the church. The German lodgers, helmets on their heads, rifles in their hands, stood at the gates of the huts where they were billeted, smiling. The peasants scratched their heads. Some declared they had nothing, others flung their caps on the ground.

"God knows we have no grain! We have none! Cut us to pieces—we have nothing!"

And now the bailiff came in sight on the road, driving a gig.

It was not so much the soldiers or the gendarmes the peasants feared, as those gold-rimmed glasses, for Grigori Karlovich knew all, saw all.

He reined in his horse. The police captain came up to the gig. The two men conversed. The police officer barked an order to the gendarmes, who entered the nearest yard and immediately found grain at the bottom of the dung heap. Grigori Karlovich's glasses flashed when he heard the cries of the owner.

Alexei was walking up and down his yard in a state of confusion pitiable to see. Matryona, her kerchief over her eyes, was crying in the porch.

"What do I want with their money, their marks?" cried Alexei, picking up now a fragment of wood, now a bit of a wheel, and chucking them into the nettles growing beside the fence. Catching sight of a cock he stamped his foot and swore at it. He shook the padlock on the door of the barn. "What will we have to eat? Those marks of theirs? It means they've decided to make beggars of us altogether! To ruin us utterly! To drive us back to the yoke!"

Semyon, who was sitting next to Matryona, said:

"It'll get worse.... They'll take your gelding."

"Oh, no, they won't! I'll use my axe, if they try that!"

"Too late, too late!"

"Oh-oh-oh!" wailed Matryona. "I'll tear their throats with my teeth!" Someone rammed on the gate with the butt of a rifle. The lodger came in, the fat German, serene, jolly, thoroughly at home. He was followed by six gendarmes and a civilian with a trident (the hetman's cockade) on his official cap, and a register under his arm.

"There's plenty here," said the German, nodding towards the barn, "lard, *Brot*...."

Alexei cast a wild glance at him, stepped back and flung the great rusty key with all his strength at the feet of the hetman's clerk.

"Take care, you swine!" cried the latter. "D'you want the rod, you son-of-a-bitch?"

Semyon thrust Matryona back with his elbow and rushed out of the porch but was instantly met by the broad blade of a bayonet at his chest.

"Halt!" shouted the German in harsh, imperious tones. "Back, Russian!"

The military carts were being loaded all day, and only departed late in the night. The village was thoroughly cleaned out. No lamps were lit, nobody sat down to supper. The women were wailing in the darkness of the huts, paper marks crumpled in their fists.

What would be the good of a man and his wife going to the town with those marks? They would find all the stalls empty: not so much as a nail, not a yard of stuff, not a scrap of leather. The factories at a standstill. Grain, sugar, soap, raw materials, all taken away to Germany in trains. The muzhik and his wife had no use for a grand piano, an old Dutch canvas, or a Chinese tea-pot. All they could do was to eye the forelocks, dropping moustaches, blue cloaks, and red-crowned fur caps of the Gaidamaks, and rub shoulders in the principal street with the blue-jowled, bowler-hatted dealers in air and currency, sigh heavily, and go home no better off than they had set out. And on the way home, the train would stop,—the axles getting overheated after the first twenty miles, and there being no machine oil, for the Germans had taken it all. Sand would be sprinkled, they would go on again, only to be stopped once more by the overheating of the axles.

It was all this which made the women wail with the crumpled Reichsmarks in their hands, and the men hide the cattle in forest gullies, out of harm's way—who could tell what sort of a notice would be pasted up on the morrow!

There were no lights in the village, all the huts were dark, but beyond the copse, on the other side of the lake, the windows of the great house shone brightly. The bailiff was giving a supper in honour of the German officers. There were sounds of military music, and the strains of German waltz tunes floated eerily over the dark village. Like a burning string, a rocket soared high up in the sky for the amusement of the German soldiers, as they stood about the courtyard of the mansion, where a barrel of beer had been rolled out for them. The burning string exploded, and straw thatches, orchards, willow trees, the white belfry, and the wattle fences were lighted up by the slowly falling stars. Many a glum countenance was raised towards them. Their light was so brilliant that every sullen wrinkle stood out. A pity they could not have been photographed in such moments by some invisible camera! Such photographs would have given the German General Staff much food for thought.

Even in the fields, over a mile from the village, it was as light as day. A few persons stole up to a lonely haystack and immediately threw themselves on the ground. Only one of them did not lie down behind the haystack. Raising his head to look at the lights falling from the sky, he laughed:

"Just look at that!"

The lights went out before they reached the ground, and it was pitch-dark again. The men around the haystack drew closer, their rifles clattering as they let them drop.

"How many altogether?"

"Ten sawed-off guns, Comrade Kozhin, four rifles."

"Not enough."

"There wasn't enough time. We'll bring some more tomorrow night."

"And where are the cartridges?"

"Here they are—in our pockets. There's plenty of cartridges."

"Hide them under the stack, then, lads. Grenades, bring grenades! The sawed-off gun is only fit for old men hiding in a ditch behind a bush. They shoot once, wet their trousers, and it's all over. The young fighter needs a rifle, and above all, hand grenades. Understand? And a sword for those who know how to handle it. That's the weapon of weapons."

"We could start this very night, Comrade Kozhin, strike me dead, if we couldn't!"

"We could raise the whole village.... There's such a lot of ill feeling.... Look, they've taken our very hearts' blood.... We'd go against them with pitchforks and scythes, we'd use all our everyday implements.... It'd be easy to do them in while they're sleepy...."

"Who's the commander—you?" cried Kozhin in cutting tones. Then he fell silent. When he spoke again his voice, at first soft and insinuating, grew louder and louder: "Who's the commander here? I should like to know that.... Am I speaking to fools? That's what I want to know.... Shall I go away this instant, and let the Germans and Gaidamaks beat and plunder you?" (Here he let out a string of obscenities.) "Haven't you any discipline? Many a head have I cut off with my own sword for this very thing! When you join the detachment you'll have to swear complete, unconditional obedience to the Ataman. Otherwise you'd better stay behind. There the rule is—sing, amuse yourselves, but when the Ataman cries: 'To horse!', you'll no longer belong to yourselves. Understand?" (He fell silent, and his next words, though still severe, were conciliatory.) "The Germans mustn't be touched yet, not today, nor yet the next day. Great strength is needed for that."

90

"Comrade Kozhin, if we could only get our hands on Grigori Karlovich—he never gives us a moment's peace."

"You can have a go at the bailiff, but not before next week, or I won't be able to manage. The other day a German raped one of the women in Osipovka. Good. She put a handful of needles in his fritters. He took a bite, and rushed away from the table out of doors. Then he fell down, and soon gave up the ghost. The Germans finished off the woman on the spot. The muzhiks went for their axes.... I can't bear to think of what the Germans did then.... Now you can't find the place where Osipovka used to be. That's what comes of acting on your own, without any plan. One, two, three, and it's all over! See?"

Matryona tossed and sighed in her bed. Day was beginning to break, the cocks were crowing. There was dew on the sill of the open window. A mosquito buzzed. The cat on the hearth woke up, leaped lightly down, and went to sniff at some rubbish in the corner of the room.

The brothers were sitting at the table talking under their breath. Semyon's chin was propped on his fists, and Alexei, leaning towards him, was looking into his face.

"I can't, Semyon, old boy. Matryona would never be able to manage by herself. We've been working and saving for years— how can we leave it all? Everything will go. There'd be nothing but the bare ground to come back to."

"You say you couldn't leave it, but what does it matter if you lose it? If we win we'll build a house of brick." (He laughed.) "We need guerilla warfare, and you keep on about your farm."

"Who's going to feed you? Tell me that!"

"It's not us you feed, anyhow. You feed the Germans, the hetman, and all those swine.... You're a slave...."

"Wait a minute! Didn't I fight for the revolution in 1917? Wasn't I elected to the soldiers' committee? Didn't I undermine the imperialist front? Aha! Don't be in such a hurry to cry shame on me, Semyon. And even now—if the Red Army came I'd be the first to take up my rifle. But what's the good of my going into the woods to some ataman?"

"Just now even atamans may be of use."

"Well—perhaps they may."

"My accursed wound has been holding me down." Semyon extended his arms over the table. "That's my misfortune.... Many of our Black Sea lads have joined these detachments. Only give us time and we'll set the Ukraine on fire from end to end."

"Have you seen Kozhin again?"

91

"I have."

"What does he say?"

"We've decided to light up your village soon."

Alexei glanced at his brother, turned pale, bent his head.

"That's as it should be. That accursed mansion is an eyesore.... So long as Grigori Karlovich is alive he won't give us any peace...."

Matryona leaped out of bed and approached them with nothing over her chemise but the rose-patterned shawl. She rapped on the table with her knuckles several times.

"They're taking what's mine, I won't stand it! We women will deal with those devils before you do!"

Semyon looked at her with surprised gaiety.

"Well, how are you women going to fight? Tell us!"

"We'll fight like women. When they sit down to eat—arsenic. We'll get some. I'll lure one into the hayloft or the bathhouse— haven't I got a knitting needle? I'll stick it into him, you know where—he won't make a sound. We'll know what to do—don't *you* shrink! And if needs must we can shoulder a rifle as well as you...."

Semyon stamped his foot, laughing uproariously.

"There's a wench for you, by God!"

"Let go of me!"

Her shawl waving, Matryona slipped her bare feet into her boots at the door, stumped about noisily, and went out, no doubt to see to the cows. For a long time, Semyon and Alexei sat wagging their heads, laughing and repeating: "She's a regular ataman, that wench!"

The wind which heralds the dawn came through the open window rustling the leaves of the aspidistras, and wafting muttered speech and snatches of a foreign song. It was their lodger, the German, coming back drunk from the big house, and sending up clouds of dust with his boots.

Alexei shut the window angrily.

"Why don't you go and lie down, Semyon?"

"Afraid?"

"That drunken devil might make trouble. He remembers that time you went for him."

"I'll go for him again." Semyon rose, as if to go to his room. "Alexei, Alexei, it's all because you're so hard to rouse that the revolution is perishing.... Wasn't Kornilov enough? Aren't the Gaidamaks, the Germans enough? What more do you want?" (He broke off suddenly.) "What's that?"

A low murmur came from the yard, and the sound of heavy boots tramping about uncertainly. A woman's voice cried angrily:

"Let me alone!" Then came the sound of struggling and heavy breathing, and again, still louder, as if from pain, Matryona cried out: "Semyon! Semyon!"

Semyon rushed out of the hut on his bow legs. Alexei only grasped the bench and stayed in his place. He knew what happened when a man was roused. "I left the axe in the entry yesterday—he'll use it. " Semyon gave a savage cry out in the yard. There came a crushing sound, a hissing and gurgling, and something fell heavily.

Matryona came in, white as a sheet, her shawl trailing. She leaned against the stove, her breast heaving tumultuously. Suddenly she made a pass in the air, as if unable to bear Alexei's gaze.

Semyon, calm and pale, appeared in the doorway.

"Give me a hand, brother," he said. "We must take him away and bury him...."

V

The German troops arrived at the Don and the Sea of Azov, and halted there. The Germans had occupied territory of vast natural wealth, bigger than the whole of Germany. Here, on the Don, as in the Ukraine, the German high command began immediately to interfere with political life, supporting the owners of big farms, encouraging the prosperous Cossacks—those very Cossacks who had bragged only four years ago that they would take Berlin by storm. These same stocky, broad-faced Cossacks with the red stripes on their trousers, strong and sturdy as if cast in iron, were now as docile as lambs.

The Germans had scarcely got to Rostov when a Cossack army, ten thousand strong, under the command of Field Ataman Popov, attacked Novocherkassk, the capital of the Don. In a bloody battle on the high plateau above the Don, the Red Cossacks of the Novocherkassk garrison, and the Bolshevik troops hastening to their aid from Rostov, seemed to be gaining the day. But the issue was decided by a fantastic occurrence.

The Volunteer detachment of Colonel Drozdovsky came marching out of Rumania. On the 22nd of April they unexpectedly broke into Rostov, holding the town till nightfall, when they were beaten back. They roamed the steppe, looking for Kornilov's army. On their way (it was the 25th of April), they heard the noise of battle outside Novocherkassk. Without asking who was fighting, and what it was about, they turned towards the town, made

93

their way with an armoured car into the Red reserves, where they caused havoc. The Don Cossacks, seeing help coming to them from on high, made a counterattack, overrunning and driving out the Reds. Novocherkassk was occupied by the Volunteers. The power of the Revolutionary Committee was seized by the "Saviours of the Don" Society. And after this came the Germans.

Under the auspices of the Germans, who had had the sense not to station a garrison in Novocherkassk, the "Saviours of the Don" presented the ataman's mace to General Krasnov, "personal friend of Emperor Wilhelm", as he was pleased to call himself. The bells of the cathedral pealed merrily. The Cossacks crowded on the cobbled square in front of the cathedral shouting "Hurrah!", and the village elders wished good luck to the new order.

The Germans did not penetrate beyond Rostov far into the Don and Kuban districts. Attempts were made by them to "win over" Bataisk, a village on the left bank facing Rostov, inhabited by working folk from the Rostov workshops and plants, and by the overflow of the poor from the city. But despite hurricane fire and bloody assaults, the Germans could not take the village. Bataisk, almost surrounded by flooded fields, showed desperate resistance and remained independent.

The Germans stayed where they were, contenting themselves with consolidating the power of the atamans, and supplying the ataman forces with munitions taken from the Russian depots in the Ukraine. The delicate question of the attitude to be adopted towards the two Volunteer groups—the army of Denikin and Drozdovsky's detachment—was handled with no less discretion. The Volunteers recognized two commandments: to destroy the Bolsheviks and to display their eternal loyalty to the Allies by reviving the war against the Germans. The former struck the Germans as wise and good, the latter they considered as a not particularly dangerous folly. They therefore shut their eyes to the existence of the Volunteers. And Drozdovsky's and Denikin's men, too, pretended not to notice that there were Germans on Russian soil.

Once the Drozdovsky battalion, while marching from Kishinev to Rostov, had to cross the river. On one bank, at Borislavl, were the Germans, and on the other, at Kakhovka, the Bolsheviks.

The Germans had been unable to force a crossing over the river. The Drozdovsky detachment managed this, drove the Red battalions out of Kakhovka, and proceeded on their way without waiting for the Germans to thank them.

Denikin dealt, on a much bigger scale, with situations no less paradoxical. In the end of April the remnants of the Volunteer

Army, battered as they were by the fighting at Ekaterinodar, nevertheless forced their way to the district around the villages of Yegorlitskaya and Mechetinskaya, about thirty miles from Novocherkassk. Here they found unexpected relief in the news that Rostov was in the hands of the Germans, and Novocherkassk had fallen to the ataman-led Don Cossacks.... The Reds left the Volunteers in peace, and opened a front against the new foe—the Germans.

The Volunteers had an opportunity to rest, to look after their wounded, to rally their forces. The first necessity for them was to replenish the equipment of their army.

All the railway stations, from Tikhoretskaya to Bataisk, were crammed with military materiel for the offensive which the Reds were preparing against Rostov. Generals Markov, Bogayevsky and Erdeli attacked the nearest rear of the Reds in three columns; at the Krilovskaya, Sosika, and Novo-Leushkovskaya railway stations they destroyed troop trains, blew up an armoured train, and retreated to the steppe with huge quantities of trophies. The Red Army offensive was prevented.

The dislocated shoulder, and the trifling scratches gained in fighting were healed. Roshchin regained his strength, grew sunburnt, and ate his fill, during the last few days in the quiet village.

The task he had set himself, the thought of which had been afflicting him like a mental sickness ever since he left Moscow—to avenge his disgrace at the hands of the Bolsheviks—was accomplished. He was having his revenge. One moment remained engraved in his memory. He had been running towards the railway embankment.... There had been a victory.... His knees had trembled, and there had been a hammering in his temples. He had taken off his soft cap to wipe his bayonet. He had done it involuntarily, like a veteran soldier who always keeps his arms clean. The former fanatical hatred, the feeling of a leaden ring round his head, of the blood rushing into his eyes, had vanished. He had simply overtaken an enemy, thrust his bayonet into him, withdrawn it and wiped it clean. So he had been right after all! His mind, gradually clearing, tried to understand—had he been right? Had he? And if he had, why did he have to go on asking himself this question?

It was a Sunday. Mass was being celebrated in the village church. Roshchin, who was late, found himself jostled in the porch amidst soldiers with freshly-shaven heads, and went out to wander in the old cemetery behind the church. Walking over the grass, where the dandelions were in blossom, he plucked a grass stem to nibble and seated himself on a mound. Vadim Petrovich was an honest man, and, as Katya had called him, a good man.

The singing of children came through the half-open, cobwebby window, and the deep-voiced responses of the deacon sounded wrathful and ruthless enough to put the childish voices to flight in sheer terror. Vadim Petrovich's thoughts involuntarily went back to the past, as if seeking something bright, something innocent....

He has waked up from sheer delight. Through the high, sparkling windowpanes he sees the blue sky of spring—never since has he seen such a sky. He hears the trees rustling in the garden. A new sateen shirt—blue with white spots—hangs over a chair beside the wooden bedstead. It has a Sabbath smell. He lies there, thinking how he will pass the long day, whom he will meet—and this is so alluring, so delicious, that he would like to go on lying there for ever.... He looks up at the wallpaper, on which a Chinese pagoda with a curly roof, a humpy bridge, two Chinese under umbrellas, and a third, with a hat like a lamp shade, fishing from the bridge, are endlessly repeated. The dear, funny Chinese, how happy they are in their pagoda on the stream.... That was his mother's voice in the passage: "Vadim, are you coming? I'm ready." And this serene beloved voice seems to permeate his whole life with happiness and wellbeing. Now he is standing beside his mother in the blue shirt with the white spots. She is wearing an elegant silk dress. She kisses him, takes a comb from her head and passes it through his hair. "Now you look nice. Let's go...." She descends the broad staircase, opening her parasol. On the swept drive, where the marks of the broom can be seen, the "troika" of chestnut horses can scarcely stand still in their impatience. The outrunner is being troublesome, and even the sedate shaft horse has hollowed out a small pit with his hoof. The wellfed, complacent coachman, his crimson shirt sleeves showing from beneath his velvet waistcoat, says, wagging his bushy beard: "A happy Easter to you!" His mother settles herself comfortably against the sunwarmed upholstery of the carriage. Vadim snuggles up to her, overcome by happy anticipations of the wind which will soon be blowing past his ears, and the trees which will come flying to meet them. The horses gallop on, rounding the estate. And here is the broad village street with the respectfully bowing peasants, and the scraggy hens gathering themselves up from beneath the carriage wheels. The whitewashed fence round the church, the green meadow, the birch trees, just putting out tiny buds of foliage, beneath them the slanting crosses, the mounds.... The porch, and the beggars in it ... the familiar smell of incense....

The church and the birch trees are still there. Vadim Petrovich seems to see their fretted green against the blue.... Beneath one of them—the fifth from the corner of the church—his mother has long lain, her grave surrounded by a railing. Three years before, the old sexton had written to Vadim Petrovich that the railing was broken, and the wooden cross had rotted.... And now he suddenly remembered, with profound remorse, that he had never replied to this letter.

The dear face, the kind hands, the voice waking him in the morning and filling his whole day with joy.... Her love for every hair and scratch on his body.... He knew that whatever his grief, she would be able to drown it in her love. And now all this lay mute beneath the mound under the birch tree—part of the earth itself.

Vadim Petrovich put his elbows on his knees and covered his face with his hands.

Long years passed. It always seemed as if it only needed one more effort, and he would again wake up with a joyful heart on such a blue morning. The two Chinese under their umbrellas would lead him across the humpy bridge into the pagoda with the raised roof. And there a being inexpressibly near and dear awaited him....

"My native land," thought Vadim Petrovich, and once more remembered the "troika" galloping through the village. "Russia ... that which was once Russia. There's nothing left of it, and it will never come again. The little boy in the sateen shirt has become a murderer."

He rose quickly, his hands folded at his back, and began pacing the grass, pulling at the joints of his fingers till they cracked. His thoughts had carried him back to places on which he had believed the door had finally banged. He had been sure he was going to his death.... And he had not died.... How simple it would have been to lie in some gully in the steppe, covered with flies....

"Ah, well," he thought, "death is easy, it's living that's hard.... And it is the duty of each of us to give our dying native land not just a mere bag of flesh and bones, but all the years which lie behind us, our affections, our hopes, the Chinese pagoda, and all our purity...."

He groaned, and then looked round sharply to see if anybody could have heard him. But the children's voices were still singing as before, pigeons were cooing on a rusty cornice.... Hurriedly, almost furtively, he recalled yet another moment of intolerable pity. (He had never reminded Katya of it.) It had been a year ago, in Moscow. Roshchin had discovered at the station that Ekaterina

97

Dmitrevna's husband had just been buried that day, and that she was now alone—quite alone. He had gone to her in the twilight, the servant had told him she was asleep, and he had decided to wait in the drawing room. The servant had come to him there, telling him that Ekaterina Dmitrevna was crying all the time: "Lying on her bed with her face turned to the wall, and weeping like a child—we had to shut the kitchen door, we couldn't bear it." He had made up his mind to wait all night if necessary, sitting on the sofa and listening to the distant ticking of a clock, which was bearing away time, ticking of the ruthless, inexorable seconds gradually planting wrinkles on the beloved face, silvering the hair.... It seemed to Roshchin that Katya, if she was not asleep, must be lying listening to the clock and thinking the same thoughts. Then he had heard her footsteps, feeble and uncertain, as if one of the heels of her slippers had turned under. She was walking about the bedroom, whispering to herself. Then she stood a long time motionless. Roshchin began to be afraid, as if he could penetrate through the wall into Katya's thoughts. The door creaked, and she came into the dining room, and opened a door in the sideboard, making the glasses jingle. Roshchin went taut, ready to rush to her. She opened the door a crack. "Is that you, Liza?" She was wearing a camelhair dressing gown and had a wineglass in one hand, and a wretched little phial in the other. She had intended by this means to get rid of her grief, her loneliness, to escape from inexorable time, from everything.... Her drawn, grey-eyed face was like that of a deserted child. It was she who needed to be taken into the Chinese pagoda.... Vadim Petrovich had said to her then: "My whole life is at your disposal." And she had believed him, she had believed that all her loneliness, all the rest of the years of her life would be dissolved in his pity, his love....

Ah, God, ah, God! He had known all along that Katya had never left him for a moment—not even when hatred had pressed upon his skull like a leaden ring, not even in that terrible month of battle. Like a wraith, spreading its arms wide, praying wordlessly, she had barred his way, and he, hoarse from frantic shouting, had thrust his bayonet into the Red Army coat, right through the inexorable wraith, and then taken off his cap to wipe the blade....

Mass was over. A crowd of sunburnt cadets and officers poured out of the church. Famous generals, with the customary stern expression in their eyes, in pressed and cleaned uniforms, adorned with orders and crosses, stepped out with leisurely steps: the tall, slender Adonis, with his beard parted and his cap set rakishly sideways on his head was Erdeli; the unkempt individual in the soiled fur cap was the caustic Markov; the short one, snubnosed, stocky, pigeyed, was Kutepov; and the one with the waxed and curled moustache was the Cossack Bogayevsky. After them, chatting as they walked, came Denikin and the aloof Romanovsky, with his handsome intelligent face,—the "enigma" they called him in the army. When the Commander in Chief appeared all stood erect, the smokers beneath the birch trees flinging away their cigarettes.

Denikin was no longer the wheezy old fellow in civilian clothes and worn boots, hanging about in the wake of the army without his baggage. He had straightened out, and was even smartly attired; his silvery beard inspired filial respect, and his eyes, no longer sunken, were suffused with a stern moisture, like an eagle's. Of course he was no Kornilov, but he was the most experienced and practical of all the generals. Raising two fingers to the peak of his cap, he passed with dignity through the church gate, and seated himself in the carriage beside Romanovsky.

The loose-limbed Teplov sauntered up to Roshchin. His left arm was in a sling and a creased cavalry greatcoat was thrown over his shoulders. He had shaved in honour of the Sabbath, and was in excellent spirits.

"Heard the latest, Roshchin? The Germans and Finns are on the eve of taking Petersburg. Mannerheim's in command—remember him? A staff general, a fine fellow and a brave soldier.... In Finland he had all the socialists' throats cut. And the Bolsheviks—think of that—are slinking out of Moscow with their valises, through Arkhangelsk.... It's a fact, upon my word it is! Lieutenant Sedelnikov told us, he's just come from Novocherkassk. He says the women there are marvellous.... Ten of them to each man...." He straddled his lean, knock-kneed legs and laughed till the Adam's apple showed over the collar of his tunic.

Roshchin did not encourage the description of the beauties of Novocherkassk, and Teplov turned to the political news, on which the army in the remote steppe lived.

"They say the whole of Moscow is mined—the Kremlin, the churches, the theatres, all the best buildings, whole streets—electric cables have been extended to Sokolniki—there's a mysterious house there, watched day and night by the Cheka men.... We approach, you know, and bang-bang-bang! Moscow goes up into the air." (He bent over Roshchin, and lowered his voice.) "It's a fact, upon my word it is! The Commander in Chief has taken the proper measures: special scouts have been sent to Moscow to look for these wires and to prevent an explosion when we approach

Moscow. But what a hanging we'll have! On the Red Square! Oh, my! Publicly, with drums beating...."

Roshchin rose, frowning.

"You'd better stick to your stories about girls, Teplov."

"So you don't like this sort of talk!"

"I do not."

Roshchin looked steadily into Teplov's witless red-brown eyes. The other's long mouth moved to one side.

"Aha, you don't seem to be able to forget the Red rations."

"What?" Roshchin raised his brows, astonished. "What's that you said?"

"I said what the whole regiment is saying. It's time you gave an account of your work in the Red Army."

"You blackguard!"

Nothing but the fact that Teplov had his arm in a sling, and was still considered an invalid, saved him from a blow. Instead of striking him, Roshchin put his hand behind his back, turned sharply, and, rigid, his shoulders raised, walked off among the graves.

Teplov hitched up his slipping greatcoat and looked after the erect back with a mortified smile. Captain von Mecke came up at that moment, with his inseparable companion—Valerian Onoli, the son of a Simferopol tobacco magnate—a freckled youth with big, light, dreamy eyes, wearing a shabby, stained student's greatcoat with the NCO shoulder straps.

"What's up—have you two quarrelled?" asked von Mecke, in the harsh voice common to people who are slightly deaf.

Teplov, still seething with indignation, tugged at his drooping moustache as he retailed the conversation he had had with Colonel Roshchin.

"It's strange you can still be surprised, Captain," said Onoli. "I saw from the very first that Colonel Roshchin was a spy."

"Chuck it, Valka!" Von Mecke winked, the whole left side of his face twitching—the result of concussion. "General Markov knows him personally, you see. One has to handle him with kid gloves. But I'll bet anything you like Roshchin's a Bolshevik and a louse...."

Things were comparatively quiet in the North Caucasus down till the end of May. Both sides were preparing for a decisive struggle. The Volunteers hoped to seize the main railway junctions, isolate the Caucasus, and, with the aid of the White Cossacks, clear the territory of Reds. The Central Executive Committee of the Kuban and Black Sea Republic were preparing for a struggle on three fronts: with the Germans, the White Cossacks, and the newly-resuscitated "Denikin bands".

The Red Caucasian Army, consisting in the overwhelming majority of war veterans from the former tsarist Transcaucasian Army, of settlers and landless Cossack youth, numbered as many as a hundred thousand. Its Commander in Chief, Avtonomov, was suspected by the members of the Kuban-Black Sea Central Executive Committee of aspiring towards dictatorship, and was for ever quarrelling with the government. At a huge meeting in Tikhoretskaya, he had called the Central Executive Committee German spies and *agents provocateurs*. In reply, the Central Executive Committee "branded" Avtonomov and his closest adherent Sorokin, bandits and enemies of the people, cursing them, and holding them up to eternal obloquy.

All these squabbles were paralyzing the army. The Red Army, which should have conducted a converging attack by three units against the Volunteer Army, situated in their very midst, was in a ferment. Continual meetings were held, commanders were dismissed, and the army seemed to be fit at the best for nothing but heroic disaster.

At last the decrees from Moscow overcame the obstinacy of the local authorities. Avtonomov was appointed inspector at the front, and the command of the Northern group of the army was handed over to Colonel Kalnin, a morose Latvian. Sorokin remained commander of the Western group.

It was then that Colonel Drozdovsky, with a detachment of three thousand picked officers, chosen for their ferocity, each of them worth ten rank-and-file soldiers in battle, joined up with the Volunteer Army. The mounted Cossacks from the villages began to come in gradually; officers, singly and in groups, inspirited by rumours of the fantastic "Frost Campaign", began to arrive from Petrograd, from Moscow, from all over Russia, Ataman Krasnov supplied them, somewhat charily, with arms and money. From day to day the Volunteer Army gathered strength; thanks to the skilful propaganda of the generals and their agitators, the unskilful handling of the situation by the local Soviet power, and the stories brought from the north by eye witnesses, its morale was at a high level.

By the end of May the local Red forces gave up the attempt to crush the Volunteer Army. Assuming the offensive, the Volunteers struck a terrible blow to Kalnin's Northern group at Torgovaya.

"Why aren't you singing any more, lads?"

"We've sung ourselves hoarse."

"Let me get myself a coal to light my pipe," said Ivan Ilyich Telegin seating himself at the campfire, on which the planks from a railway snow fence were merrily burning; having lit his pipe he stayed to listen.

It was late in the night. Almost all the fires along the railway lines had been put out. The night air was chill and the sky was thickly studded with stars. Puce-coloured, battered, broken-down freight vans stood out against the top of the embankment in the light cast by the flames. They had come from the shores of the Pacific, from the Arctic swamps, from the sands of Turkestan, from the Volga, from the Ukraine. Each van was marked "to be returned immediately". But all terms had long expired. These long-suffering cars, built for a life of peaceful toil, and now—their axle bars unoiled, their sides bashed in—resting beneath the stars, were destined for fantastic adventures. Whole trains of them, with everything in them, would be derailed; some, crammed with Red Army prisoners, their windows and doors boarded up, would travel thousands of miles, the words: "non-perishable freight, by slow train" chalked on them. Others would become graveyards for the victims of typhus, refrigerators for the transporting of frozen corpses. Many would go up in pillars of fire and smoke.... In the forests of Siberia, their walls and doors would be used for fences and sheds.... Many months would pass before, charred and shattered, the few survivors among them would come to the place to which they were "to be returned immediately", there to await repairs on rusty sidings.

"What do they say in Moscow, Comrade Telegin—how soon will the Civil War be over?"

"As soon as we win it."

"You see ... they believe in us...."

A handful of bearded men, with weather-beaten, sallow countenances, lay in languid poses around the campfire. No one wanted to sleep, but all were disinclined for serious conversation. One of them asked Telegin for some homegrown tobacco.

"Comrade Telegin—who are these Czechs? Where have they come from? I don't remember hearing about them before...."

Ivan Ilyich explained that the Czechs were Austrian prisoners of war, and that the tsarist government had started forming an army corps from them, to send to France, but had failed to accomplish this.

"And now the Soviet government cannot let them leave the country, since they want to fight in the imperialist war.... We demand their disarming, and they are revolting against this...."

"Does it mean, Comrade Telegin, we'll have to fight them, too?"

"Nobody can say anything at present.... We have no positive information ... I, personally, don't think we will.... There are only forty thousand of them...."

"We'll be able to polish them off."

Again there was silence by the campfire. The one who had asked for tobacco, glancing at Telegin, began talking again, obviously simply to make conversation.

"Under the tsar, we were sent to Sarakamysh. Nobody told us why we were fighting the Turks, what we were dying for. And the mountains there are terrible. You look round and tell yourself it was an evil hour when you were born.... And now everything's quite different: this war is our own war, war to the death.... And everything is clear—the how and the why...."

"Take me, for example—they call me Chertogonov," said another soldier, thickly. Supporting himself on one elbow he moved so near the flames that it seemed a miracle his beard didn't catch fire. He was a ferocious-looking individual, with black hair falling over his forehead, and a pair of round eyes burning out of his tanned face. "I've been in the Far East twice, I've been in prison for vagrancy again and again.... All right.... They put me in barracks just the same, gave me a soldier's certificate, and sent me to the war.... Six wounds.... Look here." He pushed his finger into the inside of his cheek, and pulled his mouth sideways, displaying broken stumps. "I managed to get to Moscow, to a hospital, and there were the Bolsheviks.... And all my sufferings were at an end. 'What's your social position?' they asked me. 'No need to look far back,' I told them. 'I am a hereditary farmhand, with no ancestors.' They laughed. They gave me a rifle and a mandate—me! We were patrolling the town in those days, looking for bourgeois.... You get into some grand house, the owners, of course, are frightened.... You look into their hiding places; flour, sugar.... The swine are all a-twitter, scared, but they don't say a word to us.... Sometimes you get quite mad—aren't you a human being, oilymug? Talk, swear, implore, can't you? You swear at him, and still not a word.... What's the matter I ask myself.... It's maddening—to have held one's tongue all one's life, working for them smug devils, spilling one's blood for them.... And they don't even consider one a human being.... So that's what they're like, the bourgeois! Since then I have burned with class hatred. Very well.... Once we were sent to requisition the merchant Ryabinkin's mansion. There were four of us, and we had a machine gun with us, to put the fear of God into him. We knocked at the front door. After some time a neat little maid opened the door to us—the poor thing turned pale and started tiptoeing about, crying: 'Oh, oh!...' We pushed her out of the way, and stepped into the hall—an enormous room with pillars, a table in the middle, with Ryabinkin and his guests around it, eating pancakes. It was Shrovetide, and everyone was drunk of course.... Just when the proletariat was dying of hunger!... I banged on the floor with my rifle with all my might, and shouted at them. They just sat there, smiling. Then Ryabinkin ran up to us, all red and jolly, his eyes bulging, crying: 'Dear Comrades! I've known all along that you meant to requisition my house and everything in it! Just let us finish up the pancakes, and, by the way, why not sit down with us? There's no disgrace in it—it's all public property.' He pointed to the table.... We stood, shifting our feet for a while, and then we sat down, still holding on to our rifles, and frowning. And Ryabinkin started pouring out vodka for us, and piling our plates with pancakes and all sorts of snacks.... Talking and laughing all the time... The things he told us, and so sarcastic—mimicking people to their faces.... All the guests were roaring with laughter, and we couldn't help laughing, either. All sorts of stories about the gentry were told, there was a lot of arguing, and whenever the host thought any of us looked like getting nasty, he poured out some more vodka: we drank out of tumblers—nothing smaller was used. Then they began opening bottles of champagne, and we stacked our rifles in a corner. 'Is that you, Chertogonov, stumbling about the hall, running into pillars?' I asked myself. We began singing in chorus. And in the evening we put the machine gun on the porch, so that nobody should butt in. We went on drinking for two days without stopping. I made up for my whole life as an underdog. But Ryabinkin baulked us, the wily merchant! While we were enjoying ourselves he managed to move all his diamonds, and gold and money and other valuables to a safe place—the maid helped him. All we requisitioned was the walls and the furniture... And when we were leaving, Ryabinkin said to us in farewell (of course everyone was still tipsy): 'Dear Comrades, take all, all, I grudge nothing. I came from the people, and I now return to the people....' And that very day he escaped abroad. And I was hauled up before the Cheka. 'I'm to blame—shoot me!' I told them. If they didn't shoot me it was only because they considered I wasn't class-conscious yet. And to this day I'm glad I had my fling for once. At least I have one happy memory.... "

"There are many blackguards among the bourgeoisie, but we have plenty, too."

The speaker was half-hidden by smoke, and everyone looked in his direction. The man who had asked Telegin for tobacco said:

"There's no stopping the people, since they smelled blood in 1914."

"That's not what I mean," said the voice from out of the smoke.

"Foes are foes, and blood must be spilled. I was talking about real bad lots."

"And who may you be?"

"Me? Oh—I'm one of the bad lots," replied the voice quietly.

At this all fell silent, staring at the glowing embers. A shiver ran down Telegin's spine. It was a chilly night. Some of the men round the campfire moved restlessly and lay down resting their cheeks on their caps.

Telegin got up and stretched, straightening the folds of his uniform. Now that the smoke had subsided, he could see the "bad lot" sitting cross-legged on the other side of the fire. He was chewing a stalk of wormwood. The embers lit up a long, thin countenance of an almost feminine softness, with a fair sparse down on the cheeks. A shabby cap was pushed to the back of the head and a military greatcoat was flung over the narrow shoulders; under it, he was naked to the waist. His shirt, which he had probably been searching for lice, lay beside him. Feeling that someone's eyes were on him he raised his head slowly, and gave a slow, childish smile.

Telegin recognized him. He was a man from his own company—Mishka Solomin, a peasant from the country round Elets, who had joined the Red Guard as a volunteer, and come to the Caucasus with the army of Sievers.

He met Telegin's eyes for the space of a second, and immediately lowered his own, as if embarrassed, and it was only then that Ivan Ilyich remembered that Mishka Solomin was famous in the company as a maker of verse and a hard drinker, though he was seldom seen actually drunk. He languidly hitched the coat off his shoulders, and began putting on his shirt. Ivan Ilyich climbed up the embankment to the passenger carriage, where an oil lamp burned vigilantly in the window of the compartment occupied by the commander of the regiment, Sergei Sergeyevich Sapozhkov. From the top of the embankment the stars could be more clearly descried and the dying campfires were reddish spots on the ground below.

"Come in, Telegin, there's plenty of hot water," said Sapozhkov, leaning out of the window, a pipe with a curving stem between his teeth.

The oil lamp, fixed to the wall, shed a dim light over the shabby second-class compartment, with rifles hanging from hooks, and books and military maps scattered about. Sergei Sergeyevich Sapozhkov, in a soiled calico shirt and braces, turned towards Telegin as the latter entered.

"Want a drink?"

Ivan Ilyich seated himself on the edge of the bunk. Through the open window came the cold night air, bringing with it the clucking of a quail. A soldier, stumbling half asleep out of the neighbouring van, to relieve nature, stumped past the window. A balalaika trilled softly. A cock crowed from somewhere quite near—it was past midnight.

"What was that—a cock?" asked Sapozhkov, and he stopped busying himself with the kettle. His eyes were inflamed and crimson blotches stood out on his gaunt cheeks. Fumbling behind him on the seat he found his pince-nez, and put it on to look at Telegin.

"How comes it that there is a live cock in the regiment?"

"Refugees again—I reported to the Commissar. Twenty carts loaded with women and children. It's a hell of a business!" said Telegin, stirring the tea in his mug.

"Where are they from?"

"Privolnaya. There was a whole train of them, but they were attacked by Cossacks on the way. Outsiders, all of them, the poorest of the poor. Two Cossack officers formed a detachment from men in the village, carried out a raid in the night, broke up the Soviet, hung a certain number of people.... "

"In a word, the usual story," said Sapozhkov, dropping out each syllable separately. He seemed to be extremely drunk, and had called Telegin just to have someone to unburden himself to.... Ivan Ilyich felt as if his whole being were humming with exhaustion, but it was so nice to rest on a cushioned seat and sip tea, that he did not go, though there was nothing much to be expected from a conversation with Sergei Sergeyevich.

"Where's your wife, Telegin?"

"In Petersburg."

"Queer chap. In peacetime you'd have made a perfectly prosperous citizen, with a virtuous wife, two virtuous children, and a gramophone.... What the devil made you join the Red Army? You'll be killed, you know...."

"I've told you already...."

"You're not manoeuvring to get into the Party, are you?"

"If the cause requires it, I'll join the Party."

Sapozhkov narrowed his eyes behind his blurred glasses.

"You could boil me three times over, but you'd never make a Communist of me," he said.

"If anyone's queer, it's you, Sergei Sergeyevich."

"Not at all. It's just that my brain isn't made for dialectics. I'm a savage, really, always ready to bolt back to the forest. H'm! So you consider me a queer chap!" He chuckled with evident satisfaction. "I've been fighting for the Soviets since October. H'm. Have you read Kropotkin?"

"No, I haven't."

"That's obvious.... It's all such a bore, old man.... The bourgeois world is infernally base and tedious. And if we win, the communist world will be tedious and mediocre, too—virtuous and tedious ... but Kropotkin was a dear old man ... poetry, dreams, classless society.... A most highly-cultured old gent. 'Give people anarchist liberty, loosen the bonds of the world's greatest evil, great cities, and classless humanity will build a pastoral paradise, since the basic motive power of mankind is love for one's neighbour...' ha-ha!"

Sapozhkov laughed shrilly, as if mocking an invisible opponent, the pince-nez dancing on the bony bridge of his nose. Still laughing, he stooped and brought from under the seat a tin canister of spirits. Pouring some into a cup, he took a drink and nibbled at a bit of sugar with a crunching sound.

"The tragedy of us Russian intellectuals, old boy, is that we grew up in the peaceful lap of serfdom, and the revolution, as well as almost frightening us to death, has given us a kind of cerebral nausea.... Such delicate folks ought not to be frightened so badly, ought they? We settled down in our snug arbours, to listen to the birds singing, and we said to ourselves: 'Now wouldn't it be nice if a way could be found to make everybody happy?' And that's the kind of people we are.... The Western intellectuals are brainy folk, the cream of the bourgeoisie, they carry out rigidly-defined tasks—to advance science and industry, to spread the consoling illusions of idealism through the world.... The intellectuals there know what they live for. But here—oh, my! Whom do we serve? What are our tasks? On the one hand we are part and parcel of the Slavophiles*—their spiritual heirs. D'you know what Slavophilism is? It's simply the idealism of Russian landed proprietors. On the other hand, all our money comes from our native bourgeoisie—we live on them. And with it all, we serve only the people ... the people, forsooth! It's a regular tragicomedy! We've shed so many tears over the sufferings of the people that we have none left. And when we were deprived of our tears, we had nothing left to live for. We kept telling ourselves our muzhiks would reach

---

*Slavophiles—representatives of a school of thought in Russia about the middle of the 19th century, advocating the unification of the Slavs under the leadership of Russia. In contrast to the Occidentophiles, they asserted that the Russian people had their own lines of development, quite different from those of the peoples of Western Europe.

Constantinople, climb on to the dome of St. Sophia, and plant the Orthodox cross on its minaret. We dreamed of presenting our muzhiks with the terrestrial globe. And we, the enthusiasts, the dreamers, the weepers, were met with pitchforks.... Whoever heard of such an outrage? And the mortal terror we experienced! And then, my friend, sabotage begins.... The intellectuals tried to back out, to free their necks from the yoke. 'I won't! Just you try and get on without me!...' And that, just when Russia is on the brink of an infernal abyss.... It was a great, an irreparable mistake. The gentry are too delicately bred, they can't understand revolution outside of books.... The revolution seemed so fascinating in books.... But now we see the soldiers deserting, killing their officers, tearing their Commander in Chief to pieces, burning estates, chasing after merchants' wives in railway carriages and making them cough up their diamond earrings.... No thank you! We're not going to play with such people, there was never anything about such people in the books.... And now what were we to do? Sit and weep floods of tears in our homes? Unfortunately we've lost the habit of weeping.... Our dreams were shattered, we had nothing to live for. We could only hide our heads under our pillows in fear and disgust; some escaped abroad, the more energetic took up arms.... A scandal in a respectable family....

"And the people are 70 per cent illiterate, they don't know how to express their hatred, they can only welter in blood and horrors. 'We've been sold!' they say. 'Our lives have been gambled away! Smash the mirrors, break up everything!' Only one little group of intellectuals kept their heads—the Communists. What do people do when a ship is sinking? They throw everything superfluous overboard. The first thing the Communists did was to throw overboard the old Russian idealism by the bushel. All this was the work of 'the old man', a real Russian, he is. And the people, with animal instinct felt: these are our chaps, not the gentry—they won't weep on our necks, they'll give the exploiters short shrift.... That's why I'm on their side, old boy, although I was brought up in the Kropotkin hothouse, under glass, amidst dreams.... And there are a lot like me. Don't sneer, Telegin, you're just an embryo, a light-hearted primitive.... Some of us, you know, need deliberately to turn ourselves inside out, and, having thus made ourselves sensitive to every touch, concentrate on a simple manifestation of will power—hatred.... There's no fighting without that.... We are doing all that is humanly possible, setting a goal for the people, and leading them towards it. But we are a mere handful. And the enemy is everywhere. Have you heard about the Czechs? The Commissar will be here soon, he'll tell you all about

108

them.... D'you know what I'm afraid of? I'm afraid the whole thing will turn out to be suicidal for us. We may last out another month or two, even six months, but not more. We're doomed, brother. It'll all end in going back to the generals. And it's all been the fault of the Slavophiles, mark my words! When the emancipation of the peasants began, we should have yelled: 'Help! We are perishing! We need intensive cultivation, frantic industrial development, universal education.... Let a new Pugachev,* or a Stenka Razin** come—so long as serfdom is really smashed to smithereens this time.' That's the slogan which should have been thrown to the masses, that's the way the intellectuals should have been trained to think.... But we luxuriated in floods of joyful tears. 'My God, how boundless, how unique is Russia! And now the muzhik is free as air, and the estates with the Turgenev maidens are intact, and the soul of our people is mysterious—not like that of the money-grubbing West....' And here am I trampling on dreams of any sort...."

Sapozhkov could not go on talking. His face was burning. But it was obvious he had not been able to get out what he really wanted to say. Telegin, stunned by the torrent of words, sat open-mouthed, his mug of tea cooling on his knee. Heavy steps were heard in the corridor, suggesting the approach of some ponderous body. The door of the compartment opened and a broad-shouldered man of middle height, dark hair plastered on his great forehead, stood in the opening. He seated himself silently under the lamp, and placed his enormous hands on his knees. The sparse wrinkles on his weatherbeaten face were like scars, his eyes could hardly be seen in the shadow of the deep sockets and overhanging brows. This was Comrade Gimza, head of the regiment's Special Department.

"Got hold of spirits again?" he said softly and gravely. "Take care, Comrade...."

"Spirits? To hell with you! Can't you see we're drinking tea?" said Sapozhkov.

Gimza boomed out, not moving in his seat:

"Lying only makes it worse. Your compartment fairly reeks of spirits. You can smell it a mile off. The soldiers are getting restless in the freight trucks, they can smell it, too.... As if we haven't enough trouble as it is! And I see you have raked up your rubbishy philosophy again, from which I draw the conclusion that you are drunk."

*Emelyan Ivanovich Pugachev (circa 1730-1775)—a Don Cossack who headed the great peasant war of 1772-75 against the yoke of feudalism and serfdom in Russia.

**Stepan Timofeyevich Razin (?-1671)—a Cossack from the Don, who headed the peasant war of 1667-71 against the yoke of feudalism and serfdom in Russia.

"Very well, I'm drunk ... shoot me then!"

"I could easily have you shot, you know that very well, and if I don't, it's for your fighting qualities...."

"Give us some tobacco," said Sapozhkov.

Gimza drew a cotton pouch from his pocket with stately movements. Then turning to Telegin, he went on speaking in slow tones, as if grinding corn:

"Every day the same thing: last week we shot three blackguards—I interrogated them myself ... muck, they admitted everything. And he has to go and get himself some more booze.... We shot an out-and-out blackguard today, one of Denikin's spies—he caught him hiding among the rushes himself ... so of course he has to get drunk and start philosophizing. He comes out with such a farrago—I was standing outside the window just now, and I felt as if I'd been eating offal. Another man would long ago have sent him to the Special Department for this 'philosophy', he's become utterly demoralized. After this sort of thing he's ill for two days and can't command the regiment...."

"Didn't you shoot my university comrade?"

Sapozhkov spoke with narrowed eyes, his nostrils quivering.

Gimza made no reply, as if he had not heard him. Telegin bent his head. Thrusting his perspiring nose towards Gimza's face, Sapozhkov continued:

"All right, he was a Denikin spy. But he and I used to go to the 'Philosophical Evenings' together. Why he joined the White Guards, the devil alone knows! Perhaps out of sheer desperation ... I took him to you myself.... Isn't it enough for you that I did my duty? Should I have danced a jig when he was led to the edge of the gully? I followed, I saw...."

He looked steadily into the dark hollows of Gimza's eyes. "Am I entitled to human feelings, or must I consume everything within me?"

Gimza replied in his deliberate tones:

"You are not.... I don't know about other people, but you must consume everything within you. It's precisely from feelings like yours that counterrevolution springs."

There was a long silence. The air was heavy. All sounds outside the dark window had died down. Gimza poured himself out some tea, broke off a great hunk of greyish bread and began eating it slowly, as people do when they are really hungry. Then he began to talk about the Czechs, in muffled tones. The news was disquieting. In all the trains, from Penza to Vladivostok, the Czechs were rising. Before the Soviet power had time to look round, the railways and towns were threatened. The troop trains in western

Russia had already cleared out Penza, proceeded to Syzran, seized it, and continued on their way to Samara. They were splendidly disciplined, well armed, brave and able fighters. As yet it would have been hard to say whether it was a mere case of mutiny, or whether some sort of outside influence was being exercised. Apparently it was something of both. However that might be, a new front had sprung up, like a train of gunpowder laid from the Pacific to the Volga, and was threatening appalling disasters."

Somebody approached the window from outside. Gimza stopped talking, frowned, turned.

A voice called him:

"Comrade Gimza, come here...."

"What's the matter?"

"It's confidential."

Drawing his brows down above his eye sockets, Gimza sat for a moment with his hands digging into the seat, rose with an effort, and went out, his shoulders brushing the doorway on either side. He sat down on the top step of the carriage, and leaned forward. A tall figure in a cavalry greatcoat emerged with jingling spurs from the darkness. Whoever it was whispered something hurriedly right into Gimza's ear.

When Gimza went out, Sapozhkov began taking hasty puffs at his pipe, and spat viciously several times through the window. Removing his pince-nez, he tossed it aside and gave a sudden laugh.

"The great thing is to give direct answers to all questions. Is there or is there not a God? There is not. Is it permissible to kill? It is. What is our first aim? World revolution. There you are, brother, without any complicated emotions...."

He broke off, stretching and listening. The whole carriage shook—that was Gimza banging on the wall with his fist. His voice, hoarsely fierce, rang out:

"If you're lying to me, you son-of-a-bitch...."

Sergei Sergeyevich caught at Telegin's sleeve.

"Hear him? D'you know what's the matter? Unpleasant rumours are going the rounds about our Commander in Chief, Sorokin.... That was a comrade from the Special Department who's just returned from headquarters. Now you know why Gimza is like a bear with a sore head...."

The stars were already growing pale in the dawn. The cock crowed again among the carts. Dew fell on the sleeping camp. Telegin went to his compartment, drew off his boots, and let himself down with a sigh on to his bunk, making the springs squeal.

It sometimes seemed to Telegin as if the brief happiness of his life had been a mere dream in the green steppe, going on to the accompaniment of revolving wheels.... His life had once been peaceful and successful: student days, Petersburg, vast and fathomless, his work, the carefree company of the eccentrics he had lodged in his flat on Vasilyevski Island. The future had then seemed as clear as daylight. He had never so much as thought about it. The years seemed to have flitted at an easy, leisurely pace over his head. Ivan Ilyich had known that, like thousands of his kind, he would conscientiously fulfil the task before him, and that on looking back—when his hair had gone grey, on what he had done, he would see that he had traversed a long road without deviating into any dangerous paths. And then Dasha had broken imperiously into the simple prose of his life, a fearful joy shining from her grey eyes. Even then, in his secret soul, a brief doubt had raised its head for a moment: happiness was not for him! But he had chased the doubt away, intending, as soon as the war should have passed, to make a nest of happiness for Dasha. Even when the edifice of empire had crumbled, and all was confusion, even when the people, a hundred and fifty million strong, roared out their wrath and pain, Ivan Ilyich went on believing that the storm would pass, and the meadow in front of Dasha's door would gleam peacefully after the rain.

And here he was—once more occupying a bunk in a troop train—yesterday's battle behind him, tomorrow's battle before him. It was now clear that there would be no return to the past. He was ashamed to remember how, a year ago, he had fussed over the furnishing of a flat on Kamenno-Ostrovsky Street, getting a mahogany bedstead for Dasha to bear her dead baby on.

Dasha had been the first to be caught in the whirlpool. The "hoppers" who had leaped upon her near the Summer Park, the dead baby with its hair standing on end, hunger, darkness, decrees every word of which breathed wrath and hate—that was what the revolution had meant for her. At night it had whistled over the roofs, blowing against the frozen windowpanes crying "Not-one-of-us!" to Dasha in the voices of the blizzard. Ivan Ilyich had come home in high spirits, one grey Petersburg spring day, with a damp wind blowing, the eaves dripping, and icicles crashing down from the dilapidated pipes. His coat was unbuttoned and he had looked at Dasha with eyes even brighter than usual. Dasha seemed to shrink under his gaze and said, muffled up to her chin in her shawl:

"I wish I could dash out my brains against the wall, Ivan, so that I could forget everything for ever.... Then I might be companion to you again. I simply can't go on lying down in that terrible bed every night, and facing the accursed day every morning.... I simply can't.... Don't think it's good things and all that, I'm pining for.... I only want to be able to breathe freely.... I don't want crumbs.... I've stopped loving you. I'm very sorry!"

When she had finished speaking, she turned away.

Dasha had always been austere about her emotions. Now she had become cruel.

"Perhaps we'd better part for a time, Dasha," he had said.

And then, for the first time in the whole winter, he had seen the joyous upward flight of her brows, the strange gleam of hope in her eyes, as a piteous tremor passed across her poor, thin face....

"I think it would be better for us to part, Ivan...."

Then it was that he had begun to make determined applications through Rublev to be accepted in the Red Army, and in the end of March he left with a troop train for the south. Dasha had seen him off at the October Station, crying bitterly as the window of his compartment floated past her, and covering her face with her shawl.

Since then Ivan Ilyich had covered hundreds and hundreds of miles, but neither battle, fatigue, nor deprivation, could drive away the memory of that beloved, tear-stained face among the women crowding in front of the grimy wall of the station. Dasha had bidden him farewell as if it were for ever. He racked his brains to discover in what way he had failed her. The reason for her ceasing to love him, must, of course, ultimately be found in himself—after all, she was not the only woman whose baby had died. And it could not have been the revolution which had alienated her.... He could think of more than one couple who had actually drawn closer in these difficult, perturbed times. How, then, had he been at fault?

Sometimes a wave of indignation would rise up in him: all right, my dear, try and find another man to dance round you as I did! The world is going to pieces, and all she thinks about is her own feelings. It's sheer self-indulgence—the whims of a woman used to white rolls, and unable to stomach bread made of rye and chaff.

But if all this was true—and it was, of course—the inference to be drawn was that Ivan Ilyich himself was a paragon of virtue, and not to love him was a crime. And this brought Ivan Ilyich up sharp, every time.... "After all, what is there so special about me? Physically healthy—granted. Remarkable for brains and charm? Why no, no more than the next man. A hero—a great man? An attrac-

113

tive male? No, no.... An ordinary, decent citizen, like a million others...." He had drawn a lucky ticket in the lottery of life; a charming girl, endowed with infinitely more fire and brains than himself, head and shoulders above him, had unaccountably fallen in love with him, and as unaccountably fallen out of love.

He asked himself whether the reason did not lie in the fact that he was not big enough for the times, that he even fought in a commonplace manner, as if it were bookkeeping, or copying names into files that he was engaged upon. He had known men who, whether they were good or bad, were forced to be reckoned with, striding like giants over a bloody battlefield.... "Ivan Ilyich, why can't you hate the foe with all your might, why can't you at least be really terrified of death?"

All this grieved Ivan Ilyich to the soul. He was utterly unconscious of the fact that he had become one of the most reliable, intelligent, and courageous members of the regiment. Dangerous operations were entrusted to him, and he carried them out brilliantly.

The conversation with Sergei Sergeyevich had plunged him into deep meditation. So even the light-hearted commander was a prey to unspeakable pangs.... And what about Misha Solomin ... and Chertogonov ... and a host of others he had brushed against carelessly? They all measured up to the time, huge, unkempt, disfigured by spiritual tortures. They had no words in which to express their pain, nothing but the rifle in their hands ... some found an outlet in wild debauch, followed by wilder remorse.... There's Russia for you—there's the Revolution....

"Comrade Commander—wake up!"

Telegin sat up on the bunk. The golden globe of the sun, suspended over the edge of the steppe, which was now the colour of a duckling's downy feathers—was peeping into the carriage window. The soldier, his broad, red-bearded face ruddy as the morning sun, gave Ivan Ilyich another shake.

"The Regimental Commander wants to see you at once."

In Sapozhkov's compartment the stinking oil lamp was still alight. In it were: Gimza, Commissar Sokolovsky, a black-haired, consumptive-looking individual, his dark eyes burning from insomnia; two battalion commanders; a few company commanders, and a representative of the Soldiers' Committee, whose face wore a defiant, almost injured expression. All were smoking. Sergei Sergeyevich, now in a tunic, with a holster on his belt, held a strip of telegraph tape in his shaking hand:

"...the unexpected capture of the station by the enemy has cut off our troops, and placed them under a double menace.... "

He was reading these words in a hoarse voice as Ivan Ilyich stopped in the doorway of the compartment.

"...in the name of the Revolution, in the name of the unfortunate population, threatened by inevitable death, execution and tortures if abandoned to the tender mercies of the White bands, lose not a moment, send reinforcements!"

"What can we do without orders from the Commander in Chief?" cried Sokolovsky. "I'll try once more to get him on the wire."

"Go on, then, try," said Gimza with ominous emphasis. (Everyone looked at him.) "I'll tell you what to do—take four men, take Telegin here, and rush to headquarters on a trolley. And don't come back without an order. Sapozhkov, write out a paper to Commander in Chief Sorokin."

A horseman stood on the crest of a grassy mound, gazing steadily from under his hand at a cloud of dust advancing along the railway track.

When the cloud was hidden by the bank of a cutting, the horseman touched his horse first with his shins and then with his spurs, the lean, chestnut stallion jerked its savage-looking head, and turned, descending the mound, at the foot of which, on either side, a platoon of officers of the Volunteer Army lay about, sheltering behind freshly heaped piles of earth.

"A trolley," said von Mecke, leaping from the saddle. And tapping the knees of his stallion with his riding crop he gave it the order to lie down. The horse pawed the ground restively, its ears twitching, but submitted and let itself down with a deep sigh, its muzzle touching the ground. Its gaunt side heaved and subsided.

Von Mecke was now squatting on the top of the mound beside Roshchin. Just then the trolley came into sight again from the cutting and now six men in greatcoats could be made out on it.

"Reds!" said von Mecke. "I thought so!" He turned his head to the left. "Squad!" Turning to the right he cried: "Make ready! Rapid fire at a moving object. Fire!"

The air around the mound was rent with a crackling sound, as of starched calico being torn. Through the cloud of smoke a man could be seen to fall off the trolley, turn over and over and roll down the slope at the side of the tracks, tearing at the grass with his hands.

Five men fired from the fast-vanishing trolley—three from rifles, two from revolvers. Another minute and it would be hidden by the next cutting, beyond the signal box. Von Mecke, his riding crop swishing through the air, was in a frenzy:

"They're getting away! You ought to be shooting crows! Shame! Shame!"

Roshchin was considered a crack shot. Quietly training his rifle a foot in front of the trolley, he took aim at a tall, broad-shouldered, clean-shaven man—evidently the Commander. "He's just like Telegin!" he thought. "How awful if it were he!"

Roshchin fired. The man's cap fell off, and at that very moment the trolley plunged into the second cutting. Von Mecke brandished his whip.

"Bastards! A set of bastards! You're not marksmen, gentlemen, you're a set of bastards!"

His eyes—the eyes of a sleepless murderer—bulging, he swore continuously till the officers rose to their feet, grumbling as they brushed the earth from their trousers.

"Be careful what you say, Captain, there are higher ranks than you here."

Putting in a fresh round of cartridges, Roshchin was conscious that his hands were still trembling. Why was this? Simply because he had thought the man was like Ivan Telegin? Nonsense! Telegin was in Petrograd, wasn't he?

Commissar Sokolovsky and Telegin, his head bandaged, climbed the steps to the porch of the two-storeyed brick building of the village council which stood, as was customary, opposite the church on an unpaved square, where formerly fairs had been held. Now the stalls were boarded up, the windows broken, the palings stolen. The church had been converted into a military hospital, and there were scraps of soldiers' clothing fluttering on a string in the churchyard.

The entrance hall of the village council, which was the headquarters of Commander in Chief Sorokin, was littered with cigarette ends and scraps of paper. A Red Army man, his rifle between his knees, was seated on a bentwood chair at the foot of the staircase, humming a steppe melody, his eyes closed. He had high cheekbones, and, sure sign that he was a military "tough", a lock of hair showed from under the red-banded cap pushed on to the back of his head.

"We want to see Comrade Sorokin," said Sokolovsky in rapid tones. "Where is he?"

The soldier opened his eyes, dull from drowsy boredom. He had an absurd, squashy nose. He inspected Sokolovsky from head to toe—his face, his clothes, his boots—and then did the same by Telegin. The Commissar pushed impatiently up to him.

"Answer me, please, Comrade. We want to see the Commander in Chief on the most urgent business."

"It is not allowed to speak to the sentry on duty," said the youth with the forelock.

"Oh, my God! They always have swine like that—formalists at headquarters!" cried Sokolovsky. "I insist on you giving me an answer, Comrade: is Comrade Sorokin in?"

"Can't say."

"Where's the Chief of Staff, then? Is he in the office?"

"All right—he's in the office."

Sokolovsky, pulling Ivan Ilyich by the sleeve, was for hurling himself upon the staircase. But the sentry, without getting off his chair, made a kind of lurching movement, and extricated his rifle from between his knees.

"Where are you going?"

"Where? To the Chief of Staff!"

"Have you got a pass?"

The Commissar fairly foamed at the mouth as he explained to the sentry the business for which he had dashed up on a trolley. The sentry, his gaze travelling from the machine gun at the door to the decrees, orders and notices with which the walls of the hall were plastered, heard him out in silence. Then he shook his head.

"An educated man like you," he said disgustedly. "You ought to know better! If you have a pass, you can go, if you haven't, I shall shoot you down ruthlessly."

There was nothing for it but to submit, although passes were issued somewhere on the other side of the square, and they were sure to be told, when they did get there, that the commandant had gone for the day. Sokolovsky felt beaten. But just then a short figure in a shirt slit right down to the navel, rushed from the square into the doorway, with a thunderous trampling of boots.

"Mitka—they're issuing soap...."

The sentry seemed to be swept from his chair as by a gust of wind. He leaped out into the porch. Sokolovsky and Telegin ascended unmolested to the second floor, and at last, directed to right and to left by pretty creatures in silk blouses, but rather puffy round the eyes, found the office of the Chief of Staff.

There, extended full-length on a tattered sofa, an elegantly-attired military man lay minutely inspecting his fingernails. He received them with excessive politeness, and a carefully "proletarian" approach, constantly employing the word "Comrade", which, on his lips, sounded exactly like "Count Sokolovsky", "Prince Telegin". When he had satisfied himself as to the business they had come on, he left them, with profuse apologies, his high tan boots, laced to the knee, creaking. A whispering began in the next room, a door banged in the distance, and all was quiet.

117

Sokolovsky looked at Telegin with burning eyes.

"Can you make anything of it all? Where are we? Is this White headquarters?"

He raised his bony shoulders, and his astonishment seemed to hold him frozen in that position. More whispering in the next room. Then the door was flung open and the Chief of Staff entered, a frowning, middle-aged, thickset individual, the hair retreating from above his great forehead, he wore a coarse soldier's tunic, held in over his huge stomach by a Caucasian belt. Casting a rapid keen glance at Telegin, and nodding to Sokolovsky, he sat down at the desk, laying his hairy hands in front of him with a characteristic gesture. His forehead was moist, like that of one who has just eaten and drunk his fill. Conscious of their eyes on him, he set his handsome, puffy face in lines still grimmer.

"The comrade on duty has just informed me that you have come on urgent business, Comrades," he said, with an air of chill importance. "I'm surprised that neither the regimental commander, nor you yourself, Comrade Commissar, saw fit to use the direct line...."

"I tried to get you on the direct line three times," said Sokolovsky, leaping to his feet and extracting from his pocket the telegraphic tape, which he held out to the Chief of Staff. "How can we sit back and wait while our comrades are perishing.... We have had no order from army headquarters. We are being implored for help. The 'Proletarian Freedom' Regiment is perishing, and it has two thousand refugees in its rear...."

The Chief of Staff glanced carelessly at the tape and flung it down on the desk, where it curled round the massive inkpot.

"We are well aware, Comrades, that fighting is going on near the position of the 'Proletarian Freedom' Regiment.... I admire your zeal, your revolutionary ardour." (He seemed to be picking his words.) "But I would request you, in future, not to raise a panic.... Especially since the operations of the enemy are of a casual nature.... In a word, all steps have been taken, and you can return to your duties without the least anxiety."

He raised his head. His glance was stern and calm. Telegin, who understood that no more would be said, rose. Sokolovsky remained seated, as if stunned.

"I can't go back to the regiment with such an answer," he rapped out. "The soldiers will hold a meeting this very day, this very day the regiment will rush heroically to the aid of the 'Proletarians'.... I give you warning, Comrade, that I shall speak in favour of an attack at the meeting...."

The Chief of Staff grew crimson. His huge bare forehead glistened. Pushing back his chair noisily, he rose, his army trousers drooping baggily, and thrust his hands into his belt.

"You will answer for your actions to the Revolutionary Tribunal of the army, Comrade! Remember, this is not 1917!"

"Don't try to intimidate me, Comrade!"

"Silence!"

Again the door was flung open, this time to admit a tall, remarkably slender man in a blue Circassian tunic of very fine cloth. He had dark hair falling over his forehead, and a drooping moustache, and his morose, handsome face was tinged with the delicate flush which so often goes with hard drinking and sadistic tendencies. He had moist, red lips, and the pupils of his black eyes were dilated. Waving the left sleeve of his tunic he went right up to Sokolovsky and Telegin, looking into their eyes with a savage glance. Then he turned towards the Chief of Staff, his nostrils quivering with rage.

"Again at your old-regime tricks! What d'you mean by shouting 'Silence!' at people? If they are at fault they will be shot.... But I won't have any of your general's high-handed attitudes...."

The Chief of Staff received the rebuke in silence, with a hanging head. He could not answer back—for it was Commander in Chief Sorokin himself.

"Sit down, Comrades, I'm listening," said Sorokin calmly, perching himself on the window sill.

Once again Sokolovsky embarked upon his explanation of the purpose of their journey: to get permission for the Varnav Regiment to go immediately to the help of the "Proletarians", who were posted near them. Besides being a revolutionary duty, this step was dictated by common sense: if the "Proletarians" were put out of action, the Varnav Regiment would be cut off from its base.

Sorokin only remained on the window sill a moment. He started striding from one of the doors to the other, barking out brief questions. Every time he made a sharp turn, his luxuriant locks flew in all directions. The soldiers loved him for his ardour and courage. He knew how to address meetings. In those days such qualities were often accepted as a substitute for military science. He had been a Cossack officer, with the rank of captain, and had fought in Transcaucasia under Yudenich. After the October Revolution he went back to the Kuban and organized a guerilla battalion in his native village of Petropavlovskaya, which subsequently fought successfully at the siege of Ekaterinodar. His star rose rapidly. Glory turned his head. His animal spirits bubbled, effervesced, he had enough for fighting and for carousing.

And the Chief of Staff saw to it that he was surrounded by pretty women and all the concomitants of luxury and debauch.

"What reply did you get in my staff?" he asked when Sokolovsky, mopping his brow convulsively with a soiled and crumpled handkerchief, stopped talking.

The Chief of Staff hastened to give an answer to this question.

"I replied that all measures had been taken by us for the relief of the 'Proletarian Freedom' Regiment. I said, moreover, that Varnav headquarters were interfering with the orders of army headquarters, which is absolutely inadmissible, and, moreover, that panic was being needlessly created."

"That's not the right approach, Comrade," said Sorokin, in tones unexpectedly mild. "Of course we must have discipline ... but there are things a thousand times more important than your discipline.... The will of the masses! The revolutionary impulse must be encouraged, even if it should run counter to your science.... What if the operations of the Varnav Regiment are useless, what if they are even harmful! What the hell! There's a revolution on. If you cross them nowadays, they simply call a meeting—I know those hotheads, they'll start yelling again that I am ruining the army for a drink."

He dashed over to the stove, and this time the glance he shot at Sokolovsky was full of fury.

"Hand over your report!"

Telegin immediately drew a paper from his pocket and placed it on the desk.

Pouncing upon it, the Commander in Chief ran his eyes over it and, with a shake of the pen, began writing:

"I command the Varnav Regiment to set out in marching order and perform its revolutionary duty."

When, however, he extended the paper towards his Chief of Staff, the latter, who had been regarding him with a mocking smile, retreated a step, and put his hands behind his back.

"You may have me committed to trial, but I shall not accept this order...."

Before he could finish speaking, Ivan Ilyich rushed forward and seized Sorokin by the wrist, just in time to prevent him raising his revolver. Sokolovsky shielded the Chief of Staff with his body. All four were breathing heavily. Sorokin tore himself free, thrust his revolver back into his pocket, and went out of the room, banging the door so violently that pieces of stucco flew about.

Doors banged, and the sound of the Commander in Chief's furious steps died away.

The Chief of Staff began to speak in conciliating bass tones:

120

"I assure you, Comrades—if I had signed that order, the misfortune might have assumed enormous proportions."

"What misfortune?" asked Sokolovsky huskily, clearing his throat.

The Chief of Staff looked at him queerly.

"Can't you guess what I mean?"

"No."

The corners of Sokolovsky's eyelids quivered.

"I am speaking of our army...."

"Well, what about it"

"I have no right to divulge military secrets to the commissar of a regiment. You know that, don't you, Comrade? You would be the first to have me shot for such conduct.... But we have gone too far. Very well, then.... Take full responsibility upon yourself...."

He went up to a map pinned up on the wall, with tiny flags dotted about it. Sokolovsky and Telegin moved up to him and stood behind him. The Chief of Staff's shoulder blades twitched beneath his tunic—apparently he did not quite enjoy the hot breath from two mouths on the back of his neck. But he calmly extracted a dirty toothpick from his pocket, and drew its chewed end over the map from the tricolour flags in the southern direction to the thickly concentrated red flags.

"That's where the Whites are," said the Chief of Staff.

"Where? Where?"

Sokolovsky moved close to the map, his bemused eyes roving over its surface. "Why, that's Torgovaya...."

"Yes—it's Torgovaya. And when it falls, the way will be almost clear for the Whites...."

"I don't understand. We thought the Whites were miles and miles ... to the north...."

"That's what *we* thought, Comrade Commissar—but the Whites thought differently. Torgovaya is at present being attacked from several directions. The Whites have airplanes and tanks. This is no Kornilov band.... They work along interior lines, striking at will. The initiative is in their hands.... "

"Dmitri Shelest's Iron Division is north of Torgovaya," said Telegin.

"Smashed...."

"And the cavalry brigade?"

"Smashed...."

Sokolovsky craned forward to see the map better.

"You have great self-control, Comrade," he said. "You seem to have reconciled yourself in advance to the fall of Torgovaya.

This division is smashed, that division is smashed...." He turned to the Chief of Staff. "And what about our army?"

"We are awaiting orders from the Supreme Command. Comrade Kalnin knows what he is about. What d'you think—can headquarters bang on the table and demand an order for attack from the staff of the Supreme Command? War isn't a meeting, you know."

The Chief of Staff gave a subtle smile. Sokolovsky, holding his breath, gazed into his calm, fat face. The Chief of Staff did not quail before this gaze.

"That's the way it is, Comrades," he said, going back to the desk. "And that's why I have no right to withdraw a single unit from the front, reasonable and essential though this might appear to be.... Our situation is difficult in the extreme. So you just go straight back to your unit. All that I have told you is for the present strictly confidential. Complete calm must be preserved in the army. As for the 'Proletarian Freedom' Regiment, you need not worry about its fate, I've just had reassuring information...."

The Chief of Staff's brows met over his hooked nose. He dismissed his visitors with a bend of the head. Sokolovsky and Telegin went out of the office. The officer on duty in the anteroom was now cleaning his nails at the window. He bowed politely to the departing visitors.

"Swine!" whispered Sokolovsky.

When they were outside, he seized Telegin by the sleeve.

"Well—how d'you like it?"

"Formally speaking, he's right. But actually, it's sabotage, of course."

"Sabotage? That's not it.... He's after something bigger. Let me go back and shoot him!"

"Stop that, Sokolovsky! Don't be an idiot!"

"Treachery, I tell you, there are traitors here!" muttered Sokolovsky. "Gimza gets information every day—drunkenness at headquarters. Sorokin has driven away the commissars. And just try and remonstrate! Sorokin's God and the tsar in the army, they adore him for his bravery, they regard him as their own. And you know who that Chief of Staff is? He's Belyakov, a tsarist colonel. See how it all hangs together? Come on, now.... Think we'll manage to get by?"

The Chief of Staff touched the hand bell on his desk, and the man on duty made his deferential appearance in the doorway.

"Find out what the condition of the Commander in Chief is," said Belyakov, looking severely downwards at the papers in front of him.

"Comrade Sorokin is in the dining room. Condition—slightly elevated."

The man waited for the Chief of Staff's reluctant smile before allowing a smile of profound significance to appear on his own lips.

"Zena's with him," he said.

"Very good! You can go."

After this Belyakov went to the communications department, where he looked through some telephonograms. He signed a few papers in his precise, fine hand, and went out, stopping for a moment in front of a door at the end of the corridor. From the room into which this door led came the sound of guitar strings being softly plucked. The Chief of Staff took out his pocket handkerchief, mopped his thick red neck, knocked, and entered without waiting for a response.

In the middle of the room, at a table spread with newspapers and littered with used dishes and wineglasses, sat Sorokin, the wide sleeves of his Circassian tunic turned back. His handsome countenance was still overcast. A lock of dark hair hung over his moist forehead. He glared at Belyakov from his dilated eyes. Beside him, on a stool, her legs crossed, showing her garters and a froth of lace, sat Zena, plucking at the strings of a guitar. She was a blue-eyed young woman with moist, vividly coloured lips, a fine, determined-looking nose, and fair hair piled loosely on the top of her head. But the scarcely perceptible unhealthy lines at the corners of her mouth gave her delicate face the expression of a wee beast whose teeth might be dangerous. Her passport showed that she was from Omsk, the daughter of a railwayman, but of course nobody believed this, or that she was eighteen years old, and that her name was Zenaida Kanavina. But she was a splendid typist, could drink vodka, play the guitar, and sing delightful songs. Sorokin had threatened to shoot her with his own hands if she attempted to infect headquarters with White-Guard putridity. And so nobody worried.

"A fine fellow, upon my word!" growled Belyakov, shaking his head, and keeping close to the door for safety's sake. "Look what a position you put me in! Two obvious Central Committee chaps turn up, threaten you with meetings, and you immediately go over to their side! Why not go straight to the Morse apparatus, and send a wire to Ekaterinodar—they'll immediately dispatch a nice little Jew to you, to organize a staff, and sleep beside you in your bed, and go to the privy with you, and keep check on every one of your thoughts. Oh my, ain't it terrible! Commander in Chief Sorokin has dictatorial leanings ... go on then—do it! Shoot me, if you like, but I'm not going to have you threatening me with a revolver in front of subordinates. What sort of discipline can there be after that? What the hell, after all!"

Not taking his eyes off the Chief of Staff, Sorokin stretched out a large, powerful hand for the neck of the bottle, but only clutched at the empty air. His mouth was distorted by a brief spasm, which set the moustache bristling. At last he managed to seize the bottle and pour out two wineglasses.

"Sit down and have a drink."

Shooting an oblique glance towards Zena's lacy drawers, Belyakov went up to the table.

"If you weren't such a clever chap I'd have got rid of you long ago. Discipline.... My discipline is battle. Just let any of you try to raise the masses! I can lead them, only give me time! No one else can do it, I'll crush the White-Guard scum all by myself.... The world will tremble...."

He inhaled the air through his nostrils, and purple veins began pulsating in his temples.

"I'll clear the Kuban without the C. C.—and the Don and Terek, too.... They crow loud enough in Ekaterinodar, they and their committees.... Swine, cowards! Wait till I get on my horse, into battle.... I'm dictator.... I lead the army!"

He reached out for the glass of spirits, but Belyakov overturned it with a rapid movement.

"You've had enough!"

"Aha! You giving me orders?"

"I ask you, as a friend."

Sorokin threw himself back in his chair, gave vent to a series of short sighs, and let his gaze wander till it rested on Zena. She was drawing a fingernail over the strings.

"The night was blissful," she sang, raising her eyebrows lazily.

As Sorokin listened, the veins in his temples began pulsating still more violently. Getting up, he jerked Zena's head back and rained avid kisses on her mouth. She went on plucking at the strings till the guitar slipped off her knees.

"That's better," said Belyakov in kindly tones. "Ah, Sorokin, Sorokin, I don't know why, but I love you!"

Zena managed to free herself at last, and bent down, very red in the face, to pick up the guitar. Her eyes gleamed through the tangles of her fair hair. She passed the tip of her tongue over her swollen lips.

"Faugh! You hurt me!"

"Listen, friends! I've got a bottle hidden away...."

Belyakov choked back his words. His hand, the fingers spread wide, was arrested in mid-air. A shot rang out outside the window, and a buzz of voices could be heard. Zena and her guitar seemed to be borne out of the room on a gust of wind. Sorokin went to the window, a frown on his face.

"Don't you go, I'll find out first what's up," said the Chief of Staff hastily.

Rows and shooting on the territory of headquarters had become a commonplace. Sorokin's army was composed of two basic groups: Cossacks from the Kuban, their nucleus formed by Sorokin himself the year before, and Ukrainians, the remnants of the Ukrainian Red armies which had retreated under pressure of the Germans. There was long-standing hostility between the Kuban Cossacks and the Ukrainians. The Ukrainians proved indifferent soldiers when it came to fighting on "foreign" soil, and helped themselves unabashed to fodder and provisions when passing through villages.

Rows and fights were of daily occurrence. But today's incident was of a more serious nature. The mounted Cossacks galloped up with loud cries. Startled groups of Red Army men came running up under cover of fences and orchards. The sound of desperate firing came from the direction of the station. A wounded Cossack, crawling and writhing in the dust of the square right under the windows of headquarters, was yelling frantically.

There was profound perturbation at headquarters. The telegraph, silent in the morning, had begun to pour out a stream of messages, each more fantastic than the other. All that could be ascertained was that the Whites, moving rapidly along the Sosika-Umanskaya line, were putting the Red troops to panic-stricken flight. The foremost units, having reached Army Headquarters, had begun looting at the station, and in the village. The Kuban troops were opening fire. The battle had begun.

Sorokin dashed out of the yard on a tall, fierce, chestnut mare. At his back was his escort of fifty, in Circassian tunics, the ends of their hoods streaming over their shoulders, their scimitars drawn. Sorokin sat on his horse as if he were part of it. He wore no cap, so as to enable all to recognize him immediately. His handsome head was thrown back, and the wind fluttered his hair, and the sleeves and skirts of his coat. He was still drunk, but his face was pale and resolute. The glance of his piercing eyes was terrifying. The dust rose in clouds beneath the hoofs of the galloping horses.

A few shots were heard from behind a hedge in the neighbourhood of the station. Some of the soldiers in the escort were emitting loud cries, one fell off his horse, but Sorokin did not even turn his head. His gaze was fixed upon the spot where, amidst the standing goods trains, there seethed a grey struggling mass of soldiers.

He was recognized from the distance. Many climbed up on to the roofs of the trains. Rifles were waved in the crowd, and men shouted. Without slowing down for a moment Sorokin made his horse jump the palings around the station allotment, and flew along the rails, into the very thick of the crowd. His bridle was seized instantly. Raising his hands above his head, he shouted:

"Comrades, companions-in-arms, warriors! What's the matter? What's the firing about? What's the panic for? Who's been turning your heads? Where is the bastard?"

"We have been betrayed!" cried a panic-stricken voice.

"The commanders have sold us! They have let the enemy in!" shouted many voices. The immense crowd, running into thousands, was spreading over the tracks and the fields beyond them, clambering on to trucks, and roaring out:

"We have been sold ... the army is utterly destroyed.... Down with the command! Kill the Commander in Chief!"

There was a whistling wailing sound, as if some infernal wind were blowing. The horses in the escort reared and whinnied. Distorted faces, grimy hands, began closing in upon Sorokin. And Sorokin thundered out, so that the muscles of his powerful neck bulged:

"Silence! You're not a revolutionary army ... you're a gang of bandits, a herd of swine... Show me the knaves of panic-mongers.... Show me the White-Guard spies!"

He suddenly urged on his horse and plunged into the very thick of the crowd. Then, leaning in his saddle, he pointed:

"That's the one!"

The crowd involuntarily turned towards the man pointed at—a tall, gaunt individual, with a big nose. He went pale and, spreading out his elbows, retreated a step. Whether Sorokin really knew him, or merely made a victim of the first man his eyes fell on, will never be known.... The crowd wanted blood. Drawing his scimitar, and brandishing it whistling through the air, Sorokin smote the tall man on his long neck. The blood gushed out in a powerful stream, splashing the muzzle of Sorokin's horse.

"It is thus that the revolutionary army deals with the enemies of the people!"

Sorokin again urged on his mare and, flourishing his blood-stained sword, his face pale and formidable, he darted among the crowd, abusing, swearing, reassuring.

"There hasn't been any rout.... The White scouts and spies have been trying to spread panic.... It's they who are encouraging you to plunder, it's they who are undermining discipline.... Who

126

says we've been beaten? Did you see it happen, you beast? Comrades, I have led you to battle—you know me! I bear the marks of twenty-six wounds. I demand the instant cessation of plundering! All back to your trains! Today I shall lead you to the attack. And cowards and traitors will meet with vengeance from the enraged people...."

The crowd listened. In their enthusiasm they climbed on to each other's shoulders for a look at their Commander in Chief. There were still a few dissenting voices, but most were eager for a fight. From all around could be heard: "It's true, what he says! Let him lead us! We'll follow him...." Company commanders who had been in hiding, crept back, and the soldiers gradually returned to their ranks. There was a rent in the breast of Sorokin's tunic where he had torn it open to display his scars.... His face was deathly pale. The panic died down, and machine-gun detachments were dispatched to meet the oncoming troops. Telegrams of the most determined nature flew backwards and forwards.

There was, however, no way of stemming the retreat. It took several days to restore order among the troops in the neighbourhood of the Timashevskaya railway station, and embark upon a counterattack. The Reds advanced in two columns through Viselki to Korenovskaya. And wherever the battle wavered, the Red Army men would see Sorokin galloping among them on his chestnut mare. It was as if, by his passionate will alone, he had stemmed the tide of defeat and saved the Black Sea coast.

There was nothing for the Central Executive Committee of the North Caucasian Republic to do, but give official confirmation of his command of military operations.

VI

During those very days, late in May, when the army of Denikin was launching its "Second Kuban Campaign", a new threat to the Russian Soviet Republic arose. Three Czech divisions, moving eastwards from the Ukrainian front, mutinied at almost the same moment in all the troop trains from Penza to Omsk.

This mutiny was the first of a series of carefully prepared blows dealt at the Soviet Union by the Intervention. The Czech divisions, which had begun to be formed as far back as 1914, from Czech nationals in Russia, and later from prisoners of war, constituted, after the October Revolution, a foreign body in the country, exercising armed interference in its internal affairs.

It had not been easy enough to get them to take part in an

armed attack against the Russian Revolution. The Czechs still cherished the idea of Russia as the future liberator of the Czech nation from Austrian tyranny. The Czech peasantry, fattening geese for Christmas, had become accustomed to saying, "One goose for a Russ". The Czech divisions, retreating under pressure of the German offensive in the Ukraine, got ready to transfer themselves to France, there to demonstrate at the front, in the face of the whole world, their aspirations to Czech liberty, and their right to participate in the defeat of the Austrians and Germans.

German prisoners of war, and with them the detested Hungarians, converged upon the Czech troops advancing on Vladivostok. Passions ran high at halts, when these converging bodies met. Agents of the Whites whispered to the Czechs of the insidious designs of the Bolsheviks, hinting at intentions to disarm the Czechs and betray their troops to the Germans.

On the 14th of May a serious fight broke out at the Chelyabinsk railway station, between Czechs and Hungarians. The Chelyabinsk Soviet had some of the most aggressive Czechs arrested. The whole troop train flew to arms. Red Army men at the disposal of the Chelyabinsk Soviet, were here, as all along the line, inadequately armed and were forced to yield. The tidings of the Chelyabinsk incident spread like wildfire among the troops. And there was a veritable explosion when, in response to the incident the following treacherous and inflammatory order of the Chairman of the Supreme Military Council of the Republic was issued:

"All Soviets are called upon to disarm Czechs, and will be held responsible for non-fulfilment of this order. Any Czech found armed on the railway line to be shot down, all Czechs in any troop train in which a single armed Czech is found, to be detrained and sent to a prisoner-of-war camp."

But since the Czechs had excellent discipline, morale and fighting experience, not to mention an abundance of machine guns and cannon, while the Soviets had nothing but the poorly equipped Red detachments, under inexperienced leadership, it was not the Soviets which disarmed the Czechs, but the Czechs who disarmed the Soviets, thus making themselves masters of the whole line from Penza to Omsk.

The rising began in Penza, where the Soviets sent five hundred Red Guards against fourteen thousand Czechs. The Reds attacked the railway station, and were destroyed almost to a man. The Czechs carried away from Penza the expedition's press for printing paper money, defeated the Reds in a great battle in the neighbourhood of Bezenchuk and Lipyagi, and occupied Samara.

Thus a new front was opened in the Civil War, rapidly covering vast territories in the Volga district, the Urals, and Siberia.

Dr. Dmitri Stepanovich Bulavin stood leaning out of the open window, listening to the hollow rumblings of artillery firing. The street was deserted. The pale sun beat mercilessly down upon the walls of the low houses, the grimy windows of empty shops, the useless signs over their doors, and the asphalted street with the layer of lime dust.

To the right, where the doctor's gaze was directed, protruded the wooden obelisk, covered with faded rags which had been put up over the monument to Alexander II. Next to it was a cannon, and a group of townsfolk were listlessly digging up cobblestones. Among them were the priest Slovokhotov, Notary Mishin, the pride and glory of the Samara intellectuals, Romanov, the proprietor of a food shop, Strambov, ex-member of the Zemstvo, and the landowner Kuroyedov, a grey-haired Apollo who had been a great gentleman in his day. They had all been Dmitri Stepanovich's patients at one time or another, and his partners in whist.... A Red Army man, his rifle resting between his knees, sat on a low post, smoking.

The guns were booming from the other bank of the Samarka. Windowpanes tinkled. At each of these sounds the doctor made a sour grimace, and snorted into his grey moustache. His pulse was 105. This meant the old social impulse was still alive in him. But it was dangerous as yet to allow his feelings to show themselves in any other way. Just across the road, exactly opposite, on the boards covering the broken plateglass window of Leder's jewellery shop, was an eyesore—the glaring order of the Rev. Com., threatening the shooting of counterrevolutionary elements.

The strange timorous figure of a man in a coconut-fibre hat with a peak back-and-front, and a tussore jacket of prewar cut, came into sight in the street. He was creeping along, hugging the wall, continually looking back and leaping as if a gun had gone off in his ear. His tow-coloured locks hung down to his shoulders, and his reddish beard seemed to have been glued on to his long, pallid face.

It was Govyadin, the statistician from the Zemstvo, the man who had once endeavoured vainly to awake in Dasha the "beautiful beast". He was on his way to Dmitri Stepanovich, and his errand was apparently of sufficient importance to force him to overcome his fear of the empty street and the moaning guns.

Catching sight of the doctor at the window, Govyadin waved frantically, a signal to be interpreted: "For God's sake don't look! I am being shadowed." Looking back, he crept along the wall past

129

the proclamation of the Revolutionary Committee, and suddenly plunged across the road and disappeared in the gateway. A minute later he was knocking at the doctor's back door.

"For God's sake shut the window, we are being watched," whispered Govyadin hoarsely, as he entered the dining room. "Pull down the blinds. Or perhaps better not! Dmitri Stepanovich, I've been sent to you...."

"At your service!" said the doctor ironically, seating himself at the table, covered with a soiled and scorched oilcloth. "Sit down, and tell me what you have to say."

Govyadin seized a chair, threw himself upon it, drew one foot up beneath him and whispered, hoarse and spluttering, right in the doctor's ear:

"Dmitri Stepanovich! A vote has just been passed at a secret meeting of the Committee of the Constituent Assembly, proposing to offer you the post of Under-Secretary for Public Health...."

"Under-Secretary?" interrupted the doctor, drawing down the corners of his mouth so that his chin was surrounded by wrinkles. "Well, well! For what republic?"

"Not for a republic, for the government.... We are taking the initiative for the struggle into our own hands. We are creating a front.... We are getting a press for printing paper money. With the Czechoslovakian corps at our head, we are moving upon Moscow.... We are forming a Constituent Assembly. We ... we, ourselves, understand.... There was a violent quarrel today. The S.R.'s and the Mensheviks demanded all posts. But we of the Zemstvo insisted on you, we carried your candidature through.... I'm filled with pride. Do you accept it?"

At that very moment there was such a stupendous roar from the other bank of the Samarka, that the glasses on the table rang, and Govyadin, clutching at his heart, leaped to his feet.

"That's the Czechs!" he exclaimed.

There was another explosion, and it seemed as if a machine gun was hammering away somewhere just next door. Govyadin, white as a sheet, sat down again with his foot under him.

"And that was the beastly Reds.... Their machine guns are on the grain elevator.... But there can be no doubt about it the Czechs will take the town.... They will, they will...."

"I may as well accept," said Dmitri Stepanovich, in a deep voice. "Have some tea—it's cold, I'm afraid."

Govyadin declined tea and went on whispering in a sort of trance.

"At the head of the government are patriots. The most upright people, noble individuals.... Volsky—you know him—he's a barrister from Tver, a splendid man.... Captain Fortunatov ... Klimush-kin—he's one of ours, from Samara—also a noble individual.... All S.R.'s, all implacable fighters.... They are actually expecting Chernov, but that's a dead secret.... He is fighting the Bolsheviks in the north.... In military circles everywhere, close blocs with us are being formed.... Colonel Galkin is representing the military.... They say he's second Danton.... In a word, everything is in readiness. We are only waiting for the storming to begin.... Everything seems to show that the Czechs have appointed it for tonight.... I represent the militia. It's an extremely dangerous and responsible post.... But we've got to fight .... to sacrifice ourselves...."

Through the window came the loud, discordant sound of a military band playing the *Internationale*. Govyadin doubled up in his chair and placed his head on the stomach of Dmitri Stepanovich. His tow-coloured hair was as lifeless as a doll's wig.

The sun set behind an enormous thundercloud. The approach of night brought no coolness. The stars were hidden in the mist. The artillery fire from the other side of the river became louder and more frequent. The houses shook with each explosion. The Bolshevik battery of 6-inch guns, posted behind the grain elevator, answered through the gloom. Machine guns barked from the roofs. From Red Army outposts in the suburb across the river, reached by a wooden bridge, came faint reports.

The huge cloud spread over the sky, emitting thunderous mutterings. It became pitch-dark. The only lights to be seen either in the town or on the riverbank were the flashes from the guns.

No one was asleep in the town. The Committee of the Constituent Assembly held uninterrupted session in mysterious underground premises. Volunteers from officers' organizations, fully armed, fumed and fretted in their homes. The townsmen stood at their windows, peering out into the nocturnal gloom. Street patrols called to one another intermittently. In intervals of silence could be heard the shrill dreary whistling of engines drawing eastward-bound trains.

The watchers at windows saw the forked lightning traversing the sky from end to end. The turbid waters of the Volga gleamed fitfully. Barges and steamers at the jetty stood out in momentary silhouette. High over the river, towering above the iron roofs, appeared and disappeared the vast bulk of the elevator, the slender spire of the Lutheran church, the white belfry of the convent, built, it was said, with money collected by Susanna, a nun. The lightning ceased. All was darkness....

The clouds dispersed. A wind rose, howling dismally in the chimneys. The Czechs went to the attack.

131

They advanced in thin lines from the railway station of Kryazh, by way of the railway bridge, skirting the tallow factories, upon the river suburb. The broken ground, the dike, the lowgrowing bushes of purple willow, all made rapid progress impossible.

The key to the town consisted in the two bridges—the wooden one, and the railway bridge. The Bolshevik artillery, from the ground behind the elevator, was shelling the approaches. The heavy firing and the explosions kept up the courage of the Red divisions, who had not much confidence in the military experience of their commanders.

Towards morning the Czechs had recourse to a ruse. In the hutments beside the elevator lived the remnants of Polish refugees with their wives and children. The Czechs knew of this. When the shells began to burst over the elevator, the Poles ran helterskelter from the huts and rushed hither and thither in search of shelter. The artillerymen chased them all away from the guns with oaths, and with blows from ramrods. When the 6-inch guns roared, the refugees, blinded and deafened, fled in all directions. And suddenly another crowd of women came running out of the barns, shrieking:

"Don't shoot, *Pane*—don't shoot, pity the unfortunate, we beseech you!"

They surrounded the cannon on all sides.

The odd-looking Polish women seized upon the cleaning rods and the cannon wheels; getting a firm grip on the arms of the gunners, who were half-stunned by the hubbub, the "women" hung upon them with their whole weight, caught at their hands, and dragged them to the ground.

Beneath the bodices of these women were military tunics, beneath their skirts—breeches....

"It's the Czechs, lads!" shouted a voice, and the next moment the speaker's head was shattered by a revolver shot. Some of the gunners tried to beat off newcomers, others fled headlong.... But the Czechs had removed the breech-blocks from the guns, and beaten a retreat, firing all the time. Then they disappeared into the spaces between the barns as if the earth had opened and swallowed them up.

The battery was silenced, its machine guns put out of action. The Czechs continued to advance, capturing the Samara suburb down to the very bank of the Volga.

By daybreak the clouds had dispersed. The scorching sun beat upon the unwashed windows of Dmitri Stepanovich's room. The doctor was seated at the window, fully dressed. His eyes were sunken—he had not been to bed. Slop basin, tray, and saucers were filled with cigarette ends. Every now and then he took out a broken comb and passed it through the grey curls over his forehead. A summons to the performance of his ministerial duties might be expected at any moment. He suddenly realized that he was infernally ambitious.

Wounded soldiers filed past his windows along Dvoryanskaya Street. They seemed to be passing through a city of the dead. Some sank on to the pavement, leaning against the walls, bandaged up after a fashion with bloodstained rags. They gazed up at the empty windows—there was no one from whom to beg a drink of water and a crust.

The street, which the storm of the night before had failed to cool, lay burning beneath the sun. From the other side of the river came the hellish music of the artillery.

A car dashed by, filling the street with clouds of white dust, and affording a glimpse of the distorted face and darkened lips of the military commissar. The car went downhill, and over the wooden bridge, where it was afterwards said to have been blown up by a shell with all its passengers.

Time came to a standstill, the battle seemed endless. The town held its breath. Society women, already attired in white dresses, lay covering their heads under cushions. The Committee of the Constituent Assembly was taking its morning tea, served by the proprietor of the flour mill. In the light of the cellar the faces of the ministers showed an unearthly pallor. And there was a perpetual booming and banging from the Czech artillery on the other side of the river.

At twelve noon, Dmitri Stepanovich went to the window and, panting with the effort, opened it, unable to endure the blue haze of tobacco smoke any more. There was no longer a single wounded soldier to be seen in the street. Many windows were opened a crack—here an eye peeped out from behind a curtain, there a perturbed face showed itself for a moment. Heads were thrust out from porches and withdrawn. It looked as if there really were no more Bolsheviks left.... But what did the rapid firing from the other side of the river mean? Oh, how wearing it all was! And suddenly, as by a miracle, a long-legged officer in a snow-white, high-waisted tunic came round the corner, stood still a moment, and proceeded down the middle of the street. His sword knocked against his boot tops. On his shoulders, like the sun at noon, blazed the old-regime bliss of gilt shoulder straps....

Something long forgotten stirred in Dmitri Stepanovich's heart, as if he had just remembered some cause of indignation....

He thrust his head out of the window with unaccountable animation, and shouted to the officer:

"Long live the Constituent Assembly!"

The officer winked at the chubby-faced doctor and replied enigmatically:

"We'll see about that!"

And now heads were leaning out of all the windows, calling to the officer.

"Captain! Captain! Well? Have we been taken? Have the Bolsheviks gone?"

Dmitri Stepanovich put on his white peaked cap, seized his walking stick, cast a glance at the mirror, and went out of the house. People were pouring into the street, as after a church service. And in the distance church bells were pealing merrily. The crowd jostled one another with joyful noise at the street corner. Dmitri Stepanovich's sleeve was seized by one of his patients, a lady with a triple chin, the flowers on whose heavily trimmed hat smelled of camphor balls.

"Look, doctor—the Czechs!"

At the street corner, surrounded by women, stood two Czechs, their rifles atilt. One of them had a blue shaven chin, the other, an enormous black moustache. They smiled nervously and glanced rapidly at the roofs, the windows, and the faces of the passers-by.

Their smart caps, the leather buttons on their tunics, the shields sewn on to their left sleeves, their sturdy pouches and cartridge cases, their resolute countenances—all evoked enthusiasm and respectful astonishment. The two of them seemed to have tumbled into Dvoryanskaya Street from some other planet.

A few officials in the crowd cheered:

"Hurrah for the Czechs! Toss them!"

Dmitri Stepanovich, sniffing as he pushed his way through the crowd, tried to utter a suitable greeting, but his throat had gone dry with emotion, and he hastened to the secret place where his high duties awaited him.

There seemed to be nobody and nothing in the flour-mill cellar but the smell of stale tobacco smoke and ash trays bristling with cigarette ends, and a fair-haired man, fast asleep at the end of a table, his head resting on a litter of papers scribbled all over with profiles. Dmitri Stepanovich touched his shoulder. The man gave a deep sigh, and raised a bearded face, his light-blue eyes, struggling back to consciousness wandering dazedly.

"What d'you want?"

"Where's the government?" asked Dmitri Stepanovich sternly. "You are speaking to the Under-Secretary for Public Health."

"Ah—Dr. Bulavin," said the fair man. "Damn it, I.... Well, what's going on in town?"

"The affair hasn't been completely liquidated as yet. But it's the end. There are Czech patrols on Dvoryanskaya Street."

The fair man showed his teeth in a hearty laugh.

"Splendid! Nice work, by Jove! Well, the government will meet here at three sharp. If all goes well we'll be moving into better quarters in the evening."

A sinister suspicion crossed the mind of Dmitri Stepanovich.

"Excuse me," he said, "am I speaking to a member of the Central Committee? Aren't you Avksentyev?"

The fair man gave a vague gesture, as if to say: "You said it!" The telephone rang. He picked up the receiver.

"Your place is on the street, doctor," he said. "Remember, we can't have any disorder. You're a representative of the bourgeois intellectuals—try and calm their zeal.... Otherwise—" (he winked), "there may be trouble later on."

Dr. Bulavin went out. By now the whole town was in the streets. Strangers were greeting one another, as if it were Easter day. Congratulations were exchanged. Scraps of news communicated.

"The Bolsheviks are plunging into the Samarka by the thousand, trying to get to the other side."

"And they're being shot down like the devil—"

"A lot of them have been drowned, too!"

"Yes, yes! The whole Volga is covered with corpses just outside town."

"And the Lord be thanked, say I! And I don't consider it a sin...."

"Quite right! A dog's death to a dog!"

"Have you heard, gentlemen? They threw the sexton from the belfry."

"Who did? The Bolsheviks?"

"Yes. So's he shouldn't ring the bells. That's what they call banging the door behind them.... If it was anyone of importance—but the *sexton*!"

"Where are you going, Dad?"

"Just down the street—I want to have a look at the barn, to see if it's all right."

"Are you mad? There are still Bolsheviks at the jetty."

"Dmitri Stepanovich.... We've lived to see the day.... Where are you going, looking so serious?"

"Well, you see—they've elected me Under-Secretary for Public Health!"

"Congratulations, Your Excellency!"

"Don't congratulate me yet.... Not until Moscow is taken."

"Oh, doctor, we're grateful for a breathing space!"

Gold shoulder straps floated here and there among the crowd. They symbolized all that was old, familiar, secure. An officer detachment strode by with firm steps, accompanied by grinning urchins, and the laughter of elegant ladies. The crowd turned out of Sadovaya into Dvoryanskaya Street, past the grotesque splendour of the green-tiled Kurlina mansion. Somebody plunged into the crowd....

"What's the matter? What's happened?"

"There are Bolsheviks in that yard, officer—they're hiding behind the wood pile, two of them."

"Aha! Go on, gentlemen, go on!"

"Where are those officers off to?"

"No panic, please, gentlemen, no panic!"

"They've found some Cheka men!"

"Dmitri Stepanovich, let's step aside—you never know...."

Shots rang out. The crowd swayed. People took to their heels, losing their hats and caps as they ran. Dmitri Stepanovich, panting, found himself once more in Dvoryanskaya Street. He felt responsible for all that was going on. Arrived at the square he glanced through narrowed eyes at the obelisk concealing the statue of Alexander II. Extending his arm, he declared in a loud, angry voice:

"The Bolsheviks are ready to destroy everything Russian. They want to make the Russian people forget their own history. We have here a perfectly harmless statue of the tsar-liberator. Remove those beastly boards and foul rags."

It was his first speech to the people. Some pert lads in peaked caps—shop assistants, probably—immediately began shouting:

"Break it up!"

There was a rending sound as the boards were torn off the statue. Dmitri Stepanovich proceeded further. The crowd was thinning. The shots from across the river could be heard more distinctly. A man came running towards the doctor from the direction of the river. His dark hair fell over his eyes, and he had on nothing but dripping wet hose. His broad chest was tattooed. Women ran screaming into gateways. He made a sudden turn and rushed down the slope towards the Volga. Three more appeared, and then others came running up, one at a time, wet, half-naked, panting. There were cries of:

"Bolsheviks! Kill them!"

Like snipe alarmed by the hunter's fire, they rushed blindly down the slope towards the landing stage. Dmitri Stepanovich, profoundly excited, also started running, and seized upon a sickly-looking individual with no eyelashes and a crooked nose.

"I'm a minister of the new government!" he exclaimed. "A machine gun is needed here immediately. Go for one at once, I order you to do so!"

"I don't speak Russian!" replied the sickly-looking individual with an obvious effort.

The doctor pushed him aside. The matter was of the greatest urgency. He went himself to look for a Czech with a machine gun ... and in a gateway, over which a red star hung crookedly, he came upon yet another Bolshevik—a copper-skinned man with a shaven head and a Tatar beard. His military tunic was torn, and blood was trickling from his shoulder. He was turning his head from side to side, showing his small teeth and snapping like a dog. On his face was imprinted the desperate fear of death. The crowd fell upon him, the women in particular uttering frenzied cries. Umbrellas and sticks were flourished, clenched fists were shaken.... A retired general, with an enormous cap almost slipping off his baldish head, and a medal jigging up and down at the base of his flabby throat, stood on the porch steps, brandishing his mottled fist right in the Bolshevik's face and trying to shout everyone down.

"Go on, gentlemen! He's a commissar.... Be ruthless! My own son is a Red. What a grief! Find him, gentlemen, I beseech you, bring my son to me.... I'll kill him here, in front of all of you.... I'll kill my own son.... There must be no quarter shown to this one, either...."

"In this case interference would be useless," thought Dmitri Stepanovich nervously, and moved away, looking over his shoulder.... The cries were dying down. In the place where the wounded commissar had stood was a medley of sticks and umbrellas.... Now all was quiet, the only sound was of blows.... The retired general glanced down from the porch; his cap had now slipped over his nose, and he was motioning faintly in the air above his head, like an orchestra conductor.

Dmitri Stepanovich was overtaken by Notary Mishin—puffy-faced, in a dingy jacket, buttoned up to the neck, one of the glasses of his pince-nez missing.

"They killed him. They beat him with their umbrellas. It's an awful thing, this mob law! Oh, doctor, they say there are terrible goings-on on the bank of the river now...."

"In that case, we'll go there. Did you know I was in the government?"

"Yes, and I was delighted to hear it."

Dmitri Stepanovich stopped a detachment of six officers in the name of the government, and demanded their escort to the river, where undesirable incidents were occurring. There were now Czech patrols at all street corners. Elegant ladies were adorning them with flowers, and giving them extempore lessons in the Russian language, laughing heartily the while in the endeavour to make the women, the town, and the country itself, pleasing to the foreigners, and to take away the bitter taste left by the hospitality extended to the Czechs by Russia during the years of their internment.

Dmitri Stepanovich arrived too late: the volunteers had already finished off the Reds fleeing from the suburb to the slushy banks of the Samarka. Those who had managed to cross by the wooden bridge, or by swimming the river in slanting lines, clambered on to barges and steamers and were moving upstream along the Volga. There were a few corpses in the lazy ripples at the water's edge. Hundreds of bodies had already been carried by the current into the Volga.

Govyadin was seated on a rotting, overturned boat, a tricolour band round his sleeve. His tow-coloured locks were damp with sweat. His pale eyes, the pupils mere pin points, were fixed on the sunny surface of the river. Dmitri Stepanovich approached him with the severe words:

"Assistant Chief of Militia, I have been informed that undesirable incidents have taken place here.... The government wishes..."

The doctor did not finish his speech, for his glance was arrested by the sight of an oak staff in Govyadin's hands, on which clotted blood and tufts of hair were visible. In a voice so muffled as to be almost inaudible, Govyadin muttered:

"There goes another..."

He then rose from the boat with a languid movement and went to the water's edge to get a closer look at the cropped head which was slanting down the river with the current. Five or six youths with stakes in their hands went up to Govyadin. Dmitri Stepanovich turned to his officers, who were standing and drinking Bavarian kvass from a cart driven up to the spot by a remarkably resourceful vendor, in a conspicuously clean apron. The doctor harangued the officers as to the need for putting an end to unnecessary cruelty. He pointed to Govyadin and the floating head. A long-legged cavalry captain, the one in the snow-white tunic, twitching his froth-covered moustache, raised his rifle and fired. The head disappeared beneath the water.

Dmitri Stepanovich, with the consciousness of having done all that was in his power, went back to town. He must not be late for the first sitting of the government. He raised clouds of dust with his boots as he went panting up the hill. His pulse could not have been less than a hundred and twenty. His head was filled with dazzling visions—the march on Moscow, the mellow pealing of Moscow's forty times forty churches ... who knows?—perhaps even the presidential chair.... For revolution is an unaccountable thing—once it started rolling backwards all those S.R.'s and S.D.'s would be sprawling under its chariot wheels in no time, with their stomachs ripped open.... No thank you, he had had enough of dabbling in Left politics.

VII

Ekaterina Dmitrevna sat beside the aspidistra in the low drawing room, writing a letter to her sister Dasha, her handkerchief, wet with tears, crumpled into a ball in her hand.

The rain was beating furiously against the flawed and bubbly glass of the windowpanes, and outside, the acacias were tossing in the wind. The same wind which was chasing the clouds above the Sea of Azov rustled the peeling wallpaper inside the room.

"Dasha, Dasha," wrote Katya. "I can never tell you how desperately unhappy I am. Vadim is dead. Colonel Tetkin, whose house I am living in, told me about it yesterday. I couldn't believe it, and asked him who told him. He gave me the address of Valerian Onoli, one of Kornilov's men, just back from the front. I went to his hotel in the evening. He must have been drunk, he pulled me into his room and offered me wine.... It was awful.... You simply can't imagine what people are like here.... 'Is my husband dead?' I asked him. Onoli was his brother officer, you know, his comrade, they fought side by side.... He saw him every day.... He jeered at me. 'He's dead, girlie, don't you worry! I saw the flies eating him up with my own eyes....' Then he said: 'Roshchin was under suspicion with us, he was lucky to die in battle....' He didn't tell me when it was, how it happened, or the place where Vadim was killed.... I implored him, I cried....He shouted at me: 'I can't remember where everybody was killed!' And then he offered himself to me instead.... Oh, Dasha! What horrid people! I rushed away from the hotel, out of my mind with grief....

"I can't believe there's no more Vadim, Dasha.... But it must be true—that man had no reason to lie to me. The Colonel says it must be true, too.... I only got one letter from Vadim all the time he was at the front, a very short one, not a bit like him. It came the second week after Easter. It had no beginning. Here it is, word for word: 'I am sending you money. I can't come and see you. I remember your words when we parted.... I don't know if a man

139

can stop being a murderer.... I don't know how I came to be a murderer. I try not to think, but I suppose I shall have to think, and do something about it. When all this passes, if it ever does, we can meet again....'

"And that's all. Oh, Dasha, how I cried. He went away from me to die. How could I have kept him, made him come back, saved him? What could I have done? Just hold him fast to my heart ... that was all.... But he hardly took any notice of me towards the end. The revolution—he could see and think of nothing else. Oh, I don't understand, I don't understand! Is it worth while for all of us to go on living? Everything is destroyed ... like storm-tossed birds we wander all over Russia. What for? If all the blood which has been shed, all our sufferings, our trials, could give us back our home, our nice rooms, our card games with friends.... Shall we ever be happy again? The past has gone beyond repair, gone for ever, Dasha.... Life is over for us, let others take our places. Stronger, better people...."

Katya laid down her pen and dabbed at her eyes with her crumpled-up handkerchief. Then she looked up at the rain streaming down the four windowpanes. An acacia bent and tossed as if the savage wind was tousling its hair. Katya proceeded with her letter:

"Vadim went to the front in the early spring. My whole life was just waiting for him. How sad, how utterly, utterly useless.... I remember sitting at the window one evening.... The acacia was coming out, the fat buds were bursting open. A flock of sparrows was making a great fuss in the yard. I felt such resentment, such loneliness.... As if I had no place in this world. The war passed, and the revolution will pass. Russia will never be the same again. We fight, we perish, we suffer. But the tree blossoms just as it did last spring, and many springs before that. And the tree and the sparrows, the whole of nature, seem to have retreated to some remote distance, where they live a life which is strange to me....

"Dasha, what are all our sufferings for? It can't be they are all in vain. We women, you and I, we know our own little world. But all that goes on outside it—the whole of Russia—is simply a blazing furnace. It must be that some new happiness will arise from the flames.... If people didn't believe that, they would never go in for all this hatred and destruction of one another.... I have lost all.... I have nothing to live for.... But I go on living, because I'm ashamed—not afraid, *ashamed*—to put my head under a train, or hang up a rope from a beam....

"I'm leaving Rostov tomorrow, so that there shall be nothing to remind me.... I shall go to Ekaterinoslav. I have friends there.... I am advised to go into a confectioner's. Perhaps you'll come south, too, Dasha. They say things are very bad in Petersburg now...."

"That's where a woman is so different from a man. A woman would never leave one she loved, not if it was the end of the world.... But Vadim left me.... He loved me as long as he felt sure of himself.... You remember how the sun shone on our joy that June in Petersburg.... All my life I shall never forget that pale northern sunshine. I haven't got a single photograph of Vadim, not the tiniest souvenir.... It's as if it had all been a dream. I can't believe he's dead, Dasha, I can't. I think I shall go mad. How sad, how futile my life has been...."

Katya could not go on. Her handkerchief was soaked through.... But she had to tell her sister all the ordinary everyday things people expect to be told in letters ... she committed these things to paper to the accompaniment of the sound of the falling rain, but neither her mind nor her heart was in the work. She wrote of the cost of food, of the soaring prices.... "No stuff, no thread.... A needle costs fifteen hundred rubles, or two live suckling pigs.... The girl next door, she's only seventeen years old, came back one night naked and bruised—her clothes were taken off in the street. They go mostly for shoes...." She wrote about the Germans, how they had put military bands in the town park and had the streets swept, but sent all the grain and butter and eggs to Germany.... The common people and the workers hated them, but said nothing, since they had nowhere to look to for help.

It was Colonel Tetkin who told her all these things. "He's very nice, but of course an extra mouth is a burden.... His wife doesn't even take the trouble to conceal this." Katya then added: "I was twenty-seven the day before yesterday, but you should just see me. Oh well, never mind that. It doesn't matter any more. There's no one to care...."

And again she went to work with her handkerchief.

Katya gave this letter to Tetkin. He promised to send it at the first opportunity to Petersburg. But it lay in his pocket a long time after Katya's departure. Communications with the north were very hard to arrange. The post was not working. Letters were delivered by special messengers—daredevils who took large sums for the service.

Before leaving, Katya sold the few things she had brought with her from Samara, leaving herself only one treasure—an emerald ring which had been a birthday present, long long ago, before the war, one spring morning in Petersburg. It all seemed so remote that Katya no longer felt any ties with the misty town in which her youth had flown by.... Dasha, Nikolai Ivanovich and Katya were walking along Nevsky Prospekt.... They chose a ring set with an emerald. She had placed the green flame on her finger, and now it was all that was left her of that life....

Several trains left the Rostov station in rapid succession. Katya was jostled and shoved into a third-class compartment. She got a place by the window, and settled her bundle of darned clothing on her lap. Low-lying meadows, Don swamplands, smoke on the horizon, the misty outlines of Bataisk, unconquered by the Germans, rushed by. At the foot of a steep riverbank were half-submerged fishing villages, clay huts, orchards, overturned boats, boys carrying a fishing net. Then came the milky expanse of the Sea of Azov, with a few sails slanting in the distance upon it. The cold chimneys of the Taganrog factories followed. Steppe. Mounds. Abandoned mines. Big villages scattered over the slopes of chalky foothills. Hawks against the blue sky. The whistle of the engine, as mournful as these dreary spaces themselves.... Morose peasants ... the iron helmets of the Germans at the stations.

Katya, hunched up like an old woman, looked out of the window. It must have been something extraordinarily sad and exquisite in her face that made the German soldier on the opposite seat gaze long at this unknown Russian woman. His gaunt, weary face, with the nickel-rimmed spectacles, also seemed to bear the stamp of grief.

"The guilty will be made to pay for all, *gnädige Frau*, time will come," he said softly, in German. "That's how it will be in Germany, that's how it'll be all over the world. The great judge will come ... its name is *Sozialismus*...."

At first Katya did not realize that he was speaking to her, and she merely lifted her eyes to his big, clean, nickel-rimmed glasses. The German gave her a friendly bow:

"Does the *gnädige Frau* speak German?"

"Yes," said Katya.

"When one suffers greatly, one may find consolation in the thought that one is suffering in a good cause," said the German, tucking his feet beneath the seat, and lowering his brows, so that he was now looking at Katya from over the top of his glasses. "I have gone deeply into the history of man. After a long period of quiet we are once more entering a period of catastrophe. Such are my conclusions. We are present at the beginning of the death of a great civilization. The Aryan world has already been through one such epoch. That was in the fourth century when the barbarians destroyed Rome. There are many who see in this analogies with our times. But it is not true. Rome was destroyed by the idea

142

of Christianity. The barbarians merely mutilated the corpse of Rome. Modern civilization will be transformed by socialism. It was destruction then, now it will be construction. The most destructive ideas of Christianity were: equality, internationalism, and the moral superiority of the poor over the rich. These were the ideas of the barbarians feeding that monstrous parasite, Rome, which was wallowing in luxury. That is why the Romans feared and persecuted the Christians. But there were no constructive ideas in Christianity, it did nothing to organize labour. It contented itself on earth with destruction alone, promising all the rest in heaven. Christianity was merely a sword, an instrument of destruction and punishment. Even in heaven, and in the ideal life, it could promise nothing but the hierarchical class and official state of the Roman Empire in reverse. And this was its basic defect. Rome set against it the idea of order. But at that time *disorder*, universal chaos, was the cherished dream of the barbarians awaiting the hour when they should storm the walls of Rome. And the hour did come. The cities were reduced to heaps of smoking ruins. Corpses, with stakes through their hearts, crushed by the chariots of the barbarians, lay about the roads. There was no help—Europe, Asia Minor, Africa, were in flames from end to end. The Romans hovered like birds above the conflagration of the whole world. They were slaughtered by the barbarians, torn to pieces in the forests by wild beasts, and perished in the desert from hunger, tropical heat, chill blasts. I have read in the pages of a contemporary how Proba, the wife of the Prefect of Rome, escaped at night in a boat with her two daughters, when Alaric and his Germans forced their entry into Rome. Floating down the Tiber, the Roman women saw the flames devouring the eternal city.... It was the end of the world...."

The German opened his rucksack, and extracted from the very bottom of it a bulging notebook with a rubbed leather binding, the leaves of which he turned over in silence for a short time, smiling discreetly.

"There," he said, going over to Katya's side, "this passage from Ammianus Marcellinus will give you a better idea of what the Romans were like before their downfall:

"'Their long robes of silk and purple fluttered in the wind and afforded glimpses of rich tunics embroidered with the likeness of various animals. Accompanied by enormous suites, they thundered at a breakneck speed in their covered chariots, shaking the homes and roads. When a patrician visited the baths, which were as a rule attached to shops, eating houses and pleasure gardens, he would demand in imperious tones that everything be given up to his exclusive use. On emerging from the bath he donned jewelled rings and buckles, and a sumptuous gown whose folds would have sufficed for a dozen men. On top of this came all sorts of attire conducive to his self-esteem. And he never failed to assume a pompous bearing, such as would not have been tolerated even in the great Marcellus, the conqueror of Syracuse. He actually ventured to make occasional audacious sallies with a huge suite of servants, cooks, protégés, and loathsomely disfigured eunuchs, to his Italian estates, where he indulged in shooting wild fowl and hunting the hare. On those rare occasions when, some sultry noontide, he ventured to cross the lake of Lucrin in his gilded barge, he would afterwards compare his journey to the campaigns of Caesar and Alexander. If a fly blundered through the silken curtains sheltering his deck, or a stray sunbeam penetrated their folds, he would bemoan his bad luck, regretting he had not been born in some land of eternal, Cymric gloom. Parasites and flatterers, ready to applaud every word uttered by their host, were the favourite guests of a great man. They surveyed with ecstatic admiration the marble pillars and mosaic floors of the rooms. Fish and fowl of extraordinary size evoked general astonishment. Scales were brought in to demonstrate their weight, and while the more sober-minded guests turned aside from such spectacles, the parasites clamoured for the recording of such miracles by lawyers....'"

"Yes," said the German, closing his notebook, "*sic transit...* these people were later forced to wander about the roads and the ruins of cities, in search of food. And the barbarians rolled on in great waves from the east, looting and laying waste. By fifty years or so there was not a trace of the Roman Empire left. Great Rome was overgrown with grass, goats pastured in the abandoned courtyards. Europe was plunged in darkness for almost seven centuries. And all this because Christianity could destroy, but had not conceived the idea of the organization of labour. There is not a word about labour in the Commandments. They are intended for men who neither sow nor reap, for whom slaves sowed and reaped. Christianity became the religion of emperors and conquerors. Labour remained unorganized and outside the moral code. The religion of labour is bringing new barbarians into the world, to destroy a second Rome. Have you read Spengler? He's a Roman from head to toe, but he is right in considering that the sun has set for *his* Europe. But for us it is rising. He cannot take the world proletariat into the tomb. The dying swan is said to sing, and the bourgeoisie forced Spengler to utter their own swan song. He was their idealistic trump card. The fangs of Christianity are rotting away. Ours are of steel.... We are countering the idea of Christianity with the socialist organization of labour.... We are being made to fight the Bolsheviks. But d'you think we don't understand who it is that is making us take up arms, and against whom we are being made to take up arms? Oh, we understand much more than people think.... We used to despise the Russians. Now we are beginning to admire and respect them...."

The train tore past a big village with a long-drawn whistle: wellbuilt huts with iron roofs, long haystacks, fenced orchards, shop signs, flashed by. A peasant in an unbelted soldier's tunic and a sheepskin cap was driving along the dusty road beside the train. His legs straddled, he stood in the small cart, the ends of the reins twisted in his hand. The big, sleek horse galloped along, trying to overtake the train. The peasant turned towards the windows of the carriages and shouted something with a generous display of white teeth.

"That's Gulyai-Polye," said the German. "It's a very rich village."

Katya, who had made the mistake of not getting into a through train, had to change several times. The bustle, the waiting on platforms, the stream of new faces, the steppe of a vastness she had never before seen, unfolding itself slowly past the window of the compartment, all distracted her from her sad thoughts. The German had got off long ago, with a hearty handshake in farewell. This man had been firm in his conviction of the logic of events, and seemed to have defined with precision the extent of his own participation in them. His optimism astonished and disquieted Katya. That which everybody considered ruin, horror, chaos, was for him the long-awaited beginning of a new era.

All that year Katya had heard nothing but the impotent grinding of teeth and sighs of despair, had seen nothing—as on that March morning in her father's house—but distorted faces, clenched fists. Colonel Tetkin, it is true, had neither sighed nor ground his teeth, but he had been, in his own words, a kind of God's fool, and had welcomed the revolution with a blissful faith in justice.

Everyone in Katya's set had seen in the revolution the ruin of Russia and Russian culture, the annihilation of life, spontaneous risings on a colossal scale—the promised Apocalypse. There had once been an empire whose workings were comprehensible and definite. The peasant ploughed, the miner hewed coal, factories turned out cheap and useful goods, merchants traded briskly, clerks worked diligently—everything went as if by clockwork. The people at the top derived luxurious comforts from all this. Some said it was an unjust system. But what was to be done if that was how God had ordained things? And suddenly it had all been shattered into smithereens, and

145

instead of an empire there was an exposed ant-heap. And the plain man staggered on, his eyes pale with horror....

For a long time the train waited at a halt in the midst of a profound stillness. Katya put her head out of the window. The leaves of a tall tree rustled in the darkness. The starry sky seemed to spread boundlessly over this strange land.

Katya leaned her elbows on the top of the open window. The rustle of the leaves, the stars, the warm fragrance of the earth, reminded her of one night in a park near Paris.... A few persons, almost all friends, and all from Petersburg, had gone there in two cars.... It had been delightful in the summerhouse on the lake where they had had supper. The weeping willows had hung over the water like silvery clouds.

One of the company was a man in evening dress without a hat, whom Katya did not know—a German who spoke excellent French and had lived in Russia for a long time. He was lean, with a longish, nervouslooking face, a high, sloping forehead, from which the hair retreated, and grave, heavy-lidded eyes. He sat quietly at the table, his long fingers caressing his wineglass. When Katya liked somebody, the atmosphere became one of warmth and tenderness. The July night over the lake seemed to be descending upon her partly exposed shoulders. Stars showed through the leaves of the creepers overhead. The warm glow of the candles fell on the faces of the assembled company, the moths on the tablecloth, the musing face of the new acquaintance. Katya could feel that he was looking at her thoughtfully. She must have been very beautiful that evening.

When they rose from the table, to stroll along an alley beneath the curved roof formed by towering trees, towards a terrace at the end of the park, from which the lights of Paris could be seen, the German had kept at Katya's side.

"Do you not consider, Madame," he said, "that there is something impermissible in beauty—something not to be tolerated?" he said in austere tones, making it as clear as possible that there was no latent significance in his words. Katya walked slowly on. She liked this man to be talking to her, his voice not drowning the rustle of the leafy roof overhead. Walking on her left side, the German looked in front of him into the depths of the alley, at the end of which the crimson glow of the town could be discerned. He went on talking.

"I'm an engineer. My father is very rich. I work in great concerns, I have dealings with thousands of people. I see and know much that is unknown to you. Excuse me—perhaps I'm boring you?"

Katya had turned her head towards him, smiling in silence. He could see her eyes and her smile in the faint reflection of the distant glow, and went on:

"We are living, unfortunately, at the meeting point of two eras. One, majestic and splendid, is in its decline. The other is being born in bleak, monotonous industrial districts, amidst the clatter of machinery. Its name is the masses, the masses of humanity, in whose midst all distinctions are destroyed. A man is nothing but deft hands guiding machines. Here are different laws, different calculations of time, a different truth. You, Madame, belong to the last remnants of the old era. That is why it makes me so sad to look at your face. The new era does not want it, any more than it wants anything which is useless, inimitable, capable of exciting obsolete feelings—love, self-sacrifice, poetry, tears of joy.... Beauty! What is it for? It is disturbing, it is not to be tolerated. I assure you, in the future, there will be laws against beauty. You may have heard of the conveyor system? It is the latest novelty from America. The philosophy of work at a continuously moving belt must be inculcated in the masses.... Robbery and murder must be made to appear less criminal than a moment of dreaming at the conveyor.... Just imagine now: beauty, moving, disturbing, suddenly invades the iron halls of industrial workshops! What would be the result? Movements would be confused, muscles would quiver, hands would commit the delay of a second, a split second of inexactitude ... errors of a second would grow into hours, hours into catastrophe.... My works would begin to produce output of lower quality than that of mv neighbours.... The concern would be ruined ... somewhere a bank would fail ... the stock exchange would respond with a sudden fall ... someone would put a bullet through his heart.... And all because a criminally-beautiful woman had passed through the factory, her skirts rustling."

Katya laughed. She knew nothing about conveyors. She had never been to a factory, all she knew about them was that their smoky chimneys spoiled the view. She was extremely fond of humanity in the mass, of the crowd, when she encountered it in the boulevards, and saw nothing in the least sinister in it. Two of her friends, among those who had supped beside the lake, were social-democrats. So her conscience was quite easy on that score. What her companion was saying, as he strolled along with raised head in the warm darkness of the alley, was new and interesting— as new and interesting, say, as the cubist art with which she had at one time adorned her drawing room. But that evening she was not bothering her head about philosophy....

"Beautiful women must have made you suffer," she said, "since you hate them so."

Then she laughed softly again, thinking of something else ... something that was as vague as the night, with its scent of flowers and leaves, its starlight streaming through the gaps in the tree-tops, and making the head swim with the sweet intimations of love. Not love for this new acquaintance—although it might be for him, after all, for he had aroused her desires. The thing which, such a short time ago, had seemed so difficult as to be almost hopeless, had come quite easily, and taken possession of her.

There is no knowing what might have happened to her in those days in Paris.... But there was a rude interruption ... the guns of world war boomed out.... And Katya never met the German any more.... Had he known of the imminence of war, or had it been just a guess? A little later, leaning against the stone balustrade, from which they could watch the lights of Paris shimmering like diamonds against the dark line of the horizon, the German had spoken with a kind of austere desperation of the inevitability of catastrophe. He had seemed obsessed with the idea of the futility of everything—of the beauty of the night, and Katya's charm.

She could not remember what she had said to him, but felt sure it had been some nonsense or other. But that did not matter. He had stood leaning his elbow on the top of the balustrade, his cheek almost touching Katya's shoulder. Katya knew that the night air was mingled with the fragrance of her scent, her shoulders, her hair.... No doubt—or at any rate so it seemed to her now—if he had placed his big hand on her shoulder she would not have moved away ... but nothing of the sort had happened....

The wind, fanning her cheeks and ruffling her hair, brought her back to the present. Sparks from the engine hung in the air. The train was crossing the steppe. Katya turned away from the window, unable to see anything for a moment. She retreated into her corner squeezing her cold hands together.

She felt suddenly remorseful. What was the meaning of these thoughts? Hardly a week had passed since she had heard of Vadim's death, and she had done worse than betray him.... She had given herself up to dreams of a man who had never been her lover.... The German must of course be dead ... he was an officer of the reserve. Dead, dead.... Everyone was dead, everything had perished, vanished, like that night on the terrace above the water near Paris, gone irreparably.

Katya compressed her lips to force back a moan. She closed her eyes. A rending grief tore at her breast.... There were not many people in the dirty compartment, feebly lit up by a flickering candle. Black, wakeful shadows of raised hands, tousled beards, unshod feet hanging from the upper berth, swept across the light.

148

No one was asleep, though it was very late. People spoke in under-tones.

"That's the worst district there is, I tell you...."

"What? Isn't it safe here, either?"

"Excuse me—what's that you say? Robbing going on here, too? It's astonishing—you'd think the Germans would put a stop to it. It's their duty to look after travellers ... since they've occupied the country they're bound to keep order."

"Begging your pardon, gentlemen, the Germans don't give a hoot for us.... Look after yourselves, my dears ... you began it! Oh, yes! Banditism is in our blood ... the people are swine.... "

To this a confident voice replied:

"The whole of Russian literature ought to be erased, and publicly burned. It's given us away. There isn't an honest man in the whole of Russia.... I was in Finland once, and I left my galoshes at the hotel. They sent a man on horseback after me with them. All in holes, they were.... That's an honest nation. And look how they dealt with the Communists—with the Russians as a whole! In the town of Abo, after the suppression of the rising, the Finns burned and tortured the man who was chief of the Red Guard then. You could hear that Bolshevik shrieking from the other side of the river."

"Oh, Lord, when shall we have something like order?"

"Excuse me, I've just come from Kiev. Grand shops, music in the cafes ... ladies walking about with diamonds on. That's what I call life! The bureaus for buying gold and all that sort of thing, doing a brisk trade.... The life of the streets in full swing ... a fine town...."

"And stuff for a pair of trousers costs half a year's salary. The speculators are strangling us.... And they all have such high fore-heads, you know, and blue serge suits.... They sit in the cafes selling order-sheets. You get up in the morning—no matches in the town. And a week later there they are—a ruble a box. Another time it's needles. I gave my wife two needles and a reel of cotton for her birthday. I used to give her diamond earrings.... The in-tellectuals are perishing, dying out...."

"The speculators should be ruthlessly shot down...."

"Now Mr. Comrade, none of your Bolshevism here!"

"What's the news in Kiev? Is the hetman sitting tight?"

"So long as the Germans hold out. They say another claimant to the Ukraine has appeared—Vasili Vishivanni. He's a descend-ant of the Hapsburgs, but he goes about in Ukrainian dress."

"Time to sleep, gentlemen, let's put out the candle."

"Put out the candle? We're in a train, aren't we?"

"It would be safer.... The windows can be seen from the fields, as the train passes."

Silence fell upon the compartment. The thump-thump of the wheels suddenly became very distinct. Sparks from the engine flew into the darkness of the steppe. Then somebody croaked out in the last stages of indignation:

"Who said: 'put out the candle'?" (Silence. An eerie sensation.) "Aha, the candle! So's he can rummage in the luggage. Find out who it was, and take him to the end of the carriage and chuck him out of the train."

Somebody began drearily sucking his teeth. A panic-stricken voice exclaimed:

"I was travelling last week, and a woman had two bundles stolen with the crook of a stick...."

"That's the Makhno men, you can be sure of that!"

"The Makhno men wouldn't soil their hands for two bundles. Robbing trains—that's their job."

"Don't let's start talking about them in the night, gentlemen."

Stories were told, one more horrible than the other. Blood-curdling incidents were related. It now appeared that the district through which the train was carrying them at such a leisurely pace was a perfect den of thieves, that the Germans always tried to avoid it, and that the guard had actually been removed at the previous station. In these villages the men flaunted beaver coats, the girls went in silks and velvets. Not a day passes but—rat-tat-tat—either the train is fired on from a machine gun, or the last few carriages are uncoupled and pushed along the rails, or the door opens when the train is at full speed, and bearded men with axes and sawed-off guns come in: hands up! The Russians they simply strip to their skins, but when they get hold of a Jew....

"A Jew? What have the Jews got to do with it?" shrieked out a clean-shaven man in a blue serge suit, the one who had been so enthusiastic about Kiev. "Why should the Jews be blamed for everything?"

This shriek put the finishing touch to the eerie atmosphere. Voices died down. Katya again closed her eyes. She had nothing worth stealing, unless it were the emerald ring. But she, too, was seized with an enervating fear. In order to still the painful sinkings at her heart she tried to recall once more the charm of that unfulfilled night. But she could hear nothing but the wheels beating out in the dark void: "Ka-ten-ka, Ka-ten-ka, Ka-ten-ka, everything's over and done...."

The train stopped abruptly, as if it had come up against a stone wall, the brakes emitted metallic squeals, chains rattled, glass rang, some boxes fell heavily from an upper bunk. What was most astonishing of all was that nobody so much as gasped. People leaped from their seats, looking from side to side, listening tensely. Words were unnecessary—it was clear that they were in for something unpleasant.

Rifle shots rang out in the darkness. The clean-shaven man in the blue serge suit rushed out of the compartment, plunging hither and thither in the attempt to find a hiding place. People were running past the windows beneath the banked up earth at the side of the lines. Bang-bang ... eyes were dazzled, ears deafened.... A terrifying voice cried: "No leaning out of the windows!" A hand grenade burst. The carriage swayed. The teeth of the passengers chattered, chattered.... Men were clambering on to the steps of the carriage, pushing the door open with the butt ends of their rifles. Brandishing hand grenades, their rifles knocking against one another in the crush, nine or ten men came tumbling into the compartment, breathing stertorously.

"Collect your things and get out into the fields."

"Get a move on, or else...."

"Mishka, cover the bourgeois with your hand grenade."

The passengers cowered. A fair-haired lad with a fierce pale face, threw himself forward, raising a hand grenade, standing there motionless for a moment with his hand over his head.

"We're going, we're going, we're going," moaned the voices of the passengers. And without any more protest, not uttering a word, they crept out of the train—some with suitcases, some with nothing but a pillow or a kettle.... One man, in pince-nez, his beard pushed sideways, actually smiled as he made his way through the throng of bandits.

The night air was chilly. The stars formed an exquisite canopy over the steppe. Katya sat down with her bundle on a pile of rotting sleepers. Since they hadn't started killing at once, they probably wouldn't kill them at all. She felt as weak as if she had just recovered from a fainting fit. "I might as well be sitting here on the sleepers, as roaming the streets of Ekaterinoslav without a crust of bread." She felt the chill on her shoulders, and yawned. In the train, tall peasants were dragging boxes from the luggage racks and throwing them out of the windows. The man in pince-nez made an attempt to climb up the embankment to the train.

"Gentlemen, gentlemen, I have a scientific apparatus in there, for God's sake be careful, it's very fragile...."

The others hissed at him, dragging him back by his waterproof into the crowd of passengers. Just at that moment a mounted detachment rode up in the darkness with a rattling of stirrups and stamping of hoofs. A powerfully-built man in a tall cap galloped a horse-length ahead of them, swaying in the saddle. The passengers huddled together. The detachment drew up beside the carriage with raised rifles and swords. The powerful man in the high cap cried in resonant tones:

"No losses, lads?"

"No, no! We're unloading the stuff. Send us carts," replied several voices.

The man in the tall cap turned his horse's head and rode into the crowd of passengers.

"Show your papers," he ordered, putting his horse through its paces, so that the froth from its muzzle flew into the fear-dilated eyes of the passengers. "Don't be afraid. You are under the protection of the people's army of Ataman Makhno. We'll only shoot officers and gendarmes." His voice rose menacingly, "—and speculators in the property of the people."

Again the man in the waterproof thrust himself forward, adjusting his pince-nez.

"Excuse me, I can give you my word of honour that there are no people belonging to the categories you mentioned among us. No one but peaceful citizens. My name is Obruchev, teacher of physics...."

"A teacher," said the powerful man reproachfully, "and going about with a pack of swine! Move aside! Don't touch that one, lads, he's a teacher."

A candle was brought out of the train. The inspection of papers began. And true enough there were neither officers nor gendarmes among the passengers. The clean-shaven man in the blue serge suit fidgeted about, nearer to the candle than anyone else.... He was no longer dressed in blue serge, but in a worn peasant coat and a soldier's peaked cap. Where could he have got these things? He must have had them with him in his suitcase. He patted the grim-visaged bandits on the shoulders in the friendliest manner.

"I'm a singer, glad to meet you, friends. We artistes need to study life, I'm an artiste."

He went on coughing and clearing his throat, till one of the raiders said mysteriously:

"We'll soon see what sort of an artiste you are. Till then you'd better not be too happy."

Small carts with iron-rimmed wheels drove up. The Makhno men flung suitcases, baskets and bundles on to them, and clambered up on top of everything, the drivers gave their wild cries, the well-nourished horses—three to a cart—broke into a gallop, and the carts disappeared in the steppe to the accompaniment of whistling and stamping.

The cavalry detachment galloped off too. A few Makhno men were still going to and fro in the neighbourhood of the carriage. The passengers chose a delegation by a show of hands, to ask the bandits' permission to proceed on their journey. The fair-haired lad, strung round with hand grenades, came up to them. The tuft of hair showing beneath the peak of his cap completely obscured one of his eyes. The other, blue and insolent, roved freely.

"What's this?" he said, eyeing each member of the delegation from head to foot. "Go? Where? How? You poor fools! Don't you know the engine driver has jumped off the engine and is now ten miles away in the steppe. I can't leave you here in the night, who knows what disorganized elements may be wandering about the steppe.... Citizens, attention, please!" (He came down the side of the embankment, adjusting his heavy belt. The rest of the Makhno men followed him, shouldering their rifles.) "Citizens, form fours.... Take your things and march into the steppe...."

As he passed Katya he bent over and touched her on the shoulder.

"Don't grieve, my lass," he said. "We won't hurt you.... Pick up your bundle and fall out and walk beside me...."

Her bundle in her hand, her shawl pulled down to her eyebrows, Katya began walking over the flat steppe. The youth with the tuft of hair strode on her left, glancing every now and then over his shoulder at the silent group of drearily marching captives. He whistled softly through his teeth.

"Who are you, where d'you come from?" he asked Katya.

She turned away her head without answering. She felt neither fear nor anxiety now, nothing but indifference. Everything seemed to be happening in a kind of dream. The youth repeated his question.

"So you don't want to lower yourself, you don't want to talk to a bandit," he said. "Too bad, little lady! You'll have to get rid of your aristocratic airs and graces. Times have changed .... "

Turning, he suddenly tore the rifle from his shoulders and shouted angrily at a dim figure detaching itself from the prisoners.

"Lagging behind, you swine! I'll shoot you down."

The figure plunged hastily back into the crowd. The youth gave a satisfied chuckle.

"As if he *could* run away, the fool? I suppose he only wanted to relieve nature. It's like this, little lady—you don't want to speak, but holding your tongue may be still worse, you know.... Don't be afraid, I'm not drunk. I don't talk when I'm drunk.... I'm not nice then.... Let's get acquainted!" He raised two fingers

153

to the peak of his cap. "Mishka Solomin! Deserter from the Red Army! A bandit by nature, most likely. A bad lot. You weren't mistaken there...."

"Where are we going?" asked Katya.

"To the village, to regimental headquarters. They'll investigate you, interrogate you—some they'll shoot, others they'll let go. As a young woman, you have nothing to fear.... Besides, I'm with you."

"I see you're the one I ought to fear most of all," said Katya, glancing obliquely at her companion.

She had not expected her words to sting him so. He drew himself up, breathing through his nostrils in spasmodic gusts, and his long countenance, pale beneath the starlight, broke into wrinkles. "Bitch!" he hissed. They went on in silence. As he walked, Mishka twisted himself a cigarette and lit up.

"You can swear yourself black in the face, but I know who you are. You belong to the officer class."

"Yes, I do," said Katya.

"Your husband's in the White bands, of course."

"Yes. My husband has been killed...."

"I wouldn't swear that it wasn't my bullet that finished him off."

He bared his teeth. Katya cast a rapid glance at him and stumbled: Mishka supported her elbow. She released her arm, shaking her head.

"I'm from the Caucasian front.... I've only been here four weeks, I've been fighting the White bands all the time. Plenty of bullets were lodged in aristocratic bones from this rifle."

Again Katya shook her head. He walked along in silence for a time, and then said, laughing:

"We certainly did get into a mess at the village of Umanskaya. Our Varnav Regiment was shot to smithereens. Commissar Sokolovsky was killed, Commander Sapozhkov went ahead with a handful of men, all wounded.... And I escaped through the German front to the Old Man. It's more fun here. Nobody stands over you—it's the People's Army. We're guerillas, little lady, we're not bandits. We choose our commanders ourselves.... And we get rid of them ourselves—just take out a revolver and bang-bang—off he goes! There's only one man over us all—the Old Man himself.... You think, if we plunder a train, everything will be squandered on drink? Nothing of the sort. All property is handed over to headquarters. Distribution to be made there. Some goes to the peasants, some to the army. The trains are our supply bases. And we, the People's Army, that is to say the people themselves, are in a state of war with Germany. That's how the matter stands. We cut the throats of the landowners. And the gendarmes and hetman

154

officers had better not fall into our hands—we finish them off with cold steel. Small Austrian and German detachments we push back to Ekaterinoslav. That's the sort of bandits we are."

It seemed as if there could never be an end to the stars over the steppe. But far away in the direction towards which they were travelling, the sky was turning a faint green. Katya stumbled more and more frequently, and could not always suppress a sigh. But Mishka was impervious to everything—it seemed as if he could have marched on for thousands of miles, his rifle at his back. Katya had now only one care: not to betray her growing weakness, not to give this contemptuous braggart an excuse to pity her....

"You're all rotten, all of you," she said, halting and adjusting her shawl to give herself a breathing space, and once more toiling over the wormwood and the gopher holes. "Why should we bear sons for you to kill? It's a sin to kill, and that's all there is to it."

"We know all that! That's all woman's stuff, it's as old as the hills," said Mishka glibly. "Our commissar explained it to us this way: 'look at everything from the class point of view...' you're aiming your gun at a class phenomenon, not a human being. See? Pity doesn't come in here, it would be sheer counterrevolution. There's something more important, my dear...."

Suddenly his voice changed strangely. It sounded hollow, as if he were listening to his own words.

"I shan't always be dangling about the front with a rifle. Everyone says Mishka is a lost soul, a drunkard, he'll end up at the bottom of a pit. That's the truth, but not the whole truth.... I'm in no hurry to die, in fact I don't want to die a bit.... The bullet which will finish me hasn't yet been cast."

He pushed the tuft of hair off his forehead.

"What's a man nowadays—an army coat and a rifle, is that all? Oh no, it isn't! I want ... God knows what I want.... I don't know myself.... I ask myself—is it a pile of money? No. The human being in me suffers.... Especially now—when we have a revolution, a civil war. My feet are sore, I suffer from cold, from my wounds—and all out of class-consciousness, for my own class. In March I had to lie half the day in an ice-hole, under machine-gun fire all the time.... That makes me a hero as regards the front, doesn't it? But in my own eyes—on the quiet—who am I? A man half crazy with drink, angry with the world and himself, pulling a knife out of his boot top...."

Mishka once again straightened himself, inhaling the freshness of the night. His face looked sad, almost feminine. His hands were thrust deep in his greatcoat pockets, and he seemed now to be addressing, not Katya, but some shade floating before him.

"Education ... I know all about that ... my mind is like a savage's....
My children will get education. But I'll always be what I am now—a
bad lot. That's my fate.... They write books about intellectuals. Oh,
what a lot of fine words! Why doesn't anybody write a book about
me? D'you think only an intellectual can go mad? I hear shrieks in
my sleep.... I wake up, ready to kill all over again...."

Horsemen came galloping out of the darkness, shouting from
far away: "Halt! Halt!" Mishka seized his rifle in his hands. "Halt
your.... Don't you know your own people?" Leaving Katya's side,
he went up to the horsemen and held a long consultation with
them.

The prisoners stood about, whispering anxiously to one another. Katya sat down on the ground, dropping her face on to her
knees. From the east, where the dawn was turning a lighter green,
came a whiff of damp air, laden with the smoke of burning dung,
the immemorial smell of steppe villages.

The stars of this endless night began to pale and disappear.
Katya had to get up and go on again. Soon the barking of dogs
could be heard, and strawricks, wellsweeps, and the roofs of the
village, came into sight. The sleeping geese looked like patches of
snow on the fields. The rosy dawn was reflected on the flat surface
of the lake. Mishka strode on, frowning.

"Don't go with the rest, I'll look after you myself."

"All right," replied Katya. His voice seemed to reach her from
a great distance.

She did not care where she went, so long as she could lie down
and sleep....

Through sleep-heavy lids she made out tall sunflowers against a
background of green shutters, on which were painted flowers and
birds. Mishka tapped with his nails on the flawed glass of the window. A door in the white wall of the hut opened slowly and the
tousled head of a peasant peeped out. The ends of his moustache
moved upwards as he bared his teeth in a yawn. "You can come in,
if you like," he said. Katya staggered into the hut, which rang with
the alarmed buzzing of flies. The peasant took a sheepskin coat and
pillow from behind a partition wall. "Sleep," he said, and went away.
The next thing Katya knew she was on a bed behind the partition.
It seemed to her that Mishka was bending over her, settling the pillow
under her head. Then she sank blissfully into oblivion.

The sound of wheels penetrated her dreams. They clattered
on and on. Innumerable carriages rolled by. And the sun was
reflected back on them by the windows of towering buildings.
Curved tiled roofs.... Paris. Carriages with elegant women in them

rolling by. People shouting, turning, pointing. Women waving lacy parasols ... the carriages galloping by faster and faster. Oh, God! It was pursuit. In Paris, on the boulevards! There they were! Vast shadows of shaggy horses against a greenish dawn. Nowhere to move, nowhere to escape! What a stamping of hoofs! What shouting! Terrifying....

Katya sat up on the bed. Outside the window, wheels were clattering, horses neighing. Through the uncurtained opening in the partition she could see people coming and going, armed from head to foot. The hut was filled with the humming of voices, the stamping of boots. People were crowding round the table, bending over something that lay on it. The room was filled with the sound of salty words. It was broad daylight, and a few dim rays struggled through the windows and penetrated the blue haze of tobacco smoke.

Nobody paid any attention to Katya, who sat on the bed adjusting her shawl and tidying her hair. Fresh troops appeared to have entered the village. The anxious hum arising from those crowding into the hut showed that something extremely important was afoot. A harsh, stuttering voice, with feminine overtones, cried imperiously:

"Devil take him! Call him, the skunk!"

The voices and cries flew out of the hut into the yard and the street, where three-horse wagons, saddled horses, groups of soldiers, sailors, and armed peasants were standing about.

"Petrichenko ... where's Petrichenko? Run and get him!"

"Run yourself, you bastard! Hi, call the Colonel, brother! Where can he be, damn him! There he is, asleep in a cart, drunk! Throw a pail of water over the devil.... Hi, you with the pail, go to the well—we can't wake the Colonel.... Hi, pals, water's no good—smear his mug with tar.... He's awake, he's awake.... Tell him the Old Man's in a rage.... He's coming, he's coming...."

The tall man in the high cap came into the hut. He had slept so soundly that his inflamed eyes could hardly be made out on his crimson, moustached countenance. Grumbling, he pushed his way to the table, and sat down.

"What are you at, you bastard? Selling the army? They've bought you!" stuttered the shrill, rasping voice.

"What's up? I had a sleep, that's all," boomed out the colonel, in a voice which seemed to come from the inside of a barrel.

"I'll tell you what's up ... what's up indeed!" said a choking voice. "You let the Germans through in your sleep, that's what's up."

"I let the Germans through? I didn't let anyone through."

"Where are your outposts? We marched all night, and didn't come across a single outpost. Why is the army in a trap?"

"Why shout? How do I know where the Germans are? The steppe's so vast...."

"It's your fault, you rotter!"

"Now, now!"

"It's all your fault, I say!"

"Let go of me!"

A sudden silence fell in the hut. People rushed away from the table. There was the sound of heavy breathing and a struggle. A hand holding a revolver was struck upwards. Several hands grasped it. A shot rang out. Stopping up her ears, Katya flung herself on the pillow. Bits of plaster fell from the ceiling. And once again there was a hum of voices, a cheerful one this time. Colonel Petrichenko rose, his sheepskin cap almost touching the ceiling, and went triumphantly out of the house surrounded by swaggering rowdies.

Outside the window all was stir and bustle. Men were getting into the saddle and clambering on to carts. Whips cracked, axles squeaked, men swore outrageously. The hut emptied, and then Katya realized that if she had not been able till now to see the person who had shouted so imperiously in such womanish tones, it was because he was too small. He was seated at the table, with his back to Katya, his elbows on a map.

His long, straight, chestnut-coloured hair fell over shoulders as narrow as a boy's. A munitions strap crossed his black cloth jacket, two revolvers and a sword were thrust into his leather belt, and his feet, in elegant spurred riding boots, were crossed beneath the table. Shaking his head from side to side, his greasy locks moving across his back, he was hastily writing something, his pen spluttering and making holes in the paper. The peasant who had given up his bed to Katya came cautiously into the hut. His face was pink and propitiatory, and bits of hay were clinging to his hair. Blinking foolishly, he sat down on a bench opposite the man writing, thrust his hands beneath him, and rubbed his bare feet against each other.

"All the time worrying, worrying, Nestor Ivanovich, and I was hoping you would stay to dinner. We slaughtered a calf yesterday.... I must have felt you would come...."

"I have no time ... don't disturb me...."

"Aha!" (The peasant fell silent and stopped blinking. His eyes became wise and heavy. For a short time he sat watching the writer's hand.)

"Nestor Ivanovich! Do you intend to give battle in our village?"

"We'll see...."

"Of course, in war, you can never tell.... I only thought if there is to be fighting, something ought to be done about the cattle.... Should we drive them into the farmsteads?"

The long-haired man threw down his pen and ran the fingers of his small hand through his locks as he read what he had written. Feeling an itching in his beard and under his armpits, the peasant scratched himself. This seemed to remind him of something:

"Nestor Ivanovich, and what about the material for us? You let us have cloth—good cloth.... You can see at a glance it's army cloth. Six cartloads, there were...."

"Isn't it enough? Aren't you satisfied? Isn't it enough?"

"Why, of course it's enough.... We don't know how to thank you for *that*. You know very well—we sent you forty men from the village to fight. My own son went. 'I must shed my blood for the cause of the peasants, Father,' he said. If that isn't enough we old fellows will go and fight.... Just you fight, we'll support you.... And about the cloth, if the Germans (which God forbid!) should fall on us, you know what their reprisals are—what are we to do? Can we be sure about the battle?"

The back of the long-haired man lengthened. He withdrew his hand from his head, and gripped the edge of the table. His breathing could be heard. He thrust his head forward. The peasant began cautiously retreating from him along the bench, and, taking his hands away from beneath him, sidled out of the hut.

The chair on which the long-haired man had been sitting, tilted sideways, and he kicked it out of his way. At last Katya, trembling, beheld the face of this little man in the black semi-military attire. He looked like a disguised monk. Furious, piercing, brown eyes glanced at her out of deep hollows beneath powerful brows. His face was slightly pockmarked, yellow-hued, clean-shaven—though effeminate-looking, there was something crude and fierce in it, as in the face of an adolescent. But the eyes were old and full of wisdom.

Katya would have trembled still more if she had known that she was in the presence of Makhno himself. He stared at the young woman sitting on the side of the bed, in dusty boots and a crumpled but still elegant silk dress, her black shawl tied peasant fashion: apparently he could not understand what sort of a bird had flown into the hut. His long upper lip twitched in a smile which exposed a row of widely-spaced teeth.

"Who do you belong to?" he rapped out.

Katya, who did not understand him, began to tremble. The smile disappeared from his face, and the expression it left behind made Katya's lips quiver.

"Who are you? A prostitute? If you have syphilis, I'll have you shot. Well? Can't you speak Russian? Are you ill? Are you healthy?"

159

"I'm a prisoner," said Katya scarcely audibly.

"What can you do? Can you manicure? We'll supply you with instruments."

"All right," she replied, still more softly.

"But don't start any depravity in the army ... d'you hear? You can stay. I shall come tonight after the battle—you can do my nails for me."

Many were the tales about Makhno among the people. It was said that, while doing hard labour in the prison at Akatui, he had tried several times to escape and had once succeeded, but was trapped in a shed, and fought the soldiers with an axe. After being beaten almost to a pulp with the butt ends of rifles, he was put in irons. And three years he had sat chained up, silent as a weasel, trying vainly, day and night, to tear the iron handcuffs from his wrists. It was there, while doing hard labour, that he had made friends with the anarchist Arshinov-Marin, whose disciple he had become.

Nestor Makhno was from the village of Gulyai-Polye, in the Ekaterinoslav region. His father was a carpenter. While still a mere child he served in a small general store, where he was cuffed and beaten, and nicknamed "the weasel" on account of his savage temper and brown eyes. He was sacked while still a mere urchin for throwing boiling water over the senior shop assistant in revenge for a thrashing. He then gathered a gang around him, raiding melon beds and orchards, doing all sorts of mischief, living a free life, till his father put him into a printshop. There, it was said, he was noticed by the anarchist Volin, who, eighteen years later, became chief of staff and chief adviser to Makhno. Volin was said to have taken a fancy to the lad and taught him to read and write and instructed him in anarchism, afterwards putting him to school, when Makhno had become a teacher. But this was not true. Makhno was never a teacher and it is more likely that he only got to know Volin much later, and learned about anarchism from Arshinov, while serving a sentence of hard labour.

In 1903 Makhno was once more at his tricks in Gulyai-Polye, this time, not in the orchards and vegetable plots but in the estates of the gentry, and the barns of the shopkeepers: stealing a horse, cleaning out the contents of a cellar, sometimes sending a threatening letter to a shopkeeper, ordering him to put money under a stone. He was at that time involved in a strange, drunken league with the police.

Makhno began to be held in real terror, but the peasants never gave him up to the authorities, for the nearer the time for the 1905 revolution came, the more resolutely Makhno annoyed the landowners. And when at last the estates blazed, and the peasantry sallied forth to plough the lands of the gentry, Makhno made his way to the town, and to important doings. Early in 1906 he and his followers attacked the treasury at Berdyansk, shot three officials, and seized the cashbox, but he was betrayed by a comrade and served time in Akatui....

Twelve years later, freed by the February revolution, he turned up in Gulyai-Polye again, where the peasantry, ignoring the ambiguous instructions of the Provisional Government, had chased away the landowners and shared the land among themselves. Makhno reminded them of his former services and was elected vice-chairman of the district Zemstvo. He immediately declared himself flatly for the "free peasant system", declaring at a sitting of the local authorities that those who supported the Zemstvo were bourgeois elements and Cadets. In the heat of argument he shot down a member of the administration, and appointed himself both chairman and district commissar.

The Provisional Government could do nothing with him, but a year later the Germans came, and Makhno had to flee. For some time he roamed over Russia, until, in the summer of 1918, he turned up in Moscow, at that time teeming with anarchists. Here he met many famous characters: old Arshinov, following with a jaundiced eye revolutionary events, which by some incomprehensible quirk of fate were being ruled by the Bolsheviks; that powerful theoretician and pillar of anarchy ("the mother of order"), Volin, whose beard and hair had never known a comb; then there was the ambitious and impatient Baron, Arten, Teper, Yakov Ali, Krasnokutsky, Glagson, Tsintsiper, and Chernyak and many another great men, all of whom had failed to get a footing in the revolution, and were lingering on in Moscow, penniless, with only one agenda for their daily sessions: "System of organization, and financial matters".... Subsequently, some of them became leaders in the Makhno anarchist system, while others took part in the blowing up of the Moscow Committee of Bolsheviks in Leontyevsky Lane.

The arrival of Makhno undoubtedly made an impression on the anarchists languishing in the cafes of Moscow. Makhno was a man of action and, moreover, an extremely determined individual. It was decided that he should go to Kiev, where it was planned to shoot Hetman Skoropadsky and his generals.

Makhno, with an anarchist to assist him, went to Belenikhino on the Ukrainian frontier, evading the vigilance of the terrible commissar Sayenko, who kept a watch on the roads. He disguised himself as an officer, but suddenly changed his mind about entering Kiev. The free air of the steppe lured him back, conspiracy was not in his line. He made straight for Gulyai-Polye.

11–559

In his native village he collected five or six reliable lads. With axes, knives and sawed-off rifles, they entrenched themselves in a gorge near the landowner Reznikov's estate, crept up to the house under cover of night, and quietly cut the throats of the proprietor and his three brothers, officials of the local police, and set fire to the house. By this means he laid hands on seven rifles, a revolver, horses, saddles and a few police uniforms.

Now well-armed and on horseback, he and his little band fell upon the farmsteads without the loss of a moment, and burned them from all four sides. Increasing the number of his followers, Makhno galloped from one end of the district to the other, till he had cleared it of landowners. And then he embarked upon an adventure which spread his fame far and wide.

It was Whitsuntide. The landowner Mirgorodsky, a magnate of the steppe, was marrying his daughter to one of the hetman's colonels. The wedding was attended by the bolder spirits among neighboring landowners, not afraid, even in such perilous times, to gallop over the steppe highway. There were also guests from further away in the district, and from Kiev.

The Mirgorodsky estate was strongly guarded by gendarmes. A machine gun was posted in the attic of the owner's house, and the bridegroom himself was escorted by his brother officers, tall fellows in flowing blue Turkish trousers, long enough, following an ancient custom, to sweep the ground, tunics of crimson cloth, and Astrakhan caps with a golden tassel reaching almost to the waist. The curved swords at their sides knocked against their broad-cuffed goatskin boots.

The bride was not long from England, where she had had the finishing touches put to her education in a boarding school for young ladies, but she could already speak Ukrainian tolerably, and wore embroidered blouses, bead necklaces, ribbons and high red boots. Her noble parent had just received from Kiev a velvet robe, made to order, and trimmed with fur, an exact copy of that worn by Hetman Mazeppa in the well-known portrait. Every effort was made to celebrate the wedding in the old fashion, and though century-old mead was hard to obtain in the troublous Ukraine, there was an abundance of all that was required for a sumptuous feast.

After mass had been said, the bride was led across the park to the new stone church. Her divinely beautiful bridesmaids accompanied her, singing, and she herself seemed to have come out of an old Cossack song. "Ha-ha!", said the friends of the groom to the girls, as they stood by the fence, "it looks as if the good old times had come back to the Ukraine!" Handfuls of oats were scattered over the young couple as they came out onto the church porch after the marriage ceremony. The bride's father, in his robe of Mazeppa, blessed them with an ancient icon from Mezhigorye in his hands. Champagne was drunk, to the accompaniment of hilarious toasts, the wineglasses were broken, and the young couple left for the station in a motorcar, the guests remaining to feast and drink.

Night fell over the great courtyard in front of the mansion, where the servants and gendarmes passed the time in the mazes of the dance. All the windows in the house shone merrily. The Jewish orchestra from Alexandrovsk sawed and tootled with all their might. The bride's father had already performed a fantastic *hopak*, and was drinking soda water. The girls and older ladies were cooling themselves at the open windows, and the bridegroom's friends, all Cossack officers, were returning to the supper table, their swords rattling, boasting they would go right to Moscow and kill the accursed Muscovites.

Just then there appeared amidst the merry-makers a little officer in the uniform of the hetman's gendarmes. There was nothing surprising in the police turning up on the estate on such a day. He came in modestly, bowing silently, and casting sideways glances at the musicians. Somebody may have noted that his uniform seemed to be rather big for him, and one lady said to another in a frightened voice: "Who's that? Isn't he terrible?" Although the unknown officer kept his eyes lowered as much as possible, they seemed to glow diabolically, in spite of himself. But when one has been drinking, all sorts of wild suspicions come into one's mind....

After the mazurkas and waltzes the orchestra struck up a tango. Two or three dancers in red tunics, still firm on their legs, seized their partners. Somebody gave orders for the overhead lights to be extinguished. In the half-dark, to the tender strains which seemed to be coming out of the depths of years long past, the couples languished, almost swooning as if in the throes of an ecstatic death.

Then it was that the shots rang out. The crowd of guests stood as if petrified. The music broke off. Makhno in the uniform of a police officer, stood at the supper table near the half-open window, a revolver in each hand, shooting at the red tunics. A tall, crimson-faced colonel, one of the bridegroom's friends, throwing out his arms, fell heavily against the table, which overturned under the weight of his body. The women gave piercing shrieks. Another of the male guests tried to draw his sword, but fell face down on the carpet before he could do so.... Three rushed at Makhno with drawn swords, of whom two fell instantly, while the third fled to the window, squealing like a rabbit. Two more men in police uniforms, ferocious-looking, with forelocks struggling from beneath their caps appeared in the doorway opposite, and opened fire on the guests. Women darted hither and thither in distraction. Bodies were falling. The bride's father could not rise from his chair, and Makhno, approaching him, sent a bullet right into his throat. In the courtyard and the park, too, there were loud reports, as the guests rushed to the windows and leaped out. A very few managed to hide in the bushes and among the rushes around the pond. The servants and gendarmes were slaughtered wholesale. Then Makhno's bravos harnessed carts, loading them till daybreak with all sorts of objects, including arms. The sun rose over the flaming estate.

This audacious raid made an overwhelming impression in the village. By that time the peasants were completely crushed—by the Germans, by the newly-introduced proprietors, by the vindictive promptitude of the gendarmes' reprisals. Not trusting the peasants, the landowners refused to give their lands for rent, and were demanding not merely the crops of the present harvest, but the return in kind of last year's losses. The peasants could do nothing but bemoan their plight. Then Makhno appeared and started a terror. The rumour flew from village to hamlet that a champion had arisen.

The peasants took fresh heart. Estates went up in flames. Wheat stacks blazed in the steppe. Guerilla detachments made audacious raids on steamers and barges laden with grain for Germany. The disturbance spread to the right bank of the Dnieper. Orders to quell the rioting were given to Austrian and German troops. Hundreds of punitive detachments were sent about the country. And then Makhno, with his small, but well-armed detachment, took the initiative to attacking the Austrian troops.

At that time Makhno's army was of no great size. Its permanent nucleus consisted of two or three hundred daredevils. They included Black Sea sailors, war veterans for one reason or another unable to show themselves in their native villages, lesser leaders, merging their detachments with Makhno's, and men without kith or kin, fighting for the hell of it and for a gay life.

And gradually individual anarchists, the so-called "Fighters", getting wind of the new bands roving on horseback at their own sweet will, went over to the army. Arriving at Makhno's headquarters on foot, ragged and hungry, a bomb in one pocket and a volume of Kropotkin in the other, the anarchists said to the Old Man:

"We've heard you're a genius. We want to see if it's true."

"Look your fill," the Old Man would reply.

"You see," said they, "if you're really such a wonder, you'll make the pages of world history. Who knows, you may be destined to become a second Kropotkin."

"Who knows?" echoed the Old Man.

They followed in the baggage trains of the Old Man, drank with him, uttered wonderful words, which was what he loved most of all, about history and fame. And gradually a few of them began to be promoted to responsible and conspicuous posts. And each of these had his cart full of booty, captured in battle: a case of brandy, a barrel of gold, a sack of clothing. Such individuals were Chaldon, Skoropionov, Yugolobov, Cherednyak, Engarets, "the Frenchman", and many others. During their prolonged halts they gathered around them brothels well supplied with gay young women, and got up "Athenian nights", assuring the Old Man that such an attitude to the sex question would make for the emancipated life, and that syphilis was a mere trifle, which would not matter a bit after absolute freedom had been achieved. Makhno called his anarchists reptiles, and was always threatening to have them shot, but he tolerated them for their book-knowledge, and because they understood the meaning of fame.

The army had no permanent headquarters. It hurled itself from one end of the province to another, on horseback and in military carts, as need arose. When a raid was meditated, or a battle was imminent, Makhno would dispatch messengers to the villages, himself uttering a rousing speech in some crowded place, at the end of which his followers threw lengths of cloth and print from the carts into the crowd. In a single day the nucleus of his army was increased by peasant guerillas. When the battle was over these volunteers returned no less rapidly to their villages, concealed their arms, and by the time the German artillery rattled up in search of the foe, they were lazily scratching themselves at their gates as if all this was nothing to do with them. The Austrian and German troops were invariably baffled in their search for Makhno, and this ubiquitous devil always seemed to be at their rear. The guerillas, like the nomads of old, did not fight any decisive battles, merely scattering over the plain with shouts, whistles, and volleys of firing, on horseback and in carts, only to gather together again at a spot where they were least expected, and make another attack.

The village was now deserted. Makhno followed the army in a wagon drawn by three horses, with a carpet laid over the floor of it. It was full noon. A plump girl, her face disfigured by weeping, her skirts girded high, was sweeping the hut out with a twig broom. The owner of the hut sat at the open window, sighing heavily as he glanced towards the hills, behind which all the infantry and cavalry had disappeared, and on the crest of which could now be discerned the sails of two windmills peacefully revolving: his conversation with Makhno had apparently not reassured him.

Katya went out to the well, had a wash, and set her clothing to rights. The master of the house called her to breakfast, and she ate two boiled dumplings and drank some milk. Then, not knowing what to do with herself, or what she might expect, she seated herself at the window. It was very hot. On the road, a number of hens were strutting about, pecking at the freshly dropped dung. Sunflowers drooped their golden heads behind palings, and the cherry trees were hung with fruit. Hawks hovered over the village. The master of the house cleared his throat and sighed.

"You should hike your skirt still higher over your head, shameless wench!" he said to the tear-sodden girl. "What if they *did* paw you? You're not the first."

The girl drew a sobbing breath, flung down her besom and let her skirt down over her plump white legs. The man allowed his gaze to rest on the besom for a few minutes.

"Which of them was it? Tell me, Alexandra, don't be afraid!"

"I don't know his name, the beast! It wasn't one of ours.... He wore glasses."

"There you are!" he said, as if pleased. "Glasses.... It's one of that lot—an anarchist." He turned to Katya. "My niece Alexandra.... I sent her to the barn for straw.... Know where the barn is? She came back in the morning all in rags.... Faugh!"

"He was drunk. He threatened me with his revolver. What was I to do?"

Alexandra moaned softly. Her uncle stamped his bare foot at her.

"Get out! I wonder I'm alive myself!"

The girl turned and fled. He began hawking and coughing again, his eyes on the distant hills.

"What's to be done? We don't enjoy feeding these bandits, do we? We have to give them horses for their carts.... And they gallop for eighty miles, the devils.... A horse isn't a machine, it needs loving care.... All our beasts are crippled now. Ah me, war...."

The chimney of the lamp hanging over the table rattled in its socket, the windowpanes rang softly. The hot air seemed to heave a sigh. Far-off thunder rolled over the earth. The owner of the house hastily thrust the upper part of his body out of the window and once again looked long at the hilltops where, beside the windmills, the figure of a lone horseman was silhouetted against the sky. Then, neatly bunching the tips of his fingers, he crossed himself before the picture in the corner.

"It's the German artillery firing on our lads," he said, scratching himself beneath his faded shirt. "What times, what times!"

He picked up the besom and threw it into the corner before going out of the house, his bare toes curling inwards. Once again there came a distant rumble over the village, and Katya, unable to sit any longer in the hut, went out into the midday heat. The sultry air was saturated with the smell of dung.

At that moment a nervous group of yesterday's passengers appeared in the street. In front, looking over the top of his pince-nez, strode Obruchev, the teacher of physics. He wore a rubber mackintosh and galoshes, and seemed to have constituted himself the leader, one who was trusted by the rest.

"Come and join us!" he cried to Katya.

She went up to them. The passengers were dishevelled and haggard. The two elderly ladies were puffy with weeping. The disguised speculator was not to be seen.

"One of our party has disappeared, leaving no trace, he must have been shot," said Obruchev cheerfully. "His fate awaits us all, friends, unless we can gather up sufficient energy. We must decide without delay the question: whether to await the issue of the battle, or to profit by the fact that we are apparently left unguarded, and try to reach the railway on foot. Each speaker is allowed one minute."

They all began speaking at once. Some pointed out that if the bandits overtook them in the open steppe they would undoubtedly all perish. Others, that there was, after all, a faint chance of salvation in flight. Yet others, confident that the Germans would be the victors, insisted that they should wait for the end of the battle. When a clattering again reached them from over the hills, all fell silent, straining their eyes to gaze at the place, where nothing could be seen but the lazily revolving sails of the windmills. Obruchev uttered a concise speech, in the course of which he enumerated all these conflicting ideas. The two ladies hung upon his lips as if he were a prophet. Coming to no conclusion, they all stood there among the hens and sparrows in the deserted street, where there was not a soul to take pity on their fellow countrymen—on Russians.... Not a soul! A woman with uncovered head looked out of the window, yawned, and turned away. An angry-looking peasant, coming round the corner with his shirt unbelted, passed the prisoners without a glance, picking up a lump of clay to throw with all his might at somebody's boar. Some hawks soared above the village, looking down indifferently on the plundered and unwanted townspeople.

A cloud of dust rose from beyond the hills. The horseman galloped away from the windmills and disappeared from view. One of the passengers suggested going back to the Volost office, where they had all spent the night. The two ladies were the first to act on the suggestion, but when the carts, each with three horses, came galloping headlong over the crest of the hill, the rest of the prisoners followed their example. Only Katya and the teacher of physics, his arms folded heroically beneath his mackintosh, remained in the street.

There were some four or five carts. Skirting the lake, they appeared in the village. They were bringing back wounded. The first of them drew up in front of the windows of a hut. The driver, a tall guerilla fighter in an unbuttoned leather jacket, cried out:

"Nadezhda—here's your man!"

A woman rushed out of the hut, tearing off her apron, and threw herself upon the cart with low wails. A lad with a sickly greenish countenance got off the cart, put his arm round the woman's neck and staggered into the hut, his head drooping, his body doubled up. The cart went on to the next house, from which sprang three gaudily attired girls.

"Take your man, my doves—he's slightly wounded," cried the driver to them gaily.

After this, he reined in the horses to a walk, looking for a place to take his last wounded to. In the cart sat Mishka Solomin, blinking, his head bound with the bloodstained fragments of a shirt, his teeth set. The driver suddenly halted his horses.

"Whoa.... Good heavens! Ekaterina Dmitrevna, can it be you?"

Katya was taken completely by surprise. Gasping in her agitation, she ran towards the cart. In it stood none other than Alexei Krasilnikov, his feet set well apart, one fist doubled against his side, the other holding the reins. His cheeks were partially concealed by a curly beard, his eyes were joyous. He had hand grenades in his belt, a machine-gun belt slung across his leather jacket, a cavalry rifle at his back.

"Ekaterina Dmitrevna, what are you doing here? Whose hut are you living in? That one? Mitrofan's? He's my third cousin, his name's Krasilnikov, too. Look—poor Mishka—his head's half blown away by shrapnel."

Katya walked beside the cart. Alexei was still hot and excited after the battle. His eyes and teeth gleamed....

"We beat the Germans into a cocked hat.... The silly fools.... They threw themselves three times against our machine guns. They're lying all over the field, poor devils! Now the Old Man has something to dress the army in.... Whoa! Mitrofan! Come out of your den! Take in a wounded hero. And you, Ekaterina Dmitrevna, mind you don't go away from this house. It's not healthy for you here...."

Mellow strokes pealed from the belfry. All over the village, wicket gates banged, shutters were opened, women ran into the street, peasants came out cautiously, a regular crowd of people appeared from nowhere; singing and talking they went out into the steppe to meet the victorious Makhno army.

Katya helped Alexei Krasilnikov to lift the half-dead Mishka into the Mitrofan yard, and carry him into the cool shed, where they laid him on Alexandra's cot. Katya set about changing his bandages, with difficulty removing the blood-stiffened rags from his hair. Mishka set his teeth and made no sound. When Katya began washing the terrible wound on the right side of his skull, Alexandra, who was holding the basin, groaned and staggered. Seizing the basin, Alexei pushed her aside.

"There's a sharp bone sticking out at the side, see!" he said to Katya. "Alexandra, bring the sugar nippers...."

"There aren't any—they're broken!"

Katya picked out the fragments of bones from the wound with her fingernails. She gave a pull. Mishka bellowed with pain. It must be a fragment. Her nails slipped, she plunged deeper. She pulled it out.

Alexei drew a loud sigh, and then laughed.

"That's the way we fight—the peasant way!"

Katya bandaged Mishka's head with clean linen. Covered with sweat, quivering all over, he lay beneath a sheepskin coat. Suddenly he opened his eyes. Alexei bent over him.

"Well now—are we going to live?"

"I boasted to her yesterday and this is the end of my boasting," said Mishka with a smile like that of death itself.

He looked at Katya, who was drying her hands and had also come up to bend over him. His lips moved:

"Look after her, Alyosha."

"All right, all right."

"I had evil thoughts about her.... She must be sent to the town."

Again he fixed an almost frenzied glance on Katya. Pain and fever he overcame like some trifle, mere nonsense, a passing annoyance. The proximity of death aroused in him a veritable whirlwind of passions and conflicting desires. At that moment he did not think of himself as a drunkard and an evildoer, but as a Russian soul, tossed like a bird in the storm; it seemed to him that he was no less suitable than another for heroic deeds, and that the loftiest tasks were not too high for him....

"Let him sleep," said Alexei softly. "He'll be all right. He's a fine lad, he'll sleep it off."

Katya went out of the house with Alexei. She still seemed to be living in a kind of waking trance beneath the boundless sky stretched over the sultry plain, beneath the immemorial smell of burning dung. Here once again, after an age-long halt, men were galloping over the steppe on horseback, baring their teeth to the free wind ... here passions could be quenched, as thirst is quenched, at a brimming cup.

She felt no fear. Her grief, not needed here by anyone, not needed by herself, seemed to have curled itself up for a sleep. She would have answered the call to self-sacrifice, to great deeds, with unthinking ease. If a voice had said: "Die," she would simply have sighed and raised clear eyes skyward.

"Vadim Petrovich is dead," she said, "I'm not going back to Moscow. I have nobody there ... and nothing.... I don't know what's happened to my sister. I meant to go somewhere, to Eka-terinoslav, perhaps...."

His feet set well apart, Alexei looked down at the ground.

"A pity about Vadim Petrovich," he said, shaking his head. "He was a good man."

"He was," said Katya, her eyes filling with tears. "He was a very good man."

"You wouldn't listen to me then. Of course we stand for our side and you stand for yours. There's nothing to get upset about in that. But how can you fight against the people? D'you suppose we'll ever give in? You saw the peasants today, didn't you? Still, he was a just man...."

Looking up at a heavily laden branch from a cherry tree hanging over the wattle fence, Katya said:

"Alexei Ivanovich, tell me what I am to do. One must live...."

The moment she said it, she felt afraid—her words seemed to have floated into the void. Alexei did not reply immediately.

"Do? What a question—just like the gentry! What—you, an educated woman, who can speak several languages, a beautiful woman like you—to ask a peasant what you're to do!"

An expression of supreme contempt passed over his face. He gently rattled the hand grenades dangling from his belt. Katya shrank into herself.

"You'll find plenty to do in the town," he said. "You might go to a tavern, to sing or dance. You can become a cocotte, or go into an office and do typewriting. You'll be all right."

Katya's head drooped. She felt he was looking at her, and she could not raise her head to meet his glance. And suddenly she understood, as then with Mishka, why Alexei stared so fixedly over her head. These were no times for forgiveness and sweetness. She was not on their side, so she was an enemy. She had asked how she was to live. She had asked a fighter, still hot from the

170

saddle, from the whistling of bullets, from the intoxication of victory ... how to live! The question now sounded absurd in her own ears. If she had asked him whom she could attach herself to, whose cart she should follow in its flight over the steppe, in quest of what freedom, his eyes would no doubt have responded with a cordial sparkle....

Katya understood all this, and dodged like some wild creature. For the first time in all these days she attempted to stick up for herself.

"You don't understand me, Alexei Ivanovich. It's not my fault that I'm driven like a dead leaf over the earth. What should I love? What should I cherish? I was never taught, so don't ask it of me. First teach me." (He had stopped knocking the grenades together, a sign that he was on the alert, listening.) "Vadim Petrovich joined the White Army against my will. I didn't want him to. He reproached me for having no hate, too.... I see it all, I understand, Alexei Ivanovich. But I'm ... just an onlooker. It's terrible. That's just my trouble. That's why I asked you what I was to do, how I was to live...."

She stopped speaking and looked frankly, clear-eyed, into the face of Alexei Ivanovich. He blinked. His expression became a little sheepish, embarrassed, completely baffled. His hand went up to the back of his head, as if to scratch it.

"You're right, it's a real drama," he said, wrinkling up his nose. "It's simple with us. My brother killed a German in our yard, they burned his house ... we went away. Where to? To the ataman. But you're from the gentry.... Yes, it's hard...."

Katya's ruse had succeeded. Alexei Ivanovich evidently intended to settle here and now the accursed question: whose rights was one like Katya—landless and horseless—to fight for?

A foolish way to spend the time at the wattle fence beneath the cherry tree. Katya would have liked to pick a couple of linked black cherries, and hang them over her ear like an earring, but she only stood there in front of Krasilnikov, while gleams of humour lit up her great eyes, brilliant beneath the blue sky.

"If we peasants are to feed you townsfolk," said Alexei Ivanovich, enforcing his words with a resolute gesture, "you must support us. We, the peasantry, are against the Germans, the Whites, the Communists, and for the free village Soviets. Do you understand me?"

She nodded. While he went on talking, she got on to the tips of her toes and with her left hand, because her right sleeve was torn under the armpit, picked two cherries: one she popped into her mouth, the other she twirled by its stem.

"If I were a countrywoman it would all be quite simple," she

171

said, spitting out the stone. "I have often heard the words: native land, Russia, the people, but I have never before seen for myself what they mean." She ate the other cherry, glancing at Alexei Ivanovich, at his beard, golden in the sunlight, at his jacket open over the chest, at his strong legs, his terrible weapons.

"The people," he echoed, getting more and more embarrassed, "We're nothing much, of course. But we don't mean to give up what's our own." He held firmly to a paling sticking out of the wattle fence, testing it to see if it would hold. "We'll fight ruthlessly, if we have to fight the whole world. You ought to listen to our anarchists, Ekaterina Dmitrevna, not to me—they're great hands at talking.... Only...." (His brows twitched, his gaze flitting searchingly over Katya.) "They're a bad lot, hopeless sots, drunkards.... They mustn't be allowed to set eyes on you...."

"Nonsense," said Katya.

"What d'you mean, nonsense?"

"I mean I'm not a child, I wouldn't let anyone get away with that sort of thing...."

"I'm glad to hear you say that...."

Katya's lips quivered—smiling, she stretched out her hand again to the cherry-laden branch. She could feel the hot sunshine penetrating, caressing, her whole body. And this, too, was a waking dream.

"But still," she said, "what is there I could do here, Alexei Ivanovich?"

"Well, there's education.... The Old Man's getting up a political department. They say he means to bring out his own newspaper."

"And what about you?"

"Me?" (Again he turned his attention to the paling, giving the fence a shake.) "I'm just a fighting man, a driver of a machine-gun carrier. My place is in battle.... Have a look round first, Ekaterina Dmitrevna, you mustn't make up your mind all at once. I'll take you to my sister-in-law—Matryona, my brother's wife. We might take you into the family, you know...."

"Makhno told me to be ready to do his nails for him this evening."

"*What?*"

Alexei's two hands flew to his belt, his very nose seemed to have become sharp. "His nails? And what did you say?"

"I told him I was a prisoner," said Katya calmly.

"Very well. If he sends for you—go. But I shall be there...."

Just then the fat Alexandra came running out of the hut, waving her apron.

"They're coming! They're coming!" she cried, rushing to open the gate.

Cheers, shots, the thud of hoofs could be heard in the distance. It was Makhno returning at the head of his army. Katya and Alexei went out into the street. Clouds of dust were rising above the path. Horsemen and carts drawn by three horses, were galloping over the mounds, past the windmills.

The foremost units were already in the village. Little boys were jumping about, young girls ran hither and thither. The sides of the sweating, frothing horses were distended. Makhno's men galloped by, their caps atilt, standing up in their carts, covered with dust and sweat.

Makhno drove past in the cart with the Persian carpet on its floor. Seated on an ammunition box, he swayed from side to side, holding his sheepskin cap against his thigh. His face was pale and tense, his dry lips compressed.

In the cart which came after him sat six men who looked with their short jackets, their felt hats, their straw yachting caps, like townsfolk. They all had long hair, beards, and spectacles. These were the anarchists from headquarters and the political department.

VIII

Dasha stayed all by herself in the empty rooms for five months. Before leaving for the front, Ivan Ilyich had given her a thousand rubles, but this did not last long. Fortunately the flat below, from which an important Petersburg official had fled with his family, was taken by an enterprising foreigner by the name of Matte, who bought up pictures, furniture and anything he could lay his hands on.

Dasha sold him a double bed, a few engravings, and some porcelain knicknacks. She parted with these possessions, redolent as they were of old memories, without a pang. She had severed herself entirely from her past.

She lived through the spring and summer on the proceeds of these sales. The town was getting emptier every day. The front lay within an hour's train journey from Petersburg, beyond the river Sestra. The government moved to Moscow. The palaces looked down on the Neva from empty, shattered windowframes. The streets were not lit up. The militia were not particularly interested in preserving the security of a bourgeoisie which was doomed anyhow. Sinister beings, such as nobody had ever seen before, appeared in the streets. They peered into windows, climbed dark stairways, tried the handles of doors. Woe to him who did not take the precaution of locking and doublelocking his door! For he would soon catch the sound of surreptitious rustlings, and meet with strangers in his apartment. With a cry of "Hands up!", the strangers would throw themselves on the tenants, tie them up with lengths of electrical cord, and bear away, at their leisure, bundles of property.

There was cholera in the town. When the berries began to ripen it assumed terrible dimensions, people falling in contortions of pain in the streets and markets. Whispered rumours spread like wildfire. Incredible disasters were expected. It was said that the Red Army men were putting the five-pointed star on their cap-bands upside down—the mark of the Antichrist—and also that a "White Man" was haunting a locked chapel on Lieutenant Schmidt Bridge, signifying that disasters from the sea were to be expected. From the bridges people pointed to the cold factory chimneys sticking up against the crimson sunset like the devil's fingers.

The factories shut down. The workers joined the food detachments, or went to the villages. Grass began to show green between the paving stones.

Dasha did not go out every day, and then only in the morning, to the market where unscrupulous Finns extorted two pairs of trousers for a sack of potatoes. Red Army men were seen with increasing frequency on the markets, where shots fired into the air dispersed the survivors of the bourgeois system—the Finns with their potatoes, and the ladies with their bundles of men's clothes and windowcurtains. It became more difficult every day to get food. Sometimes the situation was saved by Matte himself, always ready to give tinned food and sugar in exchange for antiques.

Dasha ate as little as possible, to save herself trouble. She got up early every day. When she had thread she would sew, at other times she would take up some book published in 1913 or 1914, anything to stave off thought. But mostly she sat at the window, thinking—or rather allowing her thoughts to revolve around a dark spot. Her recent spiritual upheaval, her despair, her misery, seemed now to be nothing but a kind of inert lump in her brain, a remnant of illness. She had grown so thin she might have been taken for a girl of sixteen. Indeed, she felt as if she had become a girl again, but without her girlish lightness of spirits.

Summer was passing. The white nights were drawing in, and the sun set gloomily over Kronstadt. There was an extensive view from the open window of the fifth floor—abandoned streets, on which the shades of night were descending, the dark windows of the houses. No lights were lit. The footsteps of a passer-by were seldom heard.

"What next?" wondered Dasha. "When will this state of paralysis be over?" It would soon be autumn, the rain would come, the chill wind would howl over the rooftops again. There was no wood. Her winter coat was sold. Perhaps Ivan Ilyich would return.... But that would only mean the same old wretchedness, the dim red glow of the lamps, a useless existence.

Oh, to find the strength to shake off this paralysis, to leave this house in which she was buried alive, to get away from this dying town! Then surely something new would happen.... It was the first time for a whole year that Dasha had allowed herself to think of "something new". Catching herself in the thought, she was moved and agitated, as if reflections from some radiant expanse, like those which had once warmed her on a Volga steamer, had suddenly appeared through the curtain of hopeless misery.

Then came days of regret for Ivan Ilyich. She began to pity him in a new way, like a sister, remembering with tenderness his patient care, his imperturbable, innocuous good nature.

One day she went to the bookshelf and hunted out the three white volumes of Bessonov's poems, those receptacles of utterly burned-out memories. She read them before the dark fell, in the stillness, with swallows darting past the window like black arrows. In the poems she found the words of her own grief, her loneliness, the dark wind which would one day whistle over her grave.... Giving herself up to reverie, Dasha wept. The next morning she took the dress she had had made for her wedding out of the moth balls in the trunk where it was put away, and began altering it. The swallows were still swooping by as they had the day before; and a pale sun was shining. In the stillness, infrequent distant blows could be heard, and an occasional rending sound, followed by the fall of something heavy on the road—probably a wooden house being broken up in some side street.

Dasha went on sewing with leisured movements. Her finger had grown so thin that her thimble kept falling off. Once it almost fell out of the window. She could remember sitting on a trunk in the hall of Katya's flat with this very thimble on her finger, eating bread and marmalade. That had been in 1914. Katya had quarrelled with her husband and was leaving for Paris. She had on a little hat with a tiny feather in it, which somehow had a pathetically self-sufficient air. She had turned round in the doorway, only remembering about Dasha when she caught sight of her on the trunk. "Come with me, Dasha...." But Dasha had not gone. And now ... should she try to get to Paris? Dasha knew it from Katya's letters: blue, silky, smelling like the box in which a bottle of scent is packed.... She went on sewing, giving an unconscious sigh in her agitation. Leave Russia! There were said to be no trains, nobody was allowed to go abroad.... One might try going on foot, trudging, knapsack on back, through forests, over hills, fields, blue rivers, from country to country, till one got to the divine, elegant city.... The tears rolled down her cheeks. What folly!... Everywhere was war. The Germans were firing on Paris from enormous cannon. Dreams, dreams. Was it right not to allow a person to lead a quiet, happy life? "What did I ever do to them?" The thimble rolled beneath an armchair, the sunshine swam through her tears, the swallows swooped past with their hollow cries: they're all right, all they need is flies and mosquitoes.... "I will go—I will!" sobbed Dasha.

Just then there was a series of insistent, separate knocks on the door. Dasha placed the needle and scissors on the window sill, rolled her sewing into a ball and wiped her eyes on it, then flung it into the armchair and went to see who it was that had knocked....

"Does Darya Dmitrevna Telegina live here?"

Instead of replying, Dasha bent down to the keyhole. Someone was bending down on the other side, too, and a cautious voice said into the keyhole: "A letter for her from Rostov...."

Dasha opened the door immediately. A strange man in a crumpled soldier's greatcoat and worn peaked cap, stepped across the threshold. Alarmed, Dasha retreated, extending her arms. The stranger said hastily:

"For God's sake.... Darya Dmitrevna, don't you know me?"

"No, no...."

"It's Kulichok, Nikanor Yurevich ... barrister. Don't you remember Sestroretsk?"

Dasha dropped her hands and peered into the lean, unshaven face, with the pointed nose. The wrinkles around the watchful, restless eyes spoke of habitual caution, the crooked mouth of resoluteness and cruelty. He was like some small animal on the lookout for danger.

"Surely you haven't forgotten, Darya Dmitrevna.... I used to be the assistant of Nikolai Ivanovich Smokovnikov, your sister's late husband.... I was in love with you, but you turned me down, you know.... Don't you remember?" Suddenly he smiled, and in his smile was something of forgotten, prewar days, and everything came back to Dasha: the flat, sandy shore, the mist of sunshine over the warm, drowsy gulf, her prickly self, the girlish bow on her dress, the enamoured Kulichok, whom she had despised with all her supercilious virginity.... The smell of the tall pines, rustling solemnly day and night on the sand dunes....

"You've changed so," she said in trembling tones, as she held out her hand to him. Kulichok caught it adroitly and kissed it. Despite his soldier's coat, it was obvious that he had been in the cavalry all these years.

"Allow me to hand you a letter. Allow me to go somewhere and take off my boot.... Excuse me, but it's in my boot, you see...."

He glanced round significantly and followed Dasha into an empty room, where he sat down on the floor and, frowning, began pulling at his muddy boot.

The letter was from Katya, it was the one she had handed Lieutenant Colonel Tetkin in Rostov.

At the very first lines Dasha gave a cry and clutched at her throat. Vadim was killed! Her eyes ran rapidly over the letter. Then she read it a second time, avidly. She sank on to the arm of a chair almost fainting. Kulichok stood at a respectful distance.

"Nikanor Yurevich, did you see my sister?"

"No, Darya Dmitrevna. The letter was given to me ten days ago by a certain person who told me that Ekaterina Dmitrevna had left Rostov a month before...."

"Ah, God! Where can she be? What has happened to her?"

"Unfortunately I had no opportunity of finding out."

"Did you know her husband, Vadim Roshchin? Killed.... Katya writes—oh, it's too terrible!"

Kulichok raised his eyebrows in astonishment. The letter shook so in Dasha's thin fingers that he took it and ran his eyes over the lines relating how Valerian Onoli had told Katya of the death of her husband. The corner of Kulichok's lips twitched in a crooked sneer.

"I always thought Onoli capable of baseness.... According to him, Roshchin was killed in May, wasn't he? Strange.... It seems to me I saw him rather later than that."

"When? Where?"

But here Kulichok suddenly thrust out his predatory-looking nose, and cast a searching glance at Dasha. It was a mere matter of a second. Dasha's eyes, glowing with agitation, her cold, interlaced fingers, spoke to him clearer than words: she might be the wife of a Red officer, but she would never betray him. Moving nearer to her, he asked: "Are we alone in the apartment?" ("Yes, yes," said Dasha's hurried nod.) "Darya Dmitrevna, I'm going to tell you something that might endanger my life, if...."

"Are you one of Denikin's officers?"

"Yes."

Dasha pulled at her finger joints, looking miserably out of the window at that unattainable azure....

"You needn't be afraid of me...."

177

"I was sure of that. And I want to ask you to put me up for a few days."

He said it firmly, almost threateningly. Dasha bent her head. "Very well."

"If you're afraid, however.... You're not?" (He sprang back.) "You're not?" (He advanced again.) "I quite understand.... But you have nothing to fear.... I'm very careful.... I'll only go out at night. Not a soul knows I'm in Petersburg...." (From the lining of his cap he extracted an army identity card.) "See? Ivan Svishchev. Red Army man. It's genuine. I got it with my own hands.... So you would like to know about Vadim Petrovich? I think there must be some muddle here...."

Here he seized Dasha's hands, pressing them in his own.

"It means you're on our side, Darya Dmitrevna! Thank you for that! The whole of the intellectuals, the whole of the insulted and persecuted officer class are rallying around the holy banner of the Volunteer Army. It's an army of heroes.... You'll see—Russia will be saved, and it is the white hands which will save her. And let the others take the coarse paws off Russia! There's been enough sentimentalizing. The toiling people! I've just travelled over a thousand miles on the roof of a railway carriage. I saw the toiling people. Wild beasts, that's what they are! I tell you, it's only we, a mere handful of heroes, who keep the true Russia in our hearts. And we'll fasten our law with a bayonet on the portals of the Taurida Palace."

Dasha felt stunned by the torrent of words. Kulichok stabbed the air with a black-rimmed fingernail, and froth bubbled in the corners of his lips. Apparently he was finding compensation in speech for the prolonged silence he had had perforce maintained on the roof of the railway carriage.

"Darya Dmitrevna, I won't conceal it from you.... I have been sent here, to the north, to scout and recruit. There are many who still have no conception of our forces.... In your papers we are simply spoken of as White Guard bands, a miserable handful which they will finally erase from the face of the earth in a day or two.... No wonder our officers are afraid to come.... But do you know what is really going on on the Don and Kuban? The army of the Don Ataman is increasing like a snowball. The province of Voronezh is already cleared of Reds. Stavropol will soon fall. We are waiting from day to day for Krasnov to arrive at the Volga and seize Tsaritsyn.... He is making up to the Germans, it's true, but that's just temporary.... We, Denikin's men, are advancing to the south of Kuban, as on parade. We have taken Torgovaya, Tikhoretskaya and Velikoknyazheskaya. Sorokin has been smashed into smithereens. All the villages are giving the Volunteer Army

178

an enthusiastic welcome. There was veritable carnage at Belaya Glina, we waded through such a sea of corpses that your humble servant was soaked in blood to the waist."

Looking into his eyes, Dasha turned pale. Kulichok laughed scornfully.

"You think that's all? That's only the beginning of our reprisals. The flames will spread all over the country. The Samara, Orenburg, and Ufa provinces, the whole of the Urals are ablaze. The better elements among the peasantry are organizing White armies themselves. The whole of the Middle Volga is in the hands of the Czechs. From Samara to Vladivostok the whole country is one solid rising. If it weren't for the damned Germans, Little Russia would rise as one man. The towns in the Upper Volga district are powder magazines, only waiting for the touch of a match.... I don't give the Bolsheviks another month, I wouldn't give a straw for their chances...."

Kulichok trembled with excitement. He was no longer like a small wild beast. Dasha looked at his sharp-featured face weather-beaten by the winds of the steppe, hardened in the heat of battle. Some hotblooded life had thrust itself upon her transparent solitude. She felt a sharp pain in her temples, and her heart beat violently. When Kulichok, baring his small teeth, stopped talking and began rolling home-grown tobacco into a cigarette, Dasha said:

"You will win. But war won't go on for ever ... then what will happen?"

"Then?" Inhaling, he narrowed his eyes. "Then—war against the Germans to a victorious finish, a peace congress, which we will attend as conquering heroes, and after that—with the combined forces of the Allies, of the whole of Europe—the restoration of Russia, order, lawful conduct, parliamentarism, freedom.... That's for the future.... But for now...."

Suddenly he clutched at the right side of his chest, feeling for something beneath his coat. He cautiously extracted a piece of cardboard, folded down the middle—the lid of a cigarette box—and turned it over and over between his fingers. Once more his searching gaze swept over Dasha's face.

"I can't take any risks. You see how it is.... People are liable to be searched in the streets here.... I want to give you something." He unfolded the cardboard and took from it a small triangle cut out of a visiting card. There were two letters written on it: O and K.... "Put it away somewhere, Darya Dmitrevna—guard it as something sacred.... I'll teach you how to make use of it. Forgive me—you're not afraid?"

"No."

"Good girl!"

Almost unconsciously, simply drawn in by a will stronger than her own, Dasha had fallen into the very thick of the conspiracy being carried on by the so-called "League for the Protection of the Native Land and Freedom", a conspiracy which was sweeping over the two capitals and a number of other cities of Great Russia.

The behaviour of Kulichok, an emissar of Denikin's headquarters, was unbelievably reckless: to confide in a woman he hardly knew, the wife of a Red Army officer, at the very first word. But he had once been in love with Dasha, and now, gazing into her grey eyes, he could not help trusting her, for the eyes said: "You may trust me."

At that time people's minds were guided, not by calm reflection, but by intuition. The hurricane of events roared, the sea of humanity surged, each one felt himself to be the saviour of the sinking ship, and, erect on the bridge, flourished a revolver, ordering the helm to be turned now to port, now starboard. All was then illusion, and White Guard will-o'the-wisps danced over the illimitable plains of Russia. Eyes were dull with hatred. The illusions were born of brief glimpses of mirage.

Thus the imminent overthrow of the Bolsheviks seemed absolutely inevitable; the troops of the Intervention seemed to be already closing in from the four corners of the globe to the assistance of the White armies; millions of Russian peasants seemed to be eager for a Constituent Assembly; the towns of the united and indivisible empire seemed only to be waiting for a sign to break up the Soviets, and, the day after, to restore order and constitutional law.

All cherished the illusion, and were lured by the mirage: from society ladies, fleeing from Petrograd to the south with a single change of linen, to the omniscient Professor Milyukov, who awaited with supercilious smiles the issue of events which he had himself neatly arranged in historical perspective.

Some of the firmest believers in the consoling mirages were to be found in the "League for the Protection of the Native Land and Freedom", established in the early spring of 1918 by Boris Savinkov, after the suicide of the elected Ataman Kaledin and the withdrawal of Kornilov's army from Rostov. The League was a kind of secret organization of the Volunteer Army.

At its head was the elusive and skilfully disguised Savinkov, roaming Moscow with a dyed moustache, wearing an English shooting jacket, tan gaiters and a khaki-coloured coat. The League was organized on military lines: staff, divisions, brigades, regiments, counterintelligence and various service units. Staff work was entrusted to Colonel Perkhurov.

Recruiting for membership of the League was carried on with the strictest secrecy. Each member could know only four others, so that

180

in case of mishap only five at a time could be arrested, and clues would lead no further. The address of its headquarters and the names of the leaders were kept a profound secret. Anyone wishing to become a member would be visited in his home by a regimental or divisional commander, who interrogated him, gave him a sum of money, and entered his address in code on a card. These cards, bearing circles signifying the number of members and their addresses, reached headquarters weekly. Inspection of forces was carried on in the boulevards, members of organizations arriving either with their coats buttoned in a special manner, or with a ribbon on a prearranged place. Intelligence officers were given a triangle cut from a visiting card, with two letters on them standing for their password, and the town they came from. On presentation, the triangle was fitted into the card from which it had been cut. The League had quite a considerable intelligence net at its disposal. At the secret conference held in April it was resolved to stop sabotaging and work at the Soviet offices. In this way the members of the League wormed themselves into the very heart of the apparatus of State. Some of them got into the Moscow militia. They even had their own agent in the Kremlin. They wormed themselves into the higher military bodies, and even into the Supreme Military Council. The Kremlin seemed to be firmly enmeshed in their web.

At that time the seizure of Moscow by Field Marshal Eichhorn's troops seemed inevitable. And though there were strong pro-German elements in the League, who believed in nothing but the might of German bayonets, the general tendency was on the side of the Allies. The very day of the entry of the Germans into Moscow was appointed—the fifteenth of June. It was therefore resolved to give up the idea of seizing the Kremlin and Moscow, and lead the military units of the League to Kazan, blowing up bridges and reservoirs round Moscow on the way, raising rebellions in Nizhni, Kostroma, Rybinsk and Murom, joining forces with the Czechs, and forming an eastern front, to derive its supplies from the Urals and the rich Volga districts.

Dasha believed every word Kulichok told her: the Russian patriots, or, as he called them, the Knights of the Spirit, were fighting that there might be no more insolent Finns selling potatoes, that the streets of Petersburg might be brightly lit up, and thronged with gay, well-dressed people, that, in a moment of depression, one could simply put on a hat with a feather in it, and go off to Paris ... that there should be no more "hoppers" in the Summer Park, that the autumn wind should no longer moan over the grave of Dasha's son.

All this Kulichok promised her over a cup of tea. He was as hungry as a wolf and ate up half her stock of tinned food; he even ate raw flour with salt. Then he disappeared unnoticeably in the dusk, taking the key of the door with him....

Dasha went to bed. Drawing the curtain over the window, she lay down and, as often happens in the exhausting hours of sleeplessness, thoughts, images, reminiscences, sudden guesses, burning remorse, jostled one another in wild pursuit.... Dasha tossed and turned, slipped her hands under the pillow, lay now on her back, now on her stomach.... The blanket seemed to sear her flesh, the springs of the sofa forced themselves into her side, the sheets kept slipping off....

It was a bad night—as long as life itself. The dark spot in Dasha's brain came to life again, sending poisonous shoots into its inmost convolutions. But why these conscience pangs, this terrible feeling of guilt? If one could only understand!

And much later, when daylight began to show blue through the curtains, Dasha, weary from turning in a fantastic maze of thought, grew weak and, quieting down, subjected herself with the utmost honesty and simplicity to a searching analysis—everything was wrong in her, she knew that.

Raising herself in bed, she twisted her hair into a knot, dropped her thin hands on to her knees, and gave herself up to thought.... She bade good riddance to the solitary, the dreamer, the cold woman who loved no one.... It was well that she had been frightened by the "hoppers" in the Summer Park—it was not enough—she should have been given a still worse fright. And now for flight.... Now, seized by the wind, fly my soul, where you are sent, do what you are told.... You have no more will of your own.... You are one of a million million....What peace, what liberation!

Kulichok was away two whole days. In his absence several men called, all of them tall, in worn jackets, somewhat embarrassed, but extremely well-bred. Bending down to the keyhole, they would utter the password, and Dasha let them in. On being told that "Ivan Svishchev" was not in, they seemed in no hurry to go. One of them suddenly embarked upon a narration of his domestic misfortunes, another, asking permission to smoke, produced a monogrammed case filled with execrable Soviet cigarettes, and swore foully at the deputies of the "soldiery and rabble", trilling his r's in the French manner. Yet another opened his heart to her, telling her of the motor launch in readiness for him at Krestovsky Island, just in front of the Beloselsky-Belozersky Palace, of the valuables he had managed to extricate from the safe ... and then his children had caught the whooping cough ... infernal luck!

They all seemed to be glad of the opportunity to chat with the charming thin young woman with the great eyes. On leaving they kissed her hand. Only one thing astonished Dasha—these were surely extremely naive conspirators, they were just like the characters in some silly play.... All of them inquired in cautiously-worded phrases, whether "Ivan Svishchev" had not brought money for current expenses. They were all confident that "the idiotic Bolshevik game" would very soon be played out. "After all, it won't cost the Germans much effort to take Petrograd."

At last Kulichok reappeared, once again famished, dirty and extremely preoccupied. He informed himself as to who had been there in his absence. Dasha told him in detail. He bared his teeth. "The blackguards! Coming for money ... a fine Guard! They're too lazy to lift their aristocratic backsides out of their armchairs, they want the Germans to come and liberate them: this way Your Excellencies—we've just strung the Bolsheviks up, all is in order.... Outrageous, outrageous.... Of the two hundred thousand officers left alive, the only true heroes of the spirit are the three thousand under Drozdovsky, the eight thousand under Denikin, and the five thousand in the 'League for the Protection of the Native Land'. That's all.... And where are the rest? They've sold themselves, body and soul, to the Red Army. Some are making boot polish, or selling cigarettes.... Almost the entire general staff has gone over to the Bolsheviks ... a disgrace...."

After eating his fill of flour and salt, and drinking hot water, Kulichok went to bed. Early the next morning he woke Dasha up. Dressing quickly, she went into the dining room, where he was pacing up and down beside the table.

"Here you are!" he cried impatiently, when he saw Dasha. "Tell me—are you capable of running great risks, making great sacrifices, enduring endless discomforts?"

"Yes," said Dasha.

"I don't trust a soul here. Disquieting news has been received. Someone must go to Moscow. Will you?"

Dasha blinked and raised her eyebrows for all reply. Kulichok ran up to her, made her sit down at the table, sat close to her, his knees touching hers, and began telling her whom she must see in Moscow, and what she must transmit orally about the Petrograd organization. He spoke with a kind of slow fury, as if endeavouring to engrave the words in Dasha's memory. He made her repeat them after him. She did so with childlike docility.

"Splendid! Good girl!" he cried, jumping up and rubbing the palms of his hands together vigorously. "Now what about your flat? You'd better tell the House Committee you're going to Luga for a week. I'll stay here another day or two, and leave the key

183

with the chairman of the committee when I go. Will that be all right?"

All this vehemence made Dasha's head reel. To her own surprise, she realized that she was ready, without the slightest show of resistance, to go wherever she was sent, and do whatever she was told.... When Kulichok spoke about the flat she cast a rapid glance at the maple sideboard.... "Hideous, depressing sideboard—just like a coffin!" She remembered how the swallows had summoned her to the blue spaces. And it seemed to her it would be a joy to fly out of this dusty cage, towards some free, wild life....

"The flat?" she echoed. "Perhaps I'll never come back again. Do as you like about it!"

One of the men who used to come in Kulichok's absence—a lanky, amiable individual, with a long face and a drooping moustache, put Dasha into a compartment with uncushioned seats and all the windows broken. Bending over her, he murmured into her ear in a deep voice: "Your services will not be forgotten", and vanished into the crowd. Just as the train was leaving, some people came running up, and climbed in by the windows, their bundles hanging from their teeth. The compartment was now full. Some climbed on to the ledges at the top, intended for luggage, while others crawled under the seats, where they lay contentedly striking matches and smoking home-grown tobacco.

The train dragged its length slowly past misty swamps, with long-cold factory chimneys towering over them, past ponds coated with green scum. The Pulkovo Observatory floated into sight on the horizon: there, forgotten by the world, sage astronomers, among them the seventy-year-old Glazenap himself,* went on peacefully counting the number of stars in the firmament. Seedling pines, full-grown trees, summer cottages, glided by. An armed guard was posted to prevent any more people getting in when the train stopped. And despite the terrific din, all was peace in the compartment.

Dasha sat wedged in by two soldiers—veterans of battle. From the top bunk an animated countenance hung down, its owner continually joining in the conversation.

"And then what?" came from the bunk, in a voice choked with suppressed laughter. "What did you do then?"

Opposite Dasha, between two silent, careworn women, sat a lean, one-eyed peasant with a long moustache and bristly chin. He wore a straw hat, and his shirt was made from a sack, and

*S.P. Glazenap (1848-1937)—outstanding Russian astronomer.

gathered at the neck with a tape. A comb and a stump of copying-ink pencil were stuck into his belt, and a bundle of papers was thrust into the front of his shirt.

At first Dasha paid no heed to the conversation. But gradually she realized that the one-eyed man must be recounting something extremely interesting. Heads had begun to turn towards him from all the seats, and it grew quiet in the carriage. A soldier, who had his rifle with him, said with assurance:

"I know who you are—you're partisans—Makhno men."

The one-eyed man paused for a moment, smiling slily into his moustache.

"You've got the wrong sow by the ear, brother."

Thrusting his horny hand sideways beneath his moustache, as if to wipe off the smile, he continued, not without a certain solemnity:

"Makhno ... that's a kulak organization.... He works round Ekaterinoslav. Nobody farms less than a hundred acres there. We're different. We are Red partisans."

"And what do *you* do?" asked the gay-visaged fellow traveller from the top bunk.

"The Chernigov Region is the field of our activities, and the northern parts of the Nezhin Region, see? We're Communists. In our eyes Germans, Polish landowners, hetman Gaidamaks, and our own village kulaks, are all one.... So we mustn't be confused with the Makhno men. See? "

"*We* see! We're not fools—get on with your story!"

"Very well then—it was like this: after this battle with the Germans we lost heart. We retreated to the Koshelev forest, right into the heart of it, where nothing but wolves live. There we rested a bit. People from the neighbouring villages began coming to us. They told us life was getting impossible for them. The Germans had started clearing the district of partisans in earnest. And the Gaidamaks were sent to help the Germans. There wasn't a day they didn't rush into the village and thrash anyone the kulaks pointed out. These stories made our lads so furious, they almost choked. By now another detachment had joined us, and there was quite an army in the woods, about three hundred and fifty altogether. We elected Sublieutenant Golta, a Verkiev guerilla fighter, commander of our group. Then we began wondering what direction to carry on further operations in, and decided to set up observation posts along the Desna, because military supplies were sent along it to the Germans. So off we went! We took up positions where the steamers passed close to the riverbank."

"Eh-h-h! And then what?" came from the top bunk.

"Then—a steamer approaches. 'Stop!' shout our first lines. The captain does not obey the command and—bang! bang! Of course the steamer moves inshore. We're on deck in a trice; sentries are posted, papers examined."

"That's the way!" said the soldier.

"The steamer had a cargo of saddles and harness. Two colonels were in charge—one of them just a dodderer, the other a fine upstanding young man. There was a consignment of medical supplies as well as the harness. And that was just what we needed. I was on deck, going through papers, when suddenly I saw two Communists coming up to me—Pyotr and Ivan Petrovsky, from the Borodyan District. I understood at once what was up, but gave no sign of knowing them. I treated them quite officially, strictly: 'Your papers....' Petrovsky hands me his passport, with a note in it on a cigarette paper: 'Comrade Pyavka, my brother and I are leaving Chernigov for Russia—be sure to be very ruthless with us, so as not to attract attention—there are spies all round....' Very well.... After examining all papers we unloaded the harness and the saddles and the medical supplies, as well as fifteen crates of wine as a tonic for our wounded. You've got to hand it to the ship's doctor, he behaved like a hero. 'I'm not going to give up the medical supplies!' he shouted. 'It's against all laws, and it's contrary to the international code, I would have you know!' Our reply was short and to the point: 'We have wounded soldiers ourselves, so you're observing not the international, but the human code, in giving up your medical supplies.' We arrested about a dozen officers, put them ashore, and let the boat go on. The old colonel stood on the bank crying, and begging us to spare his life—he even mentioned his military services. 'Why should we hurt him?' we thought. 'He hasn't long to live anyhow.' So we released him in a fit of magnanimity, and he made for the woods...."

Peals of joyous laughter came from the top bunk. The one-eyed man waited for them to subside, and went on with his story.

"The other one—he was a staff officer—made a good impression on us, answering our questions readily, and appearing to be quite at his ease, so we let him go too.... The rest we took into the woods. We shot them for refusing to answer questions...."

Dasha stared at the one-eyed man with bated breath. His face, with its grim wrinkles, was perfectly calm. The solitary eye, shrewd, murky-grey, the pupil a mere slit, thoughtfully followed the pine trees as they flew past. He soon took up his tale again:

"We couldn't stay long on the banks of the Desna. The Germans turned our flank, and we retreated to the Drozdov woods. We distributed our booty among the peasants. We did have a mug

186

of wine each, but all the rest we sent to the hospital. Krapivyansky was operating on our left with a large detachment, and Marunya was fighting on the right. Our joint task was to break through to Chernigov, and take it by storm. If only there had been proper communications between the detachments ... but we had no real contacts, and we got there too late. The Germans sent troops, artillery, and cavalry against us day after day. Our very existence was a thorn in their flesh. For as soon as they left a village, a Revolutionary Committee would be set up, and a couple of kulaks would be strung up on an ash tree. One day I was sent to Marunya's detachment to get some money—we needed money badly. We had to pay cash for everything we got from the population, and looting was forbidden under pain of death. So I got a cart and drove to the Koshelev woods. Marunya and I discussed things, he gave me a thousand Kerensky rubles, and I started back.... I had hardly entered the valley just outside the village of Zhukovka, when two horsemen, scouts from the Zhukovka Revolutionary Committee, dashed up to me. 'Where are you going—the Germans are there!' 'Where?' 'Why, they've almost got to Zhukovka!' Back I go ... drove into a thicket, and got off the cart. We began discussing what we should do. There could be no question of mass resistance to the Germans. A whole column of them was moving up, and they had artillery...."

"Three against a column—the odds were too heavy," said the soldier.

"That's just it! So we thought we'd just try to give them a fright. We crawled forward under cover of the rye. We could see Zhukovka, and the column coming out of the woods—about two hundred men, two guns and some baggage carts, and a little way in front, a mounted patrol. The fame of our partisans must have made a great noise if they actually sent artillery against us. We dropped flat on our faces in some vegetable plots. Our morale was excellent—we were looking forward to a good laugh. When the patrol was within fifty paces of us I gave the order: 'Battalion, fire!' We fired a couple of volleys.... One horse went over backward, and the German fell into the nettles. We fired again. We rattled our rifle bolts, made as much noise as we could...."

The eyes of the face on the top bunk fairly popped, and their owner, as if fearing to miss a single word, clapped his hand over his mouth to repress a whinny of laughter. The soldier gave a satisfied chuckle.

"The patrol galloped back to the column, and the Germans turned right about, closed up their ranks and went to the attack in proper style. They had their guns off the carts in a trice, and three-inch shells began booming over the vegetable plots, where the women were hoeing potatoes....

"A shell burst, sending up the earth in showers. Our women...." (Here the one-eyed man pushed his hat over his ear with one finger, no longer able to repress his mirth, and the man on the top shelf guffawed.) "Our women scuttled out of the potato patch like hens.... And the Germans advanced on the village, at the double. Then I said: 'We've had our fun, lads—now let's get the hell out of here!' We crawled back through the rye to the gully, I got on to my cart, and drove to the Drozdov woods without any more adventures. The Zhukovka people told us afterwards what happened: 'The Germans got as far as the vegetable plots, right up to the fence, and yelled out: "Hurrah!" And there wasn't anyone behind the fence. The villagers nearly split their sides with laughing.' The Germans occupied Zhukovka, and found there neither revolutionary committee nor guerilla fighters, but they declared martial law in the village just the same. Two days later we got news in the Drozdov woods that a big German munitions convoy had entered Zhukovka. And we needed cartridges like hell. We talked it over, and the boys got all worked up, so it was decided to march on Zhukovka and seize these munitions. About a hundred of us got together. Thirty were sent to the high-road, to cut off the retreat of the Germans on Chernigov, in case we were successful. The rest marched in line formation on Zhukovka. We crept up at dusk, dropped down in the rye near the village, and sent out seven men to see how the land lay, and bring us back information, so that we could make a surprise attack in the night. We lay there as quiet as mice, no smoking was allowed. It was drizzling ... we were all sleepy ... it was awfully damp ... we waited and waited till it began to get light. Not a movement. We couldn't understand it. We saw the women beginning to drive the cattle into the fields. And then our seven scouts came crawling back, the little dears.... It turned out they got to the mill, and lay down for a rest, the rotters, and slept all night, till the women driving out the cattle came upon them. Of course there could be no question of an attack.... We were so furious, we could hardly contain ourselves. We had to hold a court martial, and sentence them, and it was unanimously decided to shoot them. But they started crying and begging for mercy, and frankly admitted their offence. They were just young chaps, and it was their first offence ... so we decided to pardon them. But they were told they must redeem their crime in the very next battle."

"A pardon does good sometimes," said the soldier.

"Yes.... So we began to discuss our plans. Since we had not

taken Zhukovka in the night, we should have to take it in the day. No easy task—and the lads knew very well what they were in for. We spread out thin and waited for the guns to start—we didn't crawl, we fairly ran on all fours...."

Loud guffaws from the top shelf.

"And instead of Germans, we were met by women with baskets on their arms. It was a Sunday, and they were going berrying. How they laughed at us! 'You're late,' they said. 'The German munition carts took the path to Kulikov two hours ago.' Then we decided unanimously to go after the Germans, even if it should cost us all our lives. We took spades for making dugouts; the women brought us pancakes and pies. And off we went. A great crowd—quite an army—joined on to us—mostly of course out of curiosity. And this is what we did: we issued stakes to them all, men and women, and formed two lines, with a distance of twenty paces between each person, in such a way that one would have a rifle, the next one just a stake or a stick, and so on, to look formidable. Our lines stretched over three miles or so. I picked fifteen men, including our luckless scouts, as well as a couple of officers we had mobilized—they were obvious counterrevolutionaries, but they had been warned to justify our trust in them if they wanted to save their skins. This group got into the path ahead of the munitions convoy.... And then a battle started, my lads, that went on and on, for days on end...." (Here he made a gesture, as if reluctant to continue.)

"How was that?" asked the soldier.

"It was like this.... Our group let the column pass and fell upon its rear—the carts. We captured about a score of ammunition carts. We hastily filled our pouches with cartridges and issued rifles to all the peasants we could, and went on with the attack. We thought we had surrounded the column, but really it was the Germans who surrounded us: they moved all their units up to this place along three roads.... We broke up into small groups, taking cover in ditches. It was our luck that the Germans conducted operations according to the rules for big-scale battles, or not one of us would have come out alive.... As it was I, and perhaps ten other partisans survived. We fought as long as the cartridges lasted. Then we decided that this was no place for us, that we should have to cross the Desna, and get into the neutral zone, to Russia. I hid my rifle and made my way to Novgorod-Severski, pretending to be a prisoner of war.... "

"And where are you off to now?"

"To Moscow for instructions."

Pyavka recounted a great deal more about the partisans and about village life. "We go on from one disaster to another. The peasant has to be like a wolf—always ready to spring." Pyavka was from Nezhin, where he had worked at sugar refineries. He had lost his eye during the Kerensky regime, in the abortive June offensive.* "Kerensky put out my eye," was the way he formulated it. It was then, in the trenches, that he first came across Communists. He was a member of the Nezhin Soviet, and of the Revolutionary Committee, and had taken part in the secret organization of the partisan movement.

His story moved Dasha profoundly. The truth behind it was so convincing. The other passengers felt this, too, and listened spellbound to the narrator.

The rest of the day, and the long night, were exhausting. Dasha sat with her feet drawn back beneath the seat, her eyes closed, thinking till her head ached, thinking to the point of desperation. There were two truths: one, the truth of the one-eyed man, of those soldiers, those snoring women, with their plain, weary faces; and the other, the truth which Kulichok was always trumpeting. But there couldn't be two truths. One of them must be wrong, fatally wrong....

The train arrived in Moscow at noon. An ancient *izvozchik* drove Dasha at a shambling trot along Myasnitskaya Street, now become grimy and shabby, the windows of its empty shops bespattered with mud. Dasha, who remembered the city in the days when vast crowds had roamed the snow-covered streets with flags and song, congratulating one another on the bloodless revolution, was astounded at its deserted state.

On Lubyanskaya Square dust was eddying in the wind. Two soldiers in unbelted tunics, their collars open at the neck, were wandering across the square. A frail, long-faced man in a velvet jacket looked at Dasha and shouted something to her; he even ran after the droshky, but soon fell back, half-blinded by the dust. The Hotel Metropole was scarred with shell holes, and here, too, dust was eddying; a bed of bright-coloured flowers, planted by an unknown hand for an unknown reason, in the middle of the refuse-strewn square, struck a note of incongruity.

In Tverskaya Street, where a few small shops were still open, things were livelier. A huge wooden cube, draped with bunting, stood in front of the building of the Moscow Soviet, where the monument to Skobelev had been. Dasha found something sinister in this. The old cab driver pointed to it with the handle of his whip:

*The June Offensive. On June 18, 1917, the Provisional Government, of which Kerensky was Prime Minister, in compliance with the will of the Anglo-French imperialists forced the soldiers at the front to embark on yet another offensive, considering this the only hope of putting an end to the revolution.

"They've pulled down the hero. I've been driving about Moscow for years, and he always stood there. But the present government doesn't like him, you see. How is anyone to live? One might as well lie down and die. Hay two hundred rubles a pood! All the gentry have run away, and there's no one left but comrades, and most of them walk.... Oh, the State, the State!" He tugged at the reins. "If only we had a king ... any sort of a king!"

Just before getting to Strastnaya Square, on the left, idle young men and languid girls could be seen through the two plateglass windows of the Cafe Bom, lolling on sofas, smoking, and sipping nondescript drinks. A long-haired, clean-shaven man, with a pipe in his mouth, stood in the open doorway leaning his shoulder against the jamb. The sight of Dasha seemed to astonish him, and he took his pipe out of his mouth. But Dasha drove past. Here was the pink spire of the Strastnoi Monastery, and there was Pushkin on his pedestal opposite. From beneath his elbow there still protruded the faded rag on the end of a stick, placed there during the era of stormy meetings. Skinny children were playing on the granite plinth, and on a bench sat a lady wearing pince-nez, her hat an exact replica of the one Pushkin was holding behind his back.

Sparse clouds were floating over Tverskoi Boulevard. A motor lorry, full of soldiers, thundered past. Nodding towards it, the driver said: "They're after plunder. Do you know Vasili Vasilievich Ovsyannikov? He was the biggest millionaire in Moscow. They went to his house yesterday, like that, in motor lorries, and cleaned up everything. Vasili Vasilievich only shook his head, and walked out—where to, nobody knows. People have forgotten God, that's how the old folk look at it...."

At the end of the boulevard the ruins of the Gagarin mansion came into sight. A solitary man in shirt sleeves was standing on the top of a wall, breaking off bricks with a pickaxe, and throwing them on the ground. To the left, the vast bulk of the burnt-out mansion seemed to be staring at the pallid sky through the empty sockets of its windows. All round were houses riddled with bullet holes. Only eighteen months before, Dasha and Katya had been hurrying along this very pavement, lambswool shawls over their heads. Splinters of ice crunched beneath their feet, and stars were reflected in the icy puddles. The sisters were hastening to the Lawyers' Club to hear a special report on the rumours about the revolution supposed to have broken out in Petersburg. There had been intoxication in the crisp, spring air.

Dasha shook her head. "I won't think about it—it's all over and past."

The droshky turned into Arbat Street and drove up a side street on the left. Dasha's heart began to beat so violently that she felt quite dizzy. There was the white two-storeyed house with the attic floor above, where she had lived with Katya and Nikolai Ivanovich after 1915. Here it was that Telegin had come after his escape from the German prison camp. Here Katya had met Roshchin. Dasha had passed through this door, with its peeling paint, on the day of her wedding, and Telegin had handed her into the rubber-tired droshky with the grey horse, and they had driven through the spring twilight, among the still faint lights, towards happiness.... Now the panes in the attic windows were broken and Dasha recognized the wallpaper in her old room, hanging in tatters. A crow flew out of a window.

"Right or left?" asked the driver.

Dasha consulted the piece of paper in her hand. The droshky stopped in front of a tall house, the front door of which was boarded up from inside. Since Dasha was not supposed to ask anybody any questions she had to go up and down back staircases a long time, looking for flat 112a. Sometimes the sound of her steps caused a door to be opened a crack, on the chain. There seemed to be a watcher posted behind each door, to warn the inhabitants of the approach of danger.

On the fifth floor Dasha rapped at a door—three times running, and then once, as she had been instructed. Cautious steps were heard, and someone looked at Dasha through the keyhole, breathing hard. Then the door was opened by a tall elderly lady with bright-blue, alarmingly prominent eyes. Dasha silently extended the paste-board triangle. The lady said:

"Oh, from Petersburg! Come in, please!"

Dasha passed through a kitchen where obviously nothing had been cooked for a long time, into a big curtained room. In the semidarkness the outlines of handsome furniture could be made out, bronze surfaces catching the light here and there, but there was an unlived-in air in this room, too. The lady invited Dasha to sit down on a sofa, and took a seat beside her, gazing at her visitor with her terrifying, wide-open eyes.

"Speak!" she said, in harsh, peremptory tones.

Dasha did her best to gather up her thoughts, and began conscientiously repeating the not very encouraging message with which Kulichok had entrusted her. The lady clasped her exquisite, ringed hands on her rigid knees, pulling at the fingers till the joints cracked.

"So they know nothing in Petrograd!" she interrupted, her deep voice quivering with emotion. "You don't know that Colonel Sidorov's house was searched last night.... Evacuation plans and

192

a few mobilization lists were found.... You don't know that Vilen-kin was arrested early this morning. "

Straightening herself with a jerk she rose from the sofa, and drew aside the portière over the door, turning towards Dasha.

"Come this way. There's someone here who wants to meet you!"

"The password!"

The curt words came from a man standing with his back to the window. Dasha held out the paste-board triangle. "Who gave you that?" (Dasha tried to explain.) "Be more concise!"

He was holding a silk handkerchief to his mouth with his left hand, concealing features which were either naturally swarthy, or made up to appear so. Washed-out, yellow-rimmed eyes gazed impatiently at Dasha. Once more he interrupted her.

"Are you aware that by entering this organization you are risking your life?"

"I am alone and free," said Dasha. "I know hardly anything about the organization. Nikanor Yurevich gave me the commission.... I can't go on doing nothing. I assure you I'm not afraid of work, or...."

"You're nothing but a child...."

The words were uttered in the same jerky tones, but Dasha's brows flew up.

"I'm twenty-four."

"Are you—a woman?" (Dasha made no reply.) "This is very important in the circumstances." (She nodded.) "You need not tell me anything about yourself, I have sized you up. I trust you. Does that surprise you?"

Dasha could only blink. The abrupt, assured phrases, the authoritative tones, the cold eyes, were rapidly enchaining her vacillating will. She felt the same sort of relief that one feels when the doctor, seating himself at one's bedside, his spectacles gleaming sagely, says: "Well, dear lady, from now on we're going to behave ourselves...."

She looked more attentively at the man with the handkerchief to his face. He was not tall, wore a soft hat, a well-cut fawn overcoat and leather leggings. His clothes and his precise movements gave him a foreign air, but he spoke with a Petersburg accent, and his voice was somewhat vague and hollow.

"Where are you staying?"

"Nowhere—I came straight from the train."

"Good. You will now go to Tverskaya Street, to the Café Bom, order something to eat. A man will come up to you—you will rec-

193

ognize him by his wearing a death's-head tiepin. He will give you the password: 'God speed you on your way.' You will then show him this." (He tore the paste-board triangle in two, handing one half to Dasha.) "Don't let anyone see you showing it. He will give you further instructions. You must obey him implicitly. Have you any money?"

He drew two thousand-ruble "Duma" notes from a pocket-book.

"Your expenses will be paid. Try and keep this money for emergencies, for bribes, or possible flight. Anything may happen to you. Go now.... But first—do you understand all I have told you?"

"Yes," faltered Dasha, folding up the money into smaller and smaller squares.

"Not a word of having seen me! Not a word to a soul that you have been here! Go now."

Dasha went on foot to Tverskaya Street. She was hungry and tired. The trees lining the boulevard, and the few sombre-looking pedestrians, seemed to float by in a mist. But she was at peace, for her agonizing inactivity was over, and incomprehensible events had caught her up as in a tornado, and were whirling her on to some wild life.

Two women in bast shoes approached her, flitting past, vague as shadows thrown on a screen. Glancing at Dasha one of them said in low tones:

"Brazen hussy—she can hardly stand!"

A tall lady floated by, her grizzled locks screwed up in a tousled knot, pitiful, tragic lines at the corners of her puffy lips. Intense bewilderment was imprinted on what must have once been a handsome countenance. Her long black skirt was conspicuously patched with a different material. She was carrying a bundle of books beneath a long shawl, the point of which trailed on the ground, and addressed Dasha under her breath as she passed:

"I have Rozanov's banned works and a complete set of Vladimir Solovyov."

A little further on she noticed three old men bending over a park bench. As she passed, Dasha saw that two Red Army men were sitting close together on the bench, fast asleep with their mouths open and their rifles between their knees. The old men were whispering foul words over them.

Beyond the trees a dry wind was chasing the dust. A solitary tram passed by, one of its steps broken loose and clattering against the cobblestones. Soldiers hung in grey swarms from the handrails, and on the brakes at the back. Blithely indifferent to revolution, the sparrows hopped about the head of the bronze Pushkin.

Dasha turned into Tverskaya Street: a cloud of dust sprang up behind her, blowing scraps of paper on to her and propelling her towards the Café Bom—the last bulwark of the old, carefree days.

Here there gathered poets of all schools, ex-journalists, literary time-servers, brisk youths, easily and adroitly adapting themselves to the troublous times, young women dazed with boredom and cocaine, anarchist small fry—all seeking for keen sensations, while ordinary citizens were attracted by the cakes to be obtained.

Dasha had hardly settled down in a seat at the back of the café, beneath the bust of a famous writer, when a man threw up his hands in astonishment, plunged through the clouds of tobacco-smoke, and slumped into a seat beside her, giggling moistly and exposing a set of rotten teeth. She recognized him as an old friend—the poet Alexander Zhirov.

"I ran after you all down Lubyanka.... I was sure it was you, Darya Dmitrevna. Wherever have you sprung from? Are you alone? Or is your husband here, too? D'you remember me? I used to be in love with you—you knew that, didn't you?"

There was an oily gleam in his eyes. It was evident that he did not expect an answer to any of his questions. He was the same as ever—still in a continuous fever of excitement. But his unhealthy-looking skin had grown flabby and his nose, wide at the base and a trifle askew, stood out on his long emaciated countenance.

"If you knew what I've been through all these years.... It's incredible.... I haven't been in Moscow long.... I belong to the Imagist group—Seryozha Esénin, Burlyuk, Kruchenikh. We are undermining everything. Did you go past Strastnoi Monastery? Did you notice the huge letters on the wall? It's unprecedented audacity.... Even the Bolsheviks were excited. Esenin and I worked on it all night. We put the Virgin Mary and Jesus Christ through it.... Such a piece of cosmic obscenity—two old ladies read it in the early morning and both of them gave up the ghost on the spot.... I'm in the anarchist 'Black Falcon' group, too, you know, Darya Dmitrevna.... We'll get you into the movement.... It's no use protesting, we *will*! Do you know who our chief is? The famous Mamont Dalsky.... He's a genius, a second Kean, a real despera-do.... Another week or two, and the whole of Moscow will be in our hands.... It'll be the beginning of a new era! Moscow under the Black Banner! D'you know how we mean to celebrate our victory? We'll announce a universal carnival ... throw open the wine cellars, have military bands playing in the squares, a million-and-a-half masked revellers. Half of them will turn up stark naked—

195

not a doubt of it! And for fireworks, we'll blow up the ordnance depots at Lossino-Ostrovskaya. It'll be an unprecedented occurrence in the history of the world."

It was the third political system Dasha had encountered during the last few days. This time she was only frightened. She even forgot her hunger. Well-pleased with the impression he had made, Zhirov entered into greater detail.

"Doesn't the vulgarity of modern towns make you want to spew blood? My friend Valet, the talented artist—you remember him, of course!—has drawn up a plan for the thorough alteration of the face of the town.... We shan't have time to break up everything and rebuild it before the carnival.... Of course a few buildings will be blown up—the Historical Museum, the Kremlin, the Sukharev Tower, the Pertsov mansion.... We mean to put up boardings along the streets, as high as the houses, painted with architectural designs in an absolutely novel, unprecedented style.... We're going to spray coloured paint over the trees—we can't leave the foliage its natural colour, you know.... Try and imagine the black lime trees along Prechistenski Boulevard, and Tverskoi Boulevard all a sinister purple! Ghastly! A national desecration of Pushkin is being got up, too.... Do you remember the 'Magnificent Blasphemies' and the 'Struggle against Convention' in Telegin's flat? People used to make fun of us then."

He recalled the past, giggling and shivering, moving nearer to Dasha, every now and then brushing against the scarcely perceptible curve of her breast as he gesticulated....

"And do you remember Elizaveta Kievna, with her sheep's eyes? She was madly in love with your fiancé, but she lived with Bessonov. She married Zhadov, a prominent fighting anarchist.... He and Mamont Dalsky are our trump cards. Antoshka Arnoldov is here, too, you know! During the Provisional Government he got the whole press into his hands ... two private cars.... Slept with women of the aristocracy.... There was one—a Hungarian from the 'Villa Rodel'—a regular beauty.... He always took his revolver with him when he went to bed with her. He went to Paris last July—was within an inch of being made ambassador.... The ass! He didn't manage to transfer his capital to a foreign bank, and now he's starving like a stray cur. Yes, Darya Dmitrevna, one must keep in step with the new era. Antoshka Arnoldov ruined himself by taking a grand apartment on Kirochnaya Street, and going in for gilt furniture and plated coffeepots and a hundred pairs of boots. We must burn, smash, tear all prejudices to pieces.... Absolute, animal, virginal freedom—that's what we need! There'll never be such a chance again.... We are making a

196

mighty experiment. All those hankering after middle-class prosperity will perish. We will crush them.... Man is mere boundless desire...." (Here he lowered his voice, and spoke right into Dasha's ear.) "The Bolsheviks are just dung. They were only worth anything for a single week, in October.... And then they turned immediately to the State principle. Russia has always been an anarchist country, the Russian peasant is a born anarchist.... The Bolsheviks want to turn Russia into a factory—nonsense! They'll never bring it off. We have Makhno. Peter the Great was a mere puppy in comparison. Makhno in the south, Mamont Dalsky and Zhadov in Moscow ... we'll surround them with fire on two sides. I'll take you to a place tonight where you'll see the scope of it all.... You *will* come, won't you?"

A pale young man with a pointed beard had been sitting at the next table for several minutes. From behind a newspaper he was gazing fixedly through his pince-nez at Dasha. She had been so stunned by Zhirov's eloquence that she had not thought of protesting: it seemed to her that these supernatural ideas were being born with lightning rapidity in the clouds of smoke, while strange faces with dilated pupils, and teeth closed upon cigarettes floated around her. What could she find to say to all that? She could only have wailed piteously that these experiments terrified her, but her wailings would have been drowned in diabolical shrieks of amusement, in taunts, in mocking laughter.

The eyes of the man with the pointed beard prodded her more and more insistently. The tiny metal death's-head in his crimson tie told her that this was the one she had to meet, but when she made as if to rise, he gave a brief shake of the head, indicating that she must stay where she was. Dasha frowned, trying to think what she should do. He looked significantly at Zhirov. She understood, and asked Zhirov to go and get her something to eat. As soon as he left, the man with the pointed beard went up to her table and said, scarcely opening his lips:

"God speed you on your way!"

Dasha opened her bag and displayed the half of the triangle. He fitted it to the other half, and then tore both halves into bits.

"How is it you know Zhirov?" he asked in rapid tones.

"I've known him for ages—in Petersburg."

"That suits us very well. People must be led to think that you belong to his set. Agree to all his proposals. And this time tomorrow—don't forget!—be at the Gogol monument at the end of Prechistenski Boulevard. Where are you spending the night?"

"I don't know."

"Stay anywhere you like, for tonight. Go with Zhirov...."

"I'm terribly tired."

Dasha's eyes filled with tears, and her hands shook, but a glance at his cold face, and at the death's-head in his tie, made her look down abashed.

"Remember—absolute secrecy! If you let fall a single word, even by accident, you'll have to be got rid of. These are perilous times."

He stressed the words "got rid of". Dasha felt her very toes shrink. Zhirov was pushing his way to the table with two plates in his hands. The man with the death's-head tiepin went up to him, his thin lips twisted in a grimace, and Dasha heard him say: "Who's the pretty girl?"

"Now, now, Yurka, hands off!" said Zhirov, sending after the other a smile which seemed to veil a threat, and which revealed his decaying teeth.

He set before Dasha black bread, sausages, and a glass full of some brownish concoction.

"What about tonight?"

"I don't care," replied Dasha, biting off a piece of sausage with poignant enjoyment.

Zhirov invited her to come to his room at the Hotel Luxe, across the road.

"You can have a sleep and a wash, and I'll come for you about ten o'clock."

He bustled about, seeing to everything, still retaining a certain wholesome fear of Dasha. His room had brocade curtains and a pink carpet, but the bed inspired so little confidence that he himself told Dasha she had better lie down on the sofa. Moving from it books, manuscripts and newspapers, he spread a sheet and a strip of dark fur, evidently once the lining of an expensive coat. Then he went out of the room, giggling. Dasha took off her shoes. Her back, her legs, her whole body were aching. She fell asleep the moment she lay down, snuggling into the thick fur, which had a faint animal smell beneath the odour of scent and moth balls. She did not hear Zhirov come in and bend over to look at her, nor the deep voice of a tall, clean-shaven man, with a Roman cast of countenance, calling out from the door: "Take her there, then—I'll give you a note."

The evening was already far gone when she heaved a profound sigh and woke up. A yellowish moon rising from behind the roof of a house opposite was reflected brokenly in the uneven surface of the windowpane. A strip of light from an electric bulb showed beneath the door. At last Dasha remembered where she was; hastily pulling up her stockings, and setting her hair and dress to rights, she went over to the washing-stand. The towel was so filthy that Dasha, after hesitating for a moment with outspread, dripping fingers, turned back the hem of her skirt and dried her hands on it.

She felt all this squalor keenly, and her throat contracted with disgust: if only she could run back to her home, to the clean window, with the swallows outside.... Turning her head she caught sight of the moon, a refracted, ominous sickle, suspended limply above Moscow. No, no! There was no going back! She could not die in solitude in her armchair at the window, overlooking the deserted Kamenny Ostrov Street, listening to the sound of doors and windows being boarded up.... No.... Come what might, there should be no going back....

There was a knock at the door, and Zhirov entered on tiptoe. "I've got a permit, come on, Darya Dmitrevna!"

Dasha did not ask him what permit he had got and where they were to go, she merely pulled on her homemade cap and pressed the bag containing the two thousand rubles to her side. They went out. One side of Tverskaya Street was in moonlight. There were no lamps burning. A patrol was slowly passing through the empty street, silent but for the sombre thudding of heavy boots.

Zhirov directed her steps into Strastnoi Boulevard. There were patches of moonlight on the uneven ground. It was terrifying to turn one's eyes towards the pitch-dark of the shade beneath the lime trees. A figure seemed to plunge into that shade. Zhirov halted, revolver in hand.

After a moment's pause, he whistled softly. A reply came from the shade. "Gangway!" said Zhirov in a slightly louder voice. "Pass, Comrade," came in a distinct drawling voice.

They turned into Malaya Dmitrovka. Two men in leather jackets hastened across the street towards them, but after a glance silently let them pass. As they neared the former Merchants' Club, from the second storey of which a black flag drooped over the entry, four men emerged from behind pillars in the porch, training revolvers on the newcomers. Dasha stumbled in her walk.

"What the hell, Comrades!" cried Zhirov angrily. "Frightening people like that! I have a permit signed by Mamont...."

"Let's see it!"

The four men, their smooth cheeks concealed by their upturned collars, their eyes hidden under the peaks of their caps, inspected the permit by the light of the moon. Zhirov's masklike features were frozen in a set smile. One of the four asked roughly:

"Who's it for?"

"For this comrade." Zhirov seized Dasha's hand. "She's an actress from Petrograd.... She must be rigged out. She's going to join our group...."

"All right.... Go in...."

Dasha and Zhirov entered a dimly-lit hall, with a machine gun perched on a staircase leading from it. The commandant, a short, chubby-faced youth, wearing the tunic of a student's uniform, and a skullcap, appeared. He turned the permit over and over in his hands, scrutinizing it earnestly, before asking Dasha gruffly:

"What articles of clothing do you need?"

Zhirov replied for her: "Mamont has given orders for her to be clothed from head to foot, with the best things obtainable."

"What d'you mean—Mamont has given orders? It's time you understood that we don't take orders here, Comrade. This isn't a shop." (Just then the commandant felt an itching on his thigh, and started scratching the place, frowning portentously.) "All right, come on then!"

He took a key from his pocket and led them to a former cloakroom, now used as the storeroom of the House of Anarchy.

"Choose what you like, Darya Dmitrevna," said Zhirov. "Don't be shy—all this belongs to the people...."

With a sweeping gesture, Zhirov indicated the coat racks, from which hung fur boas of every description, as well as coats of sable, ermine, silver fox, chinchilla, marmoset and sealskin. Others lay heaped on tables or simply piled up on the floor. Open trunks overflowed with dresses, lingerie, and boxes of shoes. A veritable treasury of luxury seemed to have been emptied into the room. The commandant perfectly indifferent to this abundant display, seated himself, yawning, on a box.

"Darya Dmitrevna," urged Zhirov, "take whatever you like, I'll carry them for you. Come upstairs, you can change there."

However complicated Dasha's emotions may have been, she was still first and foremost a woman. Her cheeks flushed. A week ago, drooping like a lily of the valley at her window, she had believed her life was over, that she had nothing more to expect—it is unlikely that she could then have been tempted by the idea of any such treasures. Now everything around her seemed to have sprung into life, and everything within her that she had considered inert and done with was in motion. She was in that delightful state when desires, awakening hopes, reach out towards the tremulous mist of the morrow, and the present lies around in ruins, like a wrecked house.

She hardly recognized her own voice, marvelled over her own replies, actions, the calmness with which she accepted the fantastic atmosphere around her. An instinct hitherto slumbering within her came to life, telling her that this was the moment to hoist her sails and throw all unnecessary ballast overboard.

She stretched out her hand to a cape of dark sable.

"Will you give me that one!"

Zhirov glanced at the commandant, who simply inflated his cheeks. Zhirov took down the necklet and threw it across his shoulder. Dasha bent over a huge open trunk—for one moment the idea of other people's clothes was hateful to her—and plunged her arm up to the elbow in a heap of lingerie.

"And shoes, Darya Dmitrevna? And take a pair of boots for wet weather! The ball dresses are in that wardrobe. Comrade Commandant, may we have the key? Ball dresses are an actress's stock in trade, you know."

"Take what you like—what do I care!" said the commandant.

Dasha, followed closely by Zhirov carrying the clothes, went up to the second storey, to a small room with a bullet-shattered mirror in it. Peering into the network of cracks on the murky surface of the glass, Dasha saw another woman, slowly drawing on silk stockings. She next slipped on a chemise of the finest lawn, and over it lace-trimmed drawers, moving her old, mended underclothes aside with the points of her shoes. She threw the fur over her slender, bare shoulders.... What do you consider yourself, old girl? A prostitute? A plunderer? A thief? You're mighty pretty, whatever you are.... So there's a good time coming! Let it come—there'll be time enough to think it all out afterwards....

The big restaurant in the Hotel Metropole was closed on account of damage during the October bombardment, but food and drink was still served in the private rooms, for a part of the hotel was occupied by foreigners, mostly Germans, and by such pertinacious speculators as had succeeded in furnishing themselves with foreign passports—Lithuanian, Polish, Persian, and so on. The carousals held in the private rooms were comparable to those in Florence during the plague. The genuine Moscow dwellers (largely actors, firmly convinced that the Moscow theatres would not even last out the season, and that both theatres and actors were doomed) were also admitted—with personal recommendations and through the back entrance. These drank in good earnest.

Mamont Dalsky, a tragedian whose name had recently been scarcely less famous than that of the great Rossi, was the soul of these nocturnal revelries. He was a man of unbridled passions, an Apollo, a gambler, a calculating madman, dangerous, majestic, wily. He was seldom seen on the stage of recent years, and then only as guest actor, but he was frequently to be met with in the gambling dens of Petersburg and Moscow, in the south, or in Siberia. Fantastic tales were told of his losses. He was beginning to show his years, and talked about leaving the stage. During the war he had been mixed up in extremely dubious speculations in army supplies. After the revolution broke out he turned up in Moscow. Sensing its dramatic potentialities, he longed to play on its vast stage the leading role in a new version of Schiller's "Robbers".

With the persuasive powers of an actor of genius, he spoke of divine anarchy, of absolute freedom, of the relativeness of moral principles, and of the right of each to take whatever he needed. He sowed spiritual unrest in Moscow. When certain groups of Moscow youths, their numbers swollen by criminal types, began requisitioning private mansions, he consolidated these scattered anarchical groups, took the Merchants' Club by force, and renamed it the House of Anarchy, confronting the Soviet authorities with a *fait accompli.* He had not, so far, declared war against the Soviet power, but it was obvious that, with his imagination, he would not stop at the storerooms of the Merchants' Club, or at those nocturnal revelries, during which, from a window in the "House", he harangued the crowd assembled in the courtyard, his classical gesture followed by a shower of trousers, boots, stuff-lengths and bottles of brandy.

The first thing Dasha saw when she and Zhirov entered the private room in the Metropole, was the set sombre face of this man, his mouth and jaw set in resolute lines, his neck encircled by a grimy soft collar. It was like a face cast in bronze, on which passions and dissipation, like a skilful sculptor, had chiselled folds and wrinkles.

The lid of the grand piano was raised. A frail, clean-shaven man in a velvet jacket, a cigarette between his teeth, his glazed eyes half concealed by the lashes, his head thrown back, was striking sepulchral chords. A handful of "celebrities" were seated at a table around innumerable empty bottles. One of them, a snubnosed man, his prominent chin propped against the palm of his hand, so that his pudgy face was squashed into a sort of pancake, was singing the tenor part of the church service. The others—a "heavy father" with a juglike countenance, a melancholy comic actor with a sagging underlip, a *jeune premier* with a three-days' growth of beard and a pointed nose, a stage lover, drunk as a lord, and a great leading man, with a lofty brow marked by deeply-engraved wrinkles, who seemed perfectly sober—came in all together with the refrains.

The archdeacon from the Church of the Saviour, a handsome, greying man in massive gold-rimmed glasses presented to him by the merchants of Moscow, was walking up and down the carpet

202

intoning the responses, the flowing sleeves of his cassock swinging. The glasses on the tables vibrated to his deep, velvety bass. The walls of the private room were upholstered in dark-red silk, and there were brocade curtains at the door, before which stood a small three-leaved screen.

Mamont Dalsky stood with his elbow on the top of the screen, a pack of cards held in one hand. He was dressed in a kind of pseudomilitary uniform—a norfolk jacket, check breeches with a leather seat, and black cavalry boots. As Dasha entered he was listening to the requiem with a grim smile.

"What a beautiful woman—enough to drive one mad!" said the man at the piano. Dasha halted timidly. Everyone but Dalsky turned to look at her.

"True Russian beauty," said the archdeacon.

"Come and sit with us, little girl," said the leading man in his velvety voice.

"Sit down, sit down," whispered Zhirov.

Dasha seated herself at the table. They crowded round her, kissing her hands and stepping back with respectful bows, as if she were Mary Stuart; then the singing went on again. Zhirov set caviare and hors d'œuvres in front of her, and made her drink something sweet and burning. It was stuffy and smoky in the room. After tossing off the thick, syrupy drink, Dasha removed her fur, and rested her bare arms on the table. The sombre chords, the ancient words of the chant, moved her strangely. She could not take her eyes off Mamont. Zhirov had told her all about him on the way. He still stood apart from the crowd, beside the screen, and it would have been hard to say whether he was in a furious temper, or dead-drunk.

"What about it, gentlemen?" he was saying, in a deep voice which filled the room. "Doesn't anybody want to play?"

"Nobody wants to play with you, we're all enjoying ourselves, and do shut up and cool down," said the man with the flattened features, in a high rapid falsetto. "Come on, Yasha—let's have the seventh chant!"

At the piano, Yasha, throwing his head well back and half closing his eyes, placed his fingers on the keyboard.

"Not for money—to hell with your money...."

"Just the same we don't want to—it's no use trying, Mamont!"

"I'll play you for shots!"

A moment of silence followed this declaration. Then the *jeune premier* with the pointed nose passed his hand over his forehead and hair, and rose in his place, buttoning up his waistcoat.

"*I'll* play for shots!"

The comedian clutched him in silence, and bringing his enormous weight to bear on him, pushed him back on to his chair.

"I'll stake my life," shouted the *jeune premier*, "that that scoundrel Mamont has marked cards! To hell, let him keep the bank! Leave go of me!"

But he had no more strength left. The "heavy father" with the juglike face said softly:

"And not a drop of wine left! That's disgrace, Mamont, old man...."

Mamont Dalsky suddenly flung the pack of cards and a big automatic revolver, on to a little table with a telephone on it. His large, chiselled countenance was pale with fury.

"No one will leave this room," he said, biting off the syllables. "We will play the way I want! These cards are not marked."

He drew in deep breaths of air through distended nostrils, thrusting out his lower lip. All realized that the moment was fraught with danger. His glance travelled over the faces around the table. Yasha picked out the tune of a popular song with one finger on the keys of the piano. Mamont's black brows suddenly flew upwards, and a look of astonishment enlivened for a moment his fathomless eyes. He had seen Dasha. Her heart turned cold beneath this glance. He went up to her with a firm step, caught up the tips of her fingers, and raised them to his parched lips—but he did not kiss her hand, merely brushed it with his lips.

"No wine, you say? You'll soon get some!"

He pressed a bell, not taking his eyes off Dasha. A Tatar waiter entered. He flung out his hands—not a single bottle of wine, everything drunk up, the cellar locked, the manager gone....

"Get out!" said Mamont, and he stepped to the telephone as though he felt the eyes of a vast audience on him. He called a number, and began talking: "Yes.... It's me ... Dalsky.... Send a detail. The Metropole. I'm here.... It's urgent.... Yes ... four men will be enough."

Slowly he put back the receiver, leant his whole figure against the wall, and folded his arms. A quarter of an hour passed. Yasha was playing Scriabine softly. The sounds, so familiar, so reminiscent of the past, made Dasha's head swim. Time vanished. The silver brocade on her bosom rose and fell, the blood pulsated in her ears. Zhirov was whispering something to her, but she did not hear him.

She was excited, conscious of the joy of freedom, the ease of youth. She felt as if she were flying like a toy balloon released from a child's perambulator, higher and higher, to dizzying heights....

The leading man was stroking her bare arm, booming out in velvety accents:

"Don't look at him so tenderly, darling, you'll be blinded.... There is undoubtedly something satanic about Mamont.... "

The folding doors suddenly flew back, revealing four heads in caps: four hands emerging from leather sleeves and tightly grasping hand grenades, appeared over the top of the screen. The four anarchists shouted threateningly:

"Don't move! Hands up!"

"Drop that! All is in order," boomed out Dalsky imperturbably. "Thanks, Comrades!" talking up to them, and bending over the screen, he explained something to them in undertones. The caps nodded and their owners departed. A few minutes later there was the sound of voices, and a muffled shriek. The walls shook perceptibly from the dull thud of an explosion.

"Those puppies must have their cheap effects," said Mamont.

He rang the bell. The waiter, pale, his teeth chattering, bounced into the room.

"Clear all this away, and bring fresh glasses," ordered Mamont. "Yasha, spare my nerves! Play something jolly!"

Hardly had the waiter laid a clean cloth, when the anarchists reappeared, laden with bottles. Placing bottles of brandy, whiskey, liqueurs and champagne on the carpet, they vanished as silently as they had come. Cries of admiration and delight came from those seated round the table.

"I gave orders for only 50% of the drinks they found in the hotel rooms to be expropriated," explained Mamont. "The other half has been left to the owners. You can be quite easy in your consciences, all is in order."

Yasha played a flourish on the piano. Champagne corks popped. Mamont seated himself next to Dasha. In the light of the lamp on the table the chiselled lines of his face seemed more significant than ever.

"I saw you in the Luxe today, you were asleep. Who are you?"

Laughing out of sheer dizziness, she replied:

"Nobody! A toy balloon."

He laid a large, hot hand on her bare shoulder and looked into her eyes. Dasha did not care, all she felt was the warm weight of his hand on her cool shoulder. She picked up her champagne glass by its slender stem and tossed off the contents.

"So you're nobody's?" he asked.

"Nobody's!"

Mamont intoned in Dasha's ear with tragic intensity:

"Live, my child, live with all the forces of your nature.... It is your good fortune that you have met me.... Fear not, I shall not sully your youth with love.... The free neither love, nor demand love.... Othello is a medieval auto-da-fe, the Inquisition, a grimace of the devil.... Romeo and Juliet.... I know you—in your soul that's what you crave for.... But that's all old-fashioned rubbish.... We are smashing everything up, from top to bottom. We will burn all the books, destroy the museums.... Man must learn to forget the centuries.... Freedom consists in one thing only: divine anarchy.... The immense conflagration of the passions.... Oh, no! Never expect peace or love from me, pretty one! I will emancipate you.... I will strike the chains of your innocence asunder.... I will give you all you can ask, between two embraces.... Ask.... Ask now.... Tomorrow may be too late."

Beneath these ravings Dasha could feel with her whole being the heavily seething passion at her side. She was seized with horror, as in a nightmare, when one is unable to move, and the fiery-eyed monster emerges from the darkness of dreams, to knock one down, to trample, crush out one's life.... Most terrible of all was the sensation that unfamiliar, searing suffocating desires were rising in response within her.... She felt she was woman through and through. She was so beautiful in her agitation that the leading man reached out to her, and, clinking glasses with her, said jealously:

"Mamont, you're torturing the child!"

Dalsky jumped up as if he had been shot, and banged on the table, so that the glasses danced and fell.

"I'll shoot anyone down who dares to lay a finger on this woman!"

He tore over to the table on which stood the telephone, with his revolver still lying beside it. The others jumped up, overturning their chairs. Yasha took cover beneath the grand piano. Mamont snatched up the revolver, and Dasha, without herself knowing how it came about, found herself hanging on to his arm, and looking up to him with pleading eyes. He clasped her slim back beneath the shoulder blades, lifting her off her feet, and glued his mouth on hers with a violence that brought their clenched teeth into contact. Dasha moaned. At that moment the telephone rang. Mamont let Dasha down on to the seat of an armchair—she covered her eyes with her forearm—and grasped the receiver.

"Yes.... What d'you want? I'm busy.... Oh! Where? Myasnitskaya Street? Diamonds? Valuable ones? I'll be round in ten minutes...."

Thrusting his revolver into the back pocket of his breeches, he went over to Dasha, framing her face in his hands and kissing her avidly again and again. Then, with a classical gesture of farewell, he went out of the room.

Dasha spent the remainder of the night in the Luxe. She slept like a log, not even taking off the dress of silver brocade. (Zhirov slept in the bathroom—for fear of Mamont.) When she got out of bed she sat huddled up at the window till noon. She would not speak to Zhirov, or answer his questions. At about four o'clock she went out and waited till five in the Prechistenski Boulevard, on the space in front of the long-nosed Gogol, where the skinny children were quietly making mud pies with dust and sand.

She was once more in her old dress and homemade cap. The sun, which seemed to be standing guard over the poverty of life, warmed her back. The pinched faces of the children had the old look which hunger gives. All around was an empty stillness. No sound of wheels, no loud voices. All the wheels had rolled away to the war, and the passers-by had fallen silent. In his granite chair, Gogol stooped beneath the weight of his cloak, all befouled with the droppings of sparrows. Two bearded men passed without paying the slightest attention to Dasha. One of them was looking at the ground, the other at the tops of the trees. Scraps of their talk floated back to her.

"Utter defeat! Terrible! *Now* what are we to do?"

"After all, Samara has been taken, Ufa has been taken...."

"I'll never believe anything again! We won't survive another winter."

"Still Denikin's having his own way on the Don...."

"I don't believe it, nothing can save us. Babylon perished, Rome perished, and we too will perish...."

"But Savinkov hasn't been arrested. Chernov hasn't been arrested."

"That's nothing! Ah, well! Russia once existed, and now she is no more...."

The same grey-haired lady whom Dasha had seen the day before, went past, timidly displaying from under her shawl the complete works of Rozanov. Dasha turned away from her. The young man with the death's-head tiepin was edging his way up to her bench. He cast rapid glances all round, adjusted his pince-nez, and seated himself next to Dasha.

"Did you spend the night in the Metropole?"

Dasha bent her head, forming the word "yes" with her lips alone.

"Good! I've got you a room. You can move in, this evening. Not a syllable to Zhirov! Now to business! Do you know Lenin by sight?"

"No."

He drew a bundle of photographs out of his pocket and stuffed them into Dasha's bag, and sat on in silence, pushing hairs from his beard between his lips. Then he took Dasha's hands, which were lying lifelessly on her lap, and gave them a shake.

"This is how matters stand.... Bolshevism is Lenin. Get that? We may crush the Red Army, but so long as Lenin is in the Kremlin there can never be victory for us. Is that clear? He's a theoretician, he's will incarnate—the greatest danger for the whole world, not just for us.... Think it over and tell me definitely: are you, or are you not, ready and willing?"

"To kill him?" asked Dasha, watching a half-naked infant which was staggering about bowlegged. The young man shuddered convulsively, looked to the right, glanced from narrowed eyelids at the children, and once more began chewing at his beard.

"Nobody says that. Even if it's what you think, you needn't say so out loud. You have been admitted into our organization.... Didn't you understand what Savinkov said to you?"

"He never spoke to me...." (The young man laughed.) "Oh, so the one with the handkerchief was...."

"Sh! Yes—that was Boris Victorovich.... Extraordinary confidence has been placed in you. We need fresh blood. There have been too many arrests. You know of course that the Kazan mobilization plan has come to grief.... The work of our centre is being transferred elsewhere.... But an organization will be left here.... Your task will be to find out whenever Lenin makes speeches in public, to attend meetings, to get into factories.... You will not be working alone.... You will be informed of his departures from the Kremlin and where he is expected to speak.... The best thing for you to do would be to pick up acquaintances among the Communists, and try and get into the Party. Read the papers and keep up with their publications. You will receive further instructions tomorrow morning, at the same place...."

After giving her a conspiratorial address to report to, a password, and the key to her room, he went away in the direction of Arbat Square. Dasha pulled one of the photographs out of her bag and examined it for a long time. But when in its stead she began to see another face, floating from behind the crimson curtains of the previous night, she closed her bag with a resolute snap, and got up, her brows knit, her lips compressed. The tiny bowlegged boy tried to toddle after her, but collapsed on to the sand, hurting his flabby little body and crying bitterly.

Dasha's room turned out to be in Sivtsev Vrazhek Street, in a small dilapidated mansion standing in a courtyard, and apparently untenanted. Dasha had to knock a long time at the back door before it was opened to her by a heavy, dumpy old woman with eyelids turned back, exposing raw-looking flesh, her whole appearance suggesting some old nurse ending her days in the house of her employers. It was a long time before she could understand what Dasha wanted, but at last she let her in, and conducted her to her room, muttering incoherently all the time.

"They've flown away, the proud falcons—Yuri Yurich has gone, and Mikhail Yurich, and Vasili Yurich ... and Vasenka only turned sixteen on the feast of St. Thomas. I've begun to pray for their souls now...."

Refusing the old dame's offer of tea, Dasha undressed and crept beneath the wadded quilt, weeping copiously in the darkness and stifling her sobs in the pillow.

The next morning beneath the statue of Gogol, she received instructions and the order to be at a factory the day after. Her first thought was to go home, but changing her mind she went instead to the Café Bom. There she found Zhirov, who hung round her, asking where she had been all this time and why she had left without her things. "I'm expecting Mamont to call—what shall I tell him about you?"

Dasha turned aside to conceal her mantling cheek. "After all, I have been instructed to keep in touch with him," she told herself, not for a moment deceived by her own lie.

"I'll go and fetch my things," she said irritably, "and then we'll see."

She went back to her room bearing a parcel containing the valuable fur cape, the underclothes and the ball dress. The sight of them, after she had unwrapped them and flung them on to her bed, threw her into a fit of trembling; her teeth chattered, and she once more felt on her shoulders the weight of his hand, the cold touch of his clenched teeth against hers.... She sank on to her knees beside the bed, burying her face in the perfumed fur. "What is it? What is it?" she reiterated dully.

The next morning, in obedience to her instructions, after donning a dark print dress brought to her by the man with the death's-head tiepin, and tying up her head in a kerchief to look like a woman of the working class (she was to give herself out as a former housemaid in a rich family, whom the master had seduced), she took the tram to the factory.

She had no pass, but the old watchman at the gate only winked at her, saying: "You've come for the meeting, lass, have you? It's in the main building."

14–559

She picked her way over rotting planks, past heaps of rusty scrap iron and slag, past huge broken windows. There was nobody about, and the chimney stacks smoked peacefully against the cloudless sky.

Somebody pointed to a grimy door in the wall. Entering, she found herself in a long hall with walls of bare brick. The murky light filtered through a smoke-blackened glass roof. Everything was naked and exposed. Chains hung from the platforms of overhead cranes. Lower down were transmission shafts, their driving belts hanging motionless from the pulleys. Her unaccustomed eye turned in astonishment from dark lathes to the squat, lanky or straddling forms of all sorts of planing, milling and mortising machinery, and the iron discs of friction clutches. She discerned the outlines of a giant steam hammer, hanging lopsided in the semi-darkness of a wide arch.

Here were made the machinery and mechanisms which supplied the life beyond the sombre walls of the factory with light, warmth, movement, significance and luxury. There was a smell of iron filings, machine oil, earth, and home-grown tobacco. A vast crowd of men and women were standing in front of a wooden platform, and many others perched on the side plates of machines and on the high window sills.

Dasha pushed her way up to the platform. A tall young fellow, turning his head, opened his mouth in a broad smile, his teeth showing white against his begrimed face; nodding towards a bench, he stretched out his hand, and Dasha climbed up beside him to the lathe beneath the window. The faces in the vast crowd—several thousand strong—were morose, the brows lined, the lips compressed. She saw such faces every day in the streets and trams, weary Russian faces, with forbidding eyes. Dasha remembered walking about the islands in Petersburg one Sunday, before the war, when her escorts—two barristers—had turned the conversation upon just such faces. "Take the Paris crowd, Darya Dmitrevna—gay, good-humoured, bubbling with fun.... And here you see nothing but scowling countenances. Look at these two workers coming towards us! Shall I go up to them, and try and joke with them? They wouldn't understand, they'd be offended. Russians are so ridiculously slow on the uptake, so heavy in hand...." And now these humourless folk stood there, agitated, sombre, tense and determined. The same faces, but dark with hunger now, the same eyes, but the expression fiery, impatient.

Dasha forgot what she was there for. The impressions accumulated during the life which she had exchanged for her lonely existence at the window in Krasniye Zori Street, Petrograd, carried her away like a storm bird, and she abandoned herself to them with pristine innocence. She was not really stupid but, like many other people, she had been left to herself, with only her own tiny store of experience to guide her. But she thirsted for truth—she thirsted for it as an individual, as a woman, as a member of the human race.

A speaker was holding forth on the situation on the various fronts. What he had to say was not particularly encouraging. The grain blockade was closing in: the Czechoslovaks were cutting off supplies from Siberia, Ataman Krasnov, from the Don. The Germans were meting out ruthless reprisals to the Ukrainian partisans. The ships of the Intervention were threatening Kronstadt and Arkhangelsk. "But the revolution is bound to win!"

The speaker flung his slogans into the air, nailed them in space with his fist, and, picking up his briefcase, ran quickly off the platform. The applause was languid—there was little inclination to clap in such a depressing state of affairs. Heads hung, eyes disappeared beneath scowling brows.

Dasha's eyes met those of the boy with the gleaming teeth, and he grinned cheerfully at her.

"Things are bad, my lass, they want to starve us out. What's to be done about it?"

"Are you afraid?" asked Dasha.

"Me? I'm scared out of my wits! What's your name?" People began looking round with cries of "sh!", "quiet, you there!"

Dasha looked at him. His black shirt was open, showing a muscular chest, he had a bull neck, a merry face, and a bright smile; his hair lay in damp curls, his round eyes were those of a confirmed philanderer, and he was covered with grease and dirt.

"You think you're a fine chap, don't you?" said Dasha. "What are you grinning at?"

"My mother dropped me when I was a baby. Look here—come with us to the front the day after tomorrow! Will you? You'll come to grief here in Moscow, anyhow.... We're taking an accordion, my lass...."

His words were drowned by a storm of applause. A new speaker had ascended the platform, a short man in a grey jacket, his waistcoat showing horizontal wrinkles. His bald, bumpy head was bent over the notes in his hand. "Comrades!" he began, and Dasha noticed that he spoke with a slight burr, and that he looked worried, screwing up his eyes as if the light was in them. His hands rested on the table, on a sheaf of notes. When he said that his subject today would be the acute crisis which was bearing down upon the whole of Europe and on Russia heaviest of all, and that

211

this subject was famine, three thousand people held their breath beneath the smoke-blackened roof.

He began with general statements, speaking in level tones, trying to establish contact with his hearers. He stepped backwards and forwards from the table. He spoke of the world war, which the two predatory groups, who had each other by the throats, neither could nor would bring to an end—of the crazy profiteering in famine. He said only the proletarian revolution could bring the war to an end....

He said there were two ways of fighting famine: one was unrestricted private trade, distending the profits of the speculators, the other—state monopoly. He moved three paces from the end of the table, and bent towards his audience, thrusting his thumbs into the armholes of his waistcoat. This pose brought into prominence his domed brow and big hands, and Dasha noticed that the index finger of his right hand was inky.

"We have always stood, and always will stand, shoulder to shoulder with the class together with which we came out against war, together with which we have overthrown the bourgeoisie, and together with which we are bearing the whole brunt of the present crisis. We must stand by grain monopoly to the end...." (At these words the young man with the grin gave an approving grunt.) "It is our task to conquer famine, or at least to lessen its burden till the coming of the harvest, to enforce the grain monopoly, the rights of the Soviet government, the rights of the proletarian State. We must gather up all grain surpluses and see that stocks are sent where most needed, and are properly distributed....

"But our main task is to keep society going and see that the stupendous work required is never relaxed—and this can only be accomplished by united, unremitting effort...."

The breathless silence was broken by a hollow exclamation, the cry of some tormented soul stumbling on the icy ascent to which the man in the grey suit was urging them all. His brow seemed to hang above the audience—beneath its protuberances the eyes were steady, inexorable.

"...We are faced with the necessity of carrying out a revolutionary socialist task, and there are enormous difficulties in our way. Our epoch is one of bitter civil war.... It is only by defeating the counterrevolution, by pursuing a socialist policy in regard to famine, and by the struggle against it, that we shall conquer both famine and the counterrevolutionaries exploiting famine...."

One of his hands flew out of the armhole of his waistcoat, as if to annihilate an invisible foe, and remained suspended over the audience.

"When the workers, their wits fuddled by the slogans of the

212

profiteers, clamour for the unrestricted sale of grain, the import of motor lorries and other transport machinery, we reply to them that this means to go to the aid of the kulaks.... We will never take that path.... We will seek the support of the workers, with whom we gained the victory in October, we will carry our decisions through only by means of imposing proletarian discipline upon all sections of workers. We are faced with a historic task. And we will fulfil it.... The most fundamental of all questions—that of bread—is dealt with in the latest decrees. These are all based upon three ruling principles. The first is the principle of centralization, or the combining of all for a single, common task under guidance from the centre.... There are many who point out to us that the grain monopoly is being thwarted at every step by private buyers and profiteers. We hear with ever increasing frequency from the intellectuals that the profiteers are doing them a great service, are keeping them alive.... Yes, that is so.... But the private traders are doing it in the *kulak* way, the way that will lead to the consolidation, the establishment, the *perpetuation* of the power of the kulaks...."

The hand, with a sweeping gesture, wiped out a situation that would never again be tolerated.

"Our second slogan is the unity of the workers. It is they who will rescue Russia from the desperate, the stupendous difficulties in which she finds herself. We will call to our aid the organizations of workers' food detachments, of the starving people from the non-agricultural famine districts, it is to them that our Commissariat for Supplies will address itself, and upon them that we will call to join our crusade for bread!"

There was heavy fury in the thunders of applause which broke out. Dasha noticed how the speaker stepped back, thrusting his hands into his pockets, and raising his shoulders. A spot of colour burned on each cheekbone, his eyelids quivered, his forehead was damp.

"We are creating a dictatorship.... We are building up a proletarian dictatorship against exploiters...."

These words, too, were drowned in applause. Silencing his hearers with a peremptory gesture, he waited for quiet to be restored, before continuing:

"...'Representatives of the poor, unite!'—that is our third slogan. We are faced with a historic task: the task of imbuing a class which is new to history with class-consciousness.... All over the world the ranks of town workers, of industrial workers, have united to a man. But practically nowhere in the world have systematic, disinterested, self-sacrificing attempts ever been made to unite those living in remote country districts, on tiny farmsteads, their minds dulled by the benighted, lonely conditions in which they are forced to live. We are faced, here, with the task of identifying the struggle against famine with the struggle for the profound and significant system of socialism. In this struggle we must be ready to use our whole strength, to stake our all, for it is the struggle for socialism, the struggle for the final state system of the toilers and the exploited...."

He passed the palm of his hand rapidly across his forehead.

"...In the districts surrounding Moscow, and in the neighbouring provinces ... even now—in Kursk, Orel, Tambov—we have, on the most conservative estimate, up to ten million poods of surplus grain. Let us attack this matter with combined forces, Comrades! Nothing but the combined forces, the uniting of those who are the greatest sufferers in the famine centres and districts, will be of any use to us, and this is the path to which the Soviet power calls you: the uniting of the workers, the uniting of the very poorest, of their vanguard, for spreading everywhere the idea of war with the kulaks for bread...."

He wiped his brow with his hand more and more frequently, and the ring had gone out of his voice. He had said all that he intended to say. He picked up a sheet of paper from the table, glanced at it, and gathered up the rest of the pile.

"And so, Comrades, if we assimilate all this, if we do all this, we are sure to win."

Suddenly his face was lit up by a frank, good-humoured smile. And everyone understood: this is one of us! They shouted, clapped, stamped. He hastened from the platform, his head seeming to shrink into his shoulders. Dasha's white-toothed neighbour bellowed out, in a voice as powerful as the bellowing of a bull.

"Long live Ilyich!"

All that Dasha could find to say was that she had heard and seen "something new". On returning from the meeting she sat down on her bed, staring with wide-open eyes at the flourishes on the wallpaper. On her pillow lay a note from Zhirov: "Mamont expects you at 11 at the Metropole." And on the floor, just over the threshold, lay another note: "Be at the Gogol monument this evening at 6."

In the first place this "something new" was austerely moral, and therefore sublime.... It was bread that had been talked about. Formerly she had known that bread could be bought, or got in exchange for something else, at a price which everybody knew: a sack of flour cost a pair of unpatched trousers. But now it appeared that the revolution repudiated such bread with fury. Such bread was unclean. Better to starve than partake of it! Three thousand hungry men and women had today repudiated this unclean bread.

"Repudiated it in the name of...." (But here everything was once more all mixed up in Dasha's poor head.) "In the name of the insulted and oppressed...." That was what he had said, wasn't it? "To devote all one's strength, to stake one's all, one's life—for the toilers and the exploited...." This is what gave them that tragic austerity....

Kulichok had told her that all over the world helping hands were being extended, hands with bread in them.... They had only to destroy the Soviet power.... Destroy it, and then there would be bread.... In the name of what? In the name of the salvation of Russia. But who was Russia to be saved from? From ourselves.... But it was not thus that they wanted to save her—she had seen that for herself....

Dasha's poor, poor head! You've come rather late to political questions, Dasha dear! "Wait a minute!" she exclaimed. "Wait a minute!" Her hands behind her back, she paced up and down the room, her eyes on the ground.

"What could be nobler than to give one's life for the oppressed and insulted? But Kulichok had said that it was the Bolsheviks who were ruining Russia, and everyone said the same...."

Dasha closed her eyes, trying to see Russia as a thing she ought to love more than herself. She remembered a picture of Serov's: two horses on a hillside, clouds barked across the sunset, a ragged straw thatch.... "But that's only how Serov sees it...." Now it was the young fellow with the gleaming teeth who appeared inside her closed eyelids, smiling his gay, free smile. Dasha started pacing the room again.... "What then is Russia? Why are people pulling it different ways? I'm only a silly woman, of course, I don't understand a thing.... My God, my God!" Dasha began smiting her bosom with bunched fingertips. But that didn't help, either.... "Go and ask Lenin? Oh, dear, I forgot I was in the other camp...."

All these alarming contradictions and soul-searchings ended in Dasha cramming her cap over her eyes at six o'clock and setting off for the Gogol monument. The man with the tiepin immediately emerged from behind a tree.

"You're three minutes late. Well? Were you there? Did you hear Lenin? Let me have the most important facts. How did he get there? Who was with him? Was there a guard on the platform?"

Dasha tried to gather up her thoughts before replying.

"Tell me, in the name of what is he to be killed?"

"What! What! Where did you get that from? Nobody has any intention.... Ha! He made an impression on you! That's natural.... That's what makes him so dangerous."

"But what he says is true."

Craning his neck, and smiling his thin, gleaming smile right into Dasha's face, he said in insinuating tones:

"Hadn't you better give it up—eh?"

Dasha shrank away. His neck seemed to be stretching like rubber, and the twinkling reflections in his glasses danced before Dasha's eyes.

"I don't know a thing," she whispered. "I don't understand anything any more.... I *must* be convinced, I *must*...."

"Lenin is an agent of the German general staff," hissed the man with the tiepin. He spent almost half-an-hour explaining to Dasha the infernal plan of the Germans: they were sending over Bolsheviks, hired at enormous sums, in sealed carriages; and these Bolsheviks were undermining the army, gulling the workers, destroying the country's industry and agriculture.... In another month or so the Germans would be able to take Russia without firing a shot.

"The Bolsheviks are now stirring up civil war, declaring that there is a grain blockade, and at the same time killing off the private traders, our saviours. They are deliberately organizing famine.... Today you have seen thousands of imbeciles hanging on Lenin's lips ... it's infuriating, maddening.... He is deceiving the masses, the entire nation.... On the physical plane he is the 'Great Provocateur' ... on the other...." (He swayed up to Dasha's ear and whispered all in one breath)—"he is the Antichrist! Remember the prophecies? Everything coincides. The north will go to war with the south. The iron horsemen of death will appear— that's the tanks.... An evil star will drop into the source of waters—that's the five-pointed star of the Bolsheviks.... And he addresses the multitude as Christ did, only in reverse.... Today he even tried to seduce your mind, but we won't give you up. I'll have you transferred to some other work."

Dasha's third question remained unanswered. (She was back in her room, lying on her bed, her eyes hidden against the crook of her elbow.) Suddenly she felt sick of all this thinking.... "Anyone would think I was a hundred years old! Am I so hideous, after all? I'll do just as I like.... Why shouldn't I go to the Metropole, if that's what I want? Why try to hide things that won't be hidden, to stifle the cries of joy in one's bosom? Why tie one's self up in agonizing knots? For whose dear sake? Fool, fool, coward! Let yourself go! Relax! What does anything matter? To hell with love, to hell with self...."

She had known all along that she was going to the Metropole. If she had pretended to hesitate, it was only because the time appointed had not yet come, and because it was dusk, when there is no escape from one's thoughts. Somewhere in the house a clock struck nine times, solemnly, as if from a church tower. Dasha bounded violently from the bed. "I won't let myself get so excited—it's humiliating!"

Undressing rapidly, she ran in her chemise to the bathroom, which was cluttered up with wood, trunks and odds and ends of all sorts. Dasha stood under the shower, catching her breath as the icy streams ran down her back. She ran back to her room, all wet, and dragged the sheet from the mattress to dry herself, her teeth chattering.

But she still could not make up her mind. Her glance travelled irresolutely from the old dress which she had thrown on the floor, to the evening frock, draped over the back of a chair. At last, telling herself again that this was mere cowardice and procrastination, she started dressing. She was thankful that there was no looking glass in the room. Flinging the sable cape round her shoulders she stole out into the street like a thief. It was now almost dark. She walked along the boulevard. Men followed her with admiring eyes, and she could hear their extremely equivocal remarks as she passed. Two men in soldiers' greatcoats, standing under a tree, shouted after her: "Hi, parasite, where are you off to in such a hurry?"

At Nikitski Square Dasha came to a stop, almost unable to breathe—there was a stabbing pain in her heart. A lighted tram—two cars coupled together—went by, its bell clanging furiously. Even the steps were crowded with passengers. One man, holding the brass handrail with his right hand, and grasping an alligator attaché case in the other, turned a powerful clean-shaven countenance upon Dasha as he was borne past. It was Mamont. She gasped and started running after the tram. He caught sight of her and the attaché case jerked convulsively from his grasp. Letting go of the handrail, he jumped off, with the tram going at full speed. Falling flat on his back, he clutched frantically at the air, the sole of one of his boots looming huge for an instant—the next moment the upper part of his body disappeared beneath the back car and the alligator case fell at Dasha's feet. She saw the convulsive upward jerk ot his knees, heard the crunching of bones, and the clattering of boots over the cobblestones. The brakes squealed and the passengers poured out of the car.

A dull film clouded her vision, the road looked as soft as a shroud, and Dasha fell to the ground unconscious, her cheek and arms on the alligator case.

217

IX

The Volunteer Army started its offensive, the so-called "Second Kuban Campaign", with an attack on the railway station of Torgovaya. The capture of this railway junction was of the utmost importance, being equivalent to the cutting off of the whole Northern Caucasus from the rest of Russia. On the 10th of June an army of 9,000, including infantry and cavalry under the command of Denikin, marched in four columns to encircle Torgovaya.

Denikin was with Drozdovsky's column. The tension was terrific. All realized that the issue of the first battle would decide the army's fate. Drozdovsky's men, their advance covered by their only gun, charged with buckshot, made a violent rush under the enemy's artillery fire to ford the river Egorlik. At the head of the column Captain Turkul, who was in command of the regiment, bounced up and down like a rubber ball in the water, spluttering and swearing. The Reds put up a stiff resistance, but allowed themselves to be surrounded by the experienced foe out of sheer ineptitude. Their posts were overthrown, on the south by the column of Borovsky, on the east by Erdeli's cavalry. The Red units, thrown into confusion, abandoned Torgovaya and began retreating northward with their huge baggage trains. But their path was cut off at Shablievka by Markov's column. The Volunteers had scored a decisive victory. Erdeli's Cossack companies scoured the steppe, cutting down the fugitives and seizing prisoners and baggage carts.

Twilight was falling. The battle was dying down. Denikin, a scowl on his crimson face, was pacing up and down the railway platform, his plump hands clasped behind his back. Cadets, laughing and jesting, as men laugh and jest who have come scatheless through mortal danger, were bringing up sacks full of sand, and stacking them on the unsheltered trucks, while others were placing machine guns on the improvised armoured train. The air was shaken every now and then by artillery fire from a Red armoured train to the north, beyond Shablievka. The last shell from that direction fell near the bridge over the Manich, where General Markov sat his grey horse. He had not slept, eaten, or even smoked for two whole days, and was annoyed because the occupation of Shablievka was not going the way he had planned it. The station was discovered to be occupied by a strong force equipped with artillery and armoured cars. The day before, and the whole of the present day, his enveloping column had been fighting stubbornly and unsuccessfully. His usual immediate luck had failed him this time. The losses had been enormous. The

Bolsheviks, occupying Shablievka, had only retreated towards evening, under pressure of the general situation.

Leaning slightly forward in his saddle, he peered at the indistinct outlines of several dead bodies, rigid in the poses in which they had been overtaken by death. They were his officers, each of them had been worth a whole platoon in battle. Several hundred of his best fighters had been killed and wounded, simply because his mind had been temporarily below par.

He heard a groan, heavy breathing, a kind of hissing, like that of a man waking out of a nightmare. An officer came into sight, climbing out of a trench in front of the bridge, but immediately fell forward over the parapet. Coughing, he held fast, and, with difficulty lifting his leg, climbed out and stood staring at a great, clear star in the dying sunset. Turning his shaven head, he groaned and took a stumbling step forward, when he suddenly caught sight of General Markov. He saluted, dropped his hand, and said:

"I've been shell-shocked, Your Excellency."

"So I see."

"I have been shot in the back."

"Too bad...."

"I was shot in the back from a revolver at close range. Volunteer Valerian Onoli fired deliberately at me...."

"Your name?" asked Markov curtly.

"Roshchin.... Lieutenant Colonel Roshchin."

At that very moment the 6-inch gun on the northward-bound Red armoured train fired one last shot. The shell flew wailing over the dark steppe. The General's grey horse, alarmed, pricked up its ears and began to get down on its haunches. Tearing across the sky, the shell exploded five paces away from Markov.

When the dust and smoke cleared away, Vadim Petrovich Roshchin, who had been flung back by the blast from the explosion, saw the grey horse on the ground, its hoofs beating the air frantically—beside it sprawled a small motionless body. Trying to rise, Roshchin shouted:

"Stretcher bearers! General Markov has been killed!"

Having occupied Torgovaya, the Volunteer Army turned north, towards Velikoknyazheskaya, with a twofold purpose: to assist Ataman Krasnov to clear the Salsk district of Bolsheviks, and to strengthen its rear in case of attack from Tsaritsyn. Velikoknyazheskaya was taken with slight losses, but it was impossible to follow up this victory, as a Budyonny cavalry detachment had overrun and routed Erdeli's Cossack units in a night engagement, thus preventing them from crossing the river Manich.

219

The first armoured train of the Volunteer Army had a narrow escape in the neighbourhood of the station. Its crew assumed that an engine coming towards them, flying a white flag, was carrying trucebearers, and the Whites held their fire. But the engine flew on, at full speed, whistling incessantly. Only at the last moment did the crew of the armoured train recover sufficient presence of mind to fire a few rounds at close range. But a collision could not be avoided, a truck was smashed, and the engine, which had previously been soaked in petrol, and hung all over with bombs, was derailed. For a few moments the combatants were spectators of a scene worthy of an American movie.

Handing over the district to the Don Cossacks, and leaving the work of finishing off the Bolsheviks to local Cossack detachments, Denikin once more turned southward, with the aim of capturing an all-important junction—the station of Tikhoretskaya, linking the Don with the Kuban, and the Black Sea with the Caspian. There were grave dangers to be contended with. In his path lay two big non-Cossack villages—Peschanokopskoye and Belaya Glina. They were both hotbeds of Bolshevism, and were being hastily fortified. The army of Kalnin was feverishly entrenching on the outskirts of Tikhoretskaya. Sorokin's army, by now recovered from its state of panic, was beginning to exert pressure from the west. Those Red units which had been thrown into confusion on the Manich had been reorganized, and were once more attacking the enemy's rear. Many villages were sending volunteer reinforcements.

All that Denikin could count on was the lack of coordination in the movements of the enemy. But even this might at any moment change, and so he had to hurry. It sometimes required his personal efforts to urge his troops forward, as they lay utterly exhausted on the field. The infantry had to be moved on carts. In front of the army went the improvised armoured train.

The whole population was fighting shoulder to shoulder with the Red Army at Peschanokopskoye. The Volunteer Army had never before encountered such a fury of opposition. The steppe rocked beneath the cannonade from morning till night. The regiments of Borovsky and Drozdovsky were twice driven out of the village, and it was only when they saw themselves surrounded on all sides by an enemy whose strength and equipment they had no means of gauging, that the Reds, to a man, abandoned the village. Units, detachments, and crowds of refugees, were now all gathered at Belaya Glina.

Here stood the Iron Division of Dmitri Shelest, reinforced by a volunteer militia ten thousand strong. Men of all ages had been called up. The approaches to the village were fortified, system and a strategic grasp of the situation being here displayed for the first time. At meetings the challenge was to victory or death.

But it was in vain. The foe was learned in warfare, and met courage and desperation with science and technique, never over-looking a single detail, planning every move with the deliberation of a chess player, and somehow always managing to turn up in the enemy's rear. At first, it is true, the White attack was a failure. Colonel Zhebrak, who was in command of the Drozdovsky col-umn, led his men in the darkness straight up to a farmstead at which the advanced lines of the Reds were lying. Despite brisk enemy fire, he rushed to the attack and fell down dead. His men retreated, making for cover. But at nine o'clock the next morning Kutepov broke into Belaya Glina from the south, supported by the Kornilov Regiment, a Drozdovsky cavalry regiment, and an ar-moured car. Borovsky approached from the direction of the cap-tured railway station. Street fighting began. The Reds, realizing that they were surrounded, fell into confusion. The armoured car cut a path through their ranks. Thatched roofs caught fire. Cattle and horses rushed about amidst flames, gunfire and shrieks....

Shelest's Iron Division, and with it the guerilla fighters and the whole population, began retreating along the only path still open to them. But there, in front of the signal box was Denikin, on horseback, shouting furious orders, shielding his mouth with his hand, for his men to cut off the retreat of the fugitives. Erdeli's cavalry galloped after them. The commander's own escort could not resist flying after them with drawn swords. The staff officers, whirling round in their saddles, galloped up like big-game hun-ters, laying about them with their swords at heads and backs. Denikin was left quite alone. Taking off his cap, he fanned his heated countenance with it. This victory would clear the way for him to Tikhoretskaya and Ekaterinodar.

Sharp volleys sounded in the twilight from the village and farm-steads: it was Drozdovsky's men taking vengeance for Zhebrak's death by shooting Red Army prisoners. Denikin sat drinking tea in a fly-infested hut. Despite the stuffiness of the night, his thick, heavily braided tunic was buttoned up to the throat. After each volley he turned towards the broken window and passed his hand-kerchief, rolled into a ball, over his forehead, and down each side of his nose.

"Vasili Vasilich," he said to his aide-de-camp, "be a good fel-low and ask Drozdovsky to come here. This can't go on, you know!"

Clicking his spurs and saluting stiffly, the aide turned on his heel and left the room. Denikin began to fill up the teapot from the samovar. A fresh volley rang out—so near this time that the windowpanes rattled. Then a long scream rent the darkness. The boiling water overflowed the teapot, carrying with it a few tea leaves. "Tut-tut," whispered Denikin, putting the lid back on the teapot. The door was jerked open, admitting a man of about thirty, deathly pale, in a crumpled tunic, the limp general's shoulder straps also crumpled. The flame of the oil lamp was dimly reflected in his eyeglasses. His square, cleft chin, covered with stubble, jutted forward, his hollow cheeks twitched. He stopped just inside the room. Denikin rose heavily from the bench on which he was sitting, and extended his hand.

"Sit down, Mikhail Grigorevich! Will you have some tea?"

"No, thank you, Sir! I have no time!"

It was Drozdovsky, who had recently been made a general. He knew why the Commander in Chief had sent for him, and, as always when he expected a reproof, it cost him an agonizing effort to suppress his rage. He stood there, with bent head and averted eyes.

"Mikhail Grigorevich, old man, I want to talk to you about these shootings...."

Drozdovsky turned still paler.

"I am unable to restrain my officers," he said in a voice unpleasantly shrill, verging on the hysterical. "You are aware, Your Excellency, that Colonel Zhebrak was bestially tortured by the Bolsheviks.... Thirty-five officers brought by me from Rumania have been tortured and mutilated.... The Bolsheviks are killing and torturing all our people ... yes, all of them...." (His voice broke, he seemed to be almost suffocated.) "I cannot restrain the men.... I refuse.... If you object.... I can send in my papers.... I should consider it a joy ... to serve in the ranks...."

"Now, now ..." said Denikin. "Don't be so touchy, Mikhail Grigorevich.... What's this about sending in your papers? Can't you see, Mikhail Grigorevich, that by shooting prisoners we are stiffening the enemy's resistance? Rumours of these shootings will spread everywhere. Why should we do harm to our own army? I'm sure you see I am right ... you do, don't you?" (Drozdovsky said nothing.) "Tell your officers what I say, and let there be no more of these incidents...."

"Very good, Sir!"

Drozdovsky went out banging the door after him.

Shaking his head, Denikin sat meditating over his glass of tea for a long time. The last volley rang out in the darkness, and all was silence and darkness.

The operation against Tikhoretskaya was part of a plan for expending the army over a front nearly forty miles in width. It was necessary to clear the terrain of isolated enemy detachments and guerilla units, a task entrusted to the youthful General Borovsky, who, covering over sixty miles in the course of two days, fighting most of the way had occupied a number of villages. This was the first so-called raid into the enemy's rear in the history of the Civil War.

The Volunteer Army could now deploy over an unencumbered terrain. On the thirtieth of June Denikin issued a brief order: "Tomorrow, the 1st of July, the station of Tikhoretskaya to be captured, and enemy ranks grouping in the Ternovskaya-Tikhoretskaya district to be broken up...." The columns moved by night, surrounding Tikhoretskaya in a wide pincer movement. After brief skirmishing the Bolsheviks began retreating to fortified positions.

This was no longer the desperate resistance of a week ago. The fall of Belaya Glina had had a depressing effect on the troops. Sorokin's offensive was halted. The losses—the thousands who had fallen in bloody conflict—had all been in vain. The enemy moved on with machine-like precision. Men's imaginations exaggerated tenfold the forces of the Volunteers. It was rumoured that officers were flocking to Denikin from all over Russia, that the cadets were showing mercy to none, that as soon as they cleared a district, the Germans would come in. Kalnin, who was in command of the Tikhoretskaya group, was sitting motionless in his train at the station of Tikhoretskaya, as if paralyzed. When he learned that the Denikin hordes were approaching at all points, he lost heart completely, and ordered a retreat.

By nine in the morning the battle was dying down, and the Red troops retreated to a fortified position extending behind Tikhoretskaya in a semicircle. Kalnin locked himself up in his compartment, and lay down for a nap, convinced that there would be no more fighting that day. Meanwhile the Volunteers were continuing their wide encirclement of the enemy, moving through fields of densely growing wheat. By noon the ends of the pincer movement met, and advanced south towards the enemy's rear. The Kornilov Regiment stormed the railway station, capturing it without sustaining any losses. The railway employees went into hiding. Kalnin disappeared—his cap and high boots were found lying about the floor of the carriage. In the next compartment his chief of staff Zverev, a former officer of the tsarist General Staff, was found lying on the floor with his skull staved in. Prone on the seat, her head covered with a shawl, lay his wife, with a bullet through her breast, but still alive.

It now only remained for the Volunteer columns to close in on the Red Army units, which had lost their command and were cut off from their supply bases and lines of communication. They bombarded it from cannon and machine guns till nightfall. Caught within the pincer movement, men flung themselves backwards and forwards in distraction, beneath a hurricane of lead from all directions. They climbed frantically out of the trenches, rushing into a bayonet attack, and meeting death on every side. Towards evening Kutepov had cut off the only path still open—that to the north—annihilating with fire and cold steel the groups of Reds making for the railway line. In the twilight, both Reds and Whites became inextricably entangled in the dense wheat. The commanders, running hither and thither in the wheat like quails, rallied their officers and went again and again to the attack. Handkerchiefs were hoisted on bayonets from somewhere in the trenches. Kutepov and his officers galloped up, only to be met with a volley of fire and a stream of obscenities. Kutepov galloped away, bending low over his horse's neck. The Commander in Chief had given orders that prisoners were not to be shot, but no one had said that there were to be any prisoners taken.

The next morning Denikin rode at a footpace all over the field of battle. As far as the eye could see the wheat was trampled and beaten down. Vultures were sailing across the exquisite blue sky. Denikin scrutinized the lines of trenches winding across the fields over ancient barrows and ravines. Hands, feet, and heads protruded from them, and dead bodies hung over the top like sacks. He was in a sentimental frame of mind and said thoughtfully, half turning, as a sign for his aide to gallop up to him:

"To think they're all Russians! Terrible! Our joy is not unsullied, Vasili Vasilich!"

The victory was complete. Kalnin's army, thirty thousand strong, was defeated, its ranks destroyed and scattered. Only seven Red troop trains had succeeded in slipping through to Ekaterinodar. Sorokin's army had been cut off. The eastern group in the Armavir District, and the Taman coastal army were thus irrevocably separated. Denikin's army secured vast stores of booty—three armoured trains, armoured cars, fifty guns, an airplane, vans full of rifles, machine guns, shells, abundant supplies of all sorts.

The effect of the victory was overwhelming. Ataman Krasnov ordered a thanksgiving service to be held in the cathedral at Novocherkassk, haranguing the troops afterwards every bit as well as his friend the Kaiser could have done it. Although Denikin lost one-fourth of his army in three weeks, its numbers were doubled

224

by the beginning of July, thanks to the steady stream of volunteers from the Ukraine, the Novorossia region, and Central Russia. Units formed from Red Army prisoners began to be used in the White Army for the first time.

After resting for two days, Denikin split up his army into three columns and began a large-scale offensive on three fronts: on the west, against Sorokin's army, on the east, against the Armavir groups, and on the south, against the remnants of Kalnin's army, which was covering Ekaterinodar. His aim was to clean up the whole rear before storming Ekaterinodar. All was thought out and planned according to the rules of the highest military science. But there was one circumstance—and that an extremely important one—which Denikin left out of consideration: he did not realize that he was faced, not by an enemy whose strength and equipment he could weigh up and estimate, but by an armed population, an incalculable force. He did not take into account the fact that every one of his victories resulted in a corresponding increase of hatred and solidarity in this army of the people; that the era of stormy meetings, at which unpopular commanders were discharged and campaigns were decided by vote, had passed, and was being replaced by a new civil war discipline, not very firm as yet, but growing stronger every day.

Everything seemed to promise easy and immediate victory. Reconnaissance reported the panic-stricken retreat of Sorokin's army in the direction of Ekaterinodar beyond the Kuban. But this was not the whole truth. Reconnaissance was misled. Those fleeing beyond the Kuban were deserters, small detachments, and cartloads of refugees. Sorokin's army of thirty thousand had been cleared of mere hangers-on, and was now disciplined and ferocious. The Bataisk front against the Germans was abandoned. The Reds awaited an encounter in the open field with Denikin's army. And it came to pass that the Volunteer Army, flushed with victory, almost within sight of its goal, very nearly perished to the last man in the ten days of bloody battle with Sorokin's troops which lay before them.

Sorokin replied to the enquiries of the Kuban-Black Sea Central Executive Committee with Napoleonic arrogance: "I need no agitators. Denikin's bands are making propaganda for me. The legendary valour of my troops will overthrow all barriers raised by the counterrevolution." Sorokin, who had succeeded, in the first days of Denikin's attack, in checking panic among his troops, seemed to have roused himself from a drunken stupor. He ranged the front day and night, by train, by railway trolley, and on hor-

15–559

seback. He reviewed the troops, shot down two officers with his own hand in the sight of the army, for lack of revolutionary zeal; rising in his stirrups, his foaming lips savagely distorted, he castigated the enemies of the people in language so foully abusive that the Red Army men, like a herd of buffaloes maddened by gadflies, interrupted him with stentorian roars. He tightened up the activities of the Military Tribunal and Special Departments, introduced the death penalty for neglect of rifles, and issued orders to the Army in which they were told: "Soldiers! The workers of the whole world are looking towards you with hope, are offering you their noblest feelings of gratitude—with open eyes and strong limbs you are marching to meet the bloody sunrise of a new historical epoch. The parasites, the crawling vermin, the bands of Denikin, and the counterrevolutionary scum of the earth, must be wiped out by fire and lead. Peace to the toilers, death to the exploiters, long live the world revolution!"

He drew up these orders himself in a sort of delirium. They were read aloud in the companies. Ukrainian peasants, Don miners, the veterans of the Caucasian army, Cossacks and outsiders—a motley, ragged, noisy, lawless clan—listened spellbound to the grandiloquent words.

Chief of Staff Belyakov, an intelligent and accomplished soldier, drew up a plan for the attack, or rather the breakthrough of the whole group, thirty thousand strong, and their retreat to the other side of the river Kuban. This, at any rate, was the idea of the Chief of Staff, who cherished not the slightest illusions as to the outcome of an encounter with Denikin. The breakthrough was to be made in the neighbourhood of the Korenovskaya railway station (between Tikhoretskaya and Ekaterinodar). When Korenovskaya was occupied it would be an easy matter to cope with the columns of Drozdovsky and Kazanovich, once they were cut off from the main forces on the south, to move on Ekaterinodar—for the rest they must trust to luck.... It was thus that the Chief of Staff reasoned. His position was one of extreme delicacy: with all his being, sleeping or waking, he detested the Reds, but an accursed fate had involved him with the Bolsheviks. To fall into the hands of Denikin, whom he regarded with uneasy, envious admiration, would spell death! To be suspected by Sorokin of lack of revolutionary zeal or of not hating Denikin enough, would no less certainly mean death. His one hope, fantastic enough, as was everything in those fantastic times, was in the frenzied ambition of Sorokin. Belyakov's game was to use all his powers to establish Sorokin as dictator. Then he would see what was to be done.

Whatever his inmost thoughts, he embarked upon the most active preparations for the attack: munitions and forage were accumulated at the Timashevskaya station, shells unloaded, long trains of carts sent into the steppe. The army was deploying in the neighbourhood of Timashevskaya, its front facing southeast, with the idea of dealing a blow simultaneously on Korenovskaya, and, to the north, on Viselki.

In the early morning of July the fifteenth the field guns of the Reds opened a hurricane fire on Korenovskaya, and an hour later Cossack cavalry squadrons attacked the village and station by lava. They slashed at the cadets with whistling blades, riding them down and only taking those prisoners who had discarded their rifles before the Reds could reach them. Infantry units marched all night, beginning to entrench the moment they arrived at Korenovskaya, not in a semicircle this time, as at Belaya Glina, but in a complete ellipse.

The sun rose white in a mist of dust and heat. The whole steppe seemed to be in motion: cavalry galloped about, infantry regiments crept up, batteries thundered by on rumbling wheels, and the air was filled with curses, blows, shots, the whinnying of horses, hoarse cries of command. The supply columns stretched right up to the horizon. The day was as hot as a furnace. Sorokin broke away from his staff and whirled about on his foam-flecked horse in the midst of the troops. Dispatch riders and aides, swift as greyhounds, flew about the field with his orders.

His hat had fallen off during his gallop, and he had discarded his Circassian tunic. The sleeves of his crimson silk shirt were rolled high above his elbows, and his blue riding breeches were drawn tightly into a leather belt. He seemed to be in several places at once, his bared teeth gleaming in his dust-grimed visage. He was inspecting, on his third fresh horse, the positions of batteries, and of the trenches, where, like moles, the infantry divisions were digging themselves into the rich black soil. Next he galloped up to the listening posts, from there to watch the arrival and unloading of the supply columns; summoning commanders to his side with a flourish of his whip, and bending, heated and ferocious, from his saddle, he listened wild-eyed to their reports. Like the conductor of some mammoth orchestra, he evoked music from the multitudinous elements of the coming battle. He left his heavily-breathing horse at the station, made his way hastily to the telegraph room, kicking out of his way a dead body with officer's shoulder straps and the skull laid open, lying across the threshold, and ran his eyes over the telegraph tape, seized with an intoxicated frenzy of excitement: the troops of Drozdovsky and Kazanovich were approaching rapidly from the south, to enter battle—they had already left the station of Dinskaya.

Drozdovsky's troops were coming up in carts, jolting all day over the steppe, through clouds of torrid dust. The troops of the late General Markov, now under the command of General Kazanovich, which had entrained together with the artillery, arrived before them, on the sixteenth at dawn, and dashed straight out of the railway trucks, to attack Korenovskaya.

General Kazanovich was standing on the rim of a well in front of a railway shed, calmly watching the able movements of the officers' lines, marching without firing a shot. His refined, subtle countenance, with the long, grizzled moustache and clipped beard (just like His Majesty the Tsar's), bore an expression of smiling absorption and there was a cold smile of almost feminine ardour in his fine eyes. He was so confident of the outcome of the battle that he had not even wished to wait for Drozdovsky's division to come up. There was a constant rivalry between him and the morbidly vain, overcautious Drozdovsky, who was slow to a fault, often to the detriment of the matter in hand, whereas Kazanovich loved war for its broad scope, the music of battle, the sounding glory of victory.

The huge globe of the sun, promising the torrid heat of a July day, was rising from behind the distant barrows of the steppe, its dazzling light full in the eyes of the Bolsheviks. Machine guns were emitting their rap-rap, and the sultry stillness was rent by constant salvoes. The enemy could be seen clambering out of the trenches in serried ranks. Markov's men, running forward, disregarding the bullets, were met by thousands of tiny crawling figures. Kazanovich lifted his field glasses to his eyes. Queer!

"Three rounds of shrapnel for the comrades!" he cried to the telephone operator, who was ensconced beside the well. Two batteries, hidden behind the embankment, opened fire. The woolly puffs of shrapnel burst low over the enemy's lines. The tiny figures at first scattered in confusion, but soon formed lines and continued to advance. The whole field was now resounding with reports. At last the batteries of the Bolsheviks gave tongue. Kazanovich smiled, puzzled, and the slim hand holding the field glasses trembled. When he saw Markov's men throw themselves on to the ground, and begin hastily digging themselves in, his face paled beneath its tan. Leaping down from the well, he squatted over the field telephone, and called General Timanovsky.

"The troops are lying prone," he shouted into the receiver. "Break up the enemy's left flank at all costs.... Every second counts!"

Instantly some of Markov's men—Timanovsky's reserves—appeared from over the railway embankment. In groups and batches, line after line, resolute, worked up to a high pitch of excitement, they disappeared into the high ripe wheat, which was already beginning to shed its grain. Timanovsky, youthful, red-cheeked, jocose, his high cap perched over one ear, in a grimy linen shirt with black general's shoulder straps, came running after the lines, holding his dangling sword out of his way. Something utterly incomprehensible was going on: the Bolsheviks were changed men—all the moments at which it had seemed inevitable for them to waver, had passed. The entire steppe was now covered by their tiny advancing figures. The machine guns of the Volunteer Army barked furiously—ever new waves of the enemy were taking the places of those who fell.

First one, then another of Timanovsky's companies were running with rifles atilt towards the outer rim of the wheat field. Kazanovich, taut as a fiddlestring, stood there on the top of the well. He could see the fierce-looking backs of Markov's men in the narrow field of vision of his glasses. What tenseness! They were falling, falling! He turned the glasses beyond the runners, and suddenly parted lips, broad faces, sailors' caps, bare, bronzed chests, swam into view.... Bolshevik sailors.... Next minute all were mixed up in an indistinguishable mass hand-to-hand fighting. A sickly smile froze on Kazanovich's chiselled lips.... The Markov men were giving ground. The remnants of the first company were running into the wheat, lying down. The second company, beaten back, flung themselves on the ground.

The General sprang from the well and ran lightly across the field. He was seen by the troops and managed to get them on to their feet again, with short cries of: "For shame, gentlemen, for shame!" He got them to charge again but the firing was so severe, and men fell in such numbers, that they once more flung themselves down.... Could it be that the battle was lost?

At nine a.m. the booming of Drozdovsky's guns was heard from the west. An armoured car made its appearance in the field, blundering forward like a grey tortoise. Drozdovsky's troops went on with their attack systematically and without haste. Kazanovich's lines rose from the ground a third time. The Volunteers were now advancing along a wide semicircular front. It seemed impossibble that the Bolsheviks would be able to withstand such an onslaught.

A horseman appeared between the Bolshevik trenches galloping furiously up and down, and flourishing a gleaming blade. Tearing up to the top of a barrow, he pulled his horse up short. He wore a crimson shirt with the sleeves rolled up, and threw back his head, shouting and waving his sword again. And instantly a cavalry lava swooped down upon the attacking lines of Drozdovsky's men. Their short-legged, vicious ponies hugged the ground in their mad rush. The firing ceased. The whistling of blades, shrieks, the tramping of hoofs, could be heard far and wide. The crimson-shirted horseman tore down the side of the barrow, giving his horse its head as he galloped past. A cloud of black dust arose, veiling the battlefield. The troops of Drozdovsky and Markov, unable to withstand the cavalry charge, were in flight. They came to a halt beside the brook Kirpeli, where they entrenched.

Ivan Ilyich Telegin, knitting his brows and shivering with pain, bandaged his head with gauze from his first-aid packet.

It was a mere scratch, the bone had not been touched, but the pain was intense—he felt as if his whole head was coming un-screwed. He was so exhausted by his efforts, that for a long lime after the bandaging he lay motionless on his back in the wheat.

It was strange to hear the grasshoppers fiddling peacefully away as if nothing had happened. Grasshoppers hidden in the cracks of the earth, the great stars in the southern night sky, and a few bearded ears of wheat suspended motionless between his eyes and the sky—this was the end of all the bloody turmoil, the shrieks, the metallic clang of battle. A short time ago a wounded man had been moaning somewhere near, now even he had fallen silent.

What a wonderful thing silence could be! The burning pain in his head was getting less, as if there were healing in the solemn majesty of night. Vivid snatches of the day, all torn to fragments by artillery fire, the yells issuing from mouths opening like the maws of wild beasts, and bursts of furious hate, when one ran and ran, seeing nothing but the tip of one's bayonet and the pale face of the man firing at one. But these memories penetrated the brain so painfully, giving such a sudden extra twist to the skull, that Ivan Ilyich could not repress a groan, and tried frantically to think of something else.

But what else was there for him to think about? Either these terrible fragments of endless occurrences, which the mind could never quite grasp—revolution, war—or that distant dream of happiness and Dasha, on which he had turned the key. He began thinking about her (truth to tell he had never stopped thinking about her), her utter defencelessness: quite alone, so unpractical, the victim of her own illusions ... her eyes so stern, but her heart fluttering and frightened like a bird's, a child, just a child....

Ivan Ilyich clutched at a sod of warm earth with his outflung hand. His eyelids closed. She had parted with him—for ever, she was sure! Little fool! Who's afraid of your stern eyes? And who will ever love you more truly than I? Little fool! What injuries you will meet with ... bitter, unforgettable....

Tears stole from beneath the eyelashes of Ivan Ilyich—he was weak from his wound. A grasshopper began chirping right at his ear. The bloody, trampled field was silvery in the starlight. All was veiled by night.... Raising himself, Ivan Ilyich sat up, clasping his knees with his arms. It was all like a dream, like a return to childhood. His heart filled with pity and tears. He got up and started walking, trying not to let his steps jolt his head.

Korenovskaya was about half-a-mile away. Here and there the light from bonfires in the village could be seen. Closer to him, in a hollow, a clear tongue of flame danced over the ground. Suddenly feeling hungry and thirsty, Ivan Ilyich moved in the direction of the fire.

Dark figures were staggering towards it from all over the field—some were slightly wounded, some were stragglers from a decimated division, some were propelling prisoners in front of them. Men were calling to one another, swearing hoarsely, breaking out into wild laughter. There was quite a crowd around the flames, which were fed by a heap of blazing sleepers.

The smell of bread came to the nostrils of Ivan Ilyich—all these grime-covered people were munching. In a cart piled with loaves, drawn up not far from the fire, stood a gaunt woman in a white head kerchief, ladling out water.

After drinking his fill and accepting a slice of bread, Ivan Ilyich stood leaning against the cart, eating and looking up at the stars. The people round the fire seemed to have quieted down, and many were asleep. But tose who had only just arrived from the field were still seething with rage. Swearing, they uttered threats in the dark, although nobody paid any attention to them. The nurse kept on serving out slices of bread and mugs of water.

A black-bearded man, stripped to the waist, dragged up his prisoner, and knocked him down beside the fire.

"Here he is, the son-of-a-bitch, the parasite.... Question him, boys."

He kicked at the prostrate form, and stepped back, hitching up his trousers, his hollow chest heaving. Ivan Ilyich recognized Chertogonov—and turned away. Several people rushed up to the man on the ground, bending over him.

"He volunteered...." (They tore off his shoulder straps and threw them on the flames.)

"Just a kid, and as vicious as a viper!"

"Went out to fight for his dad's capital.... He's one of the rich, you can see that...."

"Look how his eyes gleam, the swine!"

"What's the good of staring at him, let *me* get at him...."

"Wait a minute! He may have papers on him.... Take him to headquarters...."

"Lug him to headquarters...."

"No, you don't!" shouted Chertogonov, rushing up. "He was lying there wounded, so I went up to him—look at those boots! And he shot at me twice, I'm not going to give him up!" And in a still more ferocious voice he shouted to the prisoner: "Take off your boots!"

Ivan Ilyich cast a sidelong glance at the group. The prisoner's round, youthful, shaven head gleamed in the firelight. He was showing his teeth in a snarl, his large eyes darting from side to side, his small nose puckered up. At first he lay there as if distraught, but suddenly he leaped to his feet. His left arm hung lifeless in the torn, bloodstained sleeve. A low hissing came from between his teeth, and he thrust out his chin horribly.... Chertogonov retreated a step—so terrible was this living spectre of hatred....

"Aha!" came a deep voice from out of the crowd. "*I* know him— I worked in his dad's tobacco factory—he's the son of Onoli, the Rostov factory owner...."

There was a hum of voices: "We know him! We know him!"

Valerian Onoli scowled, moving his lowered head from side to side and shouting, in a kind of hoarse scream:

"Beasts! Scum! Red swine! I'll bash your mugs in, d'you hear, you swine! Haven't enough of you been thrashed and hung, you curs? Haven't you had enough yet? We'll string you all up, sons-of-bitches!"

Beside himself with rage, he seized Chertogonov's tousled beard and began kicking him in his bare stomach.

Ivan Ilyich quickly moved away from the cart. There was an ominous buzz of voices, their swelling fury suddenly cut across by a shrill shriek. The sprawling body of Valerian Onoli rose, kicking out violently, above the heads of the crowd, flew into the air and fell.... A pillar of fine sparks rose above the flames....

In the chill which comes before dawn in the steppe, isolated shots resounded like the cracking of whips, amidst the solemn booming of the guns. The firing came from the columns of Drozdovsky and Borovsky, once more moving to the attack from the other side of the Kirpeli, in a desperate effort to turn their luck.

That very night an order came from the Central Executive Committee at Ekaterinodar, in permanent session all this time, appointing Commander in Chief Sorokin Supreme Commander of all Red forces in the North Caucasus.

The news was brought to him by Chief of Staff Belyakov, who rushed straight to the new Supreme Commander's carriage, holding the strip of telegraph tape, pushed his legs off the seat, and read him the order by the flame of a cigarette lighter. Sorokin, unable to rouse himself, fell back on his hot pillow, blinking helplessly. Belyakov began shaking him by the shoulder.

"Wake up, Your Excellency, Comrade Supreme Commander. You're the master of the Caucasus!... Do you hear me? You're the tsar and God almighty all in one—do you hear me?"

Only then did Sorokin realize the significance of the news, and that it was his own wonderful destiny that was stamped out in dots and dashes on the narrow strip of paper curling around the fingers of his Chief of Staff. Rapidly adjusting his trousers, he threw his tunic over his shoulders and fastened his holster and sword.

"Issue the order to the army immediately.... My horse!"

At dawn Telegin, his head freshly bandaged, made his way among the carts, and went in search of his regimental headquarters. Just then a group of mounted escorts, the long ends of their Cossack hoods streaming behind them, came galloping along the road from the station. Among them was a bugler followed by two horsemen—Sorokin sawing at the mouth of his long-maned mount, and a Cossack holding a lance from which fluttered the pennon of the Supreme Commander. The riders flew by towards the place from which the firing was coming, like wraiths enveloped in whirling clouds of dust.

Heads and beards were raised drowsily from the dew-drenched carts—hoarse voices broke the silence. But the bugler was already far away in the steppe, proclaiming that the Supreme Commander was near, he was here, in the thick of battle, amidst the flying bullets.... "We will rout the foe!" sang the bugle. "On to victory and glory.... It is not death, but fame everlasting that awaits the hero.... Ta-ra-ta...."

Ivan Ilyich found Gimza in a mud hut with broken windows. There was no other member of the staff there. Gimza, huge and morose, was sitting stoopshouldered on a bench, one hand, with a wooden spoon in it, hanging between his knees. On the table was a pot of cabbage soup, beside which lay a bulging briefcase—the entire equipment of the chief of the Special Department.

Gimza seemed to be half-asleep. He turned his eyes towards Ivan Ilyich without moving.

"Wounded?"

233

"It's nothing—a mere scratch. I've been lying in the wheat half the night. I lost touch with my men—there was a lot of confusion. Where's the regiment?"

"Sit down," said Gimza. "Hungry?"

Lifting his arm stiffly, he held out the spoon to Telegin. Ivan Ilyich fell upon the pot of half-cold soup with a suppressed groan. For a moment or two he ate in silence, before bursting out:

"How our fellows fought last night, Comrade Gimza! They didn't need any urging. They made bayonet charges at a distance of three and even four hundred yards!"

"You've had enough," said Gimza. "Heard the new order?"

"No."

"Sorokin has been made Supreme Commander. What d'you think of that?"

"That's all right.... Did you see him yesterday? He flew right into the line of fire with his reins loose—in a crimson shirt, so that everyone could see him. The moment the men saw him they started cheering. But for him, I don't know how it would have been yesterday.... We were simply astonished—a regular Caesar!"

"That's just it," said Gimza. "He *is* a Caesar—a pity I can't shoot him!"

Telegin was astonished.

"You don't mean it!" he cried.

"But I do! Never mind—you wouldn't understand, anyhow." He looked at Ivan Ilyich with a heavy, unblinking gaze. "And you—you won't betray me?" (Telegin looked him steadily in the eyes.) "Well then.... I want to entrust a difficult matter to you, Comrade Telegin. It seems to me you're the best person.... You'll have to go to the Volga...."

"Very good!"

"I'll write you out all sorts of mandates. I'll give you a letter to the chairman of the Military Council. If you don't bring it off, if you don't deliver it, better go over to the Whites—don't come back. Understand?"

"Very well."

"Don't give yourself up alive. Guard that letter as your life. If you get caught by the counterintelligence, do anything, eat it, anything.... Understand?" Gimza moved forward, banging his clenched fist on the table so hard that the pot gave a jump. "You must know what there is in the letter: the army believes in Sorokin. Sorokin is a hero, the army would follow him anywhere.... And I demand that Sorokin be shot.... Immediately, before he takes the reins of the Revolution in his own hands. Remember these words—your life is at stake, Telegin.... Understand?"

He fell silent. A fly crawled across his brow.

"Good!" said Telegin. "It shall be done!"

"Get started, then, old boy. I don't know which would be the best way for you to take—it's a long journey through Svyatoi Krest, via Astrakhan.... Better go along the Don to Tsaritsyn. And it'll give you a chance to have a look at the rear of the Whites. Get yourself officer's shoulder straps, smarten yourself up. What'll you have—captain's or a lieutenant colonel's?"

Laughing he laid his hand on Telegin's knee, patting it as if Ivan Ilyich were a child.

"Get a couple of hours' sleep, and I'll write the letter...."

X

The three weeks' leave was obtained at last. Vadim Petrovich Roshchin, worn out, ill, torn by inner conflicts, was at that time in the Volunteer garrison at the station of Velikoknyazheskaya. There was no serious fighting just then, the Red forces having withdrawn further south, into the struggle with the main forces of Denikin. Here, among the villages on the rivers Manich and Sal, there were occasional outbursts, but the Cossack punitive detachments of Ataman Krasnov had a sure way of dealing with turbulent spirits—by persuasive words, the knout, or the gallows.

Vadim Petrovich avoided taking part in reprisals, pleading the injury to his head. He kept away as much as possible from the officers' revels, held to celebrate the victories of Denikin. And strange to say, in the garrison, as in the field, all treated Roshchin with the utmost caution, with concealed hostility.

Somebody had started the rumour that he was really a Red, and the epithet stuck.

In the trenches at Shablievka, Volunteer Onoli had shot at him. Roshchin remembered that moment with the utmost clarity: the humming of a shell from the armoured train, the commander's shout: "Lie down!" The explosion. And—the delayed revolver shot, the blow, as from a stick, on the back of the head, and the fierce joy in the rolling, Asiatic eyes of Onoli.

There was only one man to believe Roshchin's unsupported word—General Markov. But he was dead, and Vadim Petrovich decided not to take up the doubtful charge against the young man.

He racked his brains for an answer to the question: why, after all, this hatred of him? Couldn't everyone see that he was an honest man, that he was completely disinterested, that all his actions were guided by the sole idea of Russia's greatness? It was not for a general's epaulettes that he had gone to this appalling steppe....

Roshchin lacked the ruthlessly clear vision of things. His mind coloured the world and events according to what he himself considered the loftiest and the most important. He did not notice things which did not fit in with his conceptions and only winced when they forced themselves upon him. In his eyes the world was a finished system. This was no doubt due to the aristocratic prejudices handed down to him through generations of complacent landed proprietors. This vanished race had placed above all blessings such tranquil complacency, applying it to everyone and everything. Was a peasant being thrashed in the stables? What of it? The peasant would bawl a bit, but after the birching he would repent, and feel all the better for it, since his repentance would be followed by a sensation of peace. Were bills protested, was the estate going under the hammer? It couldn't be helped! One could live in the annex, among the dock leaves and gooseberry bushes, without noisy revellings: no doubt this would be better suited to one's old age.... Not one of the blows dealt by fate could shake the complacency of a landed proprietor, once he had adopted a point of view enabling him to see only what was beautiful and lofty.

This lack of a critical attitude towards individuals and their actions was one of Vadim Petrovich's characteristics, too, although the events of the last few years had caused considerable wear and tear to his romanticism, leaving it almost in rags. He was continually being forced to avert his gaze. And this was why, among other things, he kept away from the officers' mess as much as possible.

To his way of thinking, these people—a handful of officers and cadets—should go clad in white, like crusaders: had they not raised the sword against the insurgent rabble and its leaders— whether the servants and myrmidons of Antichrist or the Germans? It was with such ideas in his head that Roshchin found himself in the Don.

It was shocking to hear, at the officers' drinking bouts, the noisy braggings which accompanied the clinking of glasses, the gloatings over fratricide. The youthful, once refined, countenances of these "crusaders" were distorted with the impatient desire to murder, to deal out reprisals, to wreak vengeance; raising glasses of almost raw spirits, they sang a dirge to the most insignificant of mortals, one who had been shot down, his remains burnt, the ashes scattered to the winds, like those of the False Dmitri; one who, if all the blood shed in obedience to his feeble will could have been collected in one great lake, would undoubtedly have been drowned in its deep waters by the people.

This funeral dirge seemed to be the only idea in the heads of his brother officers, and again Roshchin had to avert his gaze.... To clear Russia of the Bolsheviks, to get to Moscow. Church bells.... Denikin riding into the Kremlin on a white horse.... All that was of course quite easy to understand.... But what next? That was the chief question! It would have been considered indecent even to mention the Constituent Assembly among officers. Had it all been a dirge for the dead then?

What was it that drew these people to battle and to death? Roshchin averted his gaze.... To expose their breasts to the bullets, and then drink raw spirits in the freight vans—that was not heroism. That was old stuff. The brave and the cowardly—everyone did that. It had become a commonplace to overcome the fear of death, life had become cheap.

Heroism lay in sacrificing oneself in the name of faith and truth. But here again he had to avert his glance. What truth did his brother officers believe in? What truth did he himself believe in? In the great, tragic history of Russia? But this was an axiom, not the truth. Truth lay in movement, in life—not in the well-thumbed pages of some dusty folio, but in the ever-living stream of the future.

In the name of what truth (if one disregarded the church bells of Moscow, the white horse, the flowers on bayonets, and all that) was it necessary to kill Russian peasants? This was the question which was beginning to steal into the consciousness of Vadim Petrovich, disturbing his thoughts as a stone cast into water disturbs the reflections on its surface. At this point began the agonizing splitting of his personality. He was a stranger among his brother officers, a "Red", a "Bolshie".

The memory of his last words to Katya kept recurring with increasing frequency to his mind, causing his ears to burn with shame. She had wrung her hands, breathless with emotion, as if she saw the pebbles on the edge of an abyss slipping beneath the feet of Vadim Petrovich. "Vadim, Vadim! Something quite different must be done!"

He was not yet ready to admit that Katya had been right, that he was in a state of hopelessness, that the further he went the less he was able to understand whence came the power of the "insurgent rabble", a power which was growing with nightmare rapidity; that to rush to the conclusion that the people were being deceived by the Bolsheviks was utterly absurd, since nobody knew whether it was the Bolsheviks who had called the Revolution into life, or the people the Bolsheviks; and that there was now no one for him to blame any more—unless it were himself.

Katya had been right about everything. She had brought to these troublous times from the old life only one defence, one treasure—love and pity. He remembered how she had gone about Rostov, with her shawl and her bundle—the gentle companion of his days.... So dear, so dear.... To lay one's head in her lap, to press one's face against her tender hands, to say nothing but: "I can't stand it any longer, Katya!" But an absurd pride held Vadim Petrovich in its grip. His lean figure, as rigid as if he were laced up in a corset of steel, his head, now quite grey, arrogantly erect, were conspicuous everywhere he went—in the dusty village street, in the ranks, in the officers' mess.... "The dandy!" men said of him. "Keeping up the tone, forsooth! Fancies himself a guardsman—the infantry swine!"

He had sent Katya two short notes, but had received no reply. He then decided to write to Colonel Tetkin. But just then he got his leave, and set off at once for Rostov.

He took a droshky from the station at midday. The town was changed out of all knowledge. Sadovaya Street was swept and clean, the trees were clipped, and smart women in white dresses strol]ed along the shady side of the street, admiring their reflections in the shop windows.

Roshchin turned continually on the seat, looking for Katya. He could hardly believe his eyes. The women, in their plumed hats, panamas, white boas, were like wraiths from a forgotten dream.... White-shod feet tripped over pavements washed clean by the gloomy yardmen, and there was not the tiniest stain of blood on those white stockings. So that was why covering detachments had to be posted at Velikoknyazheskaya! That was why Denikin had been fighting the Reds these four weeks! There it is, as clear as daylight! The truth of the White war.

Roshchin laughed scornfully. There were Germans in their sickeningly familiar grey-green uniforms, in brand-new caps at street corners—Germans feeling very much at home! Look at that one, his monocle falling out of his eye socket as he bends over the hand of a tall, laughing beauty in a white dress....

"Faster, coachman!"

Colonel Tetkin was standing in front of the yard gate of his house. Vadim Petrovich, driving in, leaped out of the droshky and noticed how Tetkin stepped back, his eyes round and bulgy, his chubby hand waving Roshchin off as if trying to exorcise him.

"Good morning, Colonel.... Don't you know me? I ... for God's sake, where's Katya? Is she well? Why don't...."

"For heaven's sake—*you* alive!" cried Tetkin in his shrill, feminine voice. "Vadim Petrovich, old man!" and he fell upon

Roshchin, throwing his arms round him and wetting his cheek with his tears.

"What's happened? Colonel ... tell me all...."

"I *knew* you were alive! Oh, poor Ekaterina Dmitrevna! How she suffered!"

And Tetkin began pouring out everything helter-skelter—how Katya had gone to Onoli, who had for some reason or other assured her that Roshchin was dead. He spoke of Katya's grief, of her departure.

"So that's it," said Roshchin firmly, looking down at the ground. "Where did Ekaterina Dmitrevna go?"

Tetkin made a gesture of despair, his good-natured face expressing an agonizing desire to help.

"It seems to me," he said, "she said she was going to Ekaterinoslav.... I believe she even said something about working in some confectioner's shop in despair.... I thought she would write, but there hasn't been a line, she's vanished into thin air."

Refusing to go in for a glass of tea, Roshchin went straight back to the station. There would be a train to Ekaterinoslav in the evening. He went into the first-class waiting room, sat down on a hard oak bench, and leaned forward on his elbow, shading his eyes with the palm of his hand, remaining thus motionless through the long hours of waiting....

Somebody sank down beside Vadim Petrovich with a sigh of relief, and the evident intention of remaining there for some time. Many had come and gone before him, but this latest comer sat there with his leg and thigh jerking so violently that the whole seat shook. He neither departed nor stopped shaking his leg. Without removing his hand from his eyes, Roshchin said:

"Look here—couldn't you stop shaking your leg?"

"Sorry—a bad habit," came the amiable reply.

And after that the stranger sat quite still.

The voice struck Vadim Petrovich as familiar—it seemed to be bound up with remote, exquisite memories.... Without removing his hand, Roshchin peered at his neighbour through the chinks between his fingers. It was Telegin. His legs in the muddy boots stretched out, his hands folded over his stomach, he seemed to be dozing, with the nape of his neck resting against the high back of the seat. He wore a tight tunic, which caught him under the armpits, and the lieutenant colonel's shoulder straps on it were new. On his lean, clean-shaven face was the fixed smile of a man resting after inexpressible fatigue....

Next to Katya, Telegin was the person dearest to Roshchin in the whole world—as near as a brother, a beloved friend. He dwelt in the light reflected from the charm of the sisters—Katya and Dasha.... Vadim Petrovich almost cried out in his astonishment, almost fell on the neck of Ivan Ilyich. But Telegin neither opened his eyes nor moved. The moment had passed. Roshchin realized that this was an enemy next to him. He had known by the end of May that Telegin was in the Red Army, had joined it of his own free will and was in high favour. His clothes were obviously not his own, they had probably been taken from some fallen officer whom he must have first killed. He wore the insignia of a lieutenant colonel, and Roshchin was sure he had formerly been only a captain. Roshchin was suddenly overcome with the feeling of nausea which so often ended in one of his outbursts of bitter loathing: Telegin could only be here as a Bolshevik spy....

He ought to go and inform the military commandant immediately. Two months ago he would not have hesitated for a moment. But he seemed to have grown into the bench—he felt utterly powerless. And then the disgust somehow died down.... Ivan Ilyich, a Red officer, there he was beside him, the same as ever—tired, the essence of goodness.... He wasn't doing it for money, or for his own advancement—that was nonsense! Calm, rational, if he had joined the Red Army it was because he believed the cause a good one.... "Just like me—just like me.... Denounce him—and an hour from now Dasha's husband, Katya's brother, and mine, would be sprawling on a rubbish heap at the foot of a fence, his boots dragged off...."

His throat contracted with horror. He seemed to shrink into himself.... What was he to do? Get up and go away? But Telegin might recognize him, lose his head, call out. How could he save him?

Roshchin and Ivan Ilyich sat motionless, as if asleep, side by side on the oak bench. The station was empty at this hour. The watchman closed the doors to the platforms. Then Telegin, not opening his eyes, said:

"Thanks, Vadim."

Roshchin's hand began to tremble violently. Ivan Ilyich rose lightly and walked with calm steps towards the exit to the square, never turning his head. A minute later, Roshchin rushed after him. He ran all round the station square, where, on the asphalt pavement, melting in the white rays of the sun, swarthy street vendors nodded over their trays beneath dangling bundles of smoked fish.... The leaves on the trees were burnt, the very air, saturated with the dust of the city, was burnt.

"If I could just have embraced him—nothing more!"

Red circles of torrid heat swam in front of Roshchin's eyes. Telegin seemed to have been swallowed up by the earth.

Just when the glow of sunset was fading away over the steppe, and Roshchin, clambering on to the upper berth in the railway carriage, had fallen asleep to the thudding of the wheels, she whom he was seeking, for whom his soul, sick with blood and hate, was yearning, his wife Katya, was jogging over the steppe on a cart. Her shoulders were wrapped in a shawl. Beside her sat the beauteous Matryona Krasilnikova. The rickety cart jingled metallically. The horses snorted. Innumerable carts stretched in front and behind them over the steppe, moving through the darkness of the starry night.

Alexei Krasilnikov, the reins held loosely in his hand, was sitting in front. Semyon was perched on the side of the cart, his boots slapped at by burdock leaves and clover. There was a smell of horses and wormwood. Katya's thoughts wandered in a kind of stupor. The wind was chill on her shoulders. The steppe seemed boundless, the road endless. The horses seemed to have been plodding forward, the wheels creaking, since the beginning of time, on and on like the ghosts of ancient nomads.

Happiness is nothing but infinite yearning, the edge of the steppe, azure shores, caressing waves, peace, plenty.

Matryona looked into Katya's face and gave a chuckle. And again nothing but the thudding of hoofs broke the silence. The army was emerging from encirclement. Makhno had told them to move as quietly as possible. Alexei's heavy shoulders began to droop—he, too, must have been overcome by drowsiness.

"It isn't that I want to cut adrift from you," Semyon was saying quietly. "Don't keep on at me with your 'Semyon, Semyon'...." (Matryona gave a brief sigh, turned away her face, and gazed out over the steppe.) "I tried to explain to Alexei in the spring that it's not the ribbons on the sailor's cap I care about.... It's the cause...." (Alexei said nothing.) "Who does the fleet belong to now? To us peasants. And if we all run away.... We're all fighting for the same cause—you here, we there...."

"What do they say in their letters?" asked Matryona.

"They say I've got to go back to the destroyer if I don't want to be considered a deserter, an outlaw from the revolution.... "

Matryona shrugged up one shoulder. She was obviously seething with rage. But she restrained herself, and said nothing. A short time afterwards Alexei straightened himself on his perch, as if he could hear something, and pointed into the dark with his whip.

"The Ekaterinoslav express," he said.

241

Katya looked, but she could not see the train bearing the sleeping Vadim Petrovich on an upper berth—she only heard the whistle, drawn-out, remote, evoking a piercing grief within her....

Vadim Petrovich went straight from the station at Ekaterinoslav to the confectioners' shops, trying to get news of Katya. He went into stifling cafés, with flies on the smeared windows and the butter muslin spread over the cakes. He read the cardboard signs, "Versailles", "Eldorado", "Cosy Nook", over the doors of dubious eating houses, from which there glared at him swarthy, bewhiskered individuals, with dazzling, bulging eyeballs, who looked as if they were ready, if required, to make *shashlyk* out of anything they could lay their hands on. Even here he made enquiries. Then he visited all the shops in turn.

The sun blazed pitilessly. A variegated crowd buzzed and jostled one another in the double avenues, beneath the thick foliage of the ash trees lining Ekaterininski Prospekt. Dilapidated trams clattered by. Before the war something like a new capital for the southern Ukraine had begun to spring up here. The war had halted its growth. Under the power of the hetman and the protection of the Germans, the town had come to life once more, but in a different way: in the place of offices, banks, and warehouses, there were gaming houses, exchange booths, steak shops and lemonade stands. The hum of business and the bustle of commerce had been exchanged for the hysterical activities of currency-mongers, running hither and thither from café to street corner, with unshaven chins, and caps on the backs of their heads. The cries of the innumerable bootblacks and sellers of boot polish (the manufacture of boot polish was the only industry of those times) mingled with the importunities of sinister tramps, the wailings of orchestras from the "Cosy Nooks", amidst the meaningless jostlings of the idle crowd, living on the purchase and sale of false money and non-existent commodities.

Frantic with his fruitless searchings, half-stunned and wholly exhausted, Vadim Petrovich sat down on a bench beneath an acacia. The crowd swept past: women, some elegant, some looking very odd, in dresses made from curtains, in Ukrainian national costumes; women with sweating eyelids and lines drawn beneath the eyes, the sweat pouring in streamlets down their rouged and powdered cheeks; excited profiteers, pushing their way like maniacs, with extended arms, through this crowd of women; hetman officials, with tridents on the front of their caps, pompous, absorbed in financial schemes and ideas for stealing State property; hetman Cossacks, tall and broad-shouldered, with apoplectic necks; moustached Gaidamaks in huge caps with crimson crowns, sky-blue cloaks and exaggeratedly baggy trousers, such as Ukrainian nationalist schoolmasters had been longing to wear for two centuries. Here and there sacrosanct German officers floated among the crowd, glancing over the heads of the passers-by with contemptuous smiles....

As Roshchin looked, his heart swelled with rage. "Oh, to soak them in petrol and set fire to the beastly lot...." He had a glass of fruit juice at a mineral-water stand and once more went from door to door. Only now did he begin to realise the hopelessness of his search. Katya in this half-crazed crowd—penniless, alone, unpractical, timid, broken-hearted (with keen anguish his thoughts went back again and again to the bottle of poison in the Moscow flat). The greasy hands of the money-changers, the pimps, the restaurant-keepers were touching her, loathsome glances were stealing over her.... Almost choking with rage, he elbowed his way into the thick of the crowd, heedless of cries and oaths. In the evening he took a room in a hotel at an enormous price—a dark hole, in which there was only room for an iron bedstead with a worn mattress—and taking off his boots lay down and buried his grey head in the pillows, weeping silently and tearlessly....

After crossing the frontier of the Don on foot, Telegin put his lieutenant colonel's shoulder straps into his kit-bag; he went by train as far as Tsaritsyn and from there embarked on an enormous river steamer, crammed from top deck to hold with peasants, returning soldiers, deserters, refugees. Arrived at Saratov, he showed his papers at the Revolutionary Committee, and then took a tugboat to Syzran, where the Czechoslovak front was.

The Volga was deserted, as in those half-legendary times when the cavalry of Genghis Khan had approached its sandy shores to water their steeds in the famous river. Its mirror-like expanse flowed endlessly and slowly between a framework of sandy banks, green water meadows and clumps of rose willow. The infrequent villages seemed to be abandoned. The unbroken steppe extended eastwards, appearing to dissolve in waves of heat, as in a mirage. The reflections of clouds floated slowly by. The silence was only broken by the fussy splashing of the paddle in the blue water.

Ivan Ilyich lay on the scorching deck beneath the captain's bridge. He was bare-footed, and wore an unbelted cotton blouse; a blond fuzz was beginning to appear on his jaws. Like a cat basking in the sunshine, he revelled in the quiet, the moist fragrance of swamp blossoms, the dry smell of steppe grass wafted from the low-lying banks, and the boundless flood of light. It was the most utter repose he had ever known.

The steamer was carrying firearms and munitions for the guerillas in the steppe districts. The Red Army men accompanying the cargo were sluggish from so much fresh air—some slept, some, having slept their fill, lay about singing and gazing at the expanse of water. Comrade Khvedin, a Black Sea sailor in command of the detachment, endeavoured, several times a day, to rouse the men to a sense of shame for their lack of class-consciousness, but they only clustered round him in sitting and lying positions, their chins propped on their hands.

"Try to understand, brothers," he said in his husky voice, "it's not Denikin, it's not Ataman Krasnov, it's not the Czechs we're fighting, it's the whole bloody bourgeoisie in both hemispheres.... The world bourgeoisie must be dealt a mortal blow before it has time finally to rally its own forces.... We R-r-r-russians" (he pronounced the word proudly and with emphatic distinctness) "have our blood brothers—the world proletariat—on our side.... They are only waiting for one thing—for us to finish off our own parasites, and go to their help in the class struggle.... That needs no explanation, brothers. There have never been braver men than the Russian soldiers in the whole world—excepting the seamen of the Red Fleet, so we have all the chances. D'you see, my lads? It's as simple as ABC, what I say. There'll be a fight near Samara today, and soon there'll be fighting on all continents...."

The lads listened, hanging on his lips.... Someone remarked calmly:

"That's right ... we've stirred up a hornet's nest ... all over the world!"

The Khvalinsk mountains showed blue on the left. Comrade Khvedin looked through his field glasses. The sleepy town of Khvalinsk could now be made out through clumps of trees. Here the steamer was to refuel.

The grizzled captain was standing by the man at the wheel. The river formed three streams here, skirting islets of willow herb, and the fairway was a difficult one. Khvedin approached the captain.

"Not a soul in sight in the town—what does it mean?"

"We must have oil, whatever happens."

"Go ahead then, take it."

The steamer, coming right up to an island, on which the branches of black poplars almost touched the paddle boxes, sounded its siren, and began turning. Instantly frantic voices exclaimed from the island:

"Stop! Stop! Where are you going?"

Khvedin drew his revolver from its holster. The crew retreated from the side of the boat. The water seethed beneath the threshing paddle.

"Stop! Stop!" repeated the voices.

There was a rustling in the willow herb and some men made their way to the bank of the river, revealing flushed, agitated countenances, and waving wildly in the direction of the town. There was such a din that it was impossible to make out anything. Khvedin tried swearing at them—good, round, seamen's oaths. But by then all had become clear.... Puffs of smoke were seen at the landing stage leading to the town, and shots rang out over the water. Khvalinsk was occupied by the Whites. The people on the island were the remnants of the escaping garrison and a part of the local guerillas. Some were armed, but none of them had any ammunition.

The Red Army men rushed to their cabins for rifles. Khvedin himself took the captain's place, sending such resounding oaths echoing down the river that the men on the island were immediately comforted, and smiles appeared on their faces. In the heat of the moment Khvedin wanted to make an immediate frontal attack on the town from the river, and send a landing party ashore to deal with the enemy. But Ivan Ilyich restrained him, convincing him with little difficulty that an unprepared attack must fail, that envelopment must first be carried out, and that Khvedin had no idea of the enemy's strength—perhaps they even had artillery!

Khvedin ground his teeth, but gave in. The steamer backwatered with the current beneath rifle fire, and approached the island from the west, where the town was hidden by woods. Here they moored. The men on the island—there were about fifty of them, ragged and unkempt—came rushing down to the sandy bank.

"Listen to what we have to tell you, you devils!" they shouted.

"Zakharkin is coming to our aid, with the Pugachevsk guerilla fighters."

"We sent a messenger to him the day before yesterday."

They went on to relate how, three days ago, the local bourgeoisie had seized the building of the town Soviet and the postal and telegraph offices in an armed raid. Officers had replaced their shoulder straps, fallen upon the arsenal, and seized machine guns. Schoolboys, merchants, officials, had armed, even the deacon from the church ran up and down the street with a hunting rifle. The coup had been completely unexpected, the Reds had not even had time to snatch up their rifles.

"Our commanders ran away—they betrayed us...."

"And we are running about like lost sheep."

"Oh, you!" exclaimed Khvedin, "you *landlubbers*!"

It was all he could find to say.

They all gathered together on the riverbank for a military council. Telegin was elected secretary. First it had to be decided whether to take Khvalinsk out of the hands of the bourgeoisie, or not. The decision was for taking it. The next question was whether to wait for the Pugachevsk guerillas, or to take the town with the forces at their disposal. On this point there was much argument. Some exclaimed that they ought to wait, since the guerillas had machine guns, others that they ought not to wait, since any minute White steam ships would be coming up from Samara. Khvedin, sick of arguing, waved his hand impatiently.

"Enough jabbering, Comrades! Passed unanimously: Khvalinsk to be ours by nightfall. Draw up the minutes please, Comrade Telegin!"

Just then horsemen appeared on the cliffs of the left bank: first two, then four more. Seeing the steamer they galloped off. In a short time the whole bank was covered with horsemen, and broad pikes made from scythes caught the sun's rays.

"Hi, there—who are you?" shouted the Khvalinsk people.

From the other bank came the reply:

"Zakharkin's detachment of the Pugachevsk Peasant Army."

Khvedin seized the megaphone and boomed out, the veins in his neck swelling:

"We've brought you arms, brothers—come over here to the island.... We're going to take Khvalinsk...."

From the other side came the cry:

"All right! We have a gun.... Send the steamer across for it."

The horsemen on the riverbank formed one of the detachments of the peasant guerilla army fighting in the Samara steppe against those districts which had acknowledged the power of the Samara Provisional Government.

This army sprang up immediately after the occupation of Samara by the Czechs. The town of Pugachevsk, formerly Nikolayevsk, became its organizational centre. Hither came all the hotheads who loved riding for its own sake, all who had been confined to the peasants' narrow wedge of earth by the machinations of Shekhobalov, the well-known purchaser of land, all those endeavouring to hold land in the teeth of the rich Ural Cossacks, all those whose souls—born of the boundless steppe, where the wheat murmurs eternally, where the peasant, urging on the slow-stepping bullocks, follows the clumsy plough—brimmed over with emotions which refuse to be suppressed.

The enemy sprang up everywhere, like a mirage in the steppe. A meeting would be called in the village—rich peasants, non-commissioned officers from the tsarist army, disguised agitators from Samara, cried loudly that it was an unheard-of thing for the poorest peasant, the day labourer, the landless vagabond to be allowed to rule the district, and take their land and grain away from well-to-do farmers. And the meeting ruled that messengers should be sent to neighbouring villages, bidding them to make trenches. A whole district would sometimes rise, bring weapons from secret hiding places, plough a furrow for a boundary line, and dig trenches dozens of miles long.

At some places a republic would be proclaimed, acknowledging Samara as its centre. The defence of the territory was entrusted to the cavalry, the infantry only being mobilized when Red attacks were expected. Scythes bound upright to long poles were made to serve as weapons for the cavalry. These kulak armies were a real menace. They appeared unexpectedly, out of the misty steppe, falling upon the lines and machine guns of the Reds. People fought their own flesh and blood—brother against brother, father against son, neighbour against neighbour—and therefore they fought ferociously, ruthlessly. Whenever they scored a victory over the Reds, the kulaks armed themselves with rifles and machine guns, but did not discard their scythes.

This great peasant war, fought in the steppes round Samara, where the memory of Pugachev's campaigns was still green, left no annals or military archives, but a father and son might be overheard on some religious holiday discussing the battles of yore over a bucket of vodka, taunting one another with strategic mistakes.

"Remember that time at Koldiban, when you turned the big gun on us, Yasha? 'That must be my Yasha, that son-of-a-bitch, Yasha,' I thought.... 'Should have licked the cub oftener....' Well, we managed to frighten you off that time.... You were lucky not to fall into my hands then...."

"Go on, brag away! It was we who won!"

"Just you wait—we'll be fighting on opposite sides again!"

"That we will.... You always were a kulak, and you'll stick to your bloody kulak opinions."

"Your health, Son!"

"Your health, Father!"

The steamer crossed over to the left bank. The gangway was dropped, and Zakharkin, the commander of the Pugachevsk detachment, a man with a nose hooked like the beak of a vulture, came on board. He was so strong and muscular that the planks creaked beneath his feet. His faded tunic was splitting at the armpits, and a curved sabre banged against his high riding boots. His older brothers, peasants from the Utev District, each had a division under his command. After him came six guerillas—his commanders—clad in picturesque and unusual attire: faded shirts covered with dust and tar, unbuttoned collars, some in felt boots, with spurs fixed to them, some in bast shoes, cartridge belts slung across their shoulders, hand grenades thrust into their belts, flat German bayonets, sawed-off rifles.

Zakharkin and Khvedin met on the captain's bridge, with a handshake of mutual heartiness. Cigarettes were handed round. Khvedin gave a brief summary of the military situation. Zakharkin said:

"I know who's stirring up trouble in Khvalinsk—it's Kukushkin, the chairman of the Zemstvo.... I wish I could take that swine alive...."

"About that gun," said Khvedin. "Is it in working order?"

"It fires all right, but you have to set it each time—there's no sight, you have to aim through the barrel. But the damned thing can hit! A belfry or a pump house comes down every time!"

"Good! And what's your opinion as to a landing and flanking movement, Comrade Zakharkin?"

"We'll throw the cavalry across to the other side. Can your steamboat take a hundred men?"

"Easily—in two crossings."

"Then that's all right. When it begins to get dark we'll make a cavalry landing above the town. We'll mount the gun on the steamer. And at dawn we'll attack."

Khvedin entrusted Ivan Ilyich with the command of the landing of the infantry, who were to make a frontal attack on the landing stage. In the twilight the steamer moved cautiously, with no lights showing, up the side reach of the Volga, along the island. The only sound in the stillness was the voice of the sailor taking soundings in the river. The Pugachevsk men followed the steamer along the riverbank. Rifles were issued to the Khvalinsk men, who lay down on the sand. Telegin walked backwards and forwards at the water's edge, seeing that no one smoked or showed a light. The river lapped over the sand with scarcely a murmur. There was a smell of swamp blossoms, and a humming of gnats. The men on the sand kept very quiet.

The night became ever blacker, ever more velvety, more starry. The dry smell of wormwood and the warbling "*spat-porra, spat-porra*"* of a quail were wafted over the river from the steppe. Ivan Ilyich walked up and down at the water's edge, fighting off sleep.

Just when the shades of night were beginning to disperse, the sky to lose its velvety blackness, and cocks to crow in the distance,

*"Go to bed, go to bed!"

there came the sound of paddles splashing through the faint mist rising from the water. The steamer was approaching. Ivan Ilyich examined the drum of his revolver, tightened his leather trouser-belt, and went up and down the lines of sleepers, tapping them on their legs with a cane.

"Wake up, Comrades!"

They sprang wildly to their feet, shivering, still half-asleep, and not quite understanding what was before them.... Many went to the river to drink, dipping their heads in the water. Telegin issued his commands under his breath. Cover of some sort would be required—the soldiers began stripping off their shirts, filling them with sand, and setting them along the bulwarks. They worked in silence—this was no joking matter.

Day was beginning to break. The preparations were over. The small rusty mountain gun was posted in the bows. Fifty men went on board, lying down behind the improvised sandbags. Khvedin took the wheel, crying out:

"Full steam ahead!"

The water seethed beneath the paddles. The steamer rapidly skirted the islands and made for the town along the main stream. Yellow lights could be seen here and there in the town. Behind, a vague line of mountains, shrouded in night, could be made out. The sound of cocks crowing now came quite distinctly to the ears.

Ivan Ilyich stood near the gun. He could not get used to the idea that in a short time they would have to shoot into this inviolable stillness. A Khvalinsk dweller, a harmless little man looking like a priest with a taste for fishing, who had volunteered to be gunlayer, said amiably:

"Comrade Commander, what if we were to aim right at the post office? Bang in the middle of it.... See—where those two yellow lights are...."

"Aim at the post office!" thundered the voice of Khvedin through the megaphone. "Ready! Open sights!"

The gunner squatted down, peeping along the tube of the gun, which he trained on the lights. He loaded it. Then he turned to Telegin:

"Move back a little, dear Comrade, this thing might explode."

"Fire!" barked Khvedin.

The gun went off, recoiling violently, and emitting a blinding flash. The roar boomed over the river and the hills sent back an answering rumble.

"Fire, fire!" shouted Khvedin, turning the helm. "Rapid fire from the port side! Volleys, volleys for the swine!"

He stamped, flew into a passion, thundered out fantastic oaths. Irregular volleys came from the deck. The bank on the Khvalinsk side was getting nearer and nearer. The gunner loaded his gun unhurriedly and fired again. Splinters from some sort of shed flew into the air. Now the outlines of wooden houses, orchards, and belfries could be clearly seen.

Splintering flashes of rifle fire burst out from the landing stage below. And then Telegin heard the sound he had all along been dreading: the abrupt hurried barking of a machine gun. He felt the familiar tautness in his toes, as if all his blood vessels were contracting. Squatting down beside the gun, he drew the attention of the gunner to a long structure halfway up the side of a slope.

"Try to land her over there, where those bushes are...."

"Tchk!" said the gunner. "That's a nice little house, but never mind!"

The gun boomed out a third time. The machine gun fell quiet for a moment or two, and then its rap-rap came from somewhere higher up. The steamer approached the landing stage with a sharp turn. The bullets flew high, among the funnels and masts.

"Don't wait for the ship to moor—jump! " cried Khvedin. "Hurrah, boys!"

The sides of the landing stage creaked violently. Telegin was the first to jump, turning to the Khvalinsk men who were crawling over the rail with a cry of:

"Follow me! Hurrah!"

He ran down the planks to the shore. A cheering crowd followed him, shooting, running, stumbling. The bank was deserted. A few figures seemed to be stirring in the undergrowth of some orchards. There was a little firing from rooftops. And now, quite far away, on the hills, the machine gun barked intermittently, fell silent, and fired a couple or so more rounds. The enemy refused to accept battle.

Telegin found himself on a kind of unevenly paved square. Hardly giving himself time to regain his breath, he looked round, and rallied his men. The soles of his bare feet burned, he must have grazed them on some stones. The air smelt of dust. The shutters of the wooden houses were closed. Not even the leaves of the lilacs and acacias stirred. Four pairs of long underdrawers depended from a line over a balcony on a two-storeyed corner house with a pretentious turret. "They'll be stolen," thought Telegin to himself. The town seemed to be fast asleep, and the firing, the running, the cries merely a part of its dreams.

Enquiring the locality of the post office, the telegraph office, and the water tower, Telegin dispatched parties of ten to them. The men advanced, their nerves still on edge, starting continually, levelling their rifles at every rustle. The enemy was no-where in sight. The starlings were beginning to sing, and the pigeons were flying upwards from the rooftops.

Telegin's detachment occupied the house of the town Soviet, a brick building with peeling pillars. All the doors were wide open, and the entrance hall was strewn with weapons. Telegin went out on to a balcony. Beneath him stretched luxuriant orchards, long unpainted roofs, empty, dusty streets—all the quiet of a country town. And suddenly the alarm was sounded somewhere far away: the nervous, rapid, hollow voice of a bell floated over the town. Rapid firing came from the direction of the brassy cry for help, accompanied by the explosion of hand grenades, shouts, the heavy thud of horses' hoofs, yells. It was Zakharkin's landing party cutting off the enemy's retreat to the mountains. Then horsemen came galloping along a side street, with a metallic clanging of horseshoes. And once again all was quiet.

Ivan Ilyich went down with unhurried steps to report at the steamer that the town was occupied. After hearing him out, Khvedin said:

"The Soviet power has been restored. There's nothing more for us to do here. We must go on."

He gave a friendly pat to the shoulder of the old captain, who was half-dead with fright: "So you've smelt powder, at last! Well, old fellow.... I give up the command ... take the watch!

Telegin slept till evening to the thumping of machinery and the murmuring of water. The sunset spread its transparent hazy glow over the horizon. Soft part-singing—the voices floating away into the abandoned spaces of the steppe—could be heard from the stern. The vain beauty of the sunset glow lay over the riverbanks, the water, invaded the sight, the heart....

"Why so glum, brothers?" cried Khvedin. "Why not sing something jolly while you're about it?"

He, too, had slept, and, after tossing off a tumbler of spirits, was strolling up and down the upper deck, hitching up his trousers. "If we could only take Syzran! What d'you say, Comrade Telegin? What a drubbing we'd give them!"

He was continually laughing, exposing his white teeth. What did he care for danger, for the melancholy beauty of the Volga sunset, for the fatal bullet which—in battle, or from round some corner—would put an end to his life? The thirst for life, burning energy, were seething in him.... The planks cracked beneath his bare heels.

"Just you wait, only give us time, we'll take Syzran and Samara—the whole Volga will be ours...."

A filmy veil obscured the sunset glow. The steamer showed no lights. The banks seemed to be disappearing into the night. Khvedin, seeking an outlet for his energy, invited Ivan Ilyich to play cards with him.

"If you don't want to play for money, let's play for smacks on the nose. But proper ones!"

They sat down in the captain's cabin to play for smacks. In his excitement, Khvedin overbid, ran up a tally of three hundred smacks, and was so carried away that he almost cheated, but Ivan Ilyich, who kept a sharp lookout ("You can't get away with that with me, mate!"), won. Seating himself comfortably on the stool, he began to hit his opponent's nose with the greasy cards. Khvedin's nose was very soon as red as beetroot.

"Where did you learn that?"

"I learned it when I was a German prisoner," said Telegin. "Don't turn your phiz away! Two-hundred-and-ninety-seven."

"Mind! No bending of the cards! If you do, I'll...."

"No nonsense! You're allowed to bend the last three!"

"Go on, then, you scamp!"

But before Telegin could strike again, the captain came into the cabin. His jaw was trembling. He held his cap in his hand. Drops of sweat were running down the bald top of his head.

"You can do what you like to me, Comrade-gentlemen," he said despairingly. "I'm ready for anything. But whatever you say I'm not going on any further ... it's certain death...."

Flinging down the cards, Khvedin and Telegin went on deck. In front and to the left the electric lights of Syzran shone as bright as stars. A huge river steamer, brilliantly lit up, was moving slowly along the shore: the great white St. Andrew's flag, the imposing outlines of heavy guns, the figures of officers walking up and down the deck, could be made out with the naked eye....

"We can't go back, Comrades. At all costs we must go on," whispered Khvedin. "If only we can get to Batraki, we can stop and unload."

He ordered the whole crew to gather in the hold, in readiness for a battle. The tricolour was hoisted, and the lights were lit. At last the tug was observed from the big steamer. Brief whistles ordered it to reduce speed. A voice boomed out from a megaphone:

"Who are you? Where are you headed for?"

"The tug *Kalashnikov*. Headed for Samara," replied Khvedin.

"Why did you light up so late?"

"We were afraid of the Bolsheviks." Khvedin lowered the megaphone to murmur in Telegin's ear: "If we only had a torpedo!

I sent to Astrakhan for torpedoes.... They're just a pack of daw-
dlers in the Astrakhan Soviet."

After a silence the reply came from the steamer:

"You may proceed."

The captain put on his cap with a trembling hand. Khvedin, his
teeth bared, his eyes narrowed, watched the lights of the vessel.
Then he spat and returned to the cabin.

"Go on, finish, you devil!" he shouted at Telegin, lighting a
cigarette and snapping the match in two.

An hour later they left Syzran behind them. As they neared
Batraki, Telegin was let over the side in a sloop. He took the noon
train from Batraki, and at 5 p.m. set off from the station at Samara
for Dr. Bulavin's flat. Once again he was attired in the torn and
crumpled tunic with lieutenant colonel's shoulder straps. On the
way there, striking the tops of his boots with the cane that he had
used to arouse the guerillas the night before, he read with the
most lively curiosity, as if they were things not seen for ages, the
theatre notices, appeals and advertisements he passed. They were
all in two languages: Russian (in prereform spelling) and Czech.

His glass of lemonade in hand, Dmitri Stepanovich Bulavin,
pulling out the napkin tucked into the top of his waistcoat, and
making imposing munching movements with his lips, began his
speech in the deep, significant voice recently acquired by him in
his capacity as under-secretary.

"Gentlemen, permit me...."

It was a banquet got up for the municipal representatives to
celebrate the victorious advance of the Constituent Assembly's
army in the north. Simbirsk and Kazan had been occupied. The
Bolsheviks seemed to have finally lost the Middle Volga district.
At Melekes, the remnants of the Red Cavalry, thirty-five hundred
strong, were making frantic efforts to break through encirclement.
In Kazan, which was taken by storm by the Czechs, twenty-four
thousand poods of gold, the equivalent of upwards of six hundred
million rubles—over half the State gold reserve—had been seized.
This fact was so incredible, so overwhelming, that the mind had
not yet been able to cope with its infinite consequences.

The gold was on its way to Samara. So far, no one had put in
a definite claim for it, but the Czechs had apparently decided to
place it at the disposal of the Samara Committee of members of
the Constituent Assembly. The Samara merchantry had their own
ideas as to the fate of the gold, but so far had refrained from
expressing them. The ardent admiration for the victorious Czechs
had reached fever point.

The banquet was crowded and animated. Captain Ček, the Czech Army Commander, and the hero of the day, was the centre of a smiling galaxy formed by the society ladies of Samara; among them were such stars as Arzhanova, Kurlina, and Shekhobalova, the proprietresses of five-storeyed flour mills, grain elevators, steamship companies, and whole districts of fallow black earth. They were resplendent in diamonds the size of cobnuts, and in gowns which, if no longer quite fashionable, had at any rate, in their day, come from Paris and Vienna. Like all heroes, Ček was adorably simple and gracious. True, his sturdy body was rather too warm, and the tight collar of his faultlessly-cut tunic was digging into his crimson neck, but his florid youthful face, with the short reddish moustache and blazing eyes, seemed fairly to ask for kisses on both cheeks. The enchanting smile never left his lips, as if he renounced all personal glory, as if the society of ladies was a thousand times dearer to him than the thunder of victory and the capture of provincial towns and trains full of gold.

Opposite him sat a heavy, middle-aged military man with a white aiglet. His egglike skull was naked and massive, a veritable bulwark of authority. The most noticeable feature of his fat, clean-shaven face were the thick lips: he never stopped chewing, and contracting and retracting his eyebrows, while his glance roved eagerly over the rich display of hors d'oeuvres. The wine-glass was lost in his great fist, it was obvious he was more accustomed to holding tumblers. He took brief sips, throwing back his head. His small, cunning blue eyes never rested for long on anyone, as if he were all the time on the alert here. The other military men bent towards him with respectful attention, for this was the Orenburg ataman Dutov, the hero of the Ural Cossacks, a recently-arrived visitor.

A few seats away, between two pretty women, one a light blonde, the other auburn-haired, sat M. Janeau, the French ambassador, in a light grey cutaway and dazzling shirt front. His small face, with the exquisite moustache and pointed nose, bore the signs of extreme dissipation. He was trilling away, rolling his r's, now bending over the well-exposed charms of the auburn lady (who rewarded him by a tap on his hand with a flower), now over the pink-and-pearl shoulder of the blonde, who giggled as if he were tickling her. Both ladies understood French, when not spoken too quickly. It was obvious that poor Janeau was desperately enamoured of these feminine charms. This did not, however, prevent him from turning, whenever the conversation flagged, towards Brikin, a solid flour-mill proprietor, who had only just arrived from Omsk, or from raising his glass to the bril-

liant achievements of Ataman Dutov. The interest displayed by
M. Janeau in Siberian flour and Orenburg meat and butter,
showed his passionate loyalty to the White movement: in moments
of food crisis, the French ambassador could always offer the government fifty truckloads of flour or other commodities.... There
were sceptics who declared that there would be no harm in inviting
M. Janeau, as any decent government would, to show his ambas-
sadorial credentials.... But the government preferred the more
tactful way of confidence in its allies.

There was yet another notable foreigner at table—the swarthy,
quick-eyed Signor Piccolomini (who vowed that this was his real
name). He represented, somewhat vaguely, the Italian nation, the
Italian people. His short sky-blue uniform was adorned with silver
braid, and enormous general's epaulettes swayed up and down on
his shoulders. He was supposed to be forming a special Italian
battalion in Samara. The government asked in amazement:
"Where the devil does he think he'll find Italians here?" But they
gave him money. After all, allies are allies.... No one attached the
least importance to him in bourgeois circles.

The only government representatives at the banquet were non-
party members like Dr. Bulavin, and Semyon Semyonovich Govyadin, who had risen high on the ladder of officialdom, and was now
assistant chief of counterintelligence. The time for mutual enthusiasm, when the Bolsheviks were overthrown, was past. The Constituent Assembly Committee, confirmed S.R.'s to a man, was prating
such stuff about the attainments of the revolution, that no one but
the Czechs, who really had not the faintest insight into Russian affairs, could go on believing in it. In the initial stages, when a coup
d'etat had to be brought off, and it was necessary to pacify the workers and peasants, the S.R. government had, of course, been a god-
send. The Samara tradesmen themselves had echoed the S.R. slogans. But the Volga had now been freed from Khvalinsk to Kazan.
Denikin had conquered almost the entire North Caucasus, Krasnov
was nearing Tsaritsyn, Dutov had cleared up the Urals, and imposing White atamans were turning up almost every day in Siberia—and
those long-haired tramps, Volsky, Brushvit, Klimushkin and the rest
of the crew, meeting in the splendid palace of the Samara Marshal
of Nobility, were still hankering after a Constituent Assembly.
Faugh! The big merchants had begun resolutely going over to quite
different slogans—simpler, firmer, easier to grasp.... Most of what
Dmitri Stepanovich said was addressed to the foreigners present:

"...the serpent's sting has been removed. This phenomenal
fact, in itself marking a turning point, has not been sufficiently
taken into account.... I speak of the six hundred million gold

rubles at present in our hands...." (The ends of M. Janeau's moustache stood upright. "Bravo!" he cried, waving his glass; Piccolomini's eyes burned diabolically.) "The golden sting has been removed from the Bolsheviks, gentlemen.... They can still bite, but their bite is no longer fatal. They can threaten, but people fear them no more than they would fear a beggar shaking his crutch... They have no more gold—nothing but a printing press."

Brikin, the merchant from Omsk, suddenly opened his mouth in a loud laugh, mopping his neck with his napkin, and muttering: "What a business, my God!"

"You, gentlemen, representatives of foreign countries," continued Dr. Bulavin, and a metallic note came into his voice which had not been there before. "You, gentlemen, our allies ... remember—friendship is one thing, and money is another.... Only yesterday we were merely a comic-opera organization in your eyes, a kind of temporary growth, like the swelling which is bound to follow a blow...." (Ček frowned, M. Janeau and Piccolomini made indignant gestures.... Dmitri Stepanovich gave a sly smile.)

"Today the whole world knows that we are a solid government, that we are the guardians of a State gold fund.... Now we can come to an understanding, my friends the foreign representatives...." (He rapped his knuckles sharply on the table.) "I now speak as a private individual to private individuals, in an atmosphere of intimacy. But I fully realize the gravity of the ideas I have expressed.... I foresee the movements of ships bearing munitions and textiles to Russian ports ... the formation of vast White armies ... the sword of heavy retribution descending on the band of rascals now lording it over Russia. Six hundred million is enough for that.... Foreign representatives! Aid, comprehensive, generous aid to the legitimate representatives of the Russian people!"

He put his lips to the rim of his glass and sat down again frowning and breathing heavily. Those round the table applauded warmly. The merchant Brikin shouted:

"Thanks, friend.... That's right, friend, that's right—our way, no socialism...."

Ček rose, setting his belt over his stomach with a quick tug.

"I will be brief," he said. "We have given and will continue to give our lives for the well-being of our blood brothers, the Russians. Long live Russia, the great, the mighty.... Hurrah!"

At this the whole table thundered with applause, the outstretched hands of the ladies clapping frantically among the flowers. M. Janeau rose to speak. His head was tossed backward in a noble gesture, and his luxuriant moustache lent virility to his countenance:

"Mesdames et Messieurs! We were all sure that the gallant Russian army, lost in dreams of its glorious forefathers, has been cunningly deceived by the gang of Bolsheviks. They imposed upon it unnatural ideas and ferocious instincts, and the army ceased to be an army. Mesdames et Messieurs, I will not attempt to conceal it, there was a moment when the faith of France in the sincerity of the Russian people was shaken.... This nightmare has vanished.... Today we all see that we were wrong—the Russian people are again with us.... The army has already realized its mistake.... Once again the Russian giant is ready to stand up against the attack of our common foe.... I am happy in my newly-gained confidence...."

When the clapping had died down, Piccolomini leaped to his feet, his heavy epaulettes shaking. Since, however, no one present understood Italian, his goodwill was taken for granted, and the merchant Brikin sidled up to kiss the little swarthy man. There followed speeches by the representatives of capital. The merchants expressed themselves in foggy, involved periods—laying great stress on the fact that salvation must come from Siberia.... When everyone had finished speaking, Ataman Dutov was begged to say a few words. At first he refused: "No, no, I'm a soldier, I don't know how to speak," but in the end he rose heavily amidst the instantly ensuing silence, and sighed out:

"Well, gentlemen! If our allies help us—well and good! If they won't—we'll manage to cope with the Bolsheviks on our own.... So long as there's money.... And we trust you will not try to clip our wings in this respect, gentlemen...."

"Take us, Ataman, take us, liver and lights, we grudge nothing!" howled Brikin in an access of ecstasy.

The banquet was a success. When the speeches were over, black coffee was served, with foreign brandy and liqueurs. It was very late. Dmitri Stepanovich took French leave, departing without saying goodbye to anybody.

When, having driven back in a motorcar, he was opening his front door, an officer came rapidly up to him:

"Excuse me—are you Dr. Bulavin?"

Dmitri Stepanovich cast a glance over the stranger. It was dark in the street and all he could see were the lieutenant colonel's shoulder straps.

"Yes, I am Bulavin," the doctor conceded.

"I have come to you on very important business.... I know it's not your receiving hours.... But I've been three times already, without getting an answer."

"Tomorrow from 11 o'clock at the Ministry."

17-559

"I implore you to make it today. I'm leaving by the night steamer."

Dmitri Stepanovich paused before replying. There was something very insistent and alarming about the stranger. The doctor shrugged his shoulders.

"I give you fair warning—if you've come about monetary aid it is not within my competency."

"Oh, no, I don't want any aid."

"H'm.... Go in."

Dmitri Stepanovich preceded his visitor from the hall to his study, instantly locking the door leading to the rest of the house. There was a light somewhere—somebody must be still awake. The doctor sat down at his desk, waved his visitor to a chair opposite, glanced moodily at the pile of papers for his signature, and threaded the fingers of both hands.

"Well—what can I do for you?"

The officer pressed his cap against his chest and said softly, with heart-rending tenderness:

"Where's Dasha?"

The doctor banged the back of his head against the carving on the chair. For the first time he looked into the face of his visitor. Two years ago, Dasha had sent him a snapshot of herself and her husband. This was he. The doctor turned pale, the bags beneath his eyes shook, as he echoed hoarsely:

"Dasha?"

"Yes, I'm Telegin."

And he, too, turned pale, looking into the doctor's eyes. Recovering himself, Dmitri Stepanovich, instead of making the natural gesture of welcome towards his son-in-law, whom he was meeting for the first time in his life, threw out his hands dramatically, emitting a vague sound, as if repressing a laugh.

"So you're ... Telegin! Well, what have you got to say for yourself?"

He was apparently too much astonished even to shake hands with Ivan Ilyich. He fixed his pince-nez on the bridge of his nose (not the old cracked ones with nickel frames, but imposing gold-rimmed ones) and for some reason began hastily pulling out the drawers of his desk, which were crammed with papers.

Telegin, somewhat taken aback, followed his movements with astonishment. Only a minute before he had been ready to tell Dr. Bulavin all about himself, as to his own father....

But now he thought: "The devil knows—perhaps he guesses.... I should probably be putting him in an awkward position: after all, he *is* a minister...." Letting his head droop, he said very softly:

"Dmitri Stepanovich, I haven't seen Dasha for over six months, letters never arrive.... I haven't the slightest idea where she is."

"She's alive, she's alive, she's quite well."

The doctor was bending almost under the desk, to the very lowest drawer.

"I'm in the Volunteer Army.... I've been fighting the Bolsheviks since March.... I've just been sent by headquarters to the north on a secret mission."

Dmitri Stepanovich listened to him with a bewildered expression on his face; at the words "secret mission" a smile came and went beneath his moustache.

"Aha—and what regiment may you be in?"

"'The Privates'."

Telegin felt the blood rush into his cheeks.

"Aha! So there is such a thing in the Volunteer Army! Will you be staying with us long?"

"I'm leaving tonight."

"Very good! Where for, if I may ask? Excuse me—it's a military secret of course, I don't insist.... In other words—on counter-intelligence?"

There was something so strange in Dmitri Stepanovich's voice that Telegin, despite his intense agitation, noticed it and was on his guard at once.

But now the doctor had found what he was looking for.

"Your wife is in good health.... I got this from her last week— read it. There's something about you in it." (The doctor flung several sheets of paper covered with Dasha's bold handwriting, in front of Telegin. The irregular, precious letters swam before the eyes of Ivan Ilyich.) "Excuse me, I must leave you for a moment. Make yourself at home."

The doctor hurried out, locking the door behind him. The last Ivan Ilyich heard of him was his reply to somebody in the house: "...only a petitioner".

The doctor went out of the dining room into a dark passage where there was an old-fashioned telephone. Standing with his face against the wall as he wound up the crank at the side of the telephone, he demanded under his breath the number of counter-intelligence, and called for Semyon Semyonovich Govyadin to come to the telephone himself.

Dasha's letter was written in indelible pencil, and the writing got bigger and bigger as it went on, the lines running more and more steeply downwards.

"Papa, I don't know what's going to become of me.... Every-

259

thing's as vague as ever.... You're the only person I can write to. I'm in Kazan. I may be leaving tomorrow, but I don't know if I'll get to you. I want to see you. You'll understand everything. I'll do whatever you advise me to.... It's simply a miracle that I'm still alive.... Perhaps it would be better if I weren't, after all I've been through.... Everything I was told is a pack of lies, all a disgusting fraud.... Even Nikanor Yurevich Kulichok.... I trusted him, and allowed him to persuade me to go to Moscow. (I'll tell you the details when we meet.) Yesterday, even *he* told me, in so many words: 'They're shooting men, shovelling them into the ground by the dozen ... a bullet, that's the value of a man, the world is drowning in blood, and you expect us to stand on ceremony with you. Another man wouldn't even trouble to speak about it—he'd just invite you to bed.' I resist, Papa, I do really....I can't bear to be just a treat after a glass of spirits. If I fall as low as that, what will be left of me? It would be the end—I might as well hang myself. I did try to be useful. I worked three days under fire at Yaroslavl, as a Red-Cross nurse. At night I flung myself on my bed, my hands and my dress covered with blood. Once I was waked up by somebody pulling my skirt up. I sat up and cried out. It was a boy, an officer, I shall never forget his face! He was just a wild beast, he pushed me down, squeezing my wrists, without a word. The swine! Papa! I shot him with his own revolver—I don't know how it could happen.... I suppose he fell, I didn't see, I don't remember.... I ran out into the street. A glow in the sky, the town on fire, shells bursting.... I don't know why I didn't go mad that night. It was then that I made up my mind to run away, to run, run.... I want you to understand me, to help me.... I must get out of Russia! I have an opportunity.... Only you must help me to get away from Kulichok. He's always after me, I mean he drags me about everywhere with him, and every night there's the same talk. But I'm not going to give in, not if he kills me...."

Ivan Ilyich stopped reading, drew a breath, and then slowly turned the page.

"Quite by chance I got hold of some very valuable things.... A man was run over by a tram at Nikitsky Gate in front of me. He died because of me, I know that.... When I came to myself I had an alligator briefcase in my hand: someone must have put it into my hands when I was picked up.... I only looked into it the next day: it was full of diamond and pearl jewellery. These things were stolen by that man.... He was going to meet me.... They were stolen for me—see? Papa, I'm not going into the right or wrong of it—I kept the things.... My only salvation lies in them.... Even if you convince me that I'm a thief, I intend to keep them just the

same.... Since I've seen such a lot of death, I want to go on living....
I no longer believe in the image of humanity.... Those fine people
with their grand words about the salvation of the native land are
all beasts, swine....The things I've seen! Curses on them! This is
what has happened: Nikanor Yurevich Kulichok suddenly came
to me late one night, he'd come straight from Petrograd, it seems.
He insisted that I leave Moscow with him. It appears their 'League
for the Protection of the Native Land and Freedom' was discovered by the Cheka and wholesale arrests were going on in Moscow. Savinkov and the whole staff had escaped to the Volga. They
were to have got up risings in Rybinsk, Yaroslavl and Murom.
They were in a great hurry about it: the French ambassador
wasn't giving them any more money and wanted practical proof
of the strength of the organization. They hoped to get the whole
peasantry over to their side. Nikanor Yurevich assured me the
days of the Bolsheviks were numbered—the rising was to cover
the whole of the north, all the northern Volga districts, and join
up with the Czechs. Kulichok told me my name had been found
in the lists of the organization, and said it would be dangerous for
me to stay in Moscow, and I went to Yaroslavl with him.

"There, everything was in readiness: the leading posts in the
army, the militia, the arsenal were all in the hands of their
people.... We arrived in the evening, and at dawn I was awakened
by shots.... I rushed over to the window.... It looked out on a yard,
opposite was the brick wall of a garage, a rubbish heap, and some
dogs barking at the gate.... The shots were not repeated, all was
quiet, except for distant reports and the ominous hooting of motor
bicycles.... Then bells began ringing all over the town, in all the
churches. The yard gates opened and a group of officers already
wearing shoulder straps, came in. They all had excited faces and
were waving their weapons. They were leading a stout, clean-
shaven man in a grey jacket. He had no cap on, and no collar, his
waistcoat was unbuttoned. They were hitting him in the back. His
face was red and angry, his head rolling from side to side—you
could see he was in a terrible rage. Two of the officers stayed by
the garage, holding on to him, the rest moved aside for a consultation. Just then Colonel Perkhurov came out of the back porch.
I had never seen him before—he's the chief of all the armed forces
for the rising.... They all saluted him. He's a man with a will of
iron; he is very well set up, has sunken black eyes, a lean face,
wears gloves, carries a cane. I understood at once—it meant death
for the man in the grey jacket. Perkhurov stood looking at him
from under his brows, and I saw how evilly he bared his teeth.
And the man went on swearing, threatening, demanding. Then

Perkhurov jerked up his head, gave a command, and went away immediately.... The two men who had been holding the fat man sprang away from him. He tore off his jacket, screwed it up and threw it at the officers standing in front of him—right in the face of one of them, and swore at them, getting redder and redder in the face. He shook his fists and stood there in his unbuttoned waistcoat, huge and furious. Then they shot him. He shook all over, threw out his hands, took one step, and fell. They went on shooting at him for some time as he lay on the ground. It was Nakhimson, a Bolshevik commissar. Papa, I had seen an execution! As long as I live, I shall never forget how he gasped for breath. Nikanor Yurevich assured me it was a good thing—if they hadn't shot him, he would have shot them....

"I can't remember what happened next; everything seemed to be a continuation of that execution, everything was saturated with the convulsions of that huge frame that did not want to die.... I was ordered to go to some long, yellow building with pillars in front, and there I sat and typed orders and appeals. Motor bicycles kept dashing up, dust whirling.... People ran about, losing their tempers and giving orders; the merest trifle set them shouting and gesticulating. There were alternate fits of panic and exaggerated hopes. But whenever Perkhurov appeared, with his inexorable eyes, and threw out a word or two, the fuss all died down. The next day the rumbling of cannon could be heard from outside the town. It was the Bolsheviks coming. People had been crowding into our office from morning to night, and now it was suddenly quite empty. The town seemed to have died. The only sound was the roaring of Perkhurov's car rushing past, and the noise of armed detachments passing.... Some airplanes with Frenchmen in them were expected, some troops from the north, steamers with munitions from Rybinsk.... But these hopes were not fulfilled. And soon the town was encircled by a ring of battle. Shells were bursting in the streets.... Ancient belfries toppled down, houses fell, there were fires everywhere, and no one to put them out, the sun was hidden by smoke. Nobody even cleared the streets of dead bodies. It turned out later that in Rybinsk, where there were artillery depots, Savinkov had got up a similar rising which was suppressed by the soldiers, that the villages around Yaroslavl had not the slightest intention of giving any aid, and that the Yaroslavl workers had refused to go into the trenches and fight against the Bolsheviks.... Most terrible of all was Perkhurov's face—I kept meeting him during these days. He was like Death itself, dashing in his car over the ruins of the town—all that happened seemed to be the embodiment of his will. Kulichok kept me in a basement

several days. But, Papa, I could not shake off my feeling of guilt....
I would have gone mad in that basement. I put on a kerchief with
a red cross in front and worked till the night the officer tried to
rape me....

"The day before the fall of Yaroslavl, Nikanor Yurevich and I
crossed the Volga in a rowing boat. We walked for a whole week,
trying to hide from everyone. We spent the nights under haystacks—a good thing the nights were warm. My shoes were falling
to pieces, my feet were bleeding. Nikanor Yurevich got me some
felt boots from somewhere—probably simply took them off a fence
post. One day, I don't remember exactly when, we saw a man in
a birch copse, wearing a torn cloak, bast shoes and a shaggy cap.
He looked just like a madman, marching rapidly and sullenly
ahead, leaning on a thick stick. It was Perkhurov, *he* had run away
from Yaroslavl, too. I was so frightened of him that I threw myself
face down on the grass.... We went on to Kostroma and stayed at
a house in the suburbs belonging to an official, a friend of Kulichok's, till the Czechs took Kazan. Nikanor Yurevich looked after
me all the time as if I was a child—I'm grateful to him.... But in
Kostroma he came upon my jewels, they were in a handkerchief
in my handbag, which he carried all the way in his coat pocket. I
only remembered about them in Kostroma. I had to tell him all
about it—I told him I felt like a criminal. He developed a regular
philosophic theory about this: it seems I'm not a criminal, I just
drew a certain number in the lottery of life. From that moment his
attitude towards me changed; it became very complicated. Our
relations were also affected by living in a little country house, and
leading such a pure, quiet life, drinking milk, and eating
gooseberries and raspberries. I began to get fatter. Once, after
sunset, he began talking to me in the little garden about love—he
said I was made for love, and kissed my hands. And I felt that he
was absolutely certain I would give myself to him in a minute,
there, on the bench beneath the acacias.... After everything that
had happened, Papa, just think! Instead of going into long expla-
nations, I simply said: 'It's no good—I love Ivan Ilyich.' And I
wasn't lying, Papa....''

Ivan Ilyich took out his handkerchief, wiped his face, and then
his eyes, and went on reading:

"I wasn't lying.... I haven't forgotten Ivan Ilyich. Everything
is not over between us. You know about it, don't you? We parted
in March, he went to the Caucasus, to the Red Army.... He's very
well thought of—a real Bolshevik, though he isn't a Party member.... We broke off relations, but we are still bound by the past....
I haven't broken with the past.... For Kulichok it's all very

simple—just sleeping together.... Oh, Papa, what we used to call love is nothing but the instinct of self-preservation. We fear oblivion, destruction.... That's why it's so terrible to catch the eye of a prostitute at night.... It's just the shadow of a woman.... But I'm alive, I want to be loved, remembered, I want to see myself mirrored in the eyes of a lover. I love life.... Of course, if I felt a sudden desire to give myself—on the spur of the moment, you know ... that would be quite different! But just now I feel nothing but rage, disgust, horror.... Lately something seems to have happened to my face, my figure, I've got prettier.... I feel as if I were naked all the time, and all around me hungry eyes.... A curse on beauty! I'm writing all this to you, Papa, so as not to have to say any of it when we meet.... I'm not broken yet, you see...."

Ivan Ilyich raised his head. The cautious steps of several persons, the shuffling of feet, could be heard from the other side of the door leading into the hall. The door handle was turned. He leaped to his feet, glancing towards the window....

The windows of the doctor's flat were not very far from the ground, as is the way in provincial houses. The middle window was open. Telegin ran up to it. On the asphalt pavement lay the long shadow of a man, compasslike, from which there protruded the still longer shadow of a rifle.

It was all the work of a fraction of a second. The doorknob turned, and two common-looking youths, in peaked caps, and embroidered shirts, entered the study shoulder to shoulder. Behind them the red-bearded, "vegetarian" face of Govyadin dodged from side to side. The first thing Telegin saw, as they rushed in, was the muzzles of three revolvers directed at him.

Telegin, wise in the experience of the battlefield, knew it would not do to turn his back on a strong and unbeaten foe. In the next fraction of the second he had shifted his revolver to his left hand, and plucked from his belt, beneath his tunic, a small hand grenade, to which was attached Gimza's letter.

"Put those down!" he shouted hoarsely, the blood rushing to his face.

There was something so impressive about this exclamation, and indeed about the whole appearance of Ivan Ilyich, that the bravos were smitten with confusion and fell back a few steps. The vegetarian countenance dodged aside. Another second had been won.... Telegin hung over them, brandishing the hand grenade.

"Down, I say!"

Just then something happened which none of those present, Telegin least of all, could possibly have expected.... Immediately

264

after his second shout, an agonized scream was heard from the other side of the walnut door leading from the study to the rest of the house, and a woman's voice cried out in frantic alarm.... The door opened, and Telegin saw Dasha standing there, wide-eyed, her fingers clinging to the doorjamb, her thin face quivering.

"Ivan!"

Beside her appeared the doctor, who seized her round the waist and dragged her away ... the door banged.... All this upset the aggressive and defensive plans of Ivan Ilyich in a trice.... He made for the walnut door, pushed his shoulder against it with all his might ... something gave with a cracking sound and he rushed into the dining room, still holding his lethal weapons in his hands.... Dasha was standing beside the table, clutching at the lapels of her striped dressing gown near her throat, and gulping as if she were trying to swallow something. (He noticed this with a stab of pity.) The doctor stepped back, looking like an animal at bay.

"Help! Govyadin!" he squealed in a smothered voice.

Dasha rushed up to the walnut door and turned the key in the lock.

"Oh, God, how awful this is!"

But Ivan Ilyich did not understand her words alright: awful, indeed, it had been to break in upon Dasha with these things. He hastily thrust the revolver and hand grenade into his pockets. Then Dasha seized him by the arm, saying: "Come! " and led him into the dark passage, and thence into a narrow little room in which there was a lighted candle on the seat of a chair. The room was quite unfurnished, containing nothing but Dasha's skirt hanging on a nail, and an iron bedstead with crumpled sheets against the wall.

"Are you alone, here?" whispered Telegin. "I read your letter."

He looked round. His lips widened in a smile and trembled. Without answering, Dasha dragged him to the open window.

"Run! *Run!* Are you mad?"

From the window could be indistinctly seen, the yard, the shadows and roofs of buildings stretching towards the river, and still further down, the lights of the landing stage. There was a damp wind from the Volga, smelling pungently of rain.... Dasha stood there, her whole body touching Ivan Ilyich, her terrified face raised, the lips parted....

"Forgive me, run, don't wait, Ivan!" she murmured, looking straight into his eyes.

How was he to tear himself away? The wide circle of separation had closed in. He had escaped a thousand deaths, and now he was

265

looking into that face which was the only one in the world for him. He bent down and kissed her.

Her chill lips gave no response, merely quivering slightly.

"I haven't betrayed you.... Upon my word! We'll meet when things get better.... Now run, run, I implore you!"

Never, not even in the blissful days in the Crimea, had he loved her so! It was all he could do to restrain his tears, looking at her face.

"Come with me, Dasha! Listen! I'll wait for you at the river—tomorrow night...."

She shook her head, groaning in her agony:

"No, no ... I won't!"

"You won't?"

"I can't!"

"Very well," he said. "In that case I shall stay."

He moved away and leaned against the wall.... Dasha gasped and gave a sob.

...Then she made a wild rush at him, seizing him by the hand, and dragging him back to the window. Outside, a wicket gate squeaked and the sand crunched beneath cautious footsteps. Dasha leant her warm face despairingly against his hands....

"I read your letter," he said again. "I understand everything now."

At this, she stood still for a moment, her cheek pressed against his, and her arms round his neck.

"They're in the yard already. They'll kill you, kill you!"

Her loosened hair looked golden in the light of the candle. She seemed to him a little girl, a child; she looked now just as he had thought of her that night when he had lain wounded in the wheat, clutching a sod of earth in his hand, and meditating on her stubborn, uneasy, all-too vulnerable heart.

"Why don't you come with me, Dasha? They're torturing you here. You see the sort of people they are.... Anything, however terrible, would be easier for you, with me at your side.... Little one.... Whatever happens you are with me in life and in death, you are as much a part of me as my own heart."

He said all this in hurried undertones from the dark corner. Dasha threw back her head without letting go of his hands—her tears gushed out.... /

"I'll be faithful to you till death.... But you must go!.. Try and understand—I'm not the woman you love.... But I will be, I will really!"

He heard no more—her tears, her words, the catch in her voice, made him almost drunk with joy. He pressed her to him so hard that she felt as if her very joints were cracking.

"All right, I understand everything! Goodbye!" he whispered.

He threw himself flat on the window sill, and in another moment had slipped down like a shadow, the only sound being the light impact of his boots on the wooden roof of a shed beneath the window.

Dasha leant out of the window, but there was nothing to be seen—only pitch darkness and distant yellow lights. She pressed her hands to her heart.... Not a sound from outside.... But just then two figures emerged from the shadows. Stooping low, they ran slantwise across the yard. Dasha shrieked, so piercingly, so terribly, that the figures spun round and stood still. They must have turned towards her window. And at that moment she saw Telegin climbing over the ridge of a wooden roof at the far end of the yard.

Dasha threw herself face downwards on the bed and lay there motionless for a few moments. She got up no less violently, and groping for a slipper that had come off, rushed into the dining room.

There she found the doctor and Govyadin in belligerent poses—her father clutching a small nickel-plated pistol, his friend brandishing an army revolver. "Well?" they cried, both speaking together. She clenched her fist, staring furiously into the reddish eyes of Govyadin.

"You scoundrel!" she said, shaking her fist under his pallid nose. "You'll be shot one of these days, you scoundrel, see if you aren't!"

His long face twitched and turned still paler, his beard hanging limp and lifeless. The doctor made him a sign, but Govyadin was already shaking with rage.

"Don't shake your fist at *me*, Darya Dmitrevna.... I have by no means forgotten that you were once good enough to strike me— with your shoe, if I'm not mistaken.... Put down your fist ... and I would advise you, in general, to show me a little more respect."

"Semyon Semyonovich, you're wasting time," interrupted the doctor, still making signs but trying not to let Dasha see what he was doing.

"Don't you worry, Dmitri Stepanovich, Telegin won't get away from us...."

Dasha screamed and made a rush at him.

"You wouldn't dare!" (Govyadin instantly took refuge behind a chair.)

"We'll see whether we dare or not.... I warn you, Darya Dmitrevna, the Department for Public Security takes a very great interest in you, personally.... After today's incident I won't answer for anything. It may mean trouble for you, you know!"

"Now, now, Semyon Semyonovich, don't go too far," said the doctor angrily. "That's a little too much...."

"Everything depends on personal relations, Dmitri Stepanovich.... You know my regard for you, and my long-standing admiration for Darya Dmitrevna...."

Dasha turned suddenly pale. Govyadin's features were contorted by the sneer on his lips, as if reflected in a flawed mirror. Picking up his cap, he went out, his head held rigidly erect in an endeavour not to look ridiculous from the back. The doctor sat down at the table, saying:

"Govyadin's a dangerous man."

Dasha walked up and down the room, pulling at the joints of her fingers. She halted in front of her father:

"Where's my letter?"

The doctor, who was fumbling at his silver cigarette case, hissed a reply through closed teeth; getting the case open at last, he extracted a cigarette, squeezing it in his podgy, still tremulous fingers.

"It's there ... devil take it—where *is* it? In the study, on the floor."

Dasha went out of the room, and came back immediately with the letter, again standing in front of Dmitri Stepanovich. He was trying to light up, but the flame of the match kept dancing around the tip of the cigarette.

"I only did my duty," he said, throwing the match on the floor. (Dasha said nothing.) "He's a Bolshevik, my dear ... worse—a spy.... Civil war is no joke, you know, one has to be ready to sacrifice everything. That's what we're invested in power for, and the people never forgive weakness." (Dasha began slowly tearing the letter into tiny pieces as if lost in thought.) "He came—it's as clear as daylight—to get what he wanted out of me, and do me in at the first opportunity.... Did you see how he was armed! He had a bomb. In 1906 Governor Blok was blown to pieces by a bomb before my eyes, at the corner of Moskatelnaya Street.... You should have seen what was left of him—a limbless trunk and a tuft of beard." The doctor's hands began trembling again, he flung aside the unfinished cigarette and took out another. "I never did like your Telegin, it's a good thing you left him...." (Even this Dasha let pass in silence.) "Fancy beginning with such an obvious ruse—wanted to know where you were, forsooth...."

"If Govyadin gets him...."

"There's not the slightest doubt about that—Govyadin has a first-rate personnel. You *were* sharp with Govyadin, you know.... Govyadin's a great man.... He's thought highly of, both by the Czechs and at headquarters.... In times like these we must sacrifice our personal feelings ... for the good of the country... remember the examples from the classics.... After all, you're my daughter; your head's stuffed with a lot of nonsense, it's true—" he laughed and cleared his throat. "But it's not a bad head...."

"If Govyadin gets him," said Dasha hoarsely, "you'll do all you can to save Ivan Ilyich!"

Casting a rapid glance at his daughter, the doctor sniffed. She still held the fragments of the letter in her clenched fist.

"You will, won't you, Papa?"

"No!" shouted the doctor, banging on the table with his hand. "No! Rubbish! In your own interests—no!"

"It'll be hard for you, but you'll do it, Papa."

"You're a little fool, you chit!" roared the doctor. "Telegin's scoundrel, a criminal, he'll be shot by the military tribunal."

Dasha raised her head, and her grey eyes were so unbearably bright, that the doctor grunted, knitting his brows as if to shield his own eyes. She raised her small fist, the scraps of paper still clutched in it, threateningly.

"If all Bolsheviks are like Telegin," she said, "then the Bolsheviks must be right!"

"Fool! Fool!"

The doctor, crimson-faced, shaking with rage, jumped up and stamped his foot.

"Your Bolsheviks and your Telegin ought to be hung! Strung up on the telegraph posts.... They ought to be flayed alive!"

But Dasha's temper was even more violent than her father's. Turning pale, she stepped right up to him, and fixed those unbearably bright eyes on his face.

"You hound!" she cried. "Stop your raving! You're no father of mine—depraved madman, sot!"

And she flung the fragments of the letter in his face.

That very night, just before dawn, the doctor was called to the telephone.

A gruff indifferent voice said in his ear:

"For your information: two bodies, identified as those of assistant-chief of counterespionage Govyadin, and one of his agents, have been found near the Samoletskaya landing place behind the flour depot."

The receiver was hung up at the other end. Dmitri Stepanovich

269

opened his mouth, gasping for air, and fell down beside the telephone in a violent heart attack.

XI

Sorokin, having routed the forces of Drozdovsky and Kazanovich, the best troops in the Volunteer Army, changed his original plan for crossing the Kuban River, turning north at Korenovskaya instead, and attacked the station of Tikhoretskaya, where Denikin had his headquarters.

A ruthless battle had been raging there for days. Elated by its first successes, Sorokin's army swept away all obstacles in its path. It looked as if nothing could now halt its headlong progress. Denikin hurriedly concentrated his forces, which were scattered all over the Kuban district. So great was the tension on both sides, that every skirmish ended in a bayonet charge.

But demoralization was developing within the ranks of Sorokin's army with equal rapidity. The hostility between the Kuban and Ukrainian regiments was becoming daily more acute. The Ukrainians and the war veterans devastated the Kuban villages in the line of their advance, without troubling to find out which side was supported by the inhabitants.

The utmost confusion of thought prevailed. The villagers greeted with horror the sight of troops approaching in clouds of dust from across the steppe. Denikin at least paid for fodder, but Sorokin's fellows made a clean sweep of everything. And so the young men mounted their horses and went over to Denikin, and the old ones, with the women, children, and cattle, ran for refuge to the gullies.

Whole villages began rising against Sorokin's army. The Kuban regiments shouted: "We are being sent to the slaughter, while strangers are pillaging our country!" Chief of Staff Belyakov struggled desperately in the whirlwind of events, feeling for his head to make sure that it was still on his shoulders. And no wonder! Strategy had been flung to the winds. Tactics now rested on the points of bayonets and in revolutionary fury. The vehement, irrepressible, violent mass movement of armed men was being substituted for discipline. Supreme Commander Sorokin, who lived on spirits and cocaine all through these days, was an appalling sight. His eyes inflamed, his face dark, he forged ahead as if possessed, on the shoulders of the army, shouting himself hoarse.

The inevitable happened. The Volunteer Army, defeated, continually in retreat, was nevertheless imbued with a discipline so severe, that it went to the counterattack again and again with an obedience to a single will that was almost mechanical, clinging stubbornly to every fold in the ground that could be of use to it, and finding out, with diabolical skill, the enemy's weakest points. And on the 25th of July, in the neighbourhood of Viselki, about 30 miles from Tikhoretskaya, the tenth and last day of the battle was fought to a finish.

The position of Drozdovsky's and Kazanovich's troops was even worse than it had been in the preceding days. The Reds had managed to get in the enemy's rear, and the Volunteers were caught in a trap very like that into which the Bolsheviks had fallen at Belaya Glina. But Sorokin's army was no longer what it had been nine days before. Its eager tenseness had relaxed, and the stubborn resistance of the enemy had shaken the confidence of the soldiers, instilling doubts and despair—when would victory and rest come?

Soon after 3 p.m. Sorokin's army rushed to the attack all along the front. The impact was terrific. All along the horizon the guns thundered. The troops advanced in serried ranks, never seeking cover. Tenseness, impatience, fury were reaching breaking point.

But it was the beginning of the end for Sorokin's army. The first wave of attackers was annihilated by fire and steel. The succeeding waves were thrown into confusion by enemy fire, in a welter of dead bodies and wounded and falling men. And then occurred that which could be neither foreseen, understood, or halted—the tension of the troops suddenly slackened. No more strength or zeal was left.

And the enemy's icy will continued dealing well-calculated blows, adding still further to the general confusion.... Markov's units, and a cavalry regiment from the north, Erdeli's cavalry from the south, cut their way through the disorganized Red troops. The White armoured cars crept onward, with their devastating fire, and puffs of smoke came from their armoured trains. By four o'clock the entire steppe was covered by the southward and westward retreat of Sorokin's army—an army that had ceased to exist as an efficient force.

Chief of Staff Belyakov bundled the Supreme Commander forcibly into an automobile. Sorokin's bloodshot eyes were bulging, there was froth at the corners of his lips and his blackened hand still clutched an empty revolver. The bullet-scarred, battered car drove frantically over heaps of dead bodies, and disappeared behind the hills.

The main body of Sorokin's ravaged troops fell back on Ekaterinodar, where the western group of Red troops, the so-called Taman army, under the command of Kozhukh was also beginning to retreat from the direction of the Taman peninsula. All along the line of its retreat, villages were rising, and the "outsiders", fearing the vengeance of the Cossack population, were collecting their property and their cattle, and fleeing to the Taman army for protection. The road was barred by General Pokrovsky's White cavalry. But though the Taman troops succeeded, in a furious attack, in dispersing this cavalry, it had now become impossible to move on to Ekaterinodar, and Kozhukh's army, with its train of refugees, had to wheel sharply south, towards the wild and impassable mountains, hoping to break through to Novorossiisk, where the Black Sea fleet of the Reds stood at anchor.

Nothing could have stopped Denikin now. Clearing the path before him with ease, he marched with all his forces on Ekaterinodar, still occupied by the remnants of what had once been the North-Caucasian army, and took it by storm. Thus ended the "Frost Campaign", begun six months before by Kornilov and a handful of officers.

Ekaterinodar became the White capital. The rich Black Sea districts were hastily cleared of all dangerous and subversive elements. Generals who had only a short time before been scouring their shirts for lice, restored the traditions of a Great Power, reinstated the ancient imperial scope.

The old homely methods of gaining arms by wresting weapons and ammunition from the enemy in battle, or by raids on Bolshevik stores, were, of course, not suited to the new, ambitious plans. Now the requirements were money, a steady influx of arms and ammunition, a war commissariat on a big scale, and powerful bases for an offensive into the interior of Russia.

The era of local civil warfare was over, and powerful external forces entered the arena.

The June victories of Denikin constituted a peculiar and unexpected danger for the German High Command. The Bolsheviks were a foe bound hand and foot by the treaty of Brest-Litovsk. But Denikin was a hostile force, which the Germans did not yet know and had not had time to study. By smashing Sorokin's army, Denikin had gained access to the Sea of Azov and Novorossiisk, where the whole Russian navy had been at anchor since the beginning of May.

The Germans were not protected from the Black Sea side. So long as the navy was in the hands of the Bolsheviks they had no anxiety, for they could have countered any attempt at hostile action from the sea by crossing the Ukrainian border. But fifteen destroyers and two dreadnoughts threatened, in the hands of Denikin, to transform the Black Sea into a front of the world war.

On June the tenth Germany presented an ultimatum to the Soviet Government, demanding the transfer, within the next nine days, of the whole Black Sea fleet from Novorossiisk to Sevastopol, where there was a strong German garrison. An attack on Moscow by the Germans was to be the penalty for non-fulfilment of the ultimatum.

At the same time the Chief of Staff of the Austrian occupational troops in Odessa sent the following dispatch to the Ministry for Foreign Affairs in Vienna:

"Germany is pursuing definite economic-political aims in the Ukraine. She desires to ensure for herself, for all time, a safe route to Messopotamia and Arabia, through Baku and Persia.

"The road to the East runs through Kiev, Ekaterinoslav and Sevastopol, and hence by sea from Sevastopol to Batum and Trapezund.

"Germany intends to retain the Crimea—either as a German colony, or in some other way. She will never again let the invaluable Crimean peninsula slip through her fingers. Further, the fullest use of this route demands the control of the main railways, and since the supply of coal to such railways and to the Black Sea ports from Germany would be impossible, it is essential to Germany to possess the more important mining districts in the Don coalfields. All this, Germany intends to accomplish by one means or another...."

When the German ultimatum was received in Moscow on the tenth of June, this staggering problem, by many regarded as insoluble, was solved by Lenin in one of his lightning decisions: while it was impossible as yet to fight the Germans, it was equally unthinkable to give them the fleet.'

Comrade Vakhrameyev was sent from Moscow to Novorossiisk, as a representative of the Soviet Government. He laid before a meeting of delegates and commanders from the Black Sea fleet the only Bolshevik reply to the German ultimatum: The Council of People's Commissars to dispatch an open radiogram to the Black Sea fleet, ordering it to proceed to Sevastopol and surrender to the Germans; the Black Sea fleet, however, was not to comply with this order, but to scuttle its ships in the Novorossiisk roads.

The Soviet fleet—two dreadnoughts, fifteen destroyers, and a few submarines and auxiliary vessels, condemned to idleness by the terms of the Brest-Litovsk treaty—was at anchor outside Novorossiisk.

The delegates from the fleet came ashore and heard

Vakhrameyev out in grim silence—his proposals sounded like suicide to their ears. But they could see no other way out, for the fleet had neither coal nor oil. Moscow was threatened by the Germans, Denikin was approaching from the east, the periscopes of German U-boats were already tracing lines of foam over the roadsteads, German bombers were gleaming against the azure sky. The delegates argued long and hotly.... There was only one way out: to scuttle the ships.... Faced with such a terrible decision, however, the delegates resolved that the destiny of the fleet be put to the votes of all its crews.

Monster meetings were held in the harbour of Novorossiisk. It was hard for the sailors, gazing at the steel-grey giants, anchored there, the dreadnoughts *Volya* and *Svobodnaya Rossia*, the fast destroyers, renowned in battle, the intricate network of turrets and masts, towering over the harbour and the crowds of people, to realize that all this formidable property of the Revolution, this floating, sailors' native land, was to sink to the bottom of the sea without a shot being fired, without the slightest resistance.

The Black Sea sailors were not men to accept self-destruction calmly. Frantic words were uttered, breasts smitten, singlets torn from many a tattooed chest, caps with fluttering ribbons trampled underfoot....

Dense crowds of sailors, returned soldiers, and all the varied types making up the population of the coast, thronged the waterfront in agitation from sunrise to sunset, when the sombre purple waters of that accursed sea, no longer theirs, turned crimson in the dying rays of the sun.

Commanders and ships' officers held divergent views: the majority were secretly in favour of going to Sevastopol and surrendering to the Germans; but there was a minority, headed by Senior Lieutenant Kukel, commander of the destroyer *Kerch*, which realized the inevitability of the catastrophe and its enormous significance for the future. These said:

"We must commit suicide. We must close for a time the history of the Black Sea fleet, without sullying its pages...."

At these vast meetings, as noisily spectacular as hurricanes, one set of resolutions would be passed in the morning—another in the evening. The best reception was accorded to speakers who, flinging their caps on the ground, exclaimed:

"Comrades, to hell with those Moscow fellows! Let them drown *themselves*! *We*'re not going to surrender our ships. We'll fight the Germans to the last round...."

The harbour reverberated to the thundering "hurrahs".

The confusion reached its peak when, four days before the expiration of the term mentioned in the ultimatum, two delegates arrived hotfoot from Ekaterinodar: Rubin, Chairman of the Black Sea Republic Central Executive Committee, and, representing the army, Perebiinos, a giant of frightful aspect, with four revolvers stuck in his belt. They both—Rubin in a lengthy speech, and Perebiinos in a thunderous bass, and shaking a revolver—asserted that the fleet wasn't going to be either surrendered or scuttled, that those fellows in Moscow didn't know what they were talking about, and that the Black Sea Republic would supply all the oil, shells and food the fleet needed.

"Our Goddam position at the front," yelled Perebiinos, accompanying his words with a stream of invectives, "is so Goddam good, that next week we'll be drowning that son-of-a-bitch Denikin and his cadets in the Kuban.... Don't scuttle your ships, mates—we need to feel at the front that we have a powerful fleet behind us. If you scuttle them, mates, I categorically declare in the name of the entire Kuban-Black Sea revolutionary army that we won't stand such treachery, if you drive us to desperation we'll march with forty thousand men on Novorossiisk, and we'll skewer every man of you on the ends of our bayonets, mates...."

After this meeting, all was chaos, heads reeled. Crews left their ships and ran off at their own sweet will. Suspicious characters made their appearance in the crowd in ever greater numbers. In the daytime they shouted with the loudest: "Fight the Germans to the last round!" but at night they stole in small groups on to the half-deserted destroyers, ready to pounce, to throw the crew overboard, to loot.

Semyon Krasilnikov arrived on board the destroyer *Kerch* during this time.

Semyon was polishing the brass base of the compass. The whole crew had been at work since morning, scraping, washing, cleaning up the destroyer, which was moored close to one of the piers. A hot sun was rising from behind the scorched foothills.... The flags drooped in the hot, windless air. Semyon rubbed away at his brasses, trying not to look towards the harbour. The crew were furbishing up the destroyer for its death.

In the harbour the huge funnels of the dreadnought *Volya* were sending out clouds of smoke. The guns, their tarpaulins removed, gleamed. Black smoke rose into the sky. Ship, smoke, the brown hills, and the cement works at their base, were reflected in the mirrorlike surface of the bay.

Semyon, squatting on his bare heels, rubbed diligently at the brass. He had stood watch that night, and the thought that he had better not have come, rankled in his breast. He should have listened to his brother and Matryona.... Now they would laugh at him: "So that's how you fought the Germans!" "You've sold the fleet, brothers!" they would say. And how was he to answer them? Was he to say: "I cleaned and polished and sank the *Kerch* with my own hands?"

A motor launch, with a signalman semaphoring from its bows, cast off from the *Volya*, visiting each of the ships in turn. The destroyer *Derzky* slipped her moorings, taking the *Bespokoiny* in tow, and made slowly for the roads. Still more slowly, like convalescents, the destroyers *Pospeshny*, *Zhivoy*, *Zharky* and *Gromky* followed in their wake, crawling over the smooth surface of the bay.

Then there was a break in the procession. Eight destroyers remained in the harbour. There was no sign of movement on them. Now all eyes were fixed on the *Volya*, a light-grey, steel mountain with rusty streaks on her sides. The sailors, forgetting their swabs, cloths, and hose nozzles, stood staring at her. The flag of the Commander in Chief of the Fleet, Commodore Tikhmenev, flapped lazily in the breeze.

On the deck of the destroyer *Kerch* sailors were talking anxiously, under their breath:

"You'll see ... the *Volya* will go to Sevastopol...."

"Could they be such worms, mates? Have they no revolutionary conscience left?'"

"If the *Volya* goes, brothers, who can we trust?"

"As if you didn't know Tikhmenev! He's our worst enemy, a real fox."

"She's going! Oh, the traitors!"

Anchored next to the *Volya* stood the twin destroyer, *Svobodnaya Rossia*. But she seemed to be peacefully dozing—all her guns were covered and not a soul was to be seen on deck. Boats were being rowed frantically towards her from the pier. And suddenly the boatswain's whistle rent the stillness of the bay, the *Volya*'s winches creaked, and dripping chains and silt-covered anchors slowly ascended her sides. The bows began to turn, and a network of funnels and turrets was set in motion against the sun-bleached roofs of the town.

"They're going.... To the Germans.... Oh, mates.... To surrender to the Germans!... What have you done?"

The captain of the *Kerch*, his huge peeling nose standing out on his sunburnt face, appeared on the bridge. He followed, hollow-eyed, the movements of the *Volya*. Bending over from the bridge, he gave the order:

"Hoist a signal!"

"Aye-aye!" cried the sailors readily, rushing towards the box containing the signal flags. The gay pennants flew up the mast of the *Kerch*, fluttering against the azure sky. Their combination meant:

"To the ships going to Sevastopol—shame on the betrayers of Russia!"

The *Volya*, as if the message had not been noticed, gave no answering signal, but, unmanned, disgraced, slipped past the battleships which had remained true to their honour. "She's seen the signals!" cried the sailors suddenly, for the muzzles of the two giant guns on her after-turret lifted, and the turret turned towards the destroyer.... The captain of the *Kerch*, gripping the rail, thrust out his great peeling nose to meet death. But the guns only shifted and lowered their muzzles.

Gathering speed, the *Volya* doubled the pier, and soon her proud profile disappeared beneath the horizon, only to reappear, many years later—disarmed, rusted, and eternally disgraced—in faraway Bizerta.

Commander in Chief of the Fleet Tikhmenev insisted on carrying out the order of the Council of People's Commissars to the letter, and the dreadnought *Volya* and six destroyers surrendered at discretion in Sevastopol. All the officers and sailors were allowed to leave.

The sailors made for their homes and birthplaces. They said, of course, that they had been unable to bring themselves to sink their ships, but the real reason had been their fear of the forty thousand Red Army men who threatened to bayonet the entire population of Novorossiisk.

The dreadnought *Svobodnaya Rossia*, and eight destroyers, remained in the port of Novorossiisk. The time for executing the terms of the ultimatum would expire on the morrow. German airplanes were circling high above the town. In the roads, among the prancing dolphins, appeared the periscopes of U-boats. The Germans were said to have effected a landing not far away, at Temryuk. And on the quays of Novorossiisk stormy meetings were held day and night, and suspicious characters in civilian clothes were shouting more and more insistently:

"Don't bring ruin on yourselves, mates, don't scuttle the fleet.... "

"It's only the officers who want to scuttle the fleet, and all the officers, to a man, have sold themselves to the Entente.... "

"In December you threw your officers into the sea at Sevastopol—what are you afraid of now? Why not do it again?"

An agitator would immediately take the place of the troublemonger, tearing at the front of his shirt and yelling:

"Pay no heed to enemy agents, Comrades! If you deliver up the fleet to the Germans, they will shoot you down with your own guns.... Don't give up your arms to the imperialists.... Save the world revolution!..."

How was a man to know which one to heed? After the agitator, a soldier straight from the fighting at Ekaterinodar, hung with all sorts of weapons, would jump up and repeat the threat of the forty thousand bayonets. And by the night of the 18th of June many crews had not returned to their ships. They had run away, gone into hiding, fled to the mountains.

All through that night the destroyer *Kerch* communicated with other ships by means of signals. The *Svobodnaya Rossia* answered that she was ready to scuttle herself on principle, but that she had less than a hundred of her crew of two thousand left, and that these doubted whether they would be able to get up steam for taking off.

The destroyer *Hadzhi-Bei* had blinked the news that a meeting was still raging on deck, that there were girls on board, with bottles of spirits, probably sent there on purpose, and that looting of the vessel might be expected. Only the captain and the ship's engineer remained on deck of the torpedo boat *Kaliakyria*, and there were not more than six sailors on board the *Fidonisi*. Similar answers were received from destroyers *Captain Baranov, Smetlivy, Stremitelny, Pronzitelny*. The only ships to boast a complete crew were the *Kerch* and the *Lieutenant Shestakov*.

Towards midnight a boat approached the *Kerch* and a bold voice cried:

"Comrade seamen ... a correspondent from *Izvestia*, the organ of the Central Executive Committee, speaking. We have just received a telegram from Admiral Sablin in Moscow: you are on no account either to scuttle the fleet or go to Sevastopol, but to await further instructions...."

The sailors leaned over the rail, straining their eyes to see the swaying boat in the darkness. The voice went on arguing and persuading.... Senior Lieutenant Kukel climbed on to the bridge and interrupted it:

"Show me the telegram from Admiral Sablin."

"Unfortunately I haven't got it on me, Comrade, but I can go for it...."

Then Kukel said, loudly and distinctly, so that all should hear him:

"The boat to stand away half a cable to starboard. Sheer off, there, or..."

"Excuse me, Comrade!" shouted back the bold voice. "Since you refuse to obey orders from the centre, I shall have to telegraph to Moscow...."

"...or I will sink your boat, and have you hauled up on deck. And I cannot answer for the actions of the crew."

No answer to this came from the boat, but there was a cautious splashing of oars, and the faint outline disappeared in the darkness. The sailors laughed. The captain, lean and round-shouldered, his hands behind his back, paced the bridge like a caged beast.

Few slept that night. Men lay about the dew-drenched deck; every now and then a head would be raised, and a few words dropped, effectually banishing sleep, and giving rise to muttered conversations. The stars grew pale, and dawn was beginning to light up the mountains, when Midshipman Annensky, captain of the *Lieutenant Shestakov*, came on board from ashore, reporting that not only were the crews of destroyers, port-tugs and motor boats deserting, but that even the merchant ships were left without a single seaman, and that there was not a vessel left able to take the ships into the roadstead.

"Midshipman Annensky," replied the captain of the *Kerch*, "the responsibility rests with us, we must scuttle our ships at all costs."

Midshipman Annensky shook his head. There was a brief silence, after which the midshipman went on shore again. When the sun was high over the bay, the *Lieutenant Shestakov* steered slowly off from the pier and made for the outer roads, taking the *Captain Baranov* in tow, where the scuttling was to be done. The destroyers flew the signal at their mastheads: "I go down, but I do not surrender."

Very soon they disappeared in the morning mist. All the ships seemed deserted now. Seagulls were hovering over the steel mountain of the *Svobodnaya Rossia*. Smoke was coming from the funnels of the *Kerch*. Even at this early hour there were milling crowds on the dockside, and the strip of pier was black with running figures, as if covered with clusters of flies. There was an awful crush around the ships themselves, men climbing on to one another's shoulders, some even falling into the water.

Semyon Krasilnikov was standing guard at the gangway. Soon after five, a little man, scarlet with excitement, in a black reefer jacket with no shoulder straps, stamped noisily up the gangway. Beads of sweat stood out on his scarlet face and ran in rivulets on either side of his tiny, puckered mouth.

"Is Senior Lieutenant Kukel here?" he cried to Semyon, glaring from round, merry blue eyes at the sailor barring the way with his bayonet. Patting himself on the chest and sides, he at last produced a mandate made out in the name of Comrade Shakhov, representative of the central Soviet power. The sailor lowered his bayonet with a set face.

"Pass, Comrade Shakhov!"

Kukel came to meet him and at once started telling him about the situation, which he described as all but hopeless. He spoke slowly and at length and Shakhov's eyes rolled impatiently.

"Nonsense, we've been in many a worse fix! I've been talking to the sailors, their morale is wonderful.... I'll get you a tug and anything else you need.... We'll call a meeting.... It'll all come right in the end...."

He asked for a motor-launch and had himself taken up to the *Svobodnaya Rossia*. After this, he sped from one ship to another in the launch. Semyon could see his small figure, now dangling from the accomodation ladders of merchant vessels, now leaping ashore and plunging into the crowd, from the thick of which immediately came shouts and raised hands. Once there was the roar of a thousand voices shouting "hurrah!"

Some pinnaces, crammed with sailors, sheered off from the pier and rowed up to a small rusty craft far back in the harbour; very soon thick clouds of smoke were rolling out of the little steamer's funnels as it weighed anchor and steamed up to the *Svobodnaya Rossia*. A schooner, too, raised its sails. The *Lieutenant Shestakov* had come back to take another destroyer in tow.

Soon after nine the crowd began moving up to the gangway of the *Kerch*. The general feeling seemed to have changed for the worse. Queer-looking ragamuffins were elbowing their way to the side of the ship, their hands full of smoked sausage, bread, and bacon fat. Grinning and winking at the sailors, they let them see the bottles of spirits with which they were also provided. Kukel gave the order to draw up the gangway and cast off, and the *Kerch* fled from temptation into the middle of the harbour, from where she watched the destroyers being towed away. The rusty steamer, looking like a mere empty hulk, at last managed, puffing and smoking, to move the *Svobodnaya Rossia*, which floated majestically past the thousands of watchers. Men took off their caps, as if a funeral procession were passing. The great ship passed the booms, the gates and the harbour, and moved into the roads. Everyone expected German airplanes to appear again, but all was quiet in the sky and on the sea. The destroyer *Fidonisi* was now the only vessel left in harbour.

Once more there was a turmoil in the crowd, and a caviarlike coagulation of black heads at the pier to which the *Fidonisi* was moored. A sailing-schooner with an outboard engine moved up to take her in tow. Stones were flung at the schooner from the crowd, and a few revolver shots were heard. A grey-haired man climbed a lamppost, shouting:

"Fratricides! You have betrayed Russia.... You have betrayed the army.... What are you waiting for, mates? They're selling the only ships we have left!"

The crowd roared and tore at the paving stones. Some men jumped on to the deck of the *Fidonisi*. The *Kerch* moved rapidly shorewards, ringing the battle alarm, the muzzles of its guns turned on the crowd, while the captain shouted into the megaphone:

"Back—or I open fire!"

The crowd swerved and fell back, to the accompaniment of shrieks from those trampled underfoot. There was nothing left on the deserted quay but a rising cloud of dust. The schooner made fast to the *Fidonisi* and towed her away.

The *Kerch* followed them slowly to their destination, where all the other vessels were rocking in a light swell. Semyon watched the gulls flying high above the bows, and then looked at the captain, who was standing on the bridge, gripping the rails with both hands.

It was going on for four, when the *Kerch* passed the *Fidonisi* on her starboard. The captain uttered a single word, and a torpedo slid from its sheath like a dark shadow. A strip of foam raced along a ripple, and the *Fidonisi*, heaving herself bodily upwards, broke in two, while a shaggy mountain of foaming water boiled up from the ocean depths, and a heavy rumbling roar reverberated far out to sea. When the mountain of water had subsided, there was no *Fidonisi* to be seen any more. Nothing but foam. The sinking of the fleet had begun. Demolition squads opened the sea cocks and slide valves of the destroyers, ripped the portholes from the side of the listing vessels, setting light, just before leaping into the waiting boats, to the fuses which were to detonate the ten-foot charges at the base of the turbines and boilers. The destroyers rapidly disappeared beneath the water, which was many fathoms deep here. In twenty-five minutes the roads were clear.

The *Kerch* approached the *Svobodnaya Rossia* full steam ahead, and released her torpedoes. The sailors slowly bared their heads. The first torpedo struck the bows, and the dreadnought swayed beneath the violent onrush of the water. The second

19–559

struck her sideways, amidships. Through the cloud of water and smoke the mast could be seen to sway. The great ship—more majestic than ever amidst the roaring waves and thunder of detonations—seemed to struggle for its life like a living creature. Tears ran down the sailors' cheeks. Semyon covered his face with his hands....

Captain Kukel seemed to be wasting away, until all that was left of him was his nose, turned in the direction of the dying vessel. The last torpedo struck, and the *Svobodnaya Rossia* began to keel over... For a moment, as if making one last effort, she thrust herself out of the water, and then went rapidly to the bottom in a whirlpool of foam.

The *Kerch* left the scene of death at top speed, heading for Tuapse. Early next morning her crew took to the boats, and a message was broadcast by wireless from the doomed ship:

"To all... I am going down, after having destroyed those vessels of the Black Sea fleet which preferred destruction to the disgrace of surrendering to Germany. Destroyer *Kerch*."

Its sea cocks opened, its engines blown up, the destroyer sank fifteen fathoms to the bottom of the sea.

On shore, Semyon Krasilnikov and his mates discussed their future plans. Many suggestions were made, and at last it was decided to set out for Astrakhan on the Volga, where Shakhov was said to be forming a river fleet for fighting the White Guards.

Kozhukh's Taman army, the enemy at its heels, and encircled by villages all of which had risen against the Reds, was endeavouring to break through, by mountain paths, and over pathless wastes, to the Upper Kuban.

Their way lay through Novorossiisk, occupied by the Germans since the sinking of the fleet. The Taman columns made a surprise entry into the town—before anyone knew what had happened, troops were marching through the streets, singing. The German garrison, mistaking their purpose, rushed to the ships and opened fire on the rear column, mowing down, as well as the Red troops, their appendage of drunken Cossacks in frenzied pursuit.

By way of precaution, the Germans withdrew from the town, which, after Kozhukh had fought his way through it, was occupied by Cossacks; a little later, White troops entered, and sacked the town.

Sailors, Red Army men and anyone who looked too poor, were strung up on telegraph posts without a trial. Three thousand corpses were taken to the sea on lorries during those days. Novorossiisk had become a White port.

The Taman army, encumbered by the carts of its fifteen thousand refugees and their belongings, trudged along the famine-stricken coast to Tuapse, where it turned sharply eastwards. Denikin's men were close behind them and all the mountain passes and canyons ahead were occupied by counterrevolutionary insurgents. Not a day passed without heavy fighting. Bleeding, snapping back, halfdead with hunger, the army crept on, climbed the steep slopes of hills, melting away as it marched, but plodding doggedly on.

One day, a Red Army prisoner released by General Pokrovsky was brought to Kozhukh. He bore a letter written with military frankness:

"You have disgraced all the officers of the Russian Army and Navy, you scoundrel, by joining the ranks of the Bolsheviks, the thieves and the tramps; know, then, that this is the end for you and your tramps. We have a firm grip on you, you scoundrel, and we're not going to let you slip through our fingers. If you desire mercy, that is to say, to get off with nothing worse than being sent to a convict labour company, do as I order: lay down your arms this very day, and take your gang, disarmed, two or three miles west of the Belorechenskaya railway station. Let me know when you have complied with my order, send a message immediately to signal box number 4...."

Kozhukh read the letter, sipping tea from a tin can. He glanced at the Red Army man, shoeless, his tunic unbelted, standing dejectedly before him.

"You stinker!" said Kozhukh. "How dare you bring me such a letter? Go and find your unit...."

And that very night Kozhukh struck a crushing blow at General Pokrovsky's troops, putting them to flight and pursuing them with cavalry. He then made a breakthrough to Belorechenskaya and broke out of encirclement.

Towards the end of September, the Taman army reached Armavir, which was occupied by Denikin's troops, took it by storm, and joined up with the remnants of Sorokin's army in the village of Nevinnomysskaya.

After the disasters of Viselki and Ekaterinodar, Sorokin, embittered by failure, chewing the cud of lost military glory, had no more influence with the soldiers, and retreated further and further east, caught like a chip in the vortex of what had once been divisions, brigades and regiments, but was now a mere herd fleeing in panic at the first sound of enemy fire. The soldiers destroyed everything in the line of their retreat. Their one idea was to get as far as possible from the death whose breath they could feel on their necks—to go anywhere, the farther the better. Endless processions of deserters roved the Terek steppe, along the highways of antiquity, now covered with funeral mounds and wormwood.

Almost two hundred thousand troops and refugees escaped after the battle of Ekaterinodar. Those who remained were cut to ribbons, hung, or tortured by the Cossacks. Corpses swung from the Lombardy poplars in every Cossack village. The Cossacks, now that they no longer feared the return of the Reds, revenged themselves ruthlessly on any who fell into their hands. The very word Bolshevik was being stamped out with blood and fire throughout the district.

Sorokin was a child of the revolution, and sensed its fluctuations with an almost animal instinct. He made no attempt to stem the retreat, knowing that it would be useless. The stampede towards the east was now at its height, and could only be checked when the Whites relaxed the fury of their pursuit.

All he could do now was to look morosely out of the window of the railway carriage, as the train dragged its length past the scorched steppe, dotted over with the funeral mounds of ancient Pelasgi, Celts, Teutons, Slavs, Khazars... There was a bodyguard on the train, for passing troops had been heard shouting:

"The commanders have betrayed us, mates, sold us for a drink—kill yours as we have killed ours!"

Chief of Staff Belyakov, on his occasional visits to Sorokin's compartment, would sigh and drop a few vague, cautious words as to the impossibility of going on with the struggle. "Revolutions have their phases," he repeated incessantly, passing a hand over his large forehead. "The phase of revolutionary enthusiasm is over, and we have the elemental forces against us. It is not the officers we are fighting any more, but the people themselves. We must try and save the achievements of the revolution from destruction before it is too late ... even if it means peace by compromise." And he would quote all sorts of corroboratory examples from history.

"How much money do you mean to offer me, you scoundrel?" was Sorokin's only answer to all this. He would gladly have torn Denikin into pieces if he could only have laid his hands on him. But he was angriest of all with his comrades, the members of the Black Sea Central Executive Committee, who had fled to Pyatigorsk from Ekaterinodar. Their sole care had been to find measures for checking Sorokin's dictatorial tendencies. They had disregarded the most urgent orders, interfered in everything, and tried to pry into the innermost being of the Supreme Commander with their Marx-this and Marx-that.

The blonde Zena once more appeared in Sorokin's lounge car—a mark of Belyakov's care. Zena was as rosy and seductive as ever, though now a trifle hoarse; her silk blouses and her guitar had been stolen on the march. Her bearing towards the Supreme Commander was more independent than it had been before.

During the night, when the blinds were pulled down and Sorokin surrendered to a gloomy half-drunken exultation, Zena, after strumming for a while on the balalaika, would, like Belyakov, ramble on about the imminent end of the revolution, and the brilliant career of Napoleon, who had known how to bridge the gulf between the Jacobin terror and the throne... Sorokin's eyes would burn and his heart beat wildly, sending the hot blood, thinned with spirits, to the brain... He would tear aside the blind and gaze out of the window into the darkness of the night, which seemed to be filled with the reflections of his delirious imaginings....

The onslaught of the Whites was slackening. The Red Army at last managed to gain a foothold on the left bank of the Upper Kuban, and entrench itself. By this time Commander of the Iron Division Dmitri Shelest had returned from Tsaritsyn through the Kirghiz steppe bringing with him a fleet of motor lorries, two hundred thousand rounds of ammunition, and an order for the Caucasian forces to turn north, to the aid of Tsaritsyn, now surrounded by the White Cossack army of Ataman Krasnov.

Sorokin refused point-blank to comply with this order. The Ukrainian regiments, sick of fighting so far from their homes, were chafing and deserting, deaf to his entreaties and threats. The only person able to hold some of the troops back was Shelest, who, born and bred in Poltava, could talk to them as a peasant to peasants, slowly, reasonably, meting out praise to them and to himself. The Ukrainians saw that this was no mere outsider, but one of their own elders, and obeyed him. Dmitri Shelest led them into action, and they routed a strong officers' unit at Nevinnomysskaya. And Sorokin had burned with hatred towards him ever since.

Congratulating Shelest on his victory, he appointed him commander of a sector of the front, and the same day gave secret orders to disarm his units and shoot him and his entire staff. Getting wind of this, Shelest and his Iron Division, now swollen by a following of Ukrainians, left the front, and marched across the salt steppe and shifting sands, upon Tsaritsyn, in compliance with the order of the Revolutionary Military Council of the 10th Army. Sorokin's next step was to proclaim him an outlaw, and impose the duty of shooting him on every Red Army man; he also forbade anyone to supply the Iron Division with forage. But Shelest marched off, and no man's hand was raised against him. If he found himself short of forage on the way, Shelest would ride into some village, take off his Cossack cap, and beg, with tears in his eyes, for hay, oats and bread from the Village Executive Committee, explaining that it was not he, but Supreme Commander Sorokin, who was a traitor and a White bandit.

Very soon came another blow to Sorokin's pride: Kozhukh, whom everyone had given up for lost, arrived from over the mountains and took Armavir by storm driving the Whites across the river Kuban. The Taman troops either fulfilled Sorokin's orders grudgingly, or totally disobeyed them. Hardened by the arduous march, the Taman army was now the backbone of the disorganized Sorokin forces and took up strong positions all along the Armavir—Nevinnomysskaya—Stavropol line.

Autumn had come and long, bloody battles were being fought for the rich city of Stavropol. And everywhere the Taman troops were in the forefront of the battle.

Denikin's army had received reinforcements too—a wild band of human riffraff, formed into a kind of wolf pack by the White guerilla Shkuro, himself a scamp, a cutthroat, and a desperado.

Sorokin's staff was transferred to Pyatigorsk, and he himself did not appear at the front any more. A new regime was descending upon the Caucasus, the Moscow influence had penetrated here, and was making itself felt more and more. It began with the decision of the Territorial Party Committee to call a revolutionary military council. Not venturing to oppose Moscow, Sorokin had to submit. The Revolutionary Military Council was composed of quite new elements. The authority of the Supreme Commander was transferred to its executive body. Sorokin, who realized that his very life was at stake, put up a desperate fight.

He sat silent and morose through the sessions of the Council, but whenever he did speak, he fought for every point. And he always got his own way, because the troops concentrated in Pyatigorsk were loyal to him. He was feared, and with reason. He sought an opportunity to show his power, and one was soon forthcoming. Martinov, Commander of the Second Taman Column, announced at a military conference in Armavir his refusal to obey the Supreme Commander's orders. Sorokin immediately demanded Martinov's head of the Revolutionary Military Council, threatening complete anarchy in the army. There was no way of saving Martinov, who was summoned to Pyatigorsk, arrested, and shot in front of the army. A storm raged throughout the Taman regiments, who swore vengeance.

A new staff was formed for the Supreme Commander. Belyakov was dismissed, and Sorokin made no attempt to stick up for him. The ex-Chief of Staff handed over his papers and money, and went to the quarters of his former friend to demand an explanation. Sorokin was pacing up and down the room, his hands clasped behind his back. An oil lamp stood on the table, beside it his dinner, untouched, and an opened bottle of vodka. Through the window could be seen the thicklywooded slopes of Mashuk, in dark silhouette against the sombre colours of the sunset.

Sorokin glanced up for a moment at the newcomer, and resumed his pacing of the floor. Belyakov seated himself at the table, his head bowed. Sorokin stopped in front of him, jerking up one shoulder.

"Have some vodka! Our last drink together," he said with a hoarse guffaw, quickly pouring out two glasses, and returning to his pacing up and down. "It's all up with you, old man.... And my advice to you is to make yourself scarce as fast as you can.... I shan't stick up for you.... Tomorrow I'll appoint a commission to go through your papers, see? You'll probably be shot...."

Belyakov raised a grey, haggard countenance, passed his hand across his brow, and let it drop.

"You're a contemptible little wretch, that's what you are," said Belyakov. "And to think I put my whole heart into working for you.... You skunk.... So that's the man I was training for the role of Napoleon.... A louse!..."

Sorokin took up a wineglass, his teeth clattering against the rim as he drank. Then, his hands in the pockets of his Circassian tunic, he resumed his pacing.

"There will be no inspection," he said, stopping abruptly. "Get the hell out of here! And if I don't shoot you now, mind you, it's on account of your past services. I hope you appreciate that!"

His nostrils quivered as he inhaled the air, his lips went blue, and he was trembling all over, trying to contain his fury.

Belyakov knew Sorokin's temper only too well: without taking his eyes off him, he backed towards the door, slamming it quickly after him.... He went out by the back entrance, and left Pyatigorsk that same night.

Hour followed hour, while Sorokin sat up all through the night, drinking glass after glass of vodka, and thinking. His erstwhile friend had poisoned him with a single drop of contempt, and the poison had caused him agonizing pain, intolerable suffering.

He covered his face with his hands: Belyakov was right, a thousand times right. The Napoleonic scope of June had dwindled into sittings of the Revolutionary Military Council, furtive glances at the comrades from Moscow... Belyakov had not spoken for himself alone. That was how they spoke of him in the army, in the Party. And Denikin! He remembered an item in an Ekaterinodar White newspaper, and the memory stung him afresh—it was an interview with Denikin.

"I expected to see a lion, and the lion turned out to be nothing but a cowardly cur in a lion's skin... Not that I was really surprised. Sorokin was, and remains just an ignorant Cossack cornet." Oh, Denikin! Wait... The hour will come.... You will rue this!

Sorokin squeezed his hands together and gnashed his teeth. If only he could rush to the front, carrying with him the whole army, rout, pursue and ride down the officers, set the villages blazing from end to end! Rush into Ekaterinodar... then to have Denikin brought before him—to have him brought straight from his bed, in his underclothes... "Was it you, Anton Ivanovich, who practised your wit in short newspaper articles upon a certain ignorant cornet? Well, this is he, honoured Sir, whom you see before you... Now then, shall we cut strips of skin out of your back, or will fifteen hundred strokes of the ramrod do?"

Sorokin groaned, trying to shake off the delirious dreams which haunted him. But reality was dark, vague, full of anxiety and humiliation. The time had come for him to make a decision. His old friend and former Chief of Staff had today rendered him a last service. Sorokin walked up to the window—a light breeze brought with it the dry pungency of the wormwood-covered steppe. A dark crimson strip, ushering in the dawn, but dull as yet, stood out against the sombre sky. And the giant purple bulk of Mashuk was still there.... Sorokin gave a wry smile: thanks, Belyakov.... Now, then—to hell with hesitations and vacillations.... That night Sorokin decided to stake his all.

The Revolutionary Military Council had at last, after long hesitation, voted for an offensive to be started. The supply base was moved to Svyatoi Krest, the army was to concentrate at Nevinnomysskaya, from there to move on Stavropol and Astrakhan, and join the Tenth Army, which was fighting near Tsaritsyn. This was the very plan which Dmitri Shelest had brought with him from Tsaritsyn.

The taking of Stavropol was entrusted to the Taman troops. Everything was in motion—the supply base moved northeast, the front lines northwest. Political instructors and agitators shouted themselves hoarse in their endeavours to raise the morale of the units with fiery slogans. Commanders left with their columns for the front. Pyatigorsk was deserted. Only the government stayed behind—the Central Executive Committee of the Black Sea Republic, and Sorokin with his bodyguard and staff. In the rush nobody had realized that the government was, in fact, at the mercy of the Supreme Commander.

One evening, as Sorokin, accompanied by an orderly, riding home at a brisk trot, had just turned the corner of the municipal park where the road sloped upward, his horse almost knocked down a burly, round-shouldered individual wearing a leather jacket. The pedestrian staggered, clapping his hand to his hip, from which hung a leather holster. Sorokin knit his brows furiously as he recognized Gimza, who was supposed to be at the front. Gimza took his hand from the holster. There was a strange look in his eyes, half-covered as they were by the beetling brows.... There had been a similar look in Belyakov's eyes at their last interview. And suddenly a strip of teeth made a white line across Gimza's shaven, battle-blackened face. Sorokin's heart sank— this one was laughing at him, too!

He thrust his knees into the horse's sides so violently that the animal, snorting and plunging, galloped over the ringing cobble-stones and bore his rider up the hill, right into the middle of a pungent-smelling flock of sheep, bleating and shaking their tails as they wended their homeward way. It was the evening of the twelfth of October. Sorokin summoned the chief of his bodyguard, who whispered to him, glancing nervously at the window, that Gimza had just come to Pyatigorsk to suggest that the Central Executive Committee recall two companies from the front for their protection.... "One doesn't have to be very clever, Comrade Sorokin, to understand who these measures are taken against...."

When the autumn stars rose in all their beauty over Mashuk and the dark, somnolent Pyatigorsk, Sorokin's bodyguard noiselessly entered the homes of Rubin, Chairman of the Central Executive Committee, and of Vlasov and Dunayevsky, two of its members, of Kraini, a member of the Revolutionary Military Council, and of Rozhansky, Chairman of the Cheka. Forcing them out of their beds, they drove them at the bayonet's point out of town, to the railway line, and shot them down without a word of explanation. Sorokin was standing on the step of his railway carriage at the Lermontovo railway station while this was going on. He heard the shots—five bangs in the stillness of the night. Then he heard someone's heavy breathing—the chief of his bodyguard approached him, passing his tongue over his dry lips. "Well?" asked Sorokin. "Liquidated!" answered the chief of the bodyguard, naming all the victims.

The train left. Now the Supreme Commander was flying at full speed to the front. But news of his unprecedented crime arrived before him. Some Communists from the Territorial Committee, warned by Gimza the day before, left Pyatigorsk by car before

Sorokin. On the thirteenth of October they called a military conference at Nevinnomysskaya. And so, just as Sorokin, magnificent as an Eastern potentate, with his hundred-strong guard, his buglers sounding the alert, the banner of the Supreme Commander carried in front, made his appearance before the troops, the army conference at Nevinnomysskaya was proclaiming him an outlaw, to be arrested immediately and brought to Nevinnomysskaya for trial.

The men of the Taman army shouted the news to him from the open doors of their goods vans. Sorokin returned to the station, and summoned the commanders of the columns. No one came. He waited at the station till dusk. Then he ordered a horse, and galloped off into the steppe, accompanied by the chief of his bodyguard.

The three remaining members of the Revolutionary Military Council in Pyatigorsk were at a loss what to do: the Supreme Commander had disappeared in the steppe, and the army, instead of going on with the offensive, was demanding his trial and execution.... But a strong human machine of a hundred-and-fifty thousand men is not so easily halted once it has begun functioning.... And on the twenty-third of October the Taman army began its attack on Stavropol, the Whites simultaneously beginning their counterattack. On the twenty-eighth all commanders reported that they were short of shells and cartridges, and that if supplies were not forthcoming on the morrow, victory was not to be counted on. The Revolutionary Military Council replied that there were no more shells and cartridges—"Stavropol must be taken at the bayonet point...." On the night of the twenty-ninth two shock columns were formed. Under cover of the artillery, which was using up its last shells, they approached the village of Tatarskaya, some ten miles from Stavropol, where the White front now extended. An enormous copper-coloured moon rose over the steppe—in default of rockets it served as a signal.... The guns ceased fire. The Taman lines, marching towards the enemy's trenches without firing a shot, rushed into them. At once the bugles of the military bands blared out, and the drums rolled, while to the accompaniment of music which was their only substitute for bullets and hand grenades, the two shock columns, overtaking the musicians in dense waves, surged forward, falling by the hundred under enemy machine-gun fire, and hurled themselves upon the enemy's main line of defence. The Whites fell back on the hills, but even these heights were seized in the irresistible onslaught of the Reds. The enemy fled towards the town, pursued by Red Cossack units. On the morning of the thirtieth of October the Taman army entered Stavropol.

The following day Supreme Commander Sorokin was seen riding down the principal street of Stavropol, his chief of the bodyguard beside him. He seemed quite calm, but he was pale, and kept his eyes on the ground. Seeing him, the Red Army men gaped and backed away: "Is it a devil from the nether regions?"

Sorokin dismounted in front of the house of the Municipal Soviet, on the door of which still hung a half-torn notice, bearing the inscription: "Headquarters of General Shkuro." The surviving deputies and members of the Executive Committee were gathered inside, but Sorokin went boldly up the stairs, enquiring of the startled soldier on duty where the plenary session was being held, and appeared in the hall in front of the table of the presidium. Raising his head proudly, he addressed the amazed and perplexed assembly:

"*I* am Supreme Commander. It was *my* troops which routed Denikin's bands and reinstated the Soviet power in the town and district. An unauthorized military conference at Nevinnomysskaya has had the impertinence to declare me an outlaw. On whose authority did they do this? I demand the appointment of a commission for the investigation of my alleged crimes. Pending the findings of this commission, I shall not resign my post of Supreme Commander."

With this he left the hall, intending to mount his horse again. But six Red Army men of the 3rd Taman Regiment fell upon him on the staircase, twisting his arms behind his back.

Sorokin struggled in fierce silence; Vislenko, the commander of the regiment, hit him over the head with the handle of his whip, shouting:

"This is for shooting Martinov, you cur!"

Sorokin was taken to prison. There was perturbation among the troops who feared lest he somehow get out of prison, and escape justice. When, at the interrogation which took place the next day, Sorokin saw Gimza in the chair, he realized that all was over with him. But his boundless appetite for life awoke in him, and for the last time he banged on the table with his fist, shouting, with terrible oaths:

"It is for *me* to pass judgement, you bandits! This is obstruction of discipline, anarchy, latent counterrevolution! I shall deal with you as I have dealt with that scoundrel Martinov...."

Vislenko, who, as one of the judges, was sitting next to Gimza, turned as white as a sheet. Thrusting his arm behind him, he pulled out a large automatic pistol and emptied its contents into Sorokin.

Further advance from Stavropol to the banks of the Volga was checked by the "wolves" cavalry of Shkuro which had fled to the rear, cutting off the Taman army from its base in Nevinnomysskaya. Denikin was concentrating his forces for the encirclement of Stavropol. The columns of Kazanovich, Drozdovsky and Pokrovsky, the cavalry of Ulagai, and the newly formed Kuban Cavalry Division, commanded by a former mining engineer who had been a junior officer at the beginning of the war, and was now General Wrangel, were withdrawn from the Kuban for that purpose.

The Taman army fought for twenty-eight days. Its regiments were destroyed one after another in the iron grip of a foe rich in munitions. The rains had set in, and there were not enough greatcoats, boots or cartridges to go round. There was nowhere to look for help, for the rest of the Caucasian army, cut off from Stavropol, was retreating to the east.

The men of the Taman army, encircled by the enemy, lashed out with terrific strength. Their commander, Kozhukh, succumbed to typhus. Almost all the best commanders had been wounded or killed. But by the end of November, the Taman army at last managed to break through the front. The heroic Taman army was reduced to pitiful remnants, barefoot and in rags. Relinquishing Stavropol, they fell back to the northeast upon Blagodatnoye. There was no pursuit—the bad weather and autumn rains had brought the White advance to a standstill.

XII

October marked a twelvemonth since the peoples inhabiting Russia began demanding an end to the war. The countless groans, the myriad shouts of "Down with the war! Down with the bourgeoisie prolonging it, the military caste waging it, the landowners feeding it!" merged in the single, impressive shot fired at the Winter Palace from the deck of the cruiser *Aurora*.

Who could have foreseen that the shell which landed among the tinted lead figures and ornate black vases with which the top of that detested building bristled, crashing through the roof, to explode in the royal bedroom, where the couch on which Kerensky had tossed in sleepless hysteria all night was still warm, the shell which seemed at the time to have been the final chord of a revolution whose slogan was "war on the palaces, peace to the huts", would ring out from end to end of the boundless country, and, reverberating like an echo, would gain in volume and insistency with every peal, till it attained the irresistible strength of a hurricane?

Who could have believed that a country which had only just laid down its arms would be capable of taking them up again, and of rising in a war of class against class, poor against rich? Who could have expected that an immense army like Denikin's would spring into being from a handful of Kornilov's officers, that a riot which began on Czechoslovak troop trains would develop into war involving hundreds of miles of the Volga district, and, spreading to Siberia, lead to the brief reign of Kolchak? And, again, could it have been foreseen that a blockade would get a stranglehold on the land of the Soviets, and that maps and globes would appear with onesixth of the earth's surface unpainted, unnamed—a blank space, heavily outlined in black?

Who could have believed that Russia, cut off from the seas, and the grain districts, from coal, and from oil, starving, impoverished, typhus-ridden, would put up such a fight, doggedly sending her sons to the slaughter again and again? In the previous year men were deserting at the front, and the country seemed to have become a formless swamp, but this was a mere superficial impression: in reality, potent forces of cohesion were making themselves felt throughout the country, and aspirations for justice were beginning to tinge the bare struggle for existence. Wonderful men and women, the like of whom had never before been seen, made their appearance, and their exploits were discussed everywhere with awestruck admiration.

The Soviet land was shaken by internal disturbances. At one and the same time that there were risings in Yaroslavl (subsequently spreading to Murom, Arzamas, Rostov-Veliky and Rybinsk), the "Left Socialist-Revolutionaries" were revolting in Moscow. On the sixth of July, two of them, bearing papers on which the signature of Dzerzhinsky* had been forged, called upon Count Mirbach, the German ambassador, and engaged him in conversation, in the course of which they fired at him and threw a bomb. The ambassador was killed by the last shot, which caught him in the back of the head as he was trying to escape from the room. That evening, armed sailors and Red Army men appeared all along the Chistiye Prudi and Yauza Boulevard. They stopped cars and pedestrians, searched them, took away any arms and money found on them, and took them to the Morozov mansion in Trekhsvyatitelei Street, the headquarters of the rising. Felix Dzerzhinsky, who had gone to the house in search of the murderers of Mirbach, was there, under arrest. Arrests went on through the evening and part of the night. The telegraph was in

*Felix Edmundovich Dzerzhinsky (1877-1926)—an outstanding member of the Bolshevik Party and staunch adherent of Lenin, head of the All-Russia Extraordinary Commission (the "Cheka") and talented organizer of socialist constructive works.

the hands of the insurgents. But no one dared to attack the Kremlin as yet. There were about two thousand insurgents, forming a front from the river Yauza to the Chistiye Prudi Boulevard.

The Kremlin had nothing but telephone communication and its own ancient walls to rely on. Troops were encamped in the Khodinskoye Field, and many of the men had been given leave for the holiday of Ivan Kupala. The atmosphere inside the Kremlin was tense. Towards morning, however, they were able to get hold of some eight hundred soldiers, three batteries, and a few armoured cars; the troops began the attack at 7 a.m., bombarding and completely demolishing the Morozov mansion in Trekhsvyatitelei Street. There was a lot of noise, but the victims were few, the "army of Left Socialist-Revolutionaries" escaping through side streets and backyards to some unknown destination. Their commander, Popov, a loose-lipped youth with crazed eyes, disappeared from Moscow. A year later he reappeared as the chief of Makhno's counterintelligence and · became notorious for refined cruelty.

The risings were suppressed both on the Volga and in Moscow. But rebellion lurked everywhere: rebellion against the Bolsheviks, against the Germans, against the Whites. Villages rose against towns, and looted them. Towns deposed the Soviet power. The era of independent republics began—they grew up and burst like puffballs, some so tiny that a rider could have galloped all round their boundaries in the space of twenty-four hours.

The Soviet government exerted all its powers to cope with this anarchy. And it was at such a time that it was dealt a terrible blow: on the thirtieth of August, after a meeting held at the Michelson Works, Fanny Kaplan, a Right-wing "Socialist-Revolutionary" (from the same organization as the man with the death's-head pin) shot at Lenin, wounding him dangerously.

On the thirty-first of the month, a detachment of men dressed from head to foot in black leather marched through the streets of Moscow, bearing before it on two staffs a banner with the single word: "TERROR".... Meetings were held day and night at all the factories of Moscow and Petrograd. The workers were calling for drastic measures.

On the fifth of September the Moscow and Petrograd papers came out with an ominous headline:

THE RED TERROR

"...All Soviets are required to make immediate arrests of the Right S. R.'s, representatives of the big bourgeoisie and officers, and hold them as hostages.... Any attempt at escape or incitement to rebellion to be met with mass shooting.... It is essential for us to safeguard our rear, immediately and finally, against the White-Guard curs.... Let there be no hesitation in applying terror on a mass scale...."

In those days the most rigid economy of electric power had to be practised in the cities, and whole districts were sometimes left without light. The inhabitants of expensive apartments were, therefore, terrified to see the filaments gradually reddening in their electric lamps, for this might be a kind of deathbed illumination, signifying the near approach of squads of armed workers....

The year 1918 made its exit in a roaring tempest throughout Russia. The sombre autumnal clouds were big with rain. There were fronts in all directions—in the far North, on the Volga at Kazan, the Lower Volga at Tsaritsyn, in the North Caucasus, and on the borders of the territory occupied by the Germans. Trenches extended for thousands of miles. The coming autumn brought little cheer to the Red Army men, many of whom, as they watched the clouds creeping slowly from the north, thought of their native villages, where the wind was tearing the straw from the thatches, nettles were growing all over their lands, and potatoes were rotting in the fields. And there seemed no hope of the war ever ending. Ahead was nothing but pitch-dark night and the feeble gleam from the rushlight in the hut, where fathers and sons were anxiously awaited, while stories of such fearsome doings were told that the children on the stove ledge began to cry.

After the Republic had dealt with the various risings, the Central Committee of the Party, as if in response to the autumn depression, mobilized the staunchest Communists of Moscow, Petrograd and Ivanovo-Voznesensk, and dispatched them to the army. They travelled by train towards the fronts, breaking down any sabotage, both deliberate and unintentional, which they came across on the line. The stern regime of terror was established in the army, too. Disorganized and wilting detachments were transformed into regiments subordinated to the will of the Revolutionary Military Council. Valour and prowess became the order of the day. Cowardice was regarded as tantamount to treason. The Red front took the offensive. One sharp blow accounted for Kazan, and soon after, Samara fell. The White detachments fled in panic before the Red Terror. At Tsaritsyn, where Stalin was on the Revolutionary Military Council of the Tenth Army, a vast and bloody battle was going on against the White Cossack army of Ataman Krasnov, who had the aid and connivance of German headquarters....

But all this was only the prelude to the great struggle—a review of forces before the main events of 1919.

Ivan Ilyich Telegin had fulfilled the mission entrusted to him by Gimza. During the fighting at Kazan he was appointed commander of his regiment and was one of the first to get into Samara. It was a warm autumn day when he rode his shaggy pony down Dvoryanskaya Street at the head of his regiment. They passed the square in which stood the monument to Alexander the Second—once more being hastily concealed with boards. And there was the second house from the corner.... Ivan Ilyich bent his head—he was prepared for what he would see, but his heart nevertheless contracted with pain. All the windows on the second floor—Dr. Bulavin's rooms—were smashed, and being on horseback, he could look into them: there was the walnut door, on the threshold of which Dasha had appeared, as in a dream, that time, and there the doctor's study, the bookshelves overturned and Mendeleyev's portrait on the wall crooked, its glass smashed.... But where was Dasha? What had happened to her? There was no one to answer these questions.

1928

А. Толстой
Хождение по мукам
Том II
Восемнадцатый год
Роман
На английском языке

Перевод сделан по изданию: А. Н. Толстой. Собр. соч. в 10-ти томах, т.:, М., «Художественная литература», 1983

Редактор русского текста Н. Капустина
Контрольный редактор О. Чоракаев
Художник А. Яковлев
Художественный редактор Е. Поликашин
Технический редактор С. Алимханова

ИБ № 7334

Сдано в набор 23.05.90. Подписано в печать 21.05.91. Формат 84x108/32. Бумага офсетная. Гарнитура Таймс. Печать офсет. Усл. печ. л. 15,54. Усл. кр.-отт. 16,07. Уч.-изд. л. 20,6. Тираж 3180 экз. Заказ №559. Цена 6 р. 20 к. Изд. № 7028.

Отпечатано с оригинал-макета способом фотоофсет на Можайском полиграфкомбинате В/О Совэкспорткнига Государственного комитета СССР по печати. 143200, Можайск, ул. Мира, 93.

Издательство "Радуга" В/О Совэкспорткнига Государственного комитета СССР по печати. 119859, Москва, ГСП-3, Зубовский бульвар, 17.